THE ORPHAN
A Woeful Story

THE ORPHAN
A Woeful Story

Amol Chawak

KALPAZ PUBLICATIONS
Delhi – 110 052

THE ORPHAN : A Woeful Story

(Public Interest)

Rs. 690

ISBN: 81-7835-093-9

Published in 2002 in India by
Kalpaz Publications
C-30, Satyawati Nagar
Ashok Vihar Phase-III
Delhi-110 052
E-mail: Kalpaz@hotmail.com

Laser Typesetting by: Varsha Graphics, Delhi
Printed at Chawla Offset Printers, Delhi 110 052

Dedicated to

"The Most Beautiful Lady on Earth—My Mom"

One

A hot drop of salt water oozed out of her dark eyes as he covered her cheecks with both of his hands. It was followed by another and another and soon two continuous streams started flowing over her cheeks, colliding with his hands and dispersing over his fingers. He dared to look at her eyes. It took a lot of courage for him to do the thing which he had done thousands of times earlier. Her dark eyes were surrounded by misty water, full upto the brim and overflowing.

For the two, the world had come to a standstill and for a moment the time stood frozen and space concentrated around them. He looked deep into her eyes and tried to fathom what they were speaking out. Not a single word was said for last several seconds. Perhaps they were conversing with their candid eyes and rapidly accelerating heartbeats. Perhaps that was the best way to communicate, absolutely simple yet very effective. If possible they would have stretched the moment to cover thousand millenniums. Why? If possible they would have uprooted the very cause that had put them in so queer a situation like that. But then how many things are possible for the animal who walks on two legs and boasts to posses that invaluable thing called brain? Very few indeed! Most of the time the man is as hopelessly helpless as any other inhabitant of the earth.

Never in his life was he in such a strange situation. He hated to see her shedding tears at the same time found himself inept to console her. He put forth efforts to utter something but he couldn't. By now she had coated his hands by hers and could feel her gentle touch as she wrapped her tender palms around his and pressed her fragile fingers. Lightly she moved her palms all over his strong arms and could feel the familiar curves of the solid muscles through the rough, thick shirt that he wore. She clasped his shoulders with whatever power she could collect, her eyes still focussed on his face.

He was first to recover, realising that there was no end to it. He shook his head and removed her hands as softly as possible, being very keen to prevent anything that might offend her.

Finally, somehow, she succeeded to fight back the emotional outburst or she pretended to do so.

"Come soon," her voice was trembling and badly at the verge of chocking. He nodded silently.

"Where is Nil?," he too strived to keep his posture. Because of heavy emotional stress sentences became acutely brief.

"I have sent him to playground. He won't let you go." she spoke as he observed her intently.

"I must leave now," he turned back speedily and moved a bit and then again came back to her. All the while she was watching him with her wet, almost dizzy eyes. To her, he was no less than a dynamic prince, his majestic cap no less than a crown. Why then her heart wasn't accepting the fact that like any other prince, this prince also belonged to the whole kingdom and not just the princess?

He squeezed her hands lovingly and merely said, "take care," and turning swiftly moved out of the house. She followed him. Her world had converged into her eyes which tried to steal some moments to be stored in her memory.

There was a brave soldier in Indian Army, about 28, who happened to be her husband clad in that priceless uniform not many dare to step into. His back sight drowned her mind into a spectrum of emotions. She was very proud to be a wife of a man like him, very satisfied to be in such a meaningful mode of life, very sad to bid him farewell and very puzzled not knowing how to react. But there was no time to react anymore. Before she could think about anything he opened the gate and closed it behind him, an act which hardly consumed a few seconds, covered the distance of a few yards in a dash even a tiger would envy, broke into the vehicle which was standing on the road, smiled at her through the window and waved his hands as the giant military vehicle roared past the house. At that instant she felt a painful knot being formed in her stomach. For a moment she felt as if her arteries and veins were empty with no blood at all and she was weaker than ever. She found herself not in a position to hold up her frame and sat down there itself on the stairs. But her eyes were determinedly pointing towards the road. Everything was same what she could see, except that green military vehicle. It had gone far way and with it her brave husband, Jatin. Within some hours he would be out of the city and within a day out of this country altogether, far away beyond her reach. He would land on the foreign shores of Sri Lanka, a country cursed with bloody conflicts, always in flames with guns firing, shells exploding. The land were cold blooded fights are the order of the day, bomb blasts a mere news. He would land there as a peacekeeper !

She essayed hard to do away with the chilling thoughts but in turn it was enveloping her like a snake clutching its prey. Her peacekeeper was gone, with him her peace also !

Her mind was vacillating but it was crazy all the same and her, now completely dry eyes desperately searched for that tall 5'11" figure on the deserted path. She was trying to spot that smiling face she worshipped so badly. But she couldn't find anybody but the long, vehicle bars of the iron gate that stood in front of her, as it laughing at her ironically.

Will some miracle befall and he come back? This query was almost rhetoric with its answer convert in itself. What she was thinking was utter impossible which any sober mind would dismiss as preposterous. She knew it, yet she couldn't help it. More often, under the influence of blinding emotions, the grown ups tend to be childish, biding for unfeasible things, hoping to see something happen which logic does not permit. But she was definitely not like those fools and better part of her brain was aware of the facts. Her Jatin was gone and that was the truth. He was a warrior who went to the battlefield to fight a holy war and he should not or more correctly, must not return until becoming victorious. Otherwise he should not return at all ! This horrible thought almost stopped her heartbeats and pumped fresh salt water into her eyes.

Why does it happen to her always? Why was she always coerced to part with the people who treasured her most? Those few who were truly hers, who understood her, cared for her? Her life spined around them and they only constituted her little, fascinating world. The rest of the universe, for her, was the manifestation of hell that contained horrible demons and cruel animals, something she was badly afraid of, something she always loved to hate. And it was only for her sweet little world that she lived.

Wasn't she committing a big mistake by charging the whole world to be barbarous? Perhaps. Wasn't it downright pessimism to thing so? Of course. In fact it was entirely a wrong notion. Everything in this world cannot be bad because good and bad are opposite sides of the same coin. Interestingly, she was matured enough to know these things, still she hesitated to have faith in those who, she believed, were not hers. Was she then a pighearted coward always finding excuses for not getting involved into the mainstream ? Perhaps not, she wasn't a coward. Marrying with an armyman is a work of no coward. It takes lot of guts.

Her approach was a categorical result of the circumstances under which she spent the earlier days of her life. The psychological impact of surrounding on a human mind in its budding years is enormous. When you grow up you sense this fact, yet you cannot alter your attitude, because you were casted in a particular mould and by no means can you reshape your mind. As a result you end up thinking in a similar fashion all the time, behaving in the same, rigid and predictable manner. And your responses to any stimulus based on this framework of your mind defines your character.

Engulfed in thoughts and some sweet but more bitter memories the young lady had been sitting there on the steps for hours seldom being concerned about rest of the world. It was a characteristic of her, a habit she had mastered long ago. She didn't mind forgetting the very presence of the objects surrounding her and go astray into the past, sometimes in the future. That offered her excellent opportunity to detract her mind from the anxiety caused by any disturbing incident and she would glide freely in the sky full of memories severely captivated, several mesmerised. But deplorably very few moments in her life were worth cherishing, sprinkled very scarcely, here and there in the vast pile of dislikable incidents collected in her memory. For those very few she would turn the pages of her memory book again and again. She would disengage herself a thousand miles from present and everything else would become irrelevant. The nasty curl of hair flowing wildly over the forehead, sometimes blocking her vision, the end portion of her saree slipping down her shoulder, chilling cold breeze in winter, scorching heat in summer and merciless downpouring in rainy days, everything would go unnoticed. Same was the case today. She didn't find it awkward to lay where she had been for hours together and she was still there when the darkness loomed large signalling the advent of the evening. Since it was December and as she happened to be in Delhi, bitter cold set in quickly. But the young lady remained unruffled. Nevertheless, her body mechanism forced her to enfold her saree tightly around the body by covering the head and she grabbed the shoulders with her hands by clutching her folded legs near to her stomach. It simply didn't matter what her body was subjected to. She could have braved a storm happily. After all injuries caused to the body take far lesser time to heal than those caused to your mind. Although time is a great healer, some mental wounds take the entire lifetime to heal. The young lady had so many of them that rendered her very indifferent towards physical wounds. Cold breeze is just natural and it won't harm you when you are inside home or sitting in front of fire. You can overcome the heat in many ways and protect yourself from rain. But this young lady knew greater wretchedness of life.

At a tender age of 28 she had been through horrendous affliction nobody ever experienced. And the world never cared for her. Why should then she be interested in it? However this attitude of her was more apathetic than rebellious and she didn't mind it anyway.

She was still deeply indulged in the thought process when a, familiar, sugary voice entered her ears which sounded like.

Suchita

That's how the world knew her.

"Why are you sitting outside dear? Isn't it cold around here?" It was Ma, the mother who was quickly identified at the gate by her well-versed, somewhat lean figure, although it was very much dark now.

"Oh, not really", replied Suchita. It was as if she was back to consciousness. As she stood up after a long time her thighs ached and her eyes were a little puffed up, probably due to exorbitant shedding of tears. But how profusely delighted and assuaged she was to see the lady whom she referred as 'Ma', the mother ! Ma or Mrs. Kamal Sareen was neither her real mother nor mother-in-law but as close to her as a real mother could have been. One could never believe that Mrs. Sareen who was only an aunt for anybody else but a Ma for Jatin and Suchita was just a neighbour of them. Their relationship and behaviours never revealed this fact. The old widow in her late sixties was alone, with her son accepting Canadian, citizenship and a married daughter living, in nearby Chandigarh. Despite persistent requests by her son she refused to go abroad and with the rhapsodic camaraderie of Jatin and Suchita and solid financial aid in the form of her husband's pension she hardly confronted any trouble.

"It seems Jatin has left, I'm terrible sorry, Suchita. I couldn't come here to see him off. I had gone to temple you know. The crazy women virtually snatched me to the temple". The old lady seemed apologetic as she clutched the hands of Suchita.

"It's all right Ma, he had met you in the morning. He knew you wouldn't be here in the afternoon," said Suchita.

Hand in hand both the ladies entered the house and hurridly Suchita put on the lights.

"Suchita, how often should I tell you, not to daydream like that ?", asked Ma helping herself sit on the sofa, "You are a grown up my daughter. It's time to act not dream".

"I'm sorry Ma", There was a tinge of guilt in Suchita's eyes. Her voice was strikingly low pitched, clearly indicating that she was still not recovered completely.

"Frankly speaking I didn't dare to enter the house once Jatin was gone. I didn't simply feel like that. How could I Ma?", asked a dejected Suchita who looked uncomfortable even on the foam chair.

"I understand you my child," Ma's tone was genuinely sympathetic. As a matter of fact it had always been. The old lady could observe the gloomy face of Suchita, faded like a stale flower. But she didn't have any idea how to lift up her spirits and bring smile on that face which otherwise would shine like gold.

"Why do you look so anxious Suchita ?" asked Ma. "Are you worried about Jatin ?"

This query yielded no answer from the young lady as if she had not heard anything. With no response coming forward that could imply either "yes" or "no" she went on in a voice, as soft as butter "Suchita are you OK ? You didn't say anything ?"

At that instant Suchita realised that her remaining silent wasn't a proper way to hide her feelings. Hence she forced a delicate smile on her face which, as Ma quickly recognized was not natural.

"No, why should I worry ? He is a peacekeeper and his work is to maintain peace That's a sacred job Ma, that's a god's work". With a momentary pause she continued.

"I know it is like any other profession. Like some people are doctors, some are lawyers, teachers and so on. We cannot compare these different professions because every profession is important in its own right. But what the likes of Jatin are doing is something quite unique, very unparalleled. They risk their lives so that the nation should survive. Don't you think Ma, there is a more sense of service and will to sacrifice in this field than any other profession ? Don't you think that the people associated with the cause of national interest like Jatin and those belonging to their families should be more responsible ? I'm not sure about myself but I'm really trying to be more considerate and show restraint. But one thing is certain. I'm very happy and proud to have a life partner like him and also because he got an opportunity to serve the nation. Never mind how dangerous it might be. I have no doubt he would return victorious and make me happier than ever. But then I'm also a human being. How can I be as dry as any non living thing? Sometimes I feel awfully sad and terribly depressed. I have lost so much already and I don't want to lose any more." Suchita found herself superlatively refreshed as she uttered those words. And Ma was nothing less than impressed. She knew Suchita was talking honestly, right from the bottom of her heart and she had said what she meant. Ma was surprised and equally satisfied to watch her talk like that, very candid and very pure. Indeed over the years the girl had improved a lot !

At least she didn't hesitate to speak out the real thing. Moreover her eyes as usual had been too talkative to conceal any facts. These responses from Suchita were sufficient for Ma to comprehend that, although Suchita had picked up enough courage to face any tough situation that might arise, she couldn't help being anxious about Jatin. It wasn't extraordinary considering the total dedication of the two towards each other.

"Do you know Suchita why I didn't resist much when the ladies forced me to go to the temple ?" Asked Ma and without waiting for the response went on, "Simply because it was just like any other tour that Jatin was making. He is not fighting a war. He will be doing the job of a police. Besides if one has to go by the track record of Indian peacekeepers, they have done their work effectively. Why should then, we give much importance to an event which, in fact, is quite general ? If people start giving in to sentiments so often, how do you think the affairs would go on ? Wouldn't they come . . .".

Her sentence remained incomplete as their attention swung to the half opened door which somebody pushed with a sufficiently loud bang. And when that somebody entered in both the ladies broke into laughter. It was Nil, with his face and cloths strewn with mud, his hair spread in all possible direction and his mouth bearing a cute, innocuous smile.

"Oh, what has happened to my Pele ?" asked an amused Suchita who couldn't help laughing at the sight of her child.

"They made me a goalkeeper today. Was Pele a goalkeeper ?" Nil retorted in his immensely likeable tone and at once hurried towards the bathroom. His mom followed him curiously with an obvious intension to put to order the nice little mess her Pele had created. Ma watched them with tremendous interest as Suchita gave a hefty wash to her little footballer and changed his cloths. He in turn grabbed some coconut biscuits from Suchita and sat on Ma's lap gnawing at them.

Ma could notice a sudden alteration on Suchita's face as she looked at her son with sparkling eyes filled with passion and unmanageable delight. She was glowing like sunbeams reflecting from the surface of water. It was a soothing experience for Ma to witness a sea-change in the yesterday's defenseless, coy girl who herself was badly in need of a mother a few years back. And now she had proven herself to be a worthy mother showing all the qualities for which mothers everywhere are esteemed, qualities which make them unique in all aspects of human life. Ma had every reason to feel proud as she had played a major role in bringing about this transformation. Ma not only became her mother but also made her capable to be one. Suchita's joys knew no bounds when she gave birth to Nil some five years ago. Like any other girl she too had dreamt about a family, a good, loving husband and lovable, little children. But the kind of destiny she thought she had, the fulfilment of this dream appeared as distant as moon. No wonder then, the day Nil was born she cried a lot being unable to withstand the immense joyance of experiencing something which she had imagined only in her wildest dreams. For the first time in her life she wept because of overpowering ecstasy and not on account of the stinging grief she was well acquainted with. From that day onwards Nil was her lifeline as if her own soul was inhabiting the tiny body of that boy. And how sweet he was ! He had large, dark eyes which were inherited unmistakably from his mother and his smooth somewhat curly hair were exactly similar to his father's. His fair complexion however, was a contribution of both his parents. Suchita used to spend hours watching her baby do all those fascinating movements of little hands and legs, giving an ear to soft, frequent hums her baby would produce as if to communicate with her. She would hear those sounds with the intensity of a person listening to a melodious music. She would touch the tender hands gently only to get thrilled. Just the sight of Nil would exhilarate her like a breeze carrying the fragrance of a thousand roses would do. His smile used to provide a healing touch to her soul and her heart would sink at the instant he cried.

At times she wondered, how integral a child is to a mother. And quite inevitably the painful memories of her own mother would creep into her mind. Those weren't memories at all, but just the thoughts, because you could never remember a person who died when you were as old as a brand new car even if she might be your mother. How awfully agonizing it must be for a mother to die leaving a helpless child at the greedy world's disposal ? Her mother was such a luckless one and Suchita was an ill-fated child who even, didn't have a photograph of her mother. In solitudes she tried hard to remember her face but couldn't frame any picture of her in mind.

But all her unsettling thoughts would melt away with a mere sight of Ma. At last she had a mother !

A hearty chat with Ma would remove all cobwebs from Suchita's mind and she used to find herself breathing freely like a water starved fish hurled back to sea. Today was much the same case. Ma extracted all the nervousness that shadowed her mind and she could feel herself relaxing. Nil's arrival set her adrenalin pumping that turned her as cheerful as a lily. She chose not to talk about Jatin once Nil returned home, as he was not taken into confidence about his father's whereabouts.

Ma was so profoundly engrossed in the company of Suchita and Nil that she remained completely unaware of time. Quite accidently she caught sight of the wall clock pointing 8.35 and at once rose from her chair.

"Oh it's 8.30 already, I have to leave now dear," she said.

Suchita nodded.

"Will you be OK alone in the house ?" asked Ma.

Definitely Nil was too young to be taken into consideration.

Suchita nodded again.

"Alright then. Don't worry and call me anytime if you want," saying this Ma started getting down the stairs.

"Yes Ma" said Suchita and waved her hand as she watched Ma closing the gate behind her. For a moment she stood at the door gently moving her fingers over Nil's hair and then closed the door.

She was expecting worst thing now. Nil was well aware of the time his father used to come home. But he had not enquired about his father yet. Probably he knew Jatin used to be a bit late due to some extra work or many other reasons not quite understandable to his tiny brain. But he was sure to ask Suchita about his dad sometimes later. That moment, Suchita knew, was going to impart a big worry as she knew, it was not easy to handle this little boy. Being his mother she could even read this mind and easily forecast his reaction to practically anything. Nil was quite intelligent for his age and this fact used to fill his mother's heart with pride. But he was badly stubborn who couldn't tolerate anything against his wishes, a quality that could turn this otherwise cuddly kid into a menace. Suchita distinctly remembered an occasion when Jatin forgot to buy a toy car that he promised to bring. Nil was uncontrollable and after a long futile effort to calm him down, Jatin had to go to the market at night and bring the toy car.

Suchita wondered, as she began preparing for dinner, how she would tackle such a situation now as Jatin was away. Also his being away meant a loss of a fast friend of Nil and a whole lot of trouble for his poor mother. Who in absence of Jatin was going to play football with the little Pele, at home ? Who would carry him to the park, a thing he was so accustomed to, and run untamed after him? Who would throw his tiny body into the air just for fun and bring colourful kites as per his desire ? Suchita didn't know. But her immediate concern was how she was going to inform that cute little devil who sat glued to the television set, that his father would be out of the country by the time they wake up in the next morning. Worse she didn't know when he was supposed to return back. She had no idea how to convince her child that he was not told about this in advance because of certain reasons that she could not explain.

But as a mother her heart was sinking because she did not allow that tiny body to meet his father before they separated from each other by thousands of kilometres. She did it only because she wanted Jatin to go with a peaceful mind and not with a heavy heart. But she felt as if she had betrayed her son. How dearly, she thought, a child loves its mother ! And how badly it depends on her ! Even if you put the entire world on one side and the mother on the other, any child would select its mother. The things mother tells get engraved on its brain. Even though Suchita had not lied to Nil, she had not spoken the truth either and that was what eating up her mind. Finally she came to know that she was not in a position to keep her son in dark about his father but she thought that the time was not ripe for that purpose. Hence she decided to skip it somehow, for the time being.

"Hay mom, where is Dad ?" she heard Nil saying as she served for the dinner. Suchita did what she could do the best. She kept quiet.

"Mom, where is Dad? Won't he come home today ?" Nil insisted.

"No, he has gone somewhere." As her tone sounded he could have very well gone to a movie theatre. Suchita was amazed at the way she could make it as simple as that.

"When will he return ?" It was an obvious query.

"He didn't tell." Her reply was ready.

"But why didn't he meet me before going ?" The child was about to cry.

Now there was no answer !

"He was in a hurry and you were busy playing football, honey." She tried to manage somehow in a tone that was softer than butter and sweeter than honey. But in vain ! The damage had been done already. The child realised that he had been cheated. He burst into tears.

"Why didn't you tell me ?" he kept on repeating as helpless Suchita picked him in her arms. She tried hard to alleviate his anger but without yielding any outcome. Nil was utterly headstrong, trying his best to free himself from the realm of his mother. His was a great frenzy and his fiery tussle with Suchita resulted in twisting of his body. But Nil was least bothered about it. He kept on shouting and crying. At last after about 15–20 minutes of struggle that turned the affairs of their hair and cloths into a sheer mess the boy finally gave in. After running out of energy he gradually calmed down, completely exhausted, sobbing irregularly, eventually succumbing to sleep in Suchita's arms. Her terrible ordeal was over ! She gave an anaemic look at the meals kept in front of her. There lay a tiny dinner plate, unattended and a bigger one also unattended.

There was no point in waking him up, for the dinner. And with no food in his stomach she couldn't even look at the meal. That certainly wasn't a right kind of way to end a day. She had to put some efforts to hold back the impatient water droplets collected in her eyes. Having done it, she moved into the bedroom, carefully balancing the child and softly put him into the bed. Strangely, Suchita found her legs to be worn out, almost paralysed and her movements became lethargic. She knew it wasn't a physical weakness but the result of the psychological trauma through which she had to go throughout the day that ranged from extreme depression to extreme mood elevation and again back to depression. Nervously she cleaned up the kitchen and returned back to bed only to find that her entire body was aching with extreme pain stemming from each and every bone that reached to the skin and at once disappeared. In a moment her face grew a thin layer of sweat. Hurridly Suchita got down and turned on the ceiling fan, setting it in full speed. She felt much easeful and rested against a pillow. But she knew after what had happened, it was impossible for her to sleep peacefully. She felt like calling Ma but soon discarded the thought. "Why should the old lady suffer for me ?," she thought, "She has so many things to suffer for already".

Besides theirs was not the single family, which was going through such a testing phase. There were thousands of peacekeepers who must have left their dear ones just to fight with deadly guns in unknown jungles. Somebody's son, somebody's brother, somebody's father and somebody's husband. Nobody was sure what was in store for them. But one thing was certain, the task enthrusted upon the peacekeepers was difficult and there was hardly any doubt about it. They knew very few things about the island of Sri Lanka and they were mostly unaware about the thick forest that flowered over the most part of the battlefield. Moreover the enemy was cruel, cold-blooded and absolutely inhuman. It was well aquainted with the geographical conditions in that region. Considering these facts even a kid could have predicted that entering those jungles was no less than putting your head into a lion's jaw.

Most probably the peacekeepers knew it. But they had not learnt refusing the commands of their chiefs. They didn't know, how to run away from the battlefields. They were as ferocious as tigers and contained lions' hearts in their chests. They were the part and parcel of the great Indian Army which has a record of bravery and sacrifice.

Sacrifice! Yes, Wasn't all her sufferings a part of sacrifice that a person has to make for the motherland ? Wasn't that a sacrifice every family of the peacekeepers making ? Then where was the difference ? Why did Suchita have a boundless sense of hollowness after Jatin left her ? She was deep into thoughts again. And a slight pondering yielded the answer to her inquest.

Loneliness

It was her loneliness that made her so acutely depressed. In every other family there might be a number of persons who shared the burden of grief, who console each other and try to detract each other's mind away from the heart breaking thoughts. You are badly in need of such people when you are in distress. Preferably, the elderly people who have survived many upheavals in life, people with grey hair and wrinkled faces, people with tremendous reserve of experience, people with great patience and great hearts, people who behave like light houses for the young ones lost in the ocean of life. Wasn't there anybody like that with her ? There certainly was !

Ma was no less than a whole family for Suchita. Along with Jatin she had played a major role in reconstructing Suchita from yesterday's timid girl into today's confident young lady. In fact she had a lion's share in it as she had spent a lot of time with Suchita as compared to Jatin. But the old lady had a whole host of her own problems. Their relationship was one of an emotional give and take. Ma's only son had left the country some eight years ago and settled in Canada. Despite his constant requests Ma chose to remain in India. But remaining alone gave a sense of incompleteness to her and at such an old age she badly needed support. Also she was in requirement of an outlet for her motherly affection and she found it in the young couple of Jatin and Suchita. In fact it was Jatin who first called her Ma when she moved into the house in their neighbourhood some seven years ago.

The old lady was suffering from blood pressure that resulted into a whole lot of trouble including diabetes. Death of her husband and disunion from the only son had taken its toll and over the years her conditions deteriorated. But a sight of Suchita was sufficient to shine her eyes. And a grinning Nil would make her laugh heartily. Nil was the most precious thing for her, an embodyment of joy. Whenever she went to the temple she prayed for him.

Even then Suchita was of the opinion that she had to face the situations alone, because Ma had her own grief. Astoundingly, she didn't want anybody to share it with her. On the contrary she spread happiness and bliss, whenever and wherever possible, "So why should I," Suchita thought, "give her extra burden ?"

"No. I have to bear it all alone ! I won't give a slightest hint that I am, in any way, suffering. Also, I will try to be as gleeful as her. Everybody here is blessed with something and cursed with something, ups and downs are essential parts of life. You have to be courageous enough to face it all. It's a shame being coward and run away from situation."

Suchita was amazed she could think like that. Of course most of it she owed to Ma and Jatin.

Time passed on unnoticed and Suchita's mind was travelling from India to Sri Lanka, from Ma to Jatin to Nil.

A very faint glow of the zero watt bulb filled the entire room. Suchita's eyes were firmly focussed on the ceiling fan which was spinning endlessly. With her hand lying across her forehead and mind riding high on the kite of thoughts she layed on the bed upto early hours of dawn finally falling prey to the clutches of sleep.

✣✣✣

Two

Maj. Jatin Mittal undulated his hands at Suchita, his wife, as the military vehicle advanced forward setting a slight backward thrust to its inmates. He stole some precious glimpse of his seemingly motionless lady as long as he could do it and turned his face away from the window after she withdrew from his ambit of vision in due time. But his mind still deemed about that svelte figure he left behind.

"If only I could stop this damn vehicle", contemplated the young man, "and run back to Suchita and say, look I have come back, " His thoughts drained out for a while because of such tempting desire, but soon he came back to reality.

"Never," cried his inner voice, "I'm not a coward. My father never did it. Nobody has done it. Even Suchita would become angry if I do a foolish thing like that. And how she will drive me out !" He smiled at that.

But he knew very well that he hankered to return back not because he was nerveless but because he loved Suchita very dearly. Once he had pulled her out from grave when she happened to be downcast and now he was leaving her on her own. However, he was not that worried about her this time. He had succeeded in bringing about a drastic transition in Suchita's life. Now she was not the blushing, disabled girl of yesteryears but an unassailable young lady who emerged better and resourceful over the years. She knew how to face the harsh realities of life and pull out victories in the most precarious conditions. Jatin along with Ma equipped her with every armour needed to win the war that life is. And she was doing a great job. She was fighting the battle of life along with Jatin, hand in hand, shoulder to shoulder. She left her past way behind and never shown inclination towards it. It is very tough for a person having a dreaded past to live a normal and peaceful life. For that you have to liberate yourself from the webs of the dark memories, memories hovering over your mind, memories trying to entangle you, memories rendering you incompetent to think about the present and the future memories impairing your mind and soul, diabolical memories, pitiless memories.

More often than nothing persons having such terrible pasts gravitate towards self-destruction, suffer nervous breakdowns or get insane. Suchita had chosen first choice, but having made a fiasco of her attempt she recuperated unbelievably thanks to Jatin and Ma. Although she had a dearth, which was evident in light of her sufferings, she was courageous and perhaps it was so because of the unimaginable things that she already had experienced. Moreover she was exceedingly kind. Although the world did not furnish her much she had no grudge against anybody. But she had developed a sense of indifference towards the rest of the world and she was satisfied having confined herself within a self drawn boundary.

When Jatin married Suchita he feared she might not recover from the trauma. He feared, she might not live a normal life. But much for his delight Suchita proved him wrong. She regenerated herself just like a Phoenix. And Jatin was proud of her. It was a commendable recovery indeed.

"Guru, are you in Sri Lanka ?", a voice interrupted Jatin's thinking process and he heard a loud laughter bursting into the atmosphere. Expeditiously he regained the contemporary state of mind and turned his focus on to his comrades.

"Of course not, Mr. Sam", he retorted.

"Then what were you supposed to be doing when you were looking outside the window and not listening to what we guys were talking ? I thought you were wandering in the jungles of Jaffna expecting a tiger to jump on you", Mr. Sam argued.

"Now will you hold back your tongue ?" Jatin raised his palm as if to strike it against Mr. Sam's face. Perceiving this Mr. Sam whisked away from him and sheltered his own face with his cap.

"Look comrades", he thundered displacing his cap, "he calls me his friend and look how rudely he behaves with me", and suddenly lowering his face, pretended as if he was crying.

The whole vehicle exploded with laughter. Jatin too couldn't help laughing.

Laughter was the best medicine for these men who did this work of Army which is adjudged to be as dry as a desert and Mr. Sam or formally Maj. Sameer Pande was their doctor who would regularly administer this life drug into their bodies by cracking jokes and funny comments. It was pretty sure that this was the best thing you could do to prevent yourself from getting lunatic when you have been dumped thousands of kilometres away from your land, in a place where nobody could predict what thing will explode suddenly causing your flesh to become a part of the dust. Hence it was always better not to lose a chance to laugh.

The occupants of this vehicle were all young men between the age group of 25 to 30 with most of them falling within a height range of 5' 9" to 6' 3", all heavily built wearing thick uniforms with the typical combination of green, yellow and brown colours and showed off their proud caps which indicated their identity as officers in the grand Indian Army. This was going to be their first experience of its kind, a real skirmish with a seasoned enemy who was not known to demonstrate the scantiest amiability even in the remotest of circumstances. Thus they had a tough task carved out for them. But being young they were enthusiastic and full with vigour. Moreover they all were impatient to actually pour bullets from their weaponry which otherwise used to be just like a collection of toys for them. The main purpose in bringing them together was to expose them to a warlike situation and make use of their youth power. For this they were plucked out from various regiments and given a special training together. Presently they were in the process of transportation to Sri Lanka where they were to be handed over to their respective regiments. Because of this, most of them knew each other well while some were even good friends like Jatin and Sam who belonged to the same batch of cadets.

The giant four wheeler covered every nook and corner of the city while accumulating army officers and finally landed in the Army Headquarters at 7.40 pm. This was the place, which Mr. Sam would invariably refer to as 'Central Jail'. Officers from all over the country had already gathered in the headquarters, patiently awaiting the further instructions from their bosses. The Delhi officers had just arrived when to the surprise of everyone the chief of the army staff himself appeared at the scene. Very rapidly did he come and very rapidly did he surmount their hearts by declaring that there was going to be a small farewell party. Most of them, however couldn't believe their eyes, but surely the chief wasn't anybody who could have fooled the parting officers. Subsequently there indeed was a party.

"Friends," announced Jatin grabbing a peg of rum in the party, "this one is for the good health of all of you and successful completion of the mission, we are undertaking". Mr. Sam was not to remain behind. Quickly he stepped in.

"This is not the proper way to put it", he lodged his disapproval and promptly lifted two pegs of whisky, one in each hand.

"Comrades, this one is for your good health", he raised his right hand, and this one is for the successful accomplishment of our mission", he raised his left hand at this instant. As usual his friends started laughing, but Mr. Sam was not over yet. He gulped the high voltage fluid from one of the glasses and poured another peg in his own peerless style.

"And this one is for the poor souls who will fly to the hell because of our guns," he professed in a characteristic fashion. This remark extracted a thunderous applause from his friends, which in turn attracted attention of those who were not involved in the group. Everybody started inquiring and peeping in and soon the chief himself came forward and requested Mr. Sam to repeat his act. At that instant the effect of the three pegs Mr. Sam had crammed into stomach had vanished and he forced a lump down his dry throat. But encouraged by all and keeping in mind the lively nature of the chief he duplicated what he had done and drove enormous response. Even the chief was seen clapping and laughed whole heartedly that swung the slight bulge of his stomach. This was the laugh Mr. Sam always enjoyed imitating. Mr. Sam accepted the requests of all to reproduce the toasting act as it could mean another three helpings of whisky. But the poor fellow had to be satisfied with three pegs of plain soda water this time, as his Guru Jatin didn't allow him to have drinks.

The party proved to be a fantastic refresher for the boys. They knew, for a few of them it might just turn out to be the last. So they helped themselves with a good amount of drinks and enjoyed every bit.

Just after the dinner at exactly 9.15 pm the officers were ordered to wind up. Very soon the strong Indian contingent was on board of a special Indian Airlines' carrier at the Indira Gandhi International Airport after being convoyed to the aerodrome by two army vehicles. The chief of staff also accompanied them to bid a grand farewell. The luggage of the officers had earlier been assembled and packed into the aircraft. After finishing all formal business, keeping with the army tradition of punctuality the jumbo jet airliner plunged into air at 10.00 pm sharp. Almost all the eyes were staring at the nice looking array of light visible from the windows as the giant flying machine traversed a smooth curve before securing a straight horizontal path. The eyes still remained peeping out of the windows till suddenly the sea of light turned into a dark ocean below the plane, signalling that the capital city was left way behind. The entire day was surely very exhausting for them, both physically and emotionally, but hardly anyone showed a sign of sleep. But their other activities slowed down and what remained was slight murmuring in as low a tone as possible.

Jatin still was mingled with the deep darkness below. He simply didn't have an intention to break his present state. Why ? Even the notorious Mr. Sam was seen relaxing by closing eyes and that explosive mouth of him. That gave an excellent opportunity to Jatin to become somewhat serious and think about his journey and his fate. He knew he was going to appear in the most fatiguing test of his life. But he was sure about his destiny and it was either a victorious welcome at home or an esteemed guard of honour in the shelter of the beloved tricolour. In both ways his soul was going to rest peacefully. But he could not come to comprehend what Suchita was going to do should his destiny choose to offer him the second option. By all means it would be a big blow for her fragile mind and equally fragile body. Then there was Nil ! It was not appropriate though, to allow such negative thinking creep into the mind, the responsible husband and the father in him was prevailing over the worthy soldier that he was. He didn't know what purpose they were serving by fighting a battle that didn't directly involve their motherland. He had no idea why hundreds and thousands of innocents like Suchita and Nil should suffer because of some ununderstandable political whims. What thing was worrying him most was, if such thoughts continued flowing in, there was a chance that he might loose the driving force required to win a war. He feared that instead of going after the enemy with killer's instinct, he might find ways to save his own life. If such thing happens it will haunt him for the rest of the life and seriously hamper his reputation as a soldier. Also if everybody started thinking on the same line, which by every possibility was inevitable and run away from the battlefield, victory would run away from them and slip out of their hands altogether which was not going to cater for any purpose. And what about the pride and prestige of one of the strongest armies, they all were a part of ? Finally it boiled down to only one thing, i.e., they were all helpless. It was better, therefore to follow the policy of doing the job rightly without being concerned about the result or consequences.

At a distance of about 10,000 feet above the ground there were many heads contemplating the same issue. Mr. Sam was not one of them. The guy was sure carefree ! As soon as Delhi was nowhere to be seen, this young man sitting beside his mate Jatin, was already dozing. But that helped maintain the atmosphere inside the plane below noise pollution level, but created a ghastly serious background. By now the freezing air conditioner was switched to a warmer mode and the lights were dim. Jatin tried to slip into the fine protection of sleep by closing the eyes and slowly and steadily the sleep goddess caught hold of him.

❖❖❖

"Wake up man", somebody shook his shoulder. It was Mr. Sam. Jatin could identify him even without opening the eyes.

"Colombo is fast approaching. It's 3.15 am already." Mr. Sam showed him his wristwatch as if Jatin might not believe his words.

Jatin had a slight glimpse around just to see what others were doing. Most of the boys were awake. Slightly he rubbed his eyes and tilling a bit glanced through the window. Long ahead on what seemed to be a horizon in that well lit starry night, were bright dots of glowing lights that belonged to the slept capital of Sri Lanka. It was hardly possible to distinguish between these lights and the milky white spots of stars spread all over the sky. Only what indicated the difference was the concentrated nature of the lights and the slight twinkling of stars. Otherwise it was as if a fine texture of glistening white spots arranged artistically on a deep dark cloth. Jatin stuck there for a moment and then moved towards the bathroom. He had hardly reached his seat after having a wash, when the microphone sounded instructing them to tie belts. Within few minutes the aircraft turned its nose slightly downwards making headway for landing. After another few minutes the plane flew over the city of Colombo, finally landing on the airstrip as the giant engine ceased to function gradually, making the propellers to stop the swirling motion and covered a few metres on ground before the giant jumbo jet came to a halt.

Promptly the officers were escorted from the airport to the hotels where they were permitted to resume and enjoy their earlier disturbed sleep. The army officials had booked three hotels which were a few metres apart. Jatin was given accommodation in one 'Oriental Palace' and his roommate inescapably was Mr. Sam. Sam was already quite upset over the timing of the flight which began its journey at night. As if it was not enough, he was asked to quit the sleep because Colombo happened to be so near that there was a long time for the sunrise when they reached there. All the way from airport he had been cursing all those who arranged their trip. But as soon as they checked in the 'Oriental Palace' Mr. Sam was the first to enter into the sleep mode.

❖❖❖

It was almost 9.00 am when Jatin woke up, a time which was more than what he expected. Obviously he had some excess sleep. Instantly he realised that they were in Sri Lanka and by a Sri Lankan watch it would be 9.30 am. As per the orders they were supposed to be taken out of the hotel at 11.00 am Sri Lankan Time. Sensing the urgency, he quickly jumped out of the bed. Mr. Sam was still indulged in deep slumber and if one had to go by it's intensity it could very well have been midnight. Jatin causing damage to his sleep this time, broke his sweet meditation and reminded him that they were on duty when he showed some signs of protests.

Speedily the two mates finished off their daily business and got ready long before the army carriers entered the premises of the hotel. Initially the boys were startled to see Indian Army vehicles but somebody promptly pointed out that two Indian Ships carrying vehicles, artilleries and soldiers were already been to Sri Lankan shores and that those only were the vehicles which carried them to the hotels at previous night. Without wasting much time the officers got in and left the hotels. They moved slowly through the Sri Lankan Capital which offered an excellent opportunity for them to have a good look at the city and the people therein. Most wanderers on the streets seemed to be ignorant about this parade of officers, throwing occasional glances at the vehicles only because they were heavy. But some fellows acknowledged them, watching with curious eyes, waving hands to welcome this bunch of strangers who were supposed to be risking their life for their sake. A few enthusiasts were seen fluttering white flags as the peacekeepers moved past them. After about half an hour's journey through Colombo's populated area they stopped in front of a big horizontal building which turned out to be Sri Lankan Army headquarters as they drew near. This was where they were scheduled to meet their seniors and supposed to be given the general and the specific information about their task. And this was precisely where they were to be assigned their duties and described their role in one of the most daring and exceedingly difficult peacekeeping operations over undertaken by the Indian Army.

One by one the officers entered into the main gate where their passports were thoroughly checked before letting them in. Through a long, narrow passage enclosed in the huge, concrete horizontal structure that constituted the headquarters, they were taken into a big hall. Somewhat old but stout looking steel chairs with leather covered foam sheets were nicely arranged covering most of the available area of the floor. The chairs were directed towards the front portion which contained seven–eight comparatively newer and finer chairs, a small wooden table covered with a white cloth and resting a beautiful flowerpot along with a glass of water and a pointer stick on its surface. On the wall, facing the audiences were hung two giant maps, one of Sri Lanka and the other of South Asia. The hall had a good public address system with several speakers popping up from various places and a microphone was positioned directly in front of the maps.

The officers were requested to take seats and served a light breakfast. And after some patient waiting at exactly noon the front door opened and one by one many familiar faces poured in. Col. Singh, Brig. Malik followed by Col. Gulati, Col. Choudhari, Col. Sen, Col. Joshi and finally Col. Samarsinghe as a representative from Sri Lankan side.

"Guru, be alert, here comes the broad gauge train", Mr. Sam murmured at Jatin as the senior armymen marched inside in a row, eventually settling into chairs. Jatin indicated to keep quiet by putting his forefinger on mouth.

Though very aged, all these armymen showed great military spirits while walking, with every movement emitting kingly characters and well synchronised with others.

Col. Sen. that soft spoken and very likable man took charge of the microphone and formally welcomed the Indian officers. No introduction of the just arrived men was needed because all were known to the officers except Col. Samarsinghe. Col. Sen briefly made them acquainted with him and informed that Col. Samarsinghe was one from Sri Lankan Army who would be consulted by Indian Army and help in better coordination between the two armies. Finally Col. Sen handed over the microphone to the topmost authority present at the sight, the formidable Brig. Malik. The entire auditorium filled itself with pindrop silence as this old fox rose from his chair. Unlike the Chief of Staff he was not the one who could be taken for granted. As a matter of fact he was notorious for his straightforward attitude towards the task enthrusted upon his shoulders and he meant only business.

"Friends" removing his spectacles Brig. Malik started in his characteristic voice which was as rough as a sand paper, "as you know I have been given the responsibility by our Hon. Chief of Staff to guide this phase of our operation in Sri Lanka. On my behalf I welcome you here in Colombo. At first I will give you the scenario which compelled us to carry out this operation and then I will be describing what role exactly you all individual officers would be playing to make it a success."

At this juncture the old man paused and took out a small chit of paper from his pocket which presumably contained points to be discussed, wore his specs again and after positioning the chit on the table he continued.

"I need not remind you that presently we are in a country called Sri Lanka. This one is a sufficiently big island in Indian ocean. Often, we refer it as an emerald island because of its lush greenery. Geographically, Sri Lanka is situated towards the south-east direction of the Indian Peninsula. As you can see here in this map it is quite near to the Indian shores, the least distance being 30 kms. from Rameshwaram on the Indian coast.

This country gained independence from the British rule just after our own independence, i.e., in 1948. The population here, mainly consists of two components namely Sinhalis who speak Sinhali language and the Tamils who speak Tamil language. Unfortunately, Sri Lanka has a long history of ethnic conflict as the Tamils here are fighting for more power, possibly different state. And their stronghold is the northern part of the country surrounding Jaffna. Because of the encouragement and lavish funding by the sympathisers all over the world, some Tamil fundamentalists established military outfits like EPRLF, LTTE etc. But LTTE is the most dominant force and as it is well known, it believes in Guerrilla warfare. India was also affected by the activities of these organisation but strangely the government was ignorant about it. Worse Indian government, as it seems to many, helped them directly or indirectly in initial period.

As all of us know LTTE's history of freedom struggle is a nerve wrenching story of brutal massacres brought about by sophisticated and modern military devices. Their motto seems to be finishing off the opposition by whatever means. Several political leaders of Sri Lanka were killed by them and thousands of innocent people were ruthlessly butchered.

Finally Indian Government realised what a blunder it was to ignore the activities of these outfits. Consequently a few days back Prime Minister Rajiv Gandhi struck a deal with Sri Lankan President Jayawardhane. This Rajiv–Jayawardhane pact or Indo-Sri Lanka accord as it is called, was signed on 29 July 1987. According to this India agreed to help in settlement of Sri Lankan ethnic crisis by sending an IPKF or Indian peacekeeping force. And you all are the part and parcel of it. Our mission is specified as (i) help end the hostilities and (ii) supervise surrender of arms."

Brig. Malik stopped a bit and scanned the faces of his officers with his sharp eyes that were magnified and projected large due to the thick lenses of his spectacles. Slowly he folded the chit of paper and tucked it into his pocket and gulped half of the water from the glass kept on the table.

"I think I have cleared most of the points about the reasons behind this operation," said the old man slightly whipping his face with his handkerchief, "You may or may not agree with its purpose. But one thing is sure, we don't have tradition to object the decisions of our superiors. So I expect you to perform wholeheartedly and without any misconduct. Remember, the quality and the integrity of Indian Army is at stake. You can maintain or destroy its credibility. I need not emphasize this point again and again as we believe that you are quite capable of distinguishing between right and wrong. Anyway, I haven't yet given you a chance to make your points. Yes, if you have any doubts regarding what we are doing you are free to ask."

Saying this Brig. Malik took his seat. For a moment the entire hall filled with slight murmuring and whispering. Officers were seen bending towards one another and discussing in low tones. After about 2–3 minutes a young man rose from his chair.

"Excuse me sir, you were supposed to tell us about our exact role here. But you didn't say anything about it" he said.

"Be patient young man I have not finished it yet," retorted Brig. Malik with a slight chukcle and asked him to sit down.

"Sir, if you don't mind may I ask you a question which may seem quite irrelevant in the context ?", a chirpy voice emerged from deep within the assembly. Quite inevitably it was the man whom every body referred as Mr. Sam. Instantly, almost all faces turned to him to find out what he was upto this time. Jatin seemed very anxious after this sudden query from his mate because he was not sure when this chap would cross the barrier between seriousness and mischief.

After getting a go ahead call from Brig. Malik, Sam fired his salvo.

"Sir, why was the timing of our aeroplane so odd ? We had plenty of trouble having good sleep out there. Don't you think we could have very well flown here during day time ?"

"Indeed," The old man shook his head approvingly, "By all means you could have flown here in sunlight but not without causing any trouble. See, our enemy is no fool. He has a big circuit of spies. Besides, everyone knew about possible arrival of IPKF. So, it would have been idiotic to assume that our enemy never expected us. He certainly did. That's why we preferred to travel at night just to puzzle our enemy and hide our identity. Also, if our enemy had decided to attack our plane it was easier to counter the attack at night when the air traffic as well as marine traffic usually remains low. Is that OK, young man ?"

Mr. Sam nodded at that and sat down in a familiar atmosphere of laughing crackers. If anyone was worthy to receive Nobel Prize for making people laugh it was Mr. Sam. He had made himself so much funny that people laughed at anything he used to do. But it used to please him equally.

With no further queries forthcoming Brig. Malik stood up once again.

"As nobody is coming forward may I assume that everything is properly understood ? OK, then, gentlemen we are coming to the most important thing now which is also the main purpose of our meeting here. Yes, I am talking about your task assignment. We have in all five regiments to carry out the operation and accordingly we have divided the total area of supervision into as many parts. If you look at this map of Sri Lanka, you can see the boundaries of these hypothetical regions. We will soon hand over to you the detailed map of the area designated to your respective regiment. As per the schedule, today itself you will be transported to your proper places to take the charge. What you are supposed to do there is the most important part and you should understand it very thoroughly. Our aim is to prevent the enemy from getting out of their stronghold area which is nothing but the jungle area. In other words they should not penetrate our wall in any case and come to the civilian area to cause havoc. Also if something concrete emerges out of the negotiations and the enemy decides to surrender, we will look after the smooth surrender of arms and maintain ceasefire. These objectives should be crystal clear to you and you should engrave it on your mind so that you don't loose track. Am I very clear or do you require further clarification ?"

The tone of the old man was unmistakably that of a school teacher asking his pupils to do certain exercise. Again after realising that the audience is silent for over a minute Brig. Malik went ahead.

"Right then, young men, from now onwards you are in possession of your regiments. Meet your superiors and receive further instructions. But before leaving I want to caution you, because we are not thorough enough about the conditions prevailing here. Also this is for the first time you are facing a warlike situation. So be careful. Don't believe your enemy. Never let your emotions take over your conscience. Most importantly remove all things from your mind which are related to your dear ones. Please stop worrying about them. We will ensure that they all remain in good condition.

Remember, your service is needed by our nation. It may be in whatever form, may it be on foreign land. Don't give up hope at any stage. As an incharge of this operation I want nothing but victory and I strongly believe that in the end we will meet here once again, perhaps all of us, to celebrate conquest. Finally, I wish you a grand success," saying this the old man turned abruptly and swiftly walked out with his head held high. The other gentlemen with him, followed him.

Officers were amazed to see Brig. Malik talk like that and the way he suddenly departed was quite unusual. The roughness in his manner and voice seemed to recede a bit during his concluding lines. Everybody present there knew that no army either victorious or defeated, had ever returned back in full strength. In every war some precious human diamonds are essentially lost. Even then that does not make any commander sentimental. But that old war veteran had displayed, through the media of his half choked voice, an another wonderful dimension of his personality that, in no way matched with the virtues he was popularly known for.

"So finally it has been proved that he is not a wild animal", commented Mr. Sam as soon as the programme was over.

When the officers were guessing what the next item on their agenda would be Col. Choudhari came back and asked them to divide themselves according to the regiments. He allotted some code number to every regiment. One by one different regiments were ushered into different rooms and handed over to their respective supervisors. The officers were given detailed information and maps of the area which they were supposed to guard. Their lower rank subordinates who had earlier reached Colombo joined them after lunch.

At 2.30 pm all the formalities were called off and the boys were allowed to have adequate amount of rest till 8.00 pm because the instructions of their top bosses were clear, come what may travel only at night. This policy was formulated with the sole intention of deceiving the enemy. But of course the think tank behind this operation was too intelligent to neglect the futility of the belief that their wise adversary new nothing about these movements. Their enemy was not the one which could be taken for granted. Hence each action of Indian Army was carefully planned, thought over and revised hundreds of times by some of the best brains available. That's why a stepwise and elaborate action plan was ready with every army authority. Having strong faith in that plan and its young, dynamic executioners in the form of their soldiers Brig. Malik ordered the army to move forward and at about 9.00 pm the IPKF marched past Sri Lankan Capital. Very soon this heavy fleet of vehicles moved with great pace, pressing hard the poor roads not meant for such a heavyweight brigade. Slowly their distance from Colombo was increasing, so was the uneasiness of the old Colonels and Majors. Because they knew that their enemy was foxier than a fox. Moreover it was an expert user of landmines. In its territory you never know when something bursts like a cracker if you happen to touch it. To tackle these nasty landmines the Indians had worked out a brilliant plan. They attached a long metal strip with a single wheel tied to it, to the front portion of the leading vehicles so that if at all they had a landmine laid in front of them it would blow away as soon as this wheel touched it. This would ensure that the vehicles remain safe.

All except some top officers and the Sri Lankan army representatives who were guiding the vehicles, were allowed to sleep. But most of them could not enjoy it because of the bad road conditions which was deteriorating fast with its width decreasing and the surface becoming rough. Haphazardly grown, branches of trees were crashing with the windowpanes from both sides, producing irritating noisy sound. By and by the vehicles began dispersing in various directions and vanished in deep darkness.

Jatin was in a state of partial slumber throughout the journey and woke up only in the early hours of morning. Colonel Choudhari who was accompanying them as an incharge of Regiment 103 to which both Jatin and Mr. Sam belonged, was giving instructions to the officers who were getting down at various places along with their soldiers. Soon their carrier was getting depleted of men. At about 8.15 a.m. Jatin was ordered to give up the vehicle and move towards his destination. He was provided with 10 soldiers to assist him in his duty. The men grabbed their luggage and quickly got down as Jatin waved good-by to this partner Mr. Sam who was smiling mischievously like a teasing kid, and wished him goodluck by the thumbs up sign. After acknowledging his gesture, Jatin waited till the army vehicle was out of sight. He then visually inspected the area where they had landed and took out the map provided to him to decide their future course as his 10 commandos curiously watched their boss's activity. After carefully gazing at the complicated map he folded it and took out of his lens. By standing on a nearby lump of mud Jatin could observe the area and could see nothing but an endless mat of forest which started just at a few yards from the dusty track which had brought them to their present position. Jatin ordered his men to march forward and they entered into what could be the thickest forest they had ever seen in life. Entering into it was extremely difficult while moving through it was almost impossible. The sunbeams hardly reached the ground in that forest, their path being blocked by the formidable woody giants. There were trees everywhere and whatever little space was spared, was covered by huge bushes and crawling creepers. With a heavy load of their luggage the men moved at a snail's pace, smashing the branches with the barrels of their guns and removing the irritating, giant spider webs that stuck to their uniforms. The soil was moist and loose, making it difficult to walk. Anticipating this the soldiers were priorly advised to wear gumboots that extended upto their knees. Overcoming all these hardships they covered 10–12 km before Jatin ordered them to stop. It was 2.30 pm and everyone was hungry beyond limit. They searched for a suitable place having less concentration of trees and having found such a place started cleaning the mess out there. They cut some trees and crushed the bushes. Finally a tent was laid down where the tired men had their meals and fell fast asleep. With the kind of toil they all went through on that day, they could have slept even if a thousand lions had roared in the jungle simultaneously.

When Jatin woke up it was very dark everywhere and the things only upto 1 to 2 metres from him were feebly visible. He reached for his watch, which showed that it was still around 5.20 pm. He woke up his men and ordered them to start building what would be their shelter. In that deem light by using minimum possible battery available to them the eleven Indians laboured hard for hours together and managed to build a small hut capable of providing enough space to sleep for four people. In addition to this they erected a watch tower on the top portion of four huge, nearby trees that could accommodate four persons. This meant that atleast three out of these eleven would have to be awake at any time. For the construction of these huts they used the trunks and branches of the trees which they had cut in the afternoon, nailing them and tying them with ropes to fabricate the framework. They covered these huts by the tent cloth and wood stumps to create ceiling and walls. They suspended a monkey ladder from the watch tower to climb up and down. This primitive looking compartment was equipped with ultramodern lens and a radio transmitter and receiver set. Four long range riffles stood in a corner pointing their barrels upward, waiting impatiently to eject fireballs at any impending target. An earthen pot was ready to serve water to the thirsty soldiers. Most of the luggage including food material was housed in the ground level hut. In addition to this the hut contained cloths and articles of daily needs besides huge stockpile of weapons including two machine guns, four riffles, number of hand grenades and a big storage of bullet magazines.

They spread soft grass and twigs on the floor and covered it by cotton sheets imparting a bed like appearance. The party then shifted its attention to cooking thanks to their hollow stomachs. Soon a campfire rose in the jungle and food preparation was underway. In the meantime Jatin inspected the whole arrangement made by his team. He checked wireless set by contacting Col. Choudhari and then Mr. Sam who was somewhere within a radius of 30–35 km. from Jatin's camp. Finally he settled down beside the fire slowly sipping at his cup of coffee, staring at the flames in a very pensive mood. It was the most hectic day of his life and he felt very tired, terribly exhausted and indeed hopelessly sleepy. In last 2/3 days he had got no time even to think about himself. Suddenly he started reflecting on his life some days back and memories of Suchita and Nil flashed in front of him. Although he had decided not to indulge himself into any such temptation but hardly could he control himself. Somehow he wanted to contact his beloved ones and there was no better option than to write a detailed letter. So this young men brought a paper and pen and positioned himself on that same spot. His comrades were busy and food preparation was in full swing. Red, yellow flames were hurling in air, scattering good illumination all around the place. In that light Maj. Jatin Mittal started pouring his heart on that paper which was supposed to travel thousands of kilometres before reaching its proper destination, where at this moment, a young lady was struggling to put her five year old child to sleep in her lap.

Three

"Hey, common ladies, hurry up. We are already going to be late" a stern voice echoed from the walls of a formidable stone villa. A young man of about 30 was stuffing the dicky of a snow white Ambassador with some luggage. He was being aided by two other men, supposedly his servants.

"Just a minute please," a high frequency female voice radiated from within the mansion in response to the young man's call.

Once the dicky was closed and his servants disbanded the young man waited, slightly resting his frame against the smooth metallic surface of the car, his clean shaven face competing with the smoothness of its surface. His overall countenance gave intimation of a solid individuality. He had a fair complexion that possessed a slight reddish tinge owing to the striking of sunlight. Having a plumb pointed nose and a chin that had good percentage of feminine feature he looked somewhat baby-faced. But his razor sharp eyes panetrating power through dark goggles that he donned and a massive, plump forehead proved that he was far from being a boy. With his dark gray suit and black leather shoes he stood just below six feet and his entire disposition insinuated that he was a shrewd man with a definite purpose.

The man expelled his dark goggles and gave a casual look at his wrist watch. Just then two persons came out of the front door of the villa, the same ladies this young man was impatiently waiting for. After getting unveiled to bright sunbeams outside, their bodies at once started sparkling and their skins glittered like reflecting mirror surfaces. One of them was a tall young lady of 27, clad in bright pink saree and a sizzling matching blouse, the pink colour of her cloths forming a fabulous combination with her glassy, peach complexion. Her long, black hair capable of covering the complete span of her slender body were nicely arranged, giving her an unmistakable appearance of a 70 mm goddess. Her charming face was all grace and from her genuine expression it was evident that she was a descendent of an educated and highly cultured family.

She firmly held a corner of her silk saree by her left hand while the forefinger of her right hand was tightly in possession of a tiny hand. And that tiny hand belonged to a tiny girl of about five, wearing a rich, emerald green frock topped with satin laces and milky white shoes. Her gold ear-rings peeped out of the cluster of her slight curly hair that flown all over her shoulders and her emerald green bangles created clinking noise at each step while walking. A dark coloured *bindi* that beautifully matched her dark eyes, doted her forehead and increased her face value manifold. Its alliance with her creamy, baby skin, on the other hand, added extra weightage to her innocence.

The young man stood as if hypnotized as this gorgeous mother daughter duo hastily start dismounting the marble stairs. For him it had always been enigmatic to tell who was better than whom. But any such comparison would have been absurd considering that one of them was an integral part of the other by way of origin.

As soon as they landed on the ground the little girl, freeing herself from her mother, ran towards the young man who was himself very minutely watching her movement by spreading his arms and received the child cuddling and kissing.

"Daddy, where are we going ?" asked the girl.

"Delhi" replied her daddy.

"Are there lots and lots of chocolates ?" pat came a million dollar question.

The man looked at her eyes, smiled and said "Oh, yeah !"

The face of the little girl lit up at that remark and she smiled coyly, tightly clutching her father.

By that time her mother was near to them.

"Oho, may I know what's going on between my sweetie and her dad? Is there any plot against me ?" asked the lady wittingly as she tenderly pinched the little girl's cheeks.

"Nothing of that sort. But we won't tell you right now. This is our secret", said the man and quickly deposited the child on front seat, helped the lady to sit beside and latching the door, himself occupied the driver's seat.

A brisk movement of keys and the diesel engine started gurgling. As soon as the gear was applied, the four wheeler began its motion with a slight jerk, as the watchman opened the front gate. The man drove the vehicle with the skill of a professional motorist, smoothly taking on the curves, cruising along the road with delicate grace. Indeed he was a very good controller of automobiles. But he had a slight weak point, i.e., he was a infamous lover of speed. Whenever the traffic would be clear or the road in front of him lay deserted, with a steering wheel in his hand he couldn't help but press the accelerator. This time also the young man followed the same thing. He drove slowly within the city limits but as soon as they crossed the boundary he increased the speed drastically, and within no time this vehicle was competing the velocity of air like a crazy horse, on that mirror smooth national highway. His wife turned panicky but she couldn't complain because she had so many useless feuds with her husband on this issue. Not only this lady but plenty of other people including relatives and friends had advised him against rash driving, but in vain. He did never take those advises earnestly. He couldn't, because speed was his passion and cars his favourite toy. Right from the childhood he was fond of anything that moved on its own, may it be an unassuming bike or a kingly aeroplane. Moreover being the only son of one of the richest businessmen of the city of Agra, he could manage to get whatever he wished for. He used to buy latest vehicles and actively participated in car rallies. Moreover he was a member of flying clubs. His frequent encounters with speed ended only when his father Mr Dharmesh Shrivastav handed over his business to him and retired some three years ago. And at the age of 30 this young man, Rajkumar Shrivastav was heading a handloom business empire worth 5 crores. But whenever he got chance to drive he drove wholeheartedly without caring for anybody and any damn consequences whatsoever.

He would run the car, throttling the accelerator to the fullest possible extent and his poor lady, Suhasini, would watch the shooting speedometer, rather uneasily and keep mum. She was well aware that this was one of the very few area where her counselling wasn't going to help much. Otherwise right from their marriage some seven years ago this well informed girl from Delhi was an unofficial adviser to Raj Shrivastav.

Being well educated Suhasini was eager to get any work that would make her earn but Raj was not favourable to her opting for an outside job. Instead he absorbed her in his own business and she was more than satisfied with that. Clearly handloom business was a good hunting ground for this girl who had completed a diploma course in fashion designing after becoming a commerce graduate. Then onwards Suhasini used to spend half of her daytime at home taking care of home affairs and remaining half with her husband.

Always effervescent and smiling she looked after her in-laws with great pleasure. Although they managed a good number of maids and servants, Suhasini always made it a point to dispense atleast few hours with them. The senior Shrivastav on the other hand were gratified and proud to have such a caring, sensible and worthy daughter-in-law. On the outside front Suhasini helped her husband in his business activities and more importantly kept him in good humour throughout the day to reduce dullness from his stressful life. In fact she played an amalgamated role of his boss, secretary, friend and wife. No wonder then within six months of marriage Suhasini became a cardinal part of the Shrivastav family without the consent of whom even a spoon wouldn't move from one place to another in their home.

She became even more likeable when she gave birth to a sweet child. It happened about two years after their marriage. Exceedingly cuddly, the little girl possessed large, dark eyes having a shape of a lotus petal, lustrous, somewhat curly hair and silky, white skin. Just by looking at her anybody could deduce that she was a better candidate to be a princess of any impregnable empire. Indeed with the kind of family she had handpicked to take birth in, she was destined to evolve into no less than a princess. The entry of that little girl into the small Shrivastav family made it bigger than ever ! Their joys knew no bounds. Their hearts filled with heavenly delight just at a glimpse of her enchanting face. She made them laugh, when she tried to utter any word being taught to her. She made them concerned when she refused to eat. She made them incensed when she did not take bath and just threw everything, everywhere. And she moved them into tears when after the entire day of exasperated rejoicing she slept covering her dark eyes with her ticklish eyelids.

Her twitter, her cries, her shouts and her mischievous lies everything would fill the entire villa, reaching its every corner. From the day she entered the house, she became the centre of attraction, an indisputable queen, who could wish for anything and promptly get her demand satisfied. Everything revolved around her and she revolved everything around her. And when she realised that something was happening against her wish or assent she used her birthright to cry. And when such thing would occur, the whole Shrivastav villa would rush to the spot trying to calm down the child.

As soon as Raj Shrivastav heard the news of his daughter's birth, he declared holiday to his workers and rushed to Delhi. The

Shrivastavs celebrated a lot, the incoming of the heiress to their empire. Finally when the baby was two months old they organised a big function and named her Sujata.

After the arrival of this little fairy, her grandparents got the most pleasurable job of looking after her while Raj and Suhasini dedicated their time to the business. Sujata was so fond of her grandpa and grandma ! They provided her every need and revered her very much. Early in the morning Mr. Shrivastav would lead the child to a nearby garden and play with her. Sujata used to get her favourite eatables from her granny who would attend to Sujata's wants and needs in the absence of her mother, throughout the day. The grandpa performed the function of her entertainer frolicking new and new amusing games with her, telling her fascinating stories and teaching her something someway or the other. The old couple had come to become a part and parcel of the miniature life of this little girl, without whom she would go crazy. That's why Sujata got displeased when her grandparents left for Delhi early in that morning while the child was still in her bed. Raj and his family had been invited to attend the wedding ceremony of one of his friends. Being very busy with his work Raj sent his parents in the morning along with one of his goods carrying vehicles. After finishing his work he too started off for Delhi along with his wife Suhasini and daughter Sujata.

It was almost 7 pm when the snow white Ambassador stormed into the capital city of Delhi. Raj directed the vehicle straightway to the marriage place where the Shrivastavs were warmly greeted by Parmeet, Raj's friend and his parents. Sujata's grandparents were eagerly waiting for her arrival. As soon as they spotted her stepping down the car with her parents, the old couple hurriedly reached there to pick her up in arms. But the girl firmly refused to pay attention to them. She was really very upset over what her tiny brain thought as an act of cheating on the part of her grandparents. The old couple apologized to the furious girl and did every trick to win her over. But the child didn't give in. "Why did you leave me and go away?" was her persistent inquisition.

Her grandpa laid out every possible explanation and promised her not to repeat such a thing in future. But alas ! Sujata didn't consider their points to be authentic and remained adamant. Finally not being able to sustain emotional stress for long time, the child burst into tears and soon started weeping uncontrollably. Her loud tumultuous cry attracted attention of many including her parents who ran towards her to calm her down. They laboured hard without producing any pay off. Number of people present nearby gathered around Sujata. A few of them attempted their bit to soothe her anger. But nothing seemed to work. On the contrary, sensing the fact that a huge mob had gathered around her, the child got intimidated and jumped into mother's arm, still sobbing.

Finally a young man wearing a sky blue suit and having a fine little boy in his arm stepped forward. The man was Parmeet, the groom himself who heard about this little girl and immediately rushed to the spot. Along with him was his sister's son about the same age that of Sujata.

"Hey little lady I'm your Parmeet Uncle. Very nice meeting you baby," he forwarded his hand towards Sujata who, in turn swiftly turned her face and buried it in her mother's arms.

"OK meet this young chap Mr. Chintu all the way from America."

Still no response !

"Alright, alright," Parmeet laughed heartily. So did the people gathered around.

"You know Bhabi," said Parmeet turning his attention to Suhasini, "Mr. Chintu is a champion dancer."

"Oh really ?" asked a beguiled Suhasini, "We didn't know."

"That's not enough. He has recently won a dancing competition in his school. That way he is an accomplished dancer, you know. Now who wants to see our little hero dancing ?" asked Parmeet slightly lifting the pitch of the voice.

"We do, we do," screamed the folks jumping with joy with mere reference to dancing.

"Fine, those who don't want to join us may remain stuck to their mothers," wittingly Parmeet remarked and blinked his eyes at Suhasini who tried hard to suppress her laughter. All of a sudden laughter erupted from the mob.

At that little Sujata gave a jaded look and clutched her mother with even greater force. Laughter broke out again.

At Parmeet's instance some enthusiasts arranged the chairs in circular fashion. Those who wanted to join the dance party gathered in the space between the chairs and rest of them occupied the chairs.

"So here comes ladies and gentlemen, Mr. Chintu, err... Just a minute," leaving his speech halfway Parmeet hurriedly went inside, turned the music system on and returned back.

Finally the celebrations began as Mr Chintu started dancing on the catchy rhythm of that rock music score. Soon he was joined by few other children and young boys and girls. Rest other supported them clapping and whistling.

Sujata managed to steal a look at the dancing party and slowly positioned herself on mother's lap. Everyone noticed it but nobody disclosed. Slowly the enthusiasm reached to the peak. Someone replaced the rock music by Punjabi Bhangra and one by one everybody melted into the dancing band. Suhasini handed over the little girl to her mother-in-law and she too joined dancing. This way, quite unknowingly Sujata made peace with her grandparents.

The dancing mania continued until some elderly person turned the music system off and sent the party for dinner.

Next day was the scheduled day for marriage. Throughout the day the grown ups were busy attending wedding rituals and meeting with each other. While the children got a lot of opportunity to play and enjoy. This was entirely a new experience for little Sujata. She never had experienced such an immense company of boys and girls. In Agra it was rather a different story. Being the only child of a rich man she had always been overprotected. The poor child could only gaze through the windows of her vehicle at the children playing on streets. Sujata always felt like intermingling with them and do the very same things they used to do without being concerned about the events taking place around them. Sujata's little brain captivated by their dancing in rains, muddling with mud, carelessly running here and there couldn't know exactly why she was not allowed to do such things. At the same time she was too small to apprehend that it was unqualified stupidity to equate her with those children. She had hardly any idea that she was much more blessed than those young ones playing on roads, that there lay a bright future, perhaps a good education abroad and happy settled life for her. But those playing on roads would remain there forever, playing, eating, sleeping and perhaps dying on roads. She was in no way a match for them. She would rule like an empress and they would die like animals. But at that moment the petty childhood exultance looked everything and she would fight to win that autonomy. However, she was secured in a jail that was more angelic than heaven, the invincible Shrivastav villa that is. Tens of eyes judiciously watched her every movement everyday right from her getting up on the morning to her going back to bed. Everybody, in that villa would dance to her tune. Whenever she used to fall down at least a dozen hands would compete to cuddle up and succour this child. Her wish was the supreme command, her refusal a firm veto. But whenever she coveted to do anything that would drag her away from the strict supervision, she had to hear a stark 'no'. That's why the poor girl could afford hardly any companion of her age and always required to get contended with the expensive and the most fabulous toys which waltzed, laughed and personated with a push of a button. Nevertheless she had two cousins at Delhi, who were some sort of a solace.

Precisely then, for a kid having such a terrible drought of friends the company of these children in blood and flesh at Parmeet's marriage was overwhelming. Sujata was glad beyond any limit. Riding high on vivacity and sheer ecstasy she made friendship with each and every child present. Especially Chintu had become her favourite because of all the showmanship he did to light up her face previous night. No wonder then, most of the time Sujata accompanied this curious, little lad. Exactly of the same height as that of Sujata, Chintu was a bit fatty but that in no way did restrict his swift movements while dancing. He had glinting, jolly eyes and a somewhat blunt nose. His round face would invariably flash with a mischievous smile when somebody happened to look at him. On the marriage day he was clad in a small and radiant dark blazor and tight jeans. When he spoke in a typical childish tone, the unambiguous American accent would leave its mark on his discourse and he used words like 'gotta', 'wanna', 'ain't' and 'Chicago Bulls' hundred times a day. Sujata was thoroughly fascinated by this small American. Also because of same age their frequencies were perfectly matching. Chintu told her many enchanting things about USA, Nigera falls, Empire State Building, Disney Land and all. He showed her a lot of toys and games and even presented a few to Sujata. He invited her to visit his room exclusively filled with toys and video games. Sujata couldn't but be enthralled at the astounding description this little friend of her made while informing her about his world. And how badly did she wish to be a part of such a marvellous destination ! But that was a distant dream. She knew even spending some more time with Chintu was not going to be possible because she could correlate from many such past occasions that her father was a very busy man and would not be away from his work for too long. There was no way to persuade her father to increase their stay at Delhi because when it came to his work he didn't listen to anybody. That's why, finally when Sujata heard from her mother that they had to leave on that day itself she was far from being agitated, but she couldn't prevent herself from giving a sign of displeasure.

On the other hand Raj Shrivastav was busy meeting with people and striking a few business deals in the wedding hall itself. But he was too caring a father to forget about Sujata. He loved her most, more than any damn business advantage. Ever since her birth, one corner of his mind was always focussed on his little daughter. Whatever work he might be doing, he worried about Sujata very much. Apparently Raj was very tought and his behaviour gave pretty good indication of the same. Most of the time his face would be stone cold, absolutely expressionless and sometimes he used to lose his temper quickly. Very rarely did he used to smile. He liked to engage himself in business activities and his relationships with the people were merely professional. That's why only on very few occasions did the mighty bunglow of Shrivastavs bear substantial amount of dwellers. Otherwise it used to be quiet. Painstakingly, Raj succeeded in creating his own small domain that was isolated from the outside surrounding. Indeed, this businessman had imparted to his house the look of an unbeatable fortress.

Sujata grew under a highly protected environment like this. And her father was always watching her when he was near and even when he was not. Sujata was as if a part of his heart which had been given a human shape. Raj was almost possessive about his daughter and over the years developed a soft, refining dimension to his personality because of her. It was not that he was very rough by nature but he was a shrewd businessman and looked at the world from that point of view only. After Sujata's birth he became rather sensitive and she, his weak point.

That's why Raj became quite restless with the mere sight of Sujata getting upset because her grandparents left for Delhi without taking her with them. But he, like most of the men, managed to show off a cool face and didn't even go near to his daughter when she was crying like a hell. When everybody swarmed around Sujata and played various tricks to pacify her temper, this father of her was standing aside helping himself with a cigarette that somebody had gifted to him some moments ago. Although nobody had noticed it but the fact remained that the whole attention of this man was concentrated on the responses his little daughter was furnishing to the attempts made by the people to coax her. He knew if nobody succeeded, the responsibility would eventually fall on him. And at the end when Sujata forgot her wrath, Raj was the happiest person in the world. So what if he didn't join the dance party which was obvious considering his nature, his heart was singing and dancing with joy nobody there would ever know.

Raj had noticed, by virtue of his ability to keep an eye on his daughter at all times, how absolutely delighted Sujata was in the company of the children there. Also he had observed the way in which Sujata expressed her disgruntleness when he announced that they had to leave for Agra the same day. He could very well sense therefore, the urge of his daughter to stay at Delhi for some more time. Hence Raj decided not to break her heart and straightforwardly told Sujata that if she wished she could remain there for two days more. He promised her that he would himself come there to bring her back. Raj often used to visit Delhi for business purposes and incidentally he was supposed to come there again after two days. This proposal was a welcome one for Sujata even if that meant staying away from parents and grandparents. And the grateful daughter, in her turn, conferred a warm hug and a kiss to her daddy dearest.

After the marriage ceremony was over the Shrivastavs paid a short visit to Suhasini's elder brother Vinit who worked there as a lawyer. A recently married man, he lived with his wife, two children and his widow mother. When they started returning back darkness was already casting its shadow. They dropped Sujata to Parmeet's house and without wasting any more time quickly bade farewell. At that instant Sujata didn't have the slightest idea that it was going to be a turning point in her life nor did the Shrivastavs know what was in store for them.

Standing along with her little companions, Parmeet Uncle and the newly wedded bride at the front of the house Sujata moved her tiny hands slowly to and fro, her eyelids fluttering intermittently and unknowingly. All of a sudden salty water surged ahead and filled the gap between the eyelids making the picture in front of her hazzy as a fog. Little did the poor girl know that this was the moment her brain would cherish and store it somewhere in its memory and dig its own, each and every bit to find out where it had been stored, in turn giving terribly agonizing moments to the body that wore it. This was going to be the picture that would haunt this pitiful girl forever and bestow upon her deathlike pains on several occasions in latter part of her life. Yes, this was going to be the picture, a foggy outline of a tall man and a tall woman responsible for bringing her soul into life and an old couple who made her living worthwhile as heaven. How awfully wicked the time was ! It went so fast, and how terribly betraying the salt water was ! It blocked her vision when she badly needed to run her eyes over those four figures melting into the sturdy vehicle not less attached to her emotionally, than those four dear ones. And within seconds it was all over. The next moment there existed only the exhaust gas of the diesel engine.

All of them standing at the door turned back but Sujata hesitated and finally went inside the house with strange feeling of hollowness surrounding her mind.

The snow white Ambassador of the Shrivastavs marched passed amicably through the cumbrous traffic of the capital but as soon as it crossed the border of the city it ran wildly, storming like a lunatic horse, it pierced itself through the vehicles. Moving indiscriminately, almost in a zigzag fashion, at one instant it nearly missed hitting a motorcycle.

"Be careful son," shouted Dharmesh Shrivastav. "How often should we remind you ? You are no kid now," the old man's remark with a certain degree of scolding faded in a stern 'alright' from his son. Not a single person in the car knew then, that it was going to be the last word ever spoken by any of them.

"Alright", said Raj and slowed down a bit. He maintained the vehicle at relatively low speed for quite a some time. In the meantime cold breeze was causing hazardous effect that compelled them to close the windows. The two ladies enshrouded their respective heads in sarees while Dharmesh Shrivastav slipped himself into a warm shelter of a Kashmiri shawl. All these activities passed on silently, just through the language of signs, for nobody was in a mood to waste even a slightest amount of energy by way of speaking after that exhaustive day of marriage. What they needed was a sound sleep. Ironically there was plenty of it in store for them, waiting to grip their soul.

Once the crowded phase was crossed and left way behind, Raj experienced a monumental spurt in adrenaline level. Smooth, polished path sprinkled with faint-milky moonlight enchanted him like a trap magnetizing its prey and unknowingly he went on pressing the accelerator. Soon the obedient four wheeler moved with the ease of a fish moving in water. The pointer of the speedometer stepped forward impulsively, finally vibrating just below 85 km/hr. mark.

Indeed, the vehicle had consummated a maddening speed. For a split second it seemed as if it would move round the globe in no time. Entirely governed by the speed euphoria, Raj Shrivastav violated many driving etiquettes. He didn't know that there lay, at a short distance a sharp turn of almost 90°.

And for that matter, it was transparent that he was unsuspecting of a prodigious truck driven by a psychotic driver just like him, fast approaching as if to fix the final nail to their coffin. The driver of the truck somehow managed to overcome the sharp turn and abruptly surfaced in front of the car. Raj was almost blinded by the powerful light emerging from the truck which was not more than five metres from the Ambassador. Sudden appearance of this giant vehicle cause a great panic in Raj's mind and he lost control. Terribly scared, he tried to get away from the path traced by the truck by frantically rotating the steering wheel. In this undertaking he succeeded a bit and somehow managed to hamper a head on collision. Simultaneously, he applied the breaks with full strength but the vehicle moving with a speed of about 85 km/hr simply refused to respond well. Within twinkling of an eye the right half on the car hit the truck with incredible speed. The sound resulted was deafening. Such a great was the collision that the car took a 90° turn with its back side smacking a sideby tree. It moved further, slid down the slope after loosing union with the road and finally punched the ground. It bounced a bit and came to a standstill with the front side pointing towards the sky. The unfortunate truck disorderly landed on a huge tree on the other side. The darkness of the night rudely concealed the red coloured fluid that covered the area along with the mess of flesh and bones, but it was unable to damp the heartbroken outcry of fading souls and hurtful howls of those who managed to get through the ordeal.

When the actual crash occurred the steering wheel hit Raj Shrivastav on his head and he was deceased forthwith. Later the doctors would certify him dead due to multiple fracture of the skull and severe brain damage. As the Ambassador bumped against the tree the old Shrivastav couple sitting on the rear seat suffered deadly injuries and once the car finally hit the ground they were no more. Only that side of the car where Suhasini was sitting, i.e., the front left side was not hit directly. Thus she only could manage to let out a scream. But after so many strikes she was in an unthinkably bad state and lost her consciousness the moment the car made a lunge at the ground. About 5/6 seconds of frenzied voices and mind boggling sound and everything matured as gory as a graveyard. Or could it be something other than that ? The incumbents of the truck gave painful shrieks occasionally, but within minutes they also became unconscious.

In the next morning while reading the newspaper advocate Vinit happened to come across a news of a horrible mishap that left three people dead and three seriously injured on Delhi-Agra highway. Out of curiosity he went through the news only to find that it involved an Ambassador which was identified, from some suggestive evidences, to be belonging to some Shrivastavs of Agra. Vinit almost dropped the newspaper and gasped for his breath. He dared not gaze at the list of the dead and the injured and only noted down the hospital name. Speechlessly he put on the cloths and without uttering a single word dashed off towards the hospital on his scooter, leaving his wife perplexed and guessing the reason for this unusual behaviour. At the hospital he was the first man who clearly identified the victims. He could hear his heart beating like a drum when a nurse informed him about the departed and the disfigured while showing him the victims. Vinit hardly had glimpses of their faces before pinning them down and he was boundlessly aghast to see his dear sister in that inexplicably horrifying straits. Only Suhasini's heartbeats were still on but she was critically impaired, rest being notified dead the moment they reached the hospital. Vinit was in a precarious condition and badly needed to cry but lacked that shoulder to rest his head on. And then he thought about his mother. It was impossibly hard to predict how she would react to such abrupt disaster. But when he thought about Sujata his heart sank in great despair. He kept on telling his mind that it was no time to cry even if he saw the downfall of the pillars that smoothly held his beautiful sister. Beautiful sister ! Was she even worth looking now ? Forget, would she live anymore ? Why his dear sister whom he thought to be very fortunate turned out to be so devastatingly unlucky so as to loose everything within no time ? Even she was left grappling to hold her breath. At last why this time, which was riding so calmly had become so cruel annihilating Suhasini's well flourished world in seconds ?

Thousands of questions arose in the mind of this young man that twisted and threatened to crush every nerve of his brain.

Vinit recalled everything about Suhasini in a flash, right from their infancy to recent time and his eyes flooded with tears. For next few moments he wept irrepressibly, till a doctor patted at his shoulder looking at him with kind consoling eyes. Through the silent languages of eyes he reminded Vinit that his were not the shoulders to pat on, rather they were meant to provide resting surface for many mourning heads. There was no point, waiting for his sister to die, so he came out of the hospital, wiping off his wet eyes and started off on his scooter. His next job was to look for his niece who at least, after such a tragic turn of events, thought Vinit, should remain unscathed.

From whatever minute information he had about Parmeet's residence, Vinit somehow managed to find out the whereabouts of Sujata but only after a frantic exploration of about an hour. The poor child was carelessly playing with Chintu. And she could never have surmised what had transpired. Vinit shortly explained the inconceivable happenings to an utterly stunned Parmeet. Indeed there couldn't be anything more heart breaking than the death of a friend just after one's marriage. But this was precisely what had happened and that switched the entire atmosphere of his house from celebration mood to mourning. Finally when Vinit went to terrace where Sujata was playing, the child came all the way running towards him and clung to her uncle who in turn broke down in tears immediately. The little girl got into disarray due to such an abnormal behaviour by Vinit and not being able to react just stroked his hair with tiny hands. Only after concentrating all his emotional energy Vinit could manage to fight back the outburst of tears. Now he faced a great dilemma whether to tell Sujata the truth or not, he chose the best option. For the time being he remained silent about the accident and just chatted with her very casually.

Soon they were heading towards the hospital, Vinit, Parmeet and Sujata. With Parmeet driving the scooter and Vinit steadfastly grasping the only surviving seedling of the Shrivastav family tree.

And she didn't have the slightest idea that she was going to witness the sheer destruction of her family, a catastrophe, even the strongest and the most mature persons are not designate to sustain. But one thing was favourable to her and that was her childish innocence and inability to draw conclusions from the things observed. That's why in the hospital she failed to understand where she had been brought. But the strange people in the strange uniforms and the strange odours emanating from everywhere were already making her sick.

Vinit chose not to show the badly contorted bodies of Sujata's father and grandparents to her but before allowing her to see her mother, Vinit asked the doctors about his sister's conditions. They said the chances were grim because Suhasini was already in coma and her response to the treatment was extremely poor. He settled for waiting and they didn't have to wait for too long. Within one hour of their arrival at hospital, i.e., after 14 hours of long tussle with the death she gave in quietly, breathing her last when the child she had brought to this world was wondering why everybody there wore white cloths and why the curtains were green.

They all were escorted to the room where the corpses had been kept. After mature consideration Vinit removed the cloth that covered Suhasini's body, concurrently doing his bit to suppress the tears that threatened to burst like showers. But realising that he was not in a position to regulate himself he hastily came out of the room.

Still Sujata was confused and confused beyond limit and terribly dumbfounded. She carefully watched Suhasini's corpse as Parmeet guarded her in his arms. As soon as she ascertained the identity of her mother in that awful condition she looked at Parmeet's eyes, her face showing the first sign of horror. She knew something worst had happened !

"Mom" she suddenly surged ahead, "Wake up Mom wake up."

Parmeet was in the most difficult condition and unknowingly he brought the child very near to the dead body. She spread her tiny hands over her mother's cheeks and tried to shake her face.

"Wake up mom", she went on repeating.

Her mom did never wake up ! The girl was very small to distinguish between the living and the dead but by looking at her mother wrapped in bandages, with her characteristic smile missing and face turned into a lifeless statue, she knew all was not well. A sufficient reason for a helpless child to cry. She did the same. Frantically she tried to cuddle up with the dead body. Baffled, Parmeet quickly covered the body and came out of the room with great pace. Suchita struggled like a fish out of water.

Four

Advocate Vinit Verma is a busy man. This is the unanimous opinion of all who reside around his house. Hardly ever you will spot him at home and if you do, he would be munching at his food either for breakfast, lunch or dinner or crooning in bathroom or in intimate sleep, i.e., at night. He frankly doesn't have time for purposeless things like conversing with neighbours, partaking in weekly meetings of the society or attending wedding ceremonies or any other functions. Always in a hurry he would grab his scooter early in the morning and dash off to his office. So if you are urgently in need to contact him better march into his working place directly. There he would greet you politely with a high voltage grin. But in the office too you will have to wait a bit because a huge crowd is perpetually in a queue to meet the 'Vakilsaab'. Inexhaustibly helpful and kind Adv. Vinit is popular among the masses who approach the big capital in search of justice. He would show them the right way, he would scuffle for their purpose and moreover he would be considerate enough to charge less fees to the seemingly poor clients. More than anything else what seduces the people to him is his pacific nature and always welcoming, always animated face.

If your case is impotent or if you ask him to prove anything immoral then be prepared to hear a frank 'no' from Adv. Vinit. Never in his life has he taken up such a lawsuit and tried to convert a wrong thing into a right one. Obviously never in his life has he lost a legal battle. That's why people come to him carrying great hopes and they come in big numbers. They are assured that he won't dash their hopes and if he accepts their case, their triumph is hardly a question of time.

Even if Adv. Vinit has very less communication with his neighbours and others living in their locality, nobody ever considers him arrogant or one who possesses a great deal of vanity. They know from several prior experiences that whenever anybody is in trouble, it is Vinit who forwards a helping hand before anybody else. Also when a question of fighting a legal dispute arises in the colony Adv. Vinit renders his services absolutely free of charge! So even if he seems to be arrogant, that is only a misleading indication of his nature. Perhaps such a picture of him springs up because of his extremely hard-working, almost workaholic nature. Otherwise after coming to a one to one conversation with him, you would realise how breathtaking person he is.

In more than one ways his temper matches with that of his younger sister Suhasini, who is married to a rich family in Agra. Both very compassionate, both ever smiling and ever helping, they are brother sister duo of a right kind. Just before Vinit could consummate the studies of law their father died of cardiac arrest. And not being able to sustain this blow their mother caught ill and got bedridden ever since. The period after their father's death was a difficult one, a nerve testing tribulation. Although their bank balance was good and money was not the problem, it was extremely hard to cope up with the studies for both of them. Suhasini had to forfeit a good amount of time at home while Vinit prepared for his last important examination. Somehow they managed to overcome the hard time and once Vinit started private practice, everything was brought on track.

Both Vinit and Suhasini were industrious. Through painstaking efforts only Vinit succeeded in establishing himself as the most sought after lawyer among the poor and the downcast. They would line up themselves to seek his counselling. But everything has its own price! Vinit's over occupation with his profession had taken its toll. Hardly ever did his children manage to enjoy his company. Forget about enjoying they would only watch him infused in his work and on very few occasions they got opportunity to talk to him. His enquiring about exam scores and attending school get togethers were distant dreams. Often an exasperated Leena, his wife would go alone to the parents' day gatherings at school where they were supposed to go together as a couple. Looking at the other children relishing circus shows and ice creams with parents, Vinit's children would constantly demand such pleasures but poor Leena had to bluntly refuse every time.

It was not that Vinit was unaware of these facts. He understood everything, still he couldn't help it. After all nobody can change one's nature, even the 'one' himself. But because of such a callous attitude of her husband Leena found herself alone battling the home front. And for a middle class family it is perhaps the most arduous one to handle. Leena was compelled to do all sorts of things ranging from taking care of the children to bringing grocery, doing shopping to paying electric and water bills. As if that was not enough she herself had to call a plumber if any water tap leaked or rush to a doctor if anybody needed medical attention. Moreover the ever bed ridden mother-in-law added substantial amount of hardships to her account. Unable to move out of the bed the old lady demanded constant attention and Leena found it intemperately tedious to take care of her on one hand and discharge her other duties on the other, that too simultaneously.

Leena's mother-in-law used to be an irresistible lady while in her youth. In fact, she was one of the very few women in the entire country at that time who was well educated and earning money. But unfortunately, she was forced to take up premature retirement from her job because of her illness. Death of her husband followed by the ailment had drastically reduced her vigour. It became very hard for her to adjust herself to a life confined to a small room. The feeling that she would have to depend on her daughter-in-law for rest of her life left her frustrated.

The overall effect of these circumstances was to make her an angry woman. She spent most of her time sleeping or rebuking her daughter-in-law or crying like a little girl. Often she had quarrels with Leena and both used to complain to Vinit against each other. Vinit on the other hand, like any other poor man squeezed between mother-wife jaw would merely listen to both of them silently and end up doing nothing.

Clearly this was not the life that Leena had dreamt for. In fact she had not seen such a life even in her wildest dreams! Born and brought up in the glamorous city of Mumbai, she had a crystal clear idea of happiness. She was a firm believer of 'wealth only a happy life make'. Although a progeny of a middle class family, she always wished for a plush bungalow, a car, lots of maids and servants, a life full of comfort and worldly goods, a life which a lovely princess of a big empire would relish. The companionship of high society girls in the college only served to add fuel to this fire. Soon Leena started putting up demands which were exceedingly difficult to satisfy if one had to consider her parent's income. A born short tempered girl she had come to be a burden on the shoulders of her parents and they started pondering about the means to get rid of this paranoiac girl. Surely there always was a way! And they complied with it. They simply tied her knot!

Adv. Vinit on the other hand was badly in need of a wife mainly because of the difficulties faced by his sister Suhasini in maintaining home affairs. It was a tight rope walk for the poor girl doing household chores, taking care of mother and continuing studies all at the same time. That's why when some acquaintance suggested Leena's name Vinit accepted the offer quickly. On the other side of the coin Leena shown some resistance initially, finally giving in to her parent's yearn after realising that there was no point being inflexible. After all she was not the mistress of an ethereal beauty that a handsome prince would long for. She had but average looks, just having everything at its proper place. But certainly Vinit was too good for her. Being largely successful in his career as a lawyer his future looked very promising. Besides he was a thorough gentleman and such a fine young man that any sensible girl could have gleefully accredited him as a life partner. This was main reason why Leena did not oppose much marrying with Vinit. Although Vinit was well aware that he was capable of tugging girls far better than Leena, he was in a hurry to joining in wedlock, being positively purturbed at the way his sister was put to toil. He could have hired any maid, but thrusting all the responsibility on any unknown person was very risky, especially when his mother was unable to move. Also being seniormost capable person in the house he himself had to hunt down a wife. Thus keeping aside his liking and compromising on his dreams Vinit affirmed the very first girl he was introduced with and very soon Vinit and Leena tied their nuptials.

Immediately after their marriage Vinit made his wife to take over the entire charge of the house from Suhasini. But Suhasini was too kind hearted a person to allow this impromptu transition to take place. She helped the newly wedded groom as far as possible and as long as possible. It was quite perplexing for Leena as it was pleasant. There was no motive for Suhasini to be so solicitous about her, taking into account the fact that it resulted in depletion of her priceless time. Indeed from the very first day they met, Suhasini was an absolutely odd and intriguing character for Leena. Never in her entire life-span before marriage had she seen a person like Suhasini. She was a blend of numerous qualities, a girl as lively as a lily and as effervescent as a soap bubble, having an incredible quality of turning dullness into life and foes into friends. She was a rare and perfect example of beauty with a brain, intelligence with patience. After acquiring a degree in commerce faculty she took up a diploma course in dress designing and made it to the top applying all the instinctive abilities she was blessed with along with the immense imaginative power that she possessed. But having all these worldly gifts, she also had one important quality, i.e., a stiff patience! After a prolong illness rendered her mother paralysed she gladly accepted the household job, never ever complaining.

And above all she was marvellously good looking! Perhaps it was the single most important thing giving her tremendous captivating power. She had glistening cream complexion creating a sharp contrast with shining, coal black hair curling all over her head like thin serpents. As if that was not enough, a minute, dark mole on the centre of her right cheek increased her face value thousand times. Her large, dark eyes would glint like gems with each one of them shaped like a delightful fish. Her straight pointed nose, thin ruby lips having a bow string like appearance and a delicately cleavaged chin would make her a subject of envy among many women. Her entire face as a whole and each specific organ as if carved out by a veteran Roman sculptor with at most precision, with every curve carefully chiselled imparting a smooth finish, everything tailored into perfection. If anybody was to be mistaken for a pixie it was Suhasini. And she knew it, but hardly ever her behaviour unveiled that she knew it.

Leena found it difficult to interpret how a woman possessing such a heavenly magnificence did not take pride in it. Whatever might be her opinion about Suhasini, one thing was sure that there lay deep in her mind a feeling that could best be illustrated by the word 'jealousy'. Yes, Leena's approach towards this sister-in-law of her was that of an envy. This feeling only multiplied when businessman Dharmesh Shrivastav chose Suhasini as his daughter-in-law.

It was in a marriage of Suhasini's friend at Delhi which was also frequented by Shrivastav family. Dharmesh Shrivastav who was searching for a suitable bride for his only son, caught sight of this remarkable young lady in the wedding hall. Clad in a flamboyant olive green saree decorated with highly ingenious and delicate embroidery work, she was wandering everywhere just like a butterfly flying all over a garden. Her glamorous attire designed by herself added extra flavour to her splendour. That's why although absolutely fragile in physical sense, her presence was simply vivacious. Throughout the marriage ceremony Suhasini was the centre of attraction and very very conspicuous indeed. Terribly impressed by this stunning lady, Dharmesh Shrivastav gathered information about her there itself and came to know some facts that electrified him further. Just after completion of her diploma coarse in dress designing, Suhasini received offers from many business firms to work with them. But on account of her ambition to stand on her own and the strong mental and financial support of her brother Vinit to carry on her plans, she started her independent venture taking contracts from other firms. Later she was to merge it with her husband's business.

After knowing all these things Mr. Dharmesh Shrivastav came to realise that there couldn't have been any better choice for him to select his daughter-in-law and without wasting any time he called on Adv. Vinit, keeping in front of him the offer which he couldn't resist even if he tried.

.Very soon Suhasini was the part and parcel of one of the richest and the most well known families in Agra, i.e., the Shrivastav family. Adv. Vinit was the most contended man having found an extremely fitted and worthy husband for his sister in the form of Raj Shrivastav. Leena on the other hand although apparently very happy was all envy, not being in a position to observe the things happening to Suhasini, things she had badly dreamt for herself.

And how extremely fortunate Suhasini was! Her new family was like a heart of an empire. Along with four-five other families the Shrivastavs controlled and dominated the handloom industry in and around the Agra region. They employed a large number of skilled people who would make excellent quality of hand made woven fabric. Earlier the Shrivastavs used to have collaboration with some dress designers in Delhi who would provide various patterns as per their requirements and after receiving the handloom from Shrivastav firm, they would create fabulous dresses and sarees. Finally, the Shrivastavs would pick up the finished product from them and distribute it in the domestic as well as international market. They exported these handloom cloths to various countries of Europe, North America and middle east reaping rich harvest of money in the process.

Selling handloom cloths was an age-old business of the Shrivastav family, their source of bread and butter for over five decades. But in an unfortunate tussle between Dharmesh Shrivastav and his three brothers to catch hold of the business, the big family was broken into small fractions, despite the attempts of Dharmesh Shrivastav to thwart it from eventuating. His brothers started their own individual firms, but being the eldest one and most importantly the most sensible one, all the traditional labourers of the Shrivastav family stuck to him. Consequently Dharmesh Shrivastav's business prospered and his brothers were left way behind. He tried hard to convince them that they had made a blunder by dividing themselves but nobody listened to him, thereby causing a permanent fissure among the brothers.

Entry of Suhasini into Dharmesh Shrivastav family enhanced its strength further. Actually, by choosing Suhasini as his daughter-in-law Dharmesh Shrivastav had hit two targets with a single bullet. He had found an extremely worthy wife for his son and at the same time gained a full time dress designer for his firm who wouldn't charge a penny as her royalty. But who needs a royalty while working for your own family? Suhasini's royalty was her kind and well-disposed husband Raj, her affectionate in-laws and the entire asset of the Shrivastav family. Her royalty was her dignified position in a dignified family and the continuous, inexhaustible shower of love under which she used to bathe every moment.

Vinit always used to think that his sister was going to rule like an empress. And as if it was a fortune teller's prediction, she actually did. Suhasini with all her kindness and loving nature, ruled like an empress till a tragedy struck, a fatal accident after which she was no more an empress, she was no more a human being at all. She was but a lifeless structure, a deformed human body as dead as a stone with a broken skull, fractured rib and numerous wounds on her tender, creamy skin. Countless small fractures on her slender hands and legs with large number of broken glass pieces piercing into her face and neck, converting this charming lady into a hideous blend of flesh and bone.

Vinit felt like entire atmosphere collapsing over his head at the sight of the terrible pulp his exquisite sister was reduced to. His dreams lay shattered in a moment, just like a glass article falling on the ground, breaking into hundreds of helpless pieces. It was a very very premature exit of Suhasini and that rudely ensured stinging wounds for Vinit which he would have to sustain for entire lifetime. Truly, it was a sad end of a story which had reached 'and they lived happily ever after' stage. More painful was the incident because it occurred after a period which was nothing less than a sweet dream. The cruel destiny had changed this sweet dream into a dreadful nightmare with a single stroke of its hand. Vinit could only imagine the agonizing moments his sister must have went through before death and during some desperate moments he would try to imagine this unimaginable, causing more and more damage to his mind and soul. He was left frustrated, he was left devastated. After the death of his father and ever worrying condition of his mother, it was a third deadly blow for this young man, just like a hard punch in the stomach, which knocked him down emotionally.

Ironically Vinit had an innocent piece of his sister, i.e., Suhasini's cute, little daughter Sujata, who kept on reminding him about her. The tornado struck the Shrivastav family, but it could not blow away this child and she remained as a sole survivor, surrounded by the pathetic ruins of her family, posing a grim melancholic picture. It was a savage sarcasm of nature, a rude, barbaric joke played with a helpless life that could hardly judge its meaning. The poor girl couldn't comprehend the gravity of the situation even after watching the awful mess of her mother's body. At that instant she spontaneously burst into tears because she felt herself insecure, although she couldn't tell whether her mother was dead or she was sleeping. And when her dear ones were being cremated, she played with her cousins. All the while she was waiting for a snow white Ambassador that would come all the way from Agra and a strong man would get down, pick her up in his arms and drive straightaway to Agra. She waited patiently for days together as the people around her were mourning. At times she would weep, at times she would stare at the surrounding with her dark eyes full of apprehension and suspicion. Although incapable of thinking, she came to a definite conclusion that a drastic change had occurred in her life. And this change brought about a drastic change in this little girl. Initially she often used to cry, demanding her parents and grand parents. Later she tried to force Uncle Vinit to carry her to Agra. Vinit on his part could not satisfy her former demand, while he avoided satisfying the later one. Showing her the empty domicile of Shrivastav family could have been like adding fuel to the fire. Sujata was at least staying properly at Delhi in a false hope that someday she will meet her parents. But at Agra she would have gone mad seeing all those lifeless stones and no sign of life.

With no help forthcoming from Vinit, the little girl accepted her changed life but not without a change in her behaviour. She slowly started contracting in her own shell like a touch-me-not plantlet. Slowly she lost all her vigour. She stopped smiling, she stopped crying, she stopped playing. She started losing whatever little stock of words that was accumulated in her brain during the brief period of her existence, because soon she stopped talking too. And she ate only when the food was forcefully administered into her mouth. Vinit who himself was in deep distress tried his best to revitalize the child and kept an eye on her, day in and day out. And what else could he do? He himself was a broken man having a sister who was dead, an old mother whose condition depreciated fast and now a niece who was in dire straits. Indeed Sujata's condition was pathetic. Although she retained her royal appearance, she squandered that bright shining on her face which idolized her since birth. She was reduced to a blossomless flower that had lost its bright colour and magical fragrance, but still was a flower all the same. She was but a rudderless ship that floated wretchedly on the turbulent sea surface, in the process drifting away from its true destination. She didn't know why she was living and she didn't know what living was.

Day by day Sujata grew pale like a cursed parrot put in a cage, who keeps on wondering about the days when it used derive joy from sweet fruits sitting on a swinging branch of a huge tree as a cool breeze would permeate through the atmosphere. For this bird everything was extinct. It was left with hard, ruthless bars of its cage to knock its head on. It was left with shedding its feathers like a tree disrobing its leaves in summer. It was left with squeezing out tears and counting them as they roll down the cheeks. It was left with dreaming about the day which would free it from the cage which, perhaps was the day which would free its soul from the universe, from its body. That was the only thing it was left with. That was the only thing it could do.

It was the beginning of an oppressed life, a life full of events and abrupt ups and downs. This life was destined to include many bloody battles with destiny which in Sujata's case was essentially inharmonious and on many occasions exceedingly cruel. It was as if the destiny wanted to settle its personal score with her.

Whatever might be the reason, this girl was bound to suffer beastly days and sleepless, scary nights, just on account of her being her. Alas! It was just the initiation of her life. Many more jerks were lined up for her, waiting in queue to molest this indefensible life. Her destiny would leave no place for her to rest sedately, it would spare no moment for her to breath without fear of reprisal and ensure hardships at every stage of her life. It would leave no loopholes in its attempts to invalidate this blameless life.

As an adroit commencement of its evil design the destiny had nipped the bud in the bud without giving it any opportunity to flourish into a blooming flower. What remained was to squeeze it until every drop of the juice that imparted it its life, was extracted out, leaving behind a dry, dead pulp that would eventually burn in hot sunshine and get converted into ash.

Sujata's destiny selected aunt Leena as a worthy player to carry out the next step. This lady was quite annoyed at the turn of the events which forced her to exert more. Her mother-in-law needed more attention than ever and adding to her worry was the agonising state of mind that her husband was in, because of which he was finding it difficult to concentrate on his work, consequently reducing his income. But what pinched her the most was the thought that they had to bear the responsibility of Suhasini's daughter forever. Leena always thought that Suhasini put her mind into painful state all the time. Yes, for Leena Suhasini's only intention seemed to kill her sister-in-law. At every instant she was killing her either by her stunning looks, her piercing smile or her talkative eyes. She would slit Leena's throat by the sharpness of her sight and she would hang her by her long, slender hair. Suhasini would stab her with the knife of her elegant persona and she would suffocate her by her tremendous success. As if all this was not enough, she would burn Leena with her beauty and friendly nature. After becoming the undisputed queen of Shrivastav empire, she was even more ruthless. Her rich lifestyle would hit hundreds of bullets towards Leena and leave her severely wounded.

Suhasini did it when she was alive and even after her death she was still haunting Leena. She had left her little daughter Sujata to ensure Leena's lifelong worry and this was too much for Leena to sustain. She badly burned from within and her dormant soul furiously searched for any suitable opportunity to avenge all that punishment bestowed upon her by Suhasini. She went on thinking over it again and again for several days. And suddenly one day she found her course of action. There indeed was a fine way-out to retaliate. The huge property of Shrivastav family was still there and its only owner was in her possession in the form of a tiny girl who couldn't even speak properly. Thus quite accidentally Leena stumbled upon a chance that might also make her dreams come true. If only she could remove this small obstacle of Sujata, they could take over at least some part of Shrivastav family's wealth. The internal conflict in the Shrivastav family was well known. Therefore by taking its proper advantage and doing some legal manipulation which, Leena was confident her husband would do expertly, they were sure to get some good benefit. But Leena didn't know how to proceed because there was no doubt about the fact that little Sujata would automatically catch hold of the property once she becomes major. The only solution to this problem could be to eliminate this girl and nothing was better if Leena could do it before the child could recover from the trauma of her family's destruction. It was possible to dump this girl somewhere because she was so small and defenceless, she couldn't have resisted even a mosquito from biting her. Moreover after that unfortunate incident which deprived her of her family, she was in such a strange condition that nobody could have suspected a sabotage if somebody tried to play some mischief with her. It could have been very easy to prove that the girl herself ran away from the house as she was in a bad mental condition. Other option was to legally prove that the child perished in the tragedy that claimed the lives of her family members, that she also was a victim of the fatal accident that wiped out Shrivastav family.

Leena's determination was grim, her resolve firm. She knew, it was an opportunity of a lifetime. And she had a clear-cut idea what she had to do, just get rid of Sujata come what may. Getting away with it was quite simple. It was then a matter of some legal jugglery to grab substantial portion of the Shrivastav family's estate, by proving themselves to be the closest of their relatives. No doubt they would have to compete with some others, but they were sure to get their share.

The vicious plot took its form in Leena's mind over a period of a few months. But its execution was far more difficult. Removing Sujata from their way was the most risky and utterly dangerous affair. Moreover Leena was only used to building castles in air. She had no idea what it takes to erect a real one. Again she was a born coward who couldn't stand watching a cockroach ramble in her kitchen. And there she was making tall tall claims and big big plans that she didn't know how to implement. One thing was sure, Leena didn't have a heart to slain the child. Besides, she couldn't do anything alone and Vinit providing her any help was out of question. She was even afraid of talking to him about Shrivastav family's assets. Moreover protecting Sujata from anything was the topmost priority of Vinit those days. He kept an eye on her day in and day out, leaving hardly any chance for the likes of Leena to get wrong mileage out of her sorrowful condition. Thus for the time being Leena was left with wringing her hands. Not getting discouraged she waited patiently and thought over her plans again and again. Meanwhile she maintained the role of a responsible housewife, trying to help her husband overcome his grief and showering lots of love over the little girl she secretly wished to do away with.

Finally help did come Leena's way! That too from an unexpected corner and in an unexpected way. Just a few days after the death of Suhasini, Leena's younger brother Ravi rushed to Delhi to meet her. Being an unemployed youth he had a plenty of time and more often he used to visit Delhi. Right from the beginning Ravi was well aware of the conditions his sister was forced to cope up with. This time his heart sank as Leena described her suffering and cried dejectedly in front of him. Rapidly did he come to realise that it was a time to act on something so that his sister would not have to spend rest of her life like what she was living today. Ravi was sufficiently capable and crafty to chalk out such a strategy. He camped at Delhi for the sole purpose of comforting his sister, during which period Leena made him acquainted with her plan. Ravi approved it the moment he heard it from Leena and started working for fulfilling her wishes. Soon he came up with an idea that was incredibly brilliant and not so cold blooded and his sister appreciated it gleefully, giving her nod at the very first instant.

The remarkable plot was smartly fabricated and its execution began with stringent promptness. But there was no need to show much hurry to get to the real act. Hence Leena and Ravi waited for things to settle down a bit. Much to their joy, slowly and inevitably Verma family started leaving a normal life. Nothing really had changed except for the health of Vinit's mother which was worsening day by day and the arrival of little Sujata into their family. Vinit got back to his profession with full swing after some initial hiccups. His responsibility was even more prominent now that Sujata was also to be looked after. It was as if he had given birth to yet another child, but he was glad to have that little legacy of his sister at his disposal. Although he couldn't dedicate much time to her, owing to his packed schedule, he did his best, but sadly it seemed he had no other option but to wait to see her grim face change into a lively lily which looked pointlessly of no avail.

Ravi extended his stay at Delhi, pretending that he was on a mission of searching a job at Delhi and Vinit never suspected his intentions. But this cunning fellow was pursuing his treacherous plans from the day one. Right from the moment Leena gave him permission, he started his first step of action. He started alluring Sujata. They had met 2-3 times earlier and hence getting closer to Sujata was not a big problem for him. He would play with Sujata and bring toys and chocolates for her. Every evening he would grab her in his arms and carry her to nearby gardens and places of amusement. Often Ravi used to show her circus and magic shows. Soon Ravi became her closest friend on account of the time he used to spend with her and things he did to amuse her. That's why in the camaraderie sof Ravi Uncle, Sujata seemed to open up. Ravi Uncle would narrate fantastic stories of fairies and demons, prince and princesses to Sujata and she couldn't wait to hear those interesting tales. To Sujata, Ravi Uncle was far better than Vinit Uncle, because the latter separated her from her parents and never promised to reunite them. Moreover Vinit Uncle did not spend so much time with her and cheer her up doing all the funny things Ravi Uncle used to do. Sujata had developed a strong belief that if anybody could bring back her parents, it was Ravi Uncle. On many occasions Ravi himself had hinted at such a possibility. As a result this faultless child started believing every word and every act of this young man. She had virtually become a blind follower of him. That's why Sujata couldn't stop crying when Ravi abruptly declared that he was going back to Mumbai. She simply got scared at the prospect of losing his comforting shelter. Leena and Ravi somehow managed to calm down the child only after promising that Ravi was going to bring Raj and Suhasini along with him. And thus after making the first part of his plan hugely successful Ravi went back to Mumbai.

Although very miserable at the departure of Ravi, Sujata found herself mitigated because of the feeling that finally she was going to meet her parents and they would go together to Agra in that snow white Ambassador of them. On account of such mood elevating thoughts, very soon the little girl started regaining her original lively nature. But she hid the secret behind it because while going to Mumbai, Ravi Uncle had sternly instructed not to reveal it as her Uncle Vinit might prevent the rendezvous between her and her parents. So she kept mum and waited patiently for the arrival of her parents.

Finally one day, Aunt Leena came to Sujata in the afternoon as she was engrossed in playing with her toys and informed her that her parents were arriving and so they had to rush to the railway station to receive them. Sujata jumped for joy! Merrily she slipped into a beautiful pink frock that her Aunt helped her to wear. For months together Sujata had not been so happy. She could have danced at that instant and she could have sung. But Aunt Leena asked her to keep quiet as her grandmother was sleeping and her cousins who had just returned from the school were busy finishing homework. Leena told her children that they both were going to fetch vegetables. In last so many months, she had carried Sujata along with her almost everyday whenever she went out. So nobody could have suspected anything fishy.

Leena and Sujata quickly walked down to the nearby city bus stop where they caught a bus to the railway station. Another half an hour and they reached the place. As they got down from the bus Sujata could hear her little heart beating violently. At the platform her large, dark eyes searched all the directions as she stood clutching a forefinger of her Aunt. Sujata carefully watched every face in the mob in a hope that it might turn out to be that of her father or her mother. After 10-15 minutes of desperate scrutiny of faces she gave in and started sobbing intermittently. At that moment Aunt Leena asked her to wait patiently and ordered to stop crying. The timid girl did what was told to her. At last to her joy a familiar face emerged from the crowd. No, it wasn't Raj or Suhasini. It was Ravi! Absolutely delighted to see this medium sized, thin moustached young man wearing loose shirt-pant and greenish sunglasses, Sujata at once jumped into his arms, enquiring him about her parents.

At that Ravi informed the little girl that he had met her parents, but they didn't prefer to come there and instead they had asked him to bring her to Mumbai. Initially Sujata seemed to be badly disconcerted, but now that the whereabouts of her parents were known and Ravi Uncle had pledged to take her to her parents, she started bubbling with joy. Wildly Sujata told Aunt Leena that finally she could join her parents. She was so excited, so very delighted that unknowingly her eyes moistened. It was the moment she was living for. For days together she had battled harsh moments and now she thought it was all over, a part of history. This news sent tremors down her body. She started imagining those days at Agra, her parents, grandparents, their villa, their Ambassador, everything.

Soon an announcement sounded over the microphone and Ravi quickly clutched little Sujata in arms and quickly bade farewell to Leena. Leena in her turn, quite unknowingly and surprisingly kissed the innocent child. She too, missed a heartbeat or two at that moment, partially because she didn't know what was going to be the result of these things. Deep in the heart she was scared and she felt guilty. Besides what an outstanding girl Sujata was! Even the most cold blooded devil would not have dared to harm this cuddly kid. Hence for a moment Leena lay trapped in a great dilemma. At one frenzied instant, she almost demanded back the child. But as the train slowly started moving, Leena with a firm mind, turned back.

Stations after stations passed by and Sujata remained all smile on the lap of her Ravi Uncle, once again not knowing that yet another chapter in her life was over. This had always been the irony of her life. Her mind was always dancing with joy whenever she was supposed to cry or grieve. She didn't know, her blind pursuit of the gone days was going to continue forever, that the only way to meet her parents could have been to die like them. She didn't know, now she belonged to that huge family on earth that is called 'orphans', cursed with eternal grief and life full of shattered days and dark, sobbing nights. Once you are a part of it you can never complain against anything. Anybody can toss you around like a football and you are left with rolling on the ground, sustaining scratches and bloody wounds. You cannot complain to God because sadly it is He who wrote such a destiny for you. So you must live like an animal and wait for the day when the God calls back you, terminating your chastisement and hence your life.

Sujata could not imagine these things and so she smiled and enjoyed every bit of the journey. And at Delhi, her Aunt Leena was back home , shouting and crying that Sujata was lost in the vegetable market.

Five

Even if St. Joseph's Orphanage is located in busy Matunga suburb of busy Bombay and even if it doesn't matter in this fast moving city whether the sun is in the sky or moon, its shutter closes at 9.30 pm sharp. It is the time when the Rinki Batliwala road where St. Joseph's stands, flows in full swing. Today when the clock was about to strike at 9.30, Bhiku, the old housekeeper went to close down the door as he does everyday. To his great surprise, a little girl child was hanging around the front door. Bhiku didn't try to identify her and from the fact that she was standing exactly in front of St. Joseph's entrance he judged her to be a naughty girl of their own bunch. More often these children managed to escape the watchful eyes of the governances and come out. Thinking that she was one of them, Bhiku brought her in, lifting her with arm and simultaneously scolding the child. The girl posed absolutely no resistance to his act. Straight away Bhiku went in and handed over the girl to Sister Margaret.

"A new entrance at such an odd hour? And is this the way you treat the children Bhiku?", Sister Margaret asked the old man. Bhiku got confused over the reprimanding tone in which the sister spoke.

"Hey sis, she isn't a new entrance. And you know what she was doing? She was standing at the gate. Heavens know what might have happened had she tried to cross the road", promptly he clarified his stand.

"Bhiku, my old boy, you have really grown old. She is not our child man. Quickly go back and put her where she was", Sister counterblasted.

Startled Bhiku looked at the lass. Indisputably she wasn't a St. Joseph's child. Those large, dark eyes together with creamy, white skin were through and through foreign to him. Bhiku migrated with great strides and carted the little girl outside, deposited her at her preliminary position and went back. He deferred to seal the shutter as there seemed to be no one there to whom she might belong, but finally went in, closing the door behind him. For him the episode should have been over. But it was not going to be like that. Just after an hour Bhiku went to investigate whether the girl was gone or not. She had not gone. She was stationary at the same spot, just like a statue, staring at the vehicles zipping past her. Nobody had noticed this child, shuddering in the cold breeze with her teeth generating chattering sound, even if the stood on the terra firma of Mumbai where, they joke, the winter is as acrimonious as a lotus petal. It seemed as if she sat down once in the deserted footpath, at least the polluted posterior of her pink frock was trying to suggest like that. Bhiku knew at that instant that this girl was scheduled to be a new component of the St. Joseph's. He picked her up again and brought in front of Sister Margaret.

"Now Sister! We both were right. This is a new entrance and she belongs to St. Joseph's," said Bhiku.

"Gracious God!", muttered Sister Margaret, "Why do you produce so many creatures and render them helpless?" She kissed the cross that suspended from her neck and put both her hands on the shoulders of the girl.

"May god bless you, my child", she uttered these words twice as she judiciously scrutinized the little girl. The child undeniably hailed from a good family as was evident from her cloths and this was an amazing fact. She looked like a rose thrown into mud. Her eyes were passionate and deep dark that glittered like diamonds.

"What's your name my child", Sister's voice was as if dipped in honey.

The girl stared back in response. Sensing her enigma and fright sister Margaret cuddled her up and gently patted on her back. This action of genuine love triggered a sudden spurt of emotions and the child broke down heavily that swung her tiny body to and fro. Her cry was real heart breaking that brought tears to Sister Margaret's eyes. Even Bhiku couldn't hold back his. Indeed she was dramatically able to convey her suffering through the medium of her devastating cry even if she couldn't tell the sister that she had been ditched by a person who had promised to carry her to her parents. She couldn't tell her that she was a moron who believed this betrayer and not her own uncle who stood by her always and now probably would die hurting his soul as he couldn't desist this from happening. She couldn't say it all but the touching sound of her scream was articulate enough to elucidate its meaning. After 10-15 minutes of tense moments the girl became quite, sobbing off and on and then completely stopped producing sound. Sister thought she had slept but actually she was staring at the surrounding, scanning and analysing everything with her tiny brain. She had become very suspicious after all these happenings and now she was not going to take anybody for granted. Although the girl had rested on Sister Margaret's shoulders she was not guaranteed about the intentions of this lady.

"Bhiku, bring me the entry register", ordered Sister Margaret. Bhiku nodded mutely and took out the register from a nearby drawer.

"What's your name honey?" Asked the sister.

"Su–ya–ta", surprisingly the child responded quickly. Clearly she was not in a position to pronounce her name properly, partly because of her small age and partly because of her chocked sobbing after excessive weeping. But she spoke something at last and that was a good news.

"Bhiku, what did she say?" Obviously Sister was unable to draw any conclusion from what the girl had expressed.

"What a question to ask to a deaf old man sister" Bhiku retorted," But it seems she said 'Suchita'. Didn't she?"

"You are right Bhiku, "SUCHITA", reiterated Sister Margaret and put her name in the register. This was the name by which this girl was going to be referred throughout her life. Her entire life was getting transposed. She had come to be an invalid orphan from a crowning princess. Contentiously her destiny didn't even spare her name. That was also traded. She had been baptized again and imparted a new identity. She was officially an orphan now.

"Bhiku", sister Margaret raised her head, "Call Samantha, Mary and Clair. Ask them to come quickly".

"OK Sis", Bhiku hurriedly went in.

By Samantha, Mary and Clair sister Margaret meant sister Samantha, Sister Mary and Sister Clair, those three nuns who helped sister Margaret maintain the affairs of St. Joseph's. While Sister Margaret sought to lure little Suchita Bhiku returned back bringing with him a multitude of feminine voices. But naturally that's what you get when two or more young ladies come together. Very expeditiously these women came closer to Sister Margaret who was sitting on a chair holding a little girl in her lap.

"Oh, how so cute!" Exclaimed Sister Mary.

"A new admission, isn't she?" Enquired Sister Samantha.

"Oh why didn't you call us earlier?" Complained Sister Clair.

"Could you give me a chance to speak?", it was Sister Margaret's turn now. Her admonishing tone forced the three ladies to shut their mouths.

"Yes, she is a new entrance," continued Sister Margaret, "and her name is Suchita. It's already too late now, so I want all of us to quickly pray for her as we usually do. And then put her to sleep."

The three nodded in tandem.

Suchita was then kept on a mat on the floor and all four sisters sat on their knees forming a circle surrounding her. With their eyes closed and the right hand palm spread across their chests the four nuns started reciting hymns from the holy Bible. And the puzzled little girl looked at each one of them not knowing what they were doing. She gazed at each face minutely. Sister Samantha in her late 20's was a fat one with a rounded face and a tiny nose. Her curly hair were peeping out of the cloth that was supposed to cover her head. Smooth skin and twinkling, mischievous eyes had a major say in her disposition. Sister Mary was perhaps the youngest among them having a pointed nose, bony cheeks and a thin, delicate body. With long, slender hands and fingers she was the tallest among all and wore thick rimmed spectacles. Formally good educated and blessed with sharp, unyielding memory she could be classified as a blue stocking material. On the contrary, Sister Clair who was 30 or something, had a short figure with a good built. Her stout body with glimmering tanned complexion and prominent brown eyes could stretch upto slightly over 5 feet in her slippers. Although, sentimental she was widely accepted as one who would replace Sister Margaret as a head. Sister Margaret, in turn was a matured lady nearing 60. Her organs were already giving in and almost all her hair had turned gray. What remained was her sharp sight that could identify and separate her children from thousands.

And there was Bhiku, the old man well above 70 years. Age couldn't, in any way, dither this enormous reservoir of enthusiasm. With sheer grit this man had survived grim battles with time and every time managed to emerge victorious. Even lack of education was not a hindering reason for Bhiku. He along with his wife Champa had been loyal to St.Joseph's for decades. He continued to be associated with St. Joseph's after the death of Champa a few years ago, even if his two sons managed to establish good income by driving auto rickshaw. It was this zeal of the old man that forced the St.Joseph foundation to abandon its decision to retire him and he was allowed to be with St. Joseph's till death. In many ways he was a part and parcel of the St. Joseph's and senior to even Sister Margaret, the chieftain of St. Joseph's. He commanded great respect from father Dimello, the head of St. Joseph foundation and all and sundry of St. Joseph's Orphanage. If anybody found this man, wearing milky white Dhoti and kurta on Rinki Batliwala Road, you are at a stones throw from St. Joseph's.

Suchita's new life began on a lively note. The next morning all the children rushed to her dancing like maniacs, hugging her, kissing her. The poor child would bashfully and coyly turn her face away at every such gesture. And all the while she remained stuck to Sister Clair like a baby monkey gripping its mother. Suchita observed funny things as Sister Samantha and Sister Mary bathed the children and made them ready for school. Sister Clair then took the charge and bathed smaller children including Suchita. Once the elder children were dispatched to school Sister Clair and Sister Mary began their domestic one, i.e., they started teaching the young ones who were yet to go to school. Initially Suchita faltered to take part in it but slowly she began loving the thing. Later she discovered that these teachings were a part of all the daily activities there. It was a nice thing for her and she started taking keen interest in learning. Very soon Suchita was luxuriating in her new company, the lively sisters Samantha, Mary and Clair, the naughty, witty fellow children, somewhat strict but extremely kind Sister Margaret and last but not the least Bhiku, who was like a genie in Aladin's lamp granting every wish of the children, buying them chocolates and toffees even against the orders of Sister Margaret. It was so new, it was so fresh and Suchita couldn't but like it.

At St. Joseph's maintaining smooth proceedings affairs was a responsibility of Samantha, Mary and Clair. One of them would prepare meals with the help of a maid while the other two used to take care of other things like cleaning the floor, washing the cloths, looking after kids etc. Bhiku was a chosen person to bring grocery, vegetables and whatever needed by anyone in St. Joseph's. And Sister Margaret was the administrator, the numero uno of St. Joseph's. She would see to it that every child in their family was getting proper attention. She was the one who assigned duties to Samantha, Mary,

Clair and Bhiku. She would take proper care of the children falling ill, maintain the account of St. Joseph's and handled the cash flowing in from the St. Joseph foundation. Besides this, she would carry out other functions like maintaining discipline among the children and getting engaged in useless arguments with Bhiku. Yes, perhaps it was the only thing she could do when there was nothing else to do. These two seniormost persons in St. Joseph's would quarrel over a vast range of issues ranging from 'which is the better religion, Hinduism or Christianity?' to 'is it necessary to scold anybody to maintain discipline?'. Even after being in St. Joseph's for the most part of his life Bhiku had remained a staunch Hindu and would not budge a single inch when it came to protecting a cause of Hinduism. Sister Margaret in her turn used to attack his weak point, very deliberately and caustically and what the everyone else in St. Joseph's would get was full and free entertainment. Often Bhiku used to challenge Sister Margaret's decisions leading to heated exchanges of words. Sometimes the arguments would go upto such an extent that anyone of them would stop abruptly and immediately leave the spot. And if that happened Sister Samantha, Mary and Clair along with a few prankish children who watched the high intensity drama hiding behind the door, would run away and burst into unruly laughter.

But they knew it was all superficial. In reality there was a great understanding between sister Margaret and Bhiku. In fact sometimes Bhiku managed to evoke responses like 'Brother Bhiku' from sister Margaret. And it was none other than Sister Margaret who pressed for avoiding his retirement. Whenever help was needed sister Margaret would essentially turn to Bhiku. Their relationship was so very intricate, their relationship was so very funny.

Days passed by and Suchita faced almost no difficulty to adjust herself to the new environment probably because there were a lot of children like her, some even younger than her. Besides she found the people there to be more genuine, sympathetic and very pure at heart. Once again Suchita found herself to be the centre of attraction and she found herself receiving huge quantums of love and affection from every corner of St. Joseph's. It was indeed a remarkable new onset for her. It was as if the life was back to her life.

St. Joseph's came to be a huge parkland for Suchita where she played, danced and sang merrily. She used to be all smile when Sister Clair would load her on her back like a bag of sugar and when

Sister Samantha would carry her on her back like a horse rider. Sister Mary would toss her into the air and Suchita would scream excitedly, tightly closing her eyelids. How so ever frightening it might be, it had become a favourite act for the little girl and she would demand it again and again. But strangely and unlike other children Suchita was ever willing to share the affection of elders among all and it was quite a surprising fact. Also the rapid changes in her life made her to shed that infamous stubbornness of her and poured extraordinary maturity into her character.

Suchita developed a particularly soft corner towards Bhiku as this was the man responsible for bringing her into St. Joseph's from the dusty footpath where she was left unprotected. Bhiku too became very fond of her and always expressed his displeasure over himself for scolding this innocent girl when she was standing on the footpath that night. Bhiku was one by whom Suchita's every wish was granted, her every desire was fulfilled. May it be chocolates, biscuits or toys, Bhiku would brave hostile weather, gladly accept Sister Margaret's wrath and do virtually everything to make Suchita happy. Indeed he would remove good amount of money for such purposes from the account and face scathing attacks from the volatile sister Margaret who invariably used to deduct the money from Bhiku's monthly salary. And he did never mind it because it was his age-old habit and both he himself and Sister Margaret were well accustomed to it. Thus Bhiku provided every need and demand of Suchita but when once she demanded her parents, the poor old man couldn't but offer his tears.

On the other hand Suchita's relationship with Sister Margaret was one of an intriguing and mystifying nature. Sister Margaret who would submerge herself in account books or continuously reproach somebody or other over a trivial matter, didn't miss an opportunity to kiss this little girl when she used to go near her very unknowingly while playing hide and seek with other children. Suchita was the only one who could very well slap Sister Margaret's face and smoothly get away with it without gaining a single word of rebuke. Suchita would casually go to Sister Margaret and sit on her lap, nibbling away at a biscuit crust in hand while the head of the St. Joseph's would be busy with fixing the monthly budget of the orphanage or reading some unimaginable philosophical book. Not only she would settle herself on Sister Margaret's lap but also stare at her thick glasses or lean over the book as if to know what she plied. Had anybody else disturbed Sister Margaret while she did her important works she would have exploded like an atom bomb and blaze away at the person. But contrary to such a reaction this lucky girl would get a delicate pat on her head and a childish question like "what's my naughty kid upto?" Or a soft remark like "Don't play mischief". Knowing this well Samantha, Mary, Clair and Bhiku used to tease Sister Margaret by utilising Suchita as their weapon. So whenever they felt like provoking Sister Margaret they would send Suchita to play spoilsport when the old lady would be engrossed in some Plato or Leo Tolstoy.

With the inclusion of Suchita into the St. Joseph's team the total strength of children taking shelter in this orphanage went upto 28. And this was a huge number. Whenever they used to assemble together what they would form was a monumental mob. Generation of such a mob at St. Joseph's was certain on Sundays and other holidays because during weekdays the children would remain overburdened with schools and homework. Thankfully because of wide range of age groups, the school timings were different and hence probability of all the kids being together at the same time was very rare. Nevertheless they used to be together in the evenings but that was the time when some of them would loosen up, some would go out walking and rest did their homework. Because of severe mental and physical exhaustion it wasn't possible for them to create havoc in St. Joseph's and the atmosphere there would remain restful. But on holidays the kids would wake up fresh and energetic and that's when the real trouble would start. It could have been a big deal for Samantha, Mary and Clair to keep this enormous bunch into check. But whenever these little devils threatened to go out of control some people came handy to help. That included some elder children along with Bhiku and that inimitable Sister Margaret who had a tremendous ability and reputation to convert this inflammable crowd into a flock of tamed sheep, with a slight rise in the pitch of her voice.

But the best solution was one suggested by sister Samantha to carry the children to some nearby park or recreational place so that they could get an opportunity to rejoice as well as release their huge stock of energy, while playing. It was accepted by one and all. So come holidays and St. Joseph's would celebrate picnics.

However, the most nerve testing part was vacations, the summer and winter holidays. It is the time when people go out with children who are badly fed up with schools and routine studies. For the people living in crowdy places like Bombay, it is the time to free oneself from the fast moving, stressful city life and cool off. Unfortunately such excursions were not possible for St. Joseph's folks simply because it wasn't affordable. Taking up such a leisure trip could mean welcoming a big financial crunch at least for three months, which was a hard bargain. But the tiny brains of the innocent children would almost always fail to comprehend these calculation. They used to hear fascinating experiences from the other children at school and would demand unimaginable things from Samantha, Mary and Clair. Not only the ability of other children to spend fabulous holidays but their overall luxurious lives would also haunt the St. Joseph's children. They couldn't but compare themselves with the every other child at school and usually find themselves very ill-starred.

They didn't have parents to drop them in schools or carry them over in arms. Yes, this was their main concern, the lack of existence of the figures who brought them into this world, excavating a strange hollowness in their lives. How delighted their little friends used to be to see the blossoming faces of their mothers at the end of a hectic day at school. Despite being tired they would run towards them joyfully melting into their arms. It used to be like a meeting between a cow and her calf which was missing throughout the day and somehow managed to find his mother when the sun was inclined towards west. It was the same lady about whom their friends would talk endlessly praising her for whatever she did. Almost every child would claim its mother to be the best in the world. And by overpowering pride in their moms' eyes it was quite obvious that they were the best children in the world.

Where were St. Joseph's children in that context? Why weren't they spared the right to enjoy such extremely high quality moments in life? Where were those incomparable mothers and those formidable fathers of them? Mothers, whom they heard to be so powerful, her only touch provided soothing effect that thousands of medicinal mixtures failed to create. Her smiling face would heal agonizing wounds to the body and soul in a single magical moment. Mothers whom they heard to be so caring and affectionate that people equate them to the God. Mothers whom they knew to be so nurturing, they could give rise to the great heroes as well as notorious outlaws. Mothers whom the world recognises to be a paramount of purity and genuinity and who matched the creater God in the capability of producing life by way of giving birth. Mothers, poor or rich love their children with same intensity and their affection never rust with time or circumstances. And the taste of a simple recipe cooked by her could bit the most sumptuous cuisine in the world!

The St. Joseph's children also heard a lot about fathers from the other children. Just like moms, they formed a firm opinion, a role model of fathers too. Almost every child would boast that its father was the strongest person in the world. For the cause of protecting the children and the entire family for that matter, he would battle with demons, ghosts and horrible beasts. He was the one who toiled day in and day out so that each one in the family would rest in comfort. He was the one who would gladly accept enemity with rest of the world, even become a thief or a murderer to fill the empty stomachs of his children. He was the one who would brave many sleepless nights and suffer silently to provide better future for the children may it be a good education or a suitable groom for the daughter.

Didn't each one of them require parents like those mentioned by their friends? What unforgivable sins had they committed so as to go through this severe punishment? Whenever many innocent faces used to ask such questions to Samantha, Mary and Clair the poor girls couldn't react and simply kept mum. What they could do was just to hug the children and comfort them. In worst cases they had to share their tears too. That would happen on every parents' day when all the parents would turn out to schools along with their children to take part in the celebrations. The St. Joseph's children used to attend the schools with heavy hearts and most of them were sure to break down in tears after returning from school. Samantha, Mary and Clair who were orphans themselves had to put up brave faces to confront the hard time. On that day many children would go to bed wailing, not engulfing a single bit of food.

This was the biggest and the toughest problem faced by the St. Joseph's administration. There couldn't be anything more austre to assimilate than to see those sinless and otherwise smiling faces turn gloomy and put forth the demands which could be utterly impossible to satisfy even for the most influential forces in the world. But a partial solution of this problem was very much there. Like most of the orphanages St. Joseph's also used to have trysts with those unfortunate couples who were not blessed with children and aspired to adopt any suitable boy or a girl. And Christmas was the fixed day for such encounters between these childless parents with the parentless children. It wasn't a hard and fast rule as such and the yearning couples were welcomed and gladly awaited throughout the year. But Christmas was a special occasion when the St. Joseph's people would flash advertisements in newspapers inviting the couples from various castes, creeds and religion on the Christmas eves to select and adopt any one of their children. The responses to these call used to be haphazard. Sometimes there would be a heavy turnout and some other time not a single couple would show up. But in any case Christmas used to be a difficult day for Samantha, Mary, Clair, Bhiku and Sister Margaret. If the people arrived in huge numbers they would snatch away number of children resulting in the depletion of St. Joseph's family members consequently in the source of joy for these five elders. Indeed St. Joseph's was a heaven for them only due to the presence of those heavenly descendents called kids. On the other hand if less people attended the ceremony they used to be unhappy just because many of their children would miss the well assured life with parents. In short their's was a dilemma only comparable to the father of a newly wedded bride who cannot have his daughter with him throughout the life and at the same time finds it difficult to detach her from him.

✣✣✣

Today was the first Christmas eve after Suchita's arrival in the St. Joseph's. Right from the morning the atmosphere turned magical, completely overwhelmed with the sweet scent of cakes being baked by equally sweet hands of Sister Samantha and the flowers that lay packed in baskets brought early in the morning by Bhiku. Throughout the day the elders seemed to be busy, indulged in some work or other, while the children mostly engaged theselves in celebrating holiday, quietly interfering in the elders' business and enjoying delicious sweets. As evening approached Sister Samantha, Mary and Clair took possession of them and very quickly transformed the little devils into good looking, well behaved and well mannered kids. They were washed up, neatly dressed up and informed not to involve themselves in any activity that could damage the good work done by the three sisters and make themselves soiled again. Obviously because they were to be adopted by the couples responding to the St. Joseph's call only on the basis of their innocence and good behaviours. For that Sister Margaret delivered a lengthy speech which however, mostly failed to penetrate the heads of these tiny creatures.

Suchita who was clad in a spectacular dazzling, white attire that of a Christian bride and miniature white canvas shoes looked, directly brought down from heaven. Her frock glittered with all the lavish design embossed on it and the sparkling texture of the cloth. Her smooth hair were partly tied together on the top of the head from where hung a white piece of cloth that covered her back and mixed somewhere with her gown. It was a similar white one with some delicate design but only it was transparent and her silky, slight curly hair on the periphery which were not tied, moved carelessly all over the head and sometimes covered her forehead. At times the girl would make tender movements of tiny hands to move those naughty hairlets off her forehead. As if all this was not enough, Sister Mary brought a well blossomed rose and inserted it in Suchita's hair. Now she was shining like Cindrella. Although she didn't know what all that fuss was meant for, she came to a conclusion that it was a big day, some festival or something.

Once getting ready there seemed to be nothing else to do. So she wandered all over the orphanage, carefully observing the novelty it had possessed that day. How beautifully and artistically was it decorated! Bhiku had tied a glowing garland of bulbs all across the fronts face of St. Joseph's. Consisting of different colours red, blue, green and yellow they used to glow and ceased to glow in a characteristic manner forming interesting patterns that amused the children a lot. In the interior also the decorative work was fascinating. There were candles and flowers everywhere and coloured, scintillating strips of paper swung all across the ceiling, forming complex webs. Oh, and where from those colourful balloons have come? They were not there a few minutes back! It seems Bhiku has done this fine job, well he is always up to some surprises. And the best thing is they are always pleasant. Hay, what's that tree over there? Isn't it fabulous? Look at those delicate branches sloping downwards and that pointed top of it. The branches themselves are pointed and red cherries are positioned at each point. Boy, the glowing electric lighting is also there. Sure that's some kind of a special thing.

Suchita roamed across everything like an effervescent, fluttering butterfly every now and then leaving one flower and settling itself on another. And as she wandered, she wondered about the surroundings because she hadn't seen anything like that ever before. Finally Suchita came to halt when she happened to face a portrait of a strange individual. This cryptic painting would hang above Sister Margaret's chair in the front porch. But right now it had been taken out from that position and brought into the middle hall where that marvellous tree was kept. Suchita had glimpses of that painting on many occasions but every time she found it something mysterious. It was a bearded man with shoulder long hair. His face was serene and graceful and his look glaring, palpable and absolutely convincing. His disposition was devastatingly hypnotic. That's why Suchita stood spellbound for a few moments in front of that portrait. Unable to recognise the face she reached for Sister Mary who was arranging plates on a nearby table. With her tiny hands the girl pulled Sister Mary's gown and asked the query which was haunting her for many days.

"Who is he sister?", She pointed her forefinger towards the painting.

Sister Mary smiled at her and lovingly patted on her back.

"He is Jesus Christ."

"Jesus Christ? Who?", the question remained intact.

"He is the messenger of God. If you pray for anything he can satisfy your wish."

"Oh really?", the girl looked amazed. She again gazed at the picture, this time more carefully and fired the most awaited question.

"Will he bring back my mom and dad?"

"Perhaps but in some other form and that too today itself."

"What do you mean by some other form?"

"That means they will look different."

"Ha! What's the use? I won't identify them", said Suchita despondently clasping her hands together. It was the same girl who couldn't pronounce her name properly a few months ago. Now she was talking like a wise lady. She could very well understand that this was yet another way of making a fool of her.

"Well if he is so powerful, he should return back my mom and dad in the same form".

Here Sister Mary pretended that she didn't hear anything and got interlaced with her work again. She knew it wasn't advisable to stretch the matter too far and test the limit of the child. Suchita on the other hand got disappointed and sat on a chair with her palms providing support to her chin and her elbows resting on her thighs.

For quite a some time the girl remained where she was although everybody else in St. Joseph's seemed to be in some kind of a hurry. And then suddenly a big crowd of tiny kids gushed inside the hall attracting attention of Suchita. All those faces were familiar except for one queer character in the middle of the group. It was an old man with raw cotton like white beard and similar white hair. He wore a strange red coloured garment and a funny red coloured cap, upright over his head. He carried a huge rounded bag on his shoulder and his mischievous eyes twinkled with each mention of his name by the overjoyed children. They called him 'Santa'. As soon as these people appeared, Suchita jumped out of the chair with her hands clasping her face in sheer ecstasy and marvel. She almost screamed at the sight. As she stood at the same spot the old man stepped forward towards her, an act which scared the child and forced her to retreat a few steps. Sensing her fear the old man stopped moving further and made some jolly faces to cheer up the girl.

"Don't get frightened Suchita. I'm your friend", he said in a comical tone, "I'm Santa, Santa Claus at your service Ma'm." He placed his right hand on his chest and bent his body executing a Japanese salute.

"Yeah", the children shouted hysterically.

"Now what's your demand boys and girls, tell me one by one," Santa declared.

"A doll", a chirpy sound originated from a corner.

"An aeroplane," screamed the next one.

"A football," pat came another voice.

"Micky Mouse," "a bat," "a hat," "icecream," "chocolates." Voices exploded from everywhere.

"Wait a bit", Santa placed his bag on the floor and instructed the children to quietly sit down by raising his hands.

"First of all I'll ask this little friend of ours", he turned his face to Suchita, "What do you want dear? I have everything you would like."

Suchita stared at Santa's bag full of fascinating things. Indeed it contained everything a child might desire. But Suchita's attention remained focussed on a small white coloured toy car that peeped out of the bag. For a split moment she had a blurred remembrance of something like that four wheeler and unknowingly she pointed her index finger towards it.

"Well your wish is my command Ma'm", Santa bent down again and plucked out the shining white metal car and pushed it towards Suchita. Children jumped for joy and clapped enthusiastically as the car zoomed over the floor and delicately banged Suchita's leg. The girl picked it up and couldn't move her sight away from the toy as Santa started distributing things among children.

"OK guys," he went on after emptying out his bag, "But this is not over yet. Just now you have got what you wanted. But believe me you are going to get something you really deserve. Some of you might just get their parents today". He told the boys and girls, " and those who won't, they will get them some other day".

Hardly anybody was listening to Santa. Little children didn't understand a word of what he said. Those who were somewhat grown up, knew he was talking about couples who were supposed to adopt them. So without paying much heed to Santa the kids started enjoying their new gifts. Suchita too was deeply involved with car but occasionally she would look at Santa, still being largely confused over his identity.

"Listen children," Sister Margaret suddenly arrived at the scene, "Here are Mr. Rajat Sharma and Mrs. Nalini Sharma", she made them abreast of a couple she brought along with her. "They want to choose anyone of you as their child. So for time being keep aside your games and toys and stand here as Sister Clair says".

"Sister it will be better if the formalities are over quickly. We have my old father waiting for us at home". Mr. Sharma spoke.

"No problem Mr. Sharma, just go ahead and pick the child of your choice", Sister Margaret said in an assuring tone and turned to Sister Samantha, Mary and Clair. "Clair make the children to line up here and Samantha you introduce each one of them to Mr. and Mrs. Sharma. In the meantime Mary will clean up the mess around here because many more couples are expected to come and it's not a good sign to show them all this dirty work. OK?" The young ladies nodded as usual.

"Lastly" Sister Margaret was yet to finish, "Where is Bhiku? I haven't seen that old boy for ages." This query invited a whistle from Santa who quietly came out from a bunch of children.

"Who else asked me to slip into this bulky attire Ma'm?" He enquired, "I'm Santa now and Santa is entitled to do nothing else but be Santa". He chuckled and blinked his eyes.

"Well I don't mind even if you go to sleep right away", Sister Margaret returned a sarcastic punch. "Carry on Mr. Sharma". She resumed her talk with the waiting couple, "I just fill up the register", and without waiting for any response she made her way to the front porch.

The kids formed a row as Sister Samantha informed the Sharmas about their names and ages. As this process was going on the couple took some more time when they reached Suchita, who was still dazed at the fact that Santa was nobody else but Bhiku.

"Sister she is a perfect match for us," Mrs. Sharma told Samantha after some low pitched discussion with her husband.

"As you like Ma'm," said Sister Samantha and picked Suchita in her arm. Mr. and Mrs. Sharma followed her to the front porch as Sister Mary instructed the children to follow them silently.

"Congratulations", Sister Margaret greeted the Sharmas as she cut Suchita's name from the record. The parting hour had finally arrived. One by one everybody cuddled up the child and kissed her with tears in the eyes and grief in the heart. It was a short journey, a tiny period in the time frame, yet it looked to be ages when this lovely bud adored St. Joseph's. And it was all over now, abruptly her stay was coming to an end.

"God bless you Suchita," their hearts gave a synchronous cry as nobody was able to speak out anything. Suchita cried with frenzy and tried to foil the attempts of Mrs. Sharma to clutch her in arms. But somehow the Sharmas carried her through the doorway. Soon the elders in St. Joseph's wiped out their wet eyes and got on to the business. Suchita put all her might she could gather to free herself from the Sharmas as they travel towards their home and a deserted white toy car pathetically lay alone on the floors of St. Joseph's.

Six

"And now his excellency the honourable Lt. Governor of Delhi will present the medal of bravery posthumously to Lt. Col. Omprakash Mittal who laid down his life to the divine cause of the motherland".

An emotionless voice originated from the loudspeakers and struck the eardrums of thousands of men and women assembled to celebrate the Independence day at Azad Maidan, Delhi.

"The award will be received on behalf of late Lt. Col. Mittal by his son", the announcement went on and all eyes were fixed on a teenager who was sitting in the front row. The twelve years old boy with sparkling eyes slightly moistened with the reference of his father rose from the chair as the audience exploded into clapping. He moved gently and gracefully, clad in white shirt and maroon half pant, his walking action was as majestic as it was unrivaled. Perhaps he had inherited it from his forefathers who made the army their second home and never flaundered to relinquish their lives. Till this boy came within the gamut of dais, the public applaud had assumed deafening proportions. Swiftly he ascended the dais and stood in front of the Lt. Governor. The hurrah culminated progressively as the microphone sounded again.

"Lt. Col. Mittal of 15 Rajputana Regiment was killed in an encounter with enemy forces on 14th October 1971 in North Rajasthan. He led a fierce Indian attack successfully but had to shed his own life for the great purpose. Today on the very first Independence day after the Indian victory in the recently concluded Indo-Pak war for Bangladesh liberation, the grateful nation remembers her gallant sons for their courageous deeds and invaluable sacrifices. Lt. Col. Mittal, one of such braves, is honoured by the Government of Delhi by this medal of bravery".

With this the Lt. Governor presented the award and the crowd gave a standing ovation to the little boy imperiously holding the medal, the moisture in his eyes now sufficiently large to coalesce into drops that slid down his cheeks. Soon with this kid on the stage, the national anthem began and finally the gathering ended on a patriotic fervour with loud chats of 'Vande Mataram' and 'Jai Hind' blasting into the atmosphere giving a magical touch to the surrounding. As the crowd dissipated some enthusiasts advanced towards the little son of Lt. Col. Mittal, some shaking hands with him, some tapping on his back while others gave smiling stately looks to the child. Being very coy he was finding it difficult to appreciate the unforeseen way in which he ripened into a centre of attraction. Unable to endure the change he looked for patronage which he knew was not more than a few metres away from him. Quickly the boy spotted the smiling female face watching him minutely with eyes full of pride and a bit of salt water. This young lady of 24 with neatly cut short hair and wearing an orange *'Salwar kameez'* was about 5'4" and her cheeks forged a delicate depression when she smiled. But the most likeable feature of her was her childish chastity and fairness of mind that perfectly matched with the fairness of her body.

Unburdened to see the familiar face the boy struggled to reach her while the lady moved fast, making her way through the mob and grabbing him with arm. She planted an elated kiss on his forehead just like a mother would do when her son wins a trophy. They both waited the mob to recede as the lady stood at the child's back tenderly squeezing his chin by her hand. Soon they made their way through the overcrowded place and managed to come to the main road. The duo stepped into a city bus and within 20 min. run got down in front of a rather oddly shaped but very wide house. The front portion was narrow having a single room with large glass windows. On the backside of this room the width of the house gradually broadened giving an unusual 'V' shape to the entire framework. On the top of the front room from outside was a huge wooden strip on which was painted in thick letters 'Happy Home' while the portion down below it, contained in small letters 'a government aided orphanage.'

This entire incident had left deep imprints on the mind of the little son of Lt. Col. Mittal who now himself was an Army Captain and the world recognized him as Capt. Jatin Mittal. Nothing on earth offered him so much pleasure and conceit than to conjure up the day. And he used to recollect it more often. That's why he didn't face any difficulty in depicting everything about it in minutest detail. Right now the young man was doing the same thing, i.e., portraying his confluence with glory to a young man of about 32 and an old lady in her sixties.

Yesterday Capt. Jatin Mittal had returned home from his work and as usual signed up himself in enjoying the fellowship of his swinging chair. What else could a bachelor do? This man was not only lonely but also very poor in terms of neighbours. His house being on a corner, had a road on one side while there stood a small but tidy house on the other. As if star-crossed this neighbouring house was lying evacuated for many years. Because of this Jatin felt like living in a jungle with no human beings to talk to and consequently used to spend his leisure watching the vehicles passing by or people strolling around.

But as he presided at his swinging chair yesterday evening he was startled to see lights divulging from the windows of the proximate house. Gleefully that at last he found some companions Jatin jumped for joy and darted there only to find some grieving faces. He felt terribly awkward and the smile on his face vanished into thin air as he watched a big photograph of some man who most probably had left for his heavenly abode if the sandalwood garland that hung to the photograph was some indication. Some five six grown ups and two three children were sitting in the room and they looked in deep distress with hardly any word being spoken. This unusually sombre atmosphere left Jatin in an absolutely embarrassed condition. He apologised to them for the reason only he knew, introduced himself as briefly as he could and returned back. But before that he could receive a docile smile from one of them who promised curtly to meet him the next day.

As per his assurance the same young man showed up at Jatin's house along with an old lady apparently his mother. The man was Diljeet Sareen, an NRI doctor who worked in Canada ever since he completed his medical education. Just a 15 days back his father had died of heart attack. Diljeet's married sister lived in Chandigarh and his widow mother, the same old woman accompanying him was alone now. The old lady refused to join her son and his family at Canada simply because her entire life was spent at Delhi. Also according to her, living at daughter's house was out of question. That left no choice for Diljeet and he found a new smaller house for his mother selling their old bungalow. But still he didn't have any idea how she was going to live by herself.

Jatin looked sympathetically at the lady whom he was introduced with as Mrs. Kamal Sareen. She was in her late sixties with uniform wrinkles all over the body and silky hair. She had a yellowish white complexion and large, passionate eyes indicating that she might have caused a few heartbreaks during her peak years. Going through the shock received due to husband's death the old lady still had trouble forcing a smile on face. Surprisingly she showed a keen interest in Jatin's past. Also it had something to do with the numbers of bravery medals that adored Jatin's house.

"Son you are talking as if it's a mystery story. You have told only about the medal and not about that 'Happy Home' or that young lady with you", the Mrs. Sareen asked in a voice which was comely and sweet and she spoke as if she had been talking to her own son.

"I'm coming to that Mrs. Sareen" calmly Jatin put his point. "I was admitted into the 'Happy Home' in 1973, i.e., just after my father achieved martyrdom. It was a second blow for me because at that time I had just recovered from the shock I received due to the demise of my mother. She perished in 1969 after fighting deadly leukaemia. I was just seven years old then. It seems to me, my father was not prepared to remarry. So he sent me to a hostel and kept himself busy in the army activities. In the hostel I had to struggle for initial 2/3 years to cope up with the new lifestyle. But finally I got used to live without the parents. And the fact that I had my father, although far away from me was sufficient to feel very safe. At times I used to get opportunities to meet him when he would visit my hostel. I was very proud of my father and I used to show his photographs in military outfit to my friends. You can see how he used to be", here Jatin pointed his forefinger towards a photograph kept on a sideby table. Diljeet and his mother turned to have a look at the photograph. He was ditto like Jatin the only variance being his majestic moustache that added more glitter to his face.

"Then fortunately or unfortunately the war broke out", Jatin resumed swiftly after letting out a sigh, "I never knew the whereabouts of my father. He didn't show up for months together and finally one day I received a letter from the army officials. It informed me that my father was no more. At that instant my grief knew no bounds and I simply couldn't think about my future. I think it was too hard a jolt for me as a teenager. And you can guess what must have happened to my tender mind. It almost crumbled down. But that was not the end of everything! Before any relative or well wisher could step in, the grateful Indian Army came forward and they sent me to the 'Happy Home'. Within a month or so the magical atmosphere there and the ever so kind 'Didi', yes the same young lady I was referring to, they simply transformed my life from something like a barren desert to a green oasis." Jatin stopped here and smiled at Mrs. Sareen who appeared bewildered at the every mention of Happy Home and that young lady whom Jatin called 'Didi'.

"Well, now I will tell you about 'Happy Home' and 'Didi'", he continued. "Happy Home", as I have mentioned earlier is a government aided or rather Army managed orphanage which is exclusively meant for the helpless children of those who fought for the sake of the country. And the lady who accompanied me at the award distribution ceremony was its chief in charge. And still today she is the chief in charge of Happy Home. Her name is Nilam but affectionately everybody calls her 'Didi'. Even today if you go to the 'Happy Home' you will find an office like front room which carries a shapely wooden table and some chairs. And the nameplate in front of the main chair simply reads 'Didi'.

Didi herself is an orphan and she was brought to the Happy Home when she was 3 years old. She had to leave the orphanage after turning 18 as per the law there. Nevertheless the orphanage provided her education fees and hostel charges. This girl was very unhappy leaving 'Happy Home' but soon started working in a bank once her education was over. Never satisfied with the outside world she always dreamt of the life she had spent in the 'Happy Home'. Luckily the chief in charge of the orphanage retired and the post laid vacant. Didi applied for the job and she was promptly selected. That time she knew she got the mission for her life and firmly decided to remain single and work for the orphanage throughout her life. Such was a tremendous influence of the 'Happy Home' on her life that she couldn't think about any other place to live in. And how grateful she was! As you know the 'Happy Home' is exclusively meant for the helpless children of Army personnel. But still it accepted Didi about whom no information was available. Surely she didn't have any military background but when she was spotted wandering in the street the police took hold of her and finally handed her over to the 'Happy Home'. Some people thought that she belonged to a rich family which was robbed and brutally massacred. The little girl miraculously escaped or possibly spared. But no evidence supporting this view was existing and hence her background has largely remained a mystery. However, Didi never showed interest in her past and stuck to the name 'Nilam' given to her by the orphanage. She could never forget the fact that the 'Happy Home' accepted her by making exception to their rules. For that lot of efforts were made to persuade the top government officials. Fortunately they yielded to the frequent requests and gave green signal to her acceptance. Didi on her turn decided to pay the debts by rendering her services to the cause of the orphanage and became its chief in charge who is also called manager. She was just 24 then".

Jatin desisted for a while just to note how deeply Mrs. Sareen was engrossed in his talks. Indeed she gave an ear to him with the curiosity and eagerness of a child listening to the stories told by its grandparents. Diljeet, too was listening demurely, observing the discourse between Jatin and his mother. He was cheerful because for the first time after his father's death his mother looked so abated and for the time being it seemed as if she had forgotten the shocking incident. Also he was satisfied to note the fact that she had got a good neighbour who looked as sensible as he was considerate. With the kind of interest Diljeet's mother and Jatin were taking in each other, their frequency match was palpable. That served to remove some burden off his mind.

"Life in Happy Home was entirely of different kind, quite out of the world you know. After having entered it I slowly began absorbing knowledge about life and along with my other companions I soon mastered the art of forgetting the past. The very feeling that we all in Happy Home were facing a similar kind of destiny in our life would bind us strongly. Naturally the values of universal brotherhood were automatically inculcated in our mind. Sure we were all without the support of parents but we were not supportless either.

Our family was really big and its members were of various types and creeds. Our ages were ranging from below one year to 18, including boys and girls mostly belonging to North India region. We all used to attend a nearby government school where we used to get a handsome deduction in tuition fees. The government provides some educational grant to Happy Home via its Defence Ministry. But more often it used to be inadequate to fulfil the demand of so many boys and girls. Today I don't know what is the condition in Happy Home, but when I was there we used to share our school uniforms and books among ourselves. Besides going to school and studying we all managed the entire affair of the Happy Home under the guidance of 'Didi'. You will be surprised to hear when I say that there was not a single government employee other than 'Didi', not even a maid to look after the younger ones or wash the dishes. So we used to perform these duties together, with 'Didi' at the helm. Those who were somewhat grown up, say above 12-13 years would do major works like preparing meal, bringing groceries, helping 'Didi' take care of all activities etc. While those below this age group would carry out lighter functions like cleaning and playing with kids. All these things helped to generate a sense of being in a family and at the same time made everyone capable of accepting responsibilities at a young age. In spite of getting some financial aid from the Government of India we were always looking for the means to generate our own revenue. For that some of us who were more creatively inclined used to make things of art like toys, paintings, showpieces and what not, of course whenever they got time from studies and other work".

"How amazing!" exclaimed Mrs. Sareen. "We always tend to believe that those who are orphans are living a cursed life. But it seems, you people had transformed this curse into a blessing in disguise. But don't you think, not all orphans get the privilege of living the kind of life you have experienced?".

"Perhaps you are right", said Jatin covering his lips with curved fingers, thoughtfully digesting the point raised by Mrs. Sareen. "Indeed we were fortunate to be in Happy Home. We never felt pinched due to the fact that we lacked a very important asset in life. Instead of growing on a solid foundation of parental support we grew on an altogether different foundation of Happy Home. But what is important, is the fact that we grew. Lack of parents which could have become obstruction in the path of our growth, couldn't hinder our progress. Whole credit of it goes to the Happy Home. Its culture is really fantastic. No wonder anybody would fall in love with the Happy Home the day he or she enters into it. Such a warmth is Happy Home. Such a delightful charm is Happy Home. Ever since 'Didi' took the charge of its affairs the entire atmosphere got charged up. She was well aware what it meant to be in Happy Home and how the children felt to be in Happy Home because she herself was a part of this family for years. That's why she found herself getting accommodated in Happy Home with the ease of sugar dissolving in milk. Didi never behaved as a chief in charge but as an elder member of the family, sharing the joys and sorrows of everyone, comforting those who were in tears, encouraging those who were depressed and guiding those who were wandering along wrong paths. She worked day in and day out, hardly showing any sign of exasperation. Most of us didn't know how parents behave with their children but Didi's way of conduct gave some idea about it and we could always sense that she was not different from real parents.

Didi was instrumental in bringing radical changes in the minds of the boys and girls. We hated to call ourselves orphans and we would always maintain that Happy Home was a Home and not an orphanage. Our argument was orphans are those who are supportless. But we had a lot of support, the support of each other and an immensely protective head in the form of 'Didi'. This attitude served to bring a tremendous sense of pride and self-confidence in the children. Consequently we found the Happy Home a better place to live in.

After sustaining two hard blows I could wish for nothing more. In a startling turn of events I lost everything and regained everything. Very soon I established delicate relationships with everyone in Happy Home. There was a time when I used to consider myself unfortunate because I didn't have any brother or sister. But suddenly I earned a lot of brothers and sisters both younger ones and elder ones. And how extremely happy they were when I brought the bravery award. Actually all of them were dying to accompany me for the ceremony but Didi didn't grant permission for that. The simple reason was, we had a few really small kids who deserved attention all the time. So it could have been impossible to keep an eye on everybody in the big crowd. Also it was unfair to take some children with us leaving the remaining ones at home. Finally Didi announced her decision forbidding everybody to attend the ceremony. That decision left many faces disappointed but nevertheless nobody objected to it.

In Happy Home we had big celebrations every year on the Independence day. That year a proud boy in the form of me walked in with a shining medal of bravery won by my father and that certainly added glitter to the glorious occasion. I could see a tremendous sense of pride in every eye watching me. They thought they had a lion's cub with them. But then who wasn't a lion's cub there? I still distinctly remember every face watching me with praising eyes as if I myself had won the grand medal".

Again Jatin cut short his speech for a while just to check whether he was boring the two persons sitting in front of him. Most, probably he was not. That's what the feedback given to him by their eyes seemed to suggest. The old lady was deeply involved in Jatin's story, whereas her son sat calmly and patiently. Perhaps he was more concerned about his mother's state of mind and the fact that his mother was showing interest in things other than his father's demise was a good indication for him.

"But son how was your personal relationship with your Didi? You must be having many fond memories about her and Happy Home, don't you have?", Mrs. Sareen's sentences were sprinkled with honeydews.

"Yes of course", Jatin surged ahead avidly. He was grateful because Mrs. Sareen referred her as son and it was almost after 15 years that someone had called him son. "My relationship with Didi was a special. It was one of a deep understanding and love. She was my mother, father, sister and brother all moulded into one. I admit, she had a tremendous influence on me and I was one of the greatest receiver of her affection. I remember one incident that left deep impression on my fertile mind. If my memory is not betraying me, it must have been in 1977. That year I caught a severe illness, some typhoid or something.

And it forced me to bed for about a month. I hardly know anything about that period and as far as I can remember most of my brothers and sisters would sit around me quietly doing their works or studying. Whenever I used to wake up they would cheer me up with smiling faces. Occasionally they would clutch my hands and stroke them gently. Sometimes I used to experience the drugs being administered into my mouth. Every night Didi would come to me and enquire about my health. She used to look very exhausted, heavens knew why. She would talk to me for a few minutes, giving me encouragement to get well quickly. Then blowing a kiss at my forehead she would ask me to sleep. When I used to wake up again in the morning she would have gone and not return until night.

I took almost a month to recover from the illness and the facts I came to know after that, some accidentally and some quite naturally were startling. They simply moved me to tears. My illness was not ordinary but a fairly complex one. During that period the average medical expenses of the Happy Home shot up to a very high level. We couldn't afford the doctor's bills and costly medicines within the government's assistance, that looked very paltry compared to our need. So Didi was left with no option but to cut back all other expenses and she asked the children to exert more in order to generate more money. Unfortunately I wasn't the only one who needed medical attention. Few others were also there and that made Didi's task even worse. She hardly used to take any money that was paid to her as a salary and spent that amount on Happy Home. But this time the situation was demanding more from Didi and she took up a temporary job to earn something more. Her schedule became hectic. She had to spend all the day at work and the whole night she used to be along my bed and others'. Despite all these hardships Didi remained firm and it proved that behind her fragile body there was a core of steel. The children, in their turn, supported her wholeheartedly till the ordeal was over.

Everyone in the Happy Home experiences such incidents and the heavy showers of love in some form or the other. And from my own experience I can tell you, when you undergo such a treatment at the hands of some people you feel really blessed. You get some extraordinary and very strange power. Your appetite for living the life increases many times. Your entire life gets some kind of a positive direction, and your attitude towards the world becomes one of a faith.

Many such incidents formed a lifelong bond between myself and Didi. Still today, so many years after I left the Happy Home I frequently visit Didi and I help the Happy Home by whatever way I can. Not only me but all its former members come to see Happy Home and especially Didi, whenever they get opportunity. Today Didi is in her forties but her vigour has hardly diminished. The children come and go but Didi remains there and her stock of affection never gets exhausted. I have decided from the day one after I left the Happy Home that I am going to name my daughter 'Nilam' for Nilam Didi.

"But for that you will have to give birth to your daughter", Mr. Sareen intruded on Jatin at this juncture, "And before that you need to marry young man. So go stepwise like that".

Jatin marginally plunged his head and diffidently smiled at this remark.

"OK. What happened after you left the Happy Home? And by the way when did you leave it? It must have been a terrible experience for you. Wasn't it?" asked Mrs. Sareen.

"Ya it was, it was. See, one of the strangest rule the Happy Home abided by was that they didn't allow any childless parents to adopt anybody belonging to it. Perhaps it was something to do with some anxiety of the government. It seems they wanted to ensure good future for the offsprings of those who sacrificed their lives for the country. Therefore every member of Happy Home invariably ends up leaving it after turning 18, complete the education by government funds and settle down in a job or any business. Every year some members leave the Happy Home and some join it. But departing from Happy Home is really a very terrible experience as you put it. That is a grief only comparable to that of a married girl leaving the parental house. Those remaining in Happy Home become no less sad separating from one of their family members, you know. The feeling that they also will have to leave the Happy Home one day invariably creeps into their minds.

My association with the Happy Home grew every year and I spent the most important years of my life in this orphanage. In 1978, i.e., after six years of stay I bade farewell to Happy Home with a heavy heart. Meanwhile I was pursuing a dream that my father used to see for me, i.e., a career in the Indian Army. For the purpose of fulfilling his dream I studied hard, literally day in and day out. Side by side I started working out in gym to increase my built. Fortunately I have inherited a stout body from my father and on that foundation I accumulated a good amount of muscles. Soon I successfully appeared in the N.D.A. examination and subsequently received my military training at the National Defence Academy, Khadakwasla near Pune.

I joined the Indian Army in 1983 as an officer. And Today, as you know I'm a Captain and I work in the Army Headquarters Delhi. Last year itself I purchased this house. I was always in search of such a small and tidy home in any peaceful locality. This one, I liked very much because of its excellent location. You know the army provides accommodation but I preferred to stay in civil area. Most of the officers, I mean those who belong to Delhi remain in civilian area. That way at least after returning from duty you can forget about the rules and regulations of uniform." Jatin twinkled his eyes at this moment and chuckled.

"The location of this house is excellent, no doubt", he continued. "but unfortunately I didn't have any neighbour. So I was feeling very lonely. You know, even if I didn't have the family in conventional sense parents, grandparents, brothers, sisters and all but, I was never alone in my life. That's why after shifting here I was wandering whether I had done a mistake or what. But finally after one year it seems I will be getting a good company".

"Well, well don't worry about that", Mrs. Sareen remarked, "But do you know what will be the best company for you? A wife! Again there is no need to worry. We will fix your marriage as early as possible. Just you have to give your consent".

"Oh I forgot to tell you, how I managed to live without Happy Home". Jatin deliberately pushed forward another point to drag the earlier one out of the discussion, "Would you mind hearing this last part of my story?".

"Go ahead son", Mrs. Sareen granted her approval while Diljeet showed early signs of discomfort. He did not thinking it proper to spend so much time with the neighbour in the very first meeting. But just by looking at the thorough involvement of his mother in the talks he could not even suggest to postpone their deliberation. So he chose to remain silent.

"As I have stated earlier, leaving Happy Home was a tough business. When I left it, there was hardly anybody who didn't look to be at the verge of weeping. Some actually wept. I still remember Didi crying on my shoulders, just like a little girl. You know, it becomes very difficult to say goodbye to somebody who you nurture carefully over the years. But that's what Didi does every year. But it doesn't drain out her emotional energy. She is such an extraordinary person. Sometimes she exhibits such a softness, she can make even the butter envious. On the other hand you arrange a heap of troubles in front of her and she reacts with the fierce determination of a lioness. We have experienced it all and we have seen such extreme and opposite reactions from the same person." Jatin paused for a while and again got back to the track after a momentary ponderation.

"I think I'm deviating from what I should tell you. You know when the subject returns back to Didi I can't help but talk about her. Anyway! After walking out of the Happy Home I didn't have to wait much and I got through the N.D.A. entrance exam in the very first attempt. All the while, when I was preparing for the examination and even after that, memories of my father inspired me. They used to prevent me from getting discouraged and depressed. My military training in the Defence Academy was gruelling as it is popularly known to be. It was an ultimate test of my mental and physical strength. Sometimes I used to feel really down and defeated. On such occasions I used to take out the most precious thing I had. This medal of bravery acquired by my father. I would watch it for hours together, keeping it on the table. This method served to remind me of my true identity. After all, I wasn't any ordinary person but the son of a brave soldier who preferred devoting life on a battlefield to retreating back. So fighting spirit was in my blood and there was no question of me accepting defeat at any moment of my life. Such thoughts would keep my spirits alive and remove the cobwebs from my minds".

"That's great!" appreciated Mrs. Sareen "But son you were seriously ill for about a month in Happy Home. Doesn't that imply that you were of a fragile health?".

"Common Mom! He doesn't look to be that weak. Can't you see his formidable frame?" For the first time in past 30-35 minutes Diljeet Sareen opened his mouth. It was as if he had lost his patience to keep mum and grabbed the very first opportunity to speak.

"Well what Diljeet says is right", Jatin quipped, "As far as I remember that was the only time I was bed ridden. Otherwise my health record was solid throughout in the Defence academy. Initially I used to be somewhat frail no doubt, but as I said earlier, I have inherited a good physique from my forefathers. After coming to age I worked out regularly and then only I managed to have a good built".

"It must have been very boring for you to leave alone here. Earlier you were with so many companions in Happy Home, and then in the Defence Academy." Mrs. Sareen enquired.

"Exactly" replied Jatin. "After coming here, in spite of my expectation my life became absolutely monotonous. I should say, it turned out to be as cold as a stone and as hard as a rock. Simply speaking there was no life in my life", Jatin laughed mid way in his sentence. And the other two also joined him. Mrs. Sareen was impressed and pleased with the acrobatic jugglery of words that Jatin used to describe his pathetic situation and also with his ability to laugh at himself.

"Certainly when your life comes to be rough like this you find places where from you could extract warmth and comfort. And for this purpose I would invariably turn to the Happy Home. The mesmerising atmosphere there and a chat with Didi would make my mind fresh and bring solace to my heart. More often she advises me to get married", Jatin remarked and suddenly put his head down giggling shyly. This was the point Mrs. Sareen had been stressing since beginning but Jatin never seemed to respond well to this topic. But at this juncture he himself arrived at the matter. Mrs. Sareen seemed to the very much interested in the marriage prospects of her young neighbour. This interest had aroused partly because of her concern about this bachelor man who looked pretty helpless without a woman in his house. The other thing was, a married Jatin meant a constant companion for Mrs. Sareen, 24 hrs. a day in the form of his wife. In addition to this, a married couple would definitely offer her, sooner or later, a little piece of heaven, i.e., a small, cuddly child, something which an old lady like her would die for. That's why when Jatin informed about Didi's attempts to persuade him to marry, Mrs. Sareen almost sprang up on her feet.

"There you are! Why don't you pay heed to your esteemed Didi then?" asked Mrs. Sareen wittingly.

"Well till now I had been dilly- dalling on this marriage issue. Sometimes I argue that I am too young to tie nuptials. Sometimes I would say I can't see any suitable girl for me."

"But these are not sufficient reasons to turn down your Didi's proposals, are they? They are but lame excuses", Mrs. Sareen intervened.

"What you say is true", said Jatin, "but what I said was also not wrong. Especially my point that I have not yet come across a girl best suited for me, is quite realistic".

"So you come across girls after all!" Mrs. Sareen tried to catch Jatin in a trap of words. This time she laughed a bit louder that displayed her splendid set of bright teeth, confirming that she was a beauty not affected by age. Diljeet was wonderstrucked to see his mother laughing so carelessly after a long time. He was satisfied to bring her to Jatin's house as he realised that those moments were worth spending.

"I know, I know that", commented Mrs. Sareen as Jatin shook his head disapproving her statement with a smile. "That's the main problem my child. When you never come across any girl at all, how will you find a suitable girl for you. But never mind now. I'm here to take care of it."

Jatin looked overwhelmed not because his marriage was imminent, but because of the kind of interest the old lady was taking in his well being and the purity of her affection which was unarguably motherly. The way in which she made him feel like her own son was quite fetching. For a moment he tried to compare her with his own mother, imagining how she would have treated him had she survived. It would have been in the same manner as Mrs. Sareen did, there was no doubt about it. Quite obviously because mothers everywhere are same. Still it isn't a big deal loving your own child, but showering the similar warmth on somebody you haven't given birth to, is certainly remarkable. Mrs. Sareen seemed to belong to this latter category.

"Keep one thing in mind", Mrs. Sareen spoke, "now onwards as long as you are single, you will not prepare your food. That will be my job", and just as Jatin opened his mouth to utter something in protest she went further, "Don't object to it son. I will be happy to share some of your burden and perhaps this is the only thing I'm able to do at this age. Otherwise I'm left with nothing but to take the name of the god and wait for his call. So, please don't deny me this privilege."

Jatin couldn't say anything at that and speechlessly nodded his head. He found himself terribly pressed under Mrs. Sareen's favours. In the first meeting itself she made him her own and started directing him like an elderly person in the family. And Jatin couldn't but accept this fact. To his great surprise he found himself glad to digest this new equation and felt startlingly free and relieved after having done it.

By this time it was 9.00 pm and the patience of Diljeet Sareen was giving in. He gave an anxious look at the wall clock and finally broke his silence. "It's already nine Ma. Don't forget I have to leave early tomorrow. So wind up your talks quickly."

"Oh, I'm sorry son", said Mrs. Sareen apologetically. "I was unaware of time. We were so engrossed in chitchatting you know. Let's move now".

The three of them got up from the chair as Diljeet shook hands with Jatin.

"Nice meeting you young man", he remarked, "If you don't mind I have a request for you."

"Go ahead", said Jatin.

"In my absence here, may I assume that my mother is living with her younger son", Diljeet put his point straightforwardly. His tone was somewhat anxious as he didn't think it proper to ask such a favour from anybody in the very first meeting.

"Oh there is no question about it", Jatin's reply came as a big solace to this indebted man, who pressed Jatin's hand gently.

"What should I call you Mrs. Sareen", Jatin asked as the Sareens got out of the house.

"Call me Ma" Mrs. Sareen uttered blatantly as the distance between them was somewhat big. "Diljeet and his sister call me like that."

"OK. Ma", Jatin responded in a similar loud fashion, and waved his hand.

❖❖❖

Seven

The wall clock struck at 9 pm and Saudamini Joshi sitting alone in her third floor apartment could hear her heartbeats fill out at a shattering speed, composing a brazen sound analogous to that of a moving rail. They concocted a bizzare alliance with the sound of seconds' hand of the clock. Her forehead augmented miniscule droplets of sweat on that late summer day but the reason for their formation was not the heat alone. It was owing to the same reason why her heartbeats grew. Everyday at around 9 pm she used to have such an experience. It was the time at which her husband Nishikant would return home from his office. Right from his Churchgate office to their apartment at Santacruz he would be sober, but once reaching near the house he would get down from his car and consume substantial quantity of alcohol from a nearby bar. Thus Saudamini would always greet him as an out and out drunk. This had been the everyday's practice and she knew it was not going to be anything diverse today. She was right ! The door bell resonated at perfect five past nine and as soon as she opened the door the terribly irritating but well familiar smell of alcohol filled the room and a man of about 35 years age, carrying a dark waist coat on his shoulders shudderingly entered in and stumbled upon the sofa. It was Nishi, Saudamini's husband.

No, he was not like that when they married some 8 years ago. He was then a fine gentleman, a young and dynamic chap who worked in a big private company as a marketing officer and drew huge amount of salary. It was that Nishi who hypnotized Saudamini and she willingly accepted him as a life partner. No doubt he used to drink but that was very occasional. In fact it was Saudamini who would force him to drink in parties to prove their position in high society. Slowly Nishi fell in the trap of that intoxicant and he made it a routine job to have a peg of whisky. Still, Saudamini hardly objected to his dangerous addiction, as nothing seemed to go wrong. But then arose a serious problem in their life that rendered Nishikant mentally irresolute. As they went on celebrating their wedding anniversaries they found themselves in distressing condition, as there appeared no sign that their wedding would ever produce a fruit, that Saudamini would ever bear a child. Medical checkups provided evidences to prove that their fear was not absurd. Indeed the chances of the Joshis having a child were slim. It was a tremendous blow for Nishi and soon he started drinking heavily. Even as her husband took the shelter of alcohol to burn the emotional stress Saudamini was hopeful that someday she would produce an offspring. For that she vigorously pleaded to God although that turned out to be futile. She was already overwhelmed with this grief and Nishi's deteriorating behaviour in addition to this was making her like uglier than the hell.

After closing the door Saudamini gingerly removed the waist coat from the possession of her husband. This act disturbed the state of the drunkard man who in turn grumbled a few angry words at his wife.

"To hell with you", he uttered his most liked collection of words and repeated it twice.

"To hell with me and to hell with everything except you", Saudamini shouted back.

This remark seemed to cause a furore and somehow Nishikant rose up and managed to lean against the sofa.

"Look", he pointed his shaking forefinger at his wife. "Don't dare to raise your voice again", he almost scuttered those words.

"I will and I definitely will", Saudamini retorted ferociously that turned Nishi's face red hot like a burning coal.

"You bloody bitch, I will throw you out of the window," Nishi grappled to maintain his posture as he tried to stand up. But the alcohol was in full control and the moment he left the support of the sofa his paralysed body twisted and he fell on the sofa after getting off balanced.

Saudamini laughed sardonically at her husband.

"You are going to throw me out of the window ? First learn to stand upright young man. How funny to be the weakest in the weak and roar like tigers."

Saudamini had crossed the limits she had never dared to cross before. She had made a fun of her husband, she had criticised him like never. It was Nishi's turn now. Badly hurt by Saudamini's mockery, he stood up somehow and by the moment Saudamini realised that something was going to happen, she was laying on the floor with a bang as her frantic husband hit on the face.

"I told you not to be smart with me stupid woman. Someday I really might do away with you", Nishi muttered, by vexedly looking at his wife who was still on the floor with her backside towards him. The next moment this man also went down crashing with a thud, but slightly missed hitting Saudamini.

"To hell with you", he kept on repeating.

"Now stop your drama and get me some food. I'm dying of hunger, hurry up, hurry up", he ordered in his trembling alcoholic voice.

Saudamini didn't move a bit.

"Now this is too much. I think you need some more bashing you idiot", saying this Nishi forcefully positioned himself on the floor and turned Saudamini's face towards him. He was taken aback by what he saw. Saudamini's forehead was wounded and warm blood was dripping on the floor. Clearly she had been badly hit. Her eyes were closed and she showed no movement whatsoever.

"Oh my god ! Saudamini get up please", Nishi was aghast at the sight. For a second his alcoholic influence was gone. Saudamini didn't show any sign of consciousness and her heart beats very feeble. In a surprisingly sudden and swift action, Nishi picked her up and placed her on the sofa.

Very quickly he reached for the telephone and curtly asked their family doctor to come over there. And till he arrived, Nishi could do nothing but to wring his hands after his attempts to revive. Saudamini turned unproductive. However the damn liquor was as if squeezed-out of his body because of this unexpected incident. A sharp spray of cold water on the face and he was as sedate as a priest. Meanwhile the doctor applied bandage to Saudamini's forehead and rubbed icecubes on her face. Finally she was back to senses and stared coldly at her husband who gave her a meek smile even as he felt terribly ashamed at his rude behaviour. Once the doctor was gone, Nishi tried to say something to his wife but she swiftly turned her face away.

"Sau, I'm terribly sorry for what has happened. But I was out of the senses you know. Anyway, I'm feeling extremely guilty and I promise you this won't occur again", said Nishi, with his head dropped down.

Saudamini didn't say anything but started sobbing as she pressed her face against a pillow. She knew, it could very well occur everyday.

"OK I don't mind your not talking with me. I'm going to take my wash now. Till then you have a nice rest. And after that I'll serve our supper," saying this Nishi went inside. Saudamini produced some inaudible hooting sound at this instant. She was well aware that once out of alcoholic influence Nishi was as harmless as a cow.

As soon as Nishi entered the bathroom for taking bath Saudamini quietly grabbed the telephone receiver and dialed her parents in Pune. Her mother came on line.

"Hello, it's Saudamini speaking."

"Oh Sau ! How are you my dear ? Your voice seems to be changed. Any cold or something honey ?"

"I'm not very well mom", Saudamini responded in a half choked voice, "I'm terribly upset Mom, I was beaten up by Nishi today". And she started weeping at this juncture.

"What ? Has that man gone mad or what ?" telephonic voice of her mother was capable of conveying her anxiety.

"He drinks everyday you know. He quarrels a lot of me. I'm fed up Mom, I'm done for. I only want to die now."

"Don't be silly. Now at once stop crying and tell me what's the problem basically."

"The same old story Mom. He badly wants a child. Now that we have waited this much long why not wait for some more time ? He wants to adopt a child. You tell me Mom, what is the point in raising a child when you know it's not your blood ? And who will ensure that it is from a good background ? Frankly, I'm sick of Nishi and I don't want to live here anymore. I'll come over there tomorrow".

"Sau, again you are talking like a fool. Mind well you are not going to serve any purpose by coming here. Try to convince him my child. And if he doesn't share your views act like how he demands. Don't forget, it's you who selected Nishi from all probables and now you have to stick to him come what may. If Nishi wants, go ahead and adopt a child. Isn't a better than having a drunkard husband and a punishing life ? If you are going to have your own baby nobody can prevent it. But till then save your marriage life my dear. And if still you have any problem we can think of any other alternative. You understand ?"

"Yes Mom, perhaps you are right," Saudamini's voice was betraying but her face was not. Providentially, her mother could not see her face flooded with mortification, as the only hope for any help, her own mother didn't seem to be on her side. Her last window of hope was shut off. Dejectedly she placed the receiver in its cradle even as her mother seemed to say something, and leaned over the bed. She mashed her lips tightly in between her teeth to reduce the sound of her cry as water drops rolled down her cheeks. She felt badly licked. Even after such impertinent and crude behaviour by Nishi it was Saudamini who was going to admit her lapse. But there was hardly any choice.

With her heart burning like a heap of dried grass Saudamini got back on her feet and served the dinner plates even before Nishi came out from the bathroom. Puzzled to watch her in kitchen, Nishi hurriedly went to the dining table.

"That's like a good wife !", he exclaimed excitedly.

"How great you are Sau ! I begged for your pardon and you granted it in no time. That's so nice of you."

His Sau's face was cold as a stone at this complement.

"Look Nishi," she calmly spoke, "There is no point in these useless fights. We both are suffering for the mistake of nature. Somewhere we should put a fullstop at such incidents otherwise we are going to be doomed." Saudamini was sobbing at intervals.

"Then what do you suggest ? Are you ready to adopt a child ?" Nishi asked thoughtfully.

Saudamini shook her head denoting her conformity, and Nishi's face shined like a sunbeam.

"You really mean it ?" he still couldn't believe Saudamini's words.

"Yes", somehow Saudamini hold back her tears and forced a faint smile on face.

Nishikant Joshi jumped out of chair at that and hawled like a child.

Next morning Nishikant woke up early and even after previous night's argument with Saudamini and consequent late going to bed, he felt fresh as a dew drop. Even as Saudamini was still laying in the bed this man was already in the bathroom, whistling and singing merrily. Indeed, after so many years he found himself so assuaged and contended. And why shouldn't he be ? After all he was going to be a father. At last somebody will run towards him, calling him daddy and jump into his arms, finally quenching his long lasting thirst. He would feel himself so significant at that moment !

Nishi was fully dressed up with coat and tie when Saudamini got down from the bed.

"You are ready so early ? Why didn't you inform me that you are leaving early today ?" asked a puzzled Saudamini.

"I'm not early honey, it's only you are late. By the way, I'm not going to office my dear. I'll apply for an off today. Don't forget we have to wander searching for a suitable child," Nishi clarified on the dot.

"Today itself ?" Saudamini's unrest was not concealable.

She asked this question as if they could manufacture their own child within one day so that there wasn't a need to adopt one.

"Do you mean we will wait for hundred years ?" Nishi's voice achieved a stern form and Saudamini hurriedly went in, without making an eye contact with her husband. The fire within her was burning fervently even if she tried to suppress it.

"Get ready soon", Nishi instructed his wife and grabbed the telephone. He took out some paper cuttings from his pocket and dialled a number from one of them.

"Hellow, is it St. Joseph's foundation ?"

"Yes, who do you want ?"

"I want to talk to father Dimello please."

"Go ahead, you are talking to him already."

"Hellow father, I'm Nishikant, Nishikant Joshi from Santacruz. I have contacted you in connection with one advertisement appeared in the *Times of India*, dated 24 December. It says 'come and share the God's gift this Christmas by adopting a child from St. Joseph's orphanage'. Sir, I'm aspiring to adopt one child. Can I have one of your children today ? Sorry I'm a bit late."

"No problem Mr. Joshi, anytime you are most welcome. By the way, congratulations for your brave decision."

"Thank you sir, thank you very much."

"May god bless you," saying this father Dimello disconnected the call.

Unbelievably delighted, Nishi scanned the address mentioned in the chit of paper, St. Joseph's Orphanage.

17, Rinki Batliwala Road,
Matunga (W).

"Done", he told to himself raising his fist. By the time Saudamini got ready, putting on fascinating costume on the body and all that feminine stuff on the face, Nishi had already informed his boss that he wasn't available for the job because of some important personal work. And his boss willingly granted his wish because Nishi wasn't a man who took leaves over trivial issues. Still Nishi thought that it was because the stars were favouring him and he could very well be the king of the world that day.

Vehemently and bubbling with strange power Nishi escorted his wife to their sky blue fiat and soon they made headways towards St. Joseph's.

✣✣✣

18th Feb, 10.45 am a sky blue fiat, parting slightly from the continuous flow of automobiles on the Rinki Batliwala Road came to a halt in front of St. Joseph's Orphanage. An old man of about 75 was sitting outside, on a chair, enjoying the rat race among the four wheelers.

He watched minutely as the occupants of the car started getting down. When it became sure that they were approaching St. Joseph's itself, the old man called Bhiku yelled at them.

"Hey, that's not a proper way to put your vehicle there. That cop at the square will dump your pretty thing in the dustbin."

Nishi couldn't hold back his laughter at that remark.

"Then what should I do old boy ?" He enquired.

"Park it over there", Bhiku pointed towards an empty spot a few yards away, "And you call yourself educated and cultured."

"Ha, Ha," Nishi was amused at the old man.

Perhaps that was a crude way to receive a visitor but Nishi was no way in a mood to get angry at such remarks. But Saudamini made strange annoyed faces at Bhiku.

"Well, I guess, you have come to take one of our precious babies along with you," said Bhiku leading the couple through the main entrance.

"You are right on target old man," said Nishi.

"In that case, may I have the privilege to welcome you to this wonderful home," Bhiku quipped tongue in cheek.

"But I didn't recognise you. Are you the seniormost kid around here ?" Jokingly Nishi remarked and forced the old man to laugh heartily.

"Perhaps you are right, no, no you are very true," Bhiku flashed his toothless smile.

Just as they entered into the first room, Sister Margaret who was busy reading a newspaper lowered the page in front of her on hearing the footsteps and stared at the incoming couple through the specs.

"Meet Sister Margaret, our head," Bhiku began the introduction, "She is the sole controller of the affairs here. And sis he is... err... in fact I don't know who he is. So let him do the job himself," Bhiku passed on the batton to Nishi.

"Hellow Sister, I'm Nishikant Joshi and she is my wife Saudamini. I work in a private firm as a marketing officer," said Nishi sitting on a chair placed in front of Sister Margaret, "Eight years have gone after our marriage but we couldn't have a child yet. So now we have decided to go for adopting a child. That's why we are here today."

"You have arrived at a very good decision Mr Joshi. In fact you could have come here earlier. Nevertheless, it's never too late in life," sister Margaret gave her thoughtful opinion.

Just then, a gang of little boys and girls came out from inside, with Sister Clair trying to restrict the noise they were propagating. Sudden advent of them all clad in school uniforms and carrying school bags, water bags and lunch boxes, attracted attention of Nishi and Saudamini even if Sister Margaret and Bhiku were expecting them as it was the time of going to school.

After conscientiously watching those faces Nishi's sight glued to one particular girl as everyone rocked hands at Sister Margaret and Bhiku. The girl was around 10 years old, her slight curly hair were tightly tied by ribbons to form two distinct tails which danced on her back with each step. She had large, dark, passionate eyes and baby smooth cream complexion. Her entire disposition was full of innocence and in her school uniform consisting of white shirt, maroon skirt and maroon tie she looked absolutely graceful. Nishi could hear her feeble yet sweet "bye Sister Margaret, bye Bhiku" among all voices. And as soon as she became aware of the presence of Nishi and Saudamini she shyly retreated back towards Sister Clair. Finally all the children were gone, so was she.

"Who was that girl with large, dark eyes Sister ?", Saudamini pinched her husband's hand at the mention of a 'girl' as Nishikant asked this question to Sister Margaret. At that Sister Margaret and Bhiku laughed and that flummoxed this man.

"So you are also among them !", said Sister Margaret.

"Everytime any couple comes to St. Joseph's they first enquire about this kid. Indeed she is a remarkable girl, but if you want to adopt her, you better quit the thought. Just imagine she has been around here for last 5/6 years. But this girl is not ready to leave St. Joseph's."

"It's quite obvious Sister, any child will behave like that itself. But it does not mean that they should spoil their life by remaining orphans forever," asked Nishi.

"You are right Mr Joshi, but this girl is something different. Everytime she was forced out of St. Joseph's she responded strangely. She stopped talking, she stopped eating and what not. It has happened 3/4 times. Finally we decided that we ourselves will not allow any parents to get hold of her," said Sister Margaret.

"That was a past Sister but the future is, this girl is going to be my daughter, yes Sister she is destined to be my daughter. You just see how she accepts our home."

Sister Margaret was surprised to hear those words. It was easy to judge that the man was getting emotional.

"If it happens Mr Joshi, we'll be grateful to you. Believe me nothing will be better than this. And if you have such an intense urge to give shelter to this tiny supportless life, I'm sure you will be able to win her over."

As the conversation moved ahead, Saudamini was tending to look more and more nervous. Since beginning she was opposed to adopting a child and her discomfort only grew at the prospect of having a girl at her disposal. Once in a while she tried to show her negation but she had no other alternative than to give in to her husband's wishes, consequently she kept mum and she was only left with wringing her hand.

"What's her name Sister ?" Nishi's voice had a large percentage of impatience.

"Suchita. At least that's what she said when we found her six years ago."

"Any information about her past ?"

"Nothing. That's the sad story here, Mr Joshi. You don't know your past and you don't want to accept your future. This life is so aimless, you die hundred deaths every moment. It's like trying to walk in a stark darkness. You never know when you will stumble upon a stone and end up fracturing your skull. I've seen it all Mr. Joshi. I've seen children crying like a hell. I've seen them posing difficult questions that people like me and you cannot answer. That's why I say, if you are helping atleast one innocent life here you will straightway land up in heaven, believe me."

"I understand sister, how awful it must be to live a life like that. I regret, I should have come here earlier," Nishi looked pathetically guilty.

"Noble you ! May god bless you my son."

Sister Margaret was amazed at such an odd couple of Nishi and Saudamini. The husband seemed to be so overenthusiastic to have a child and on the other hand there was no limit to the indifference of the wife.

"When are the children supposed to return Sister ?" asked Nishi.

"Oh, they will be back home by 2:30. I'm afraid, you'll have to wait that longer."

"That's no problem Sister, we'll just make a move now and we will be back again by that time," said Nishi as he stood up from the chair, "But please make sure that Suchita doesn't go anywhere."

"No she won't."

✣✣✣

The Joshis, instead of going back to home, wandered all over the nearby area in their slick, sky blue vehicle. They had their lunch at a restaurant and returned back to St. Joseph's at sharp 2.30 pm. Sister Margaret greeted them at the door.

"Now go and meet your daughter to be," she chuckled as the Joshis made their way into the orphanage.

"Oh definitely, but if you don't mind I want to meet her alone. I won't prefer anybody else with us." Nishi expressed his wish.

"As you like Mr. Joshi," Sister Margaret showed him the way, as Nishi instructed Saudamini to sit there in the front porch. Sister Margaret ushered him into a small room, which appeared to be a kind of playground for the young ones. A wide mattress was spread across the room and some toys lay scattered here and there. Nishi removed his shoes and positioned himself on the mat. Just then Sister Clair entered into the room with Suchita.

"Hellow Mr. Joshi, here she is and I leave her at your disposal," said Sister Clair. "If she creates any problem just ask me. I'm sitting outside."

"Thank you Sister, I'm sure I won't need your help," Nishi looked confident to convince the child. Sister Clair smiled at that and went back. Suchita didn't try to follow her. It seemed Sister Margaret had given her a lesson or two. She stood beside the door staring at her legs.

"Suchita come here and sit," Nishi spoke in as soft a tone as possible. The girl quietly obeyed him.

"You know who I'm ? I'm your father," he straightaway got on to the business.

At that Suchita gazed into his eyes with her large ones, "I know who you are," her tone was ruthless. "Everytime Sister Margaret brings somebody, he calls himself my father. I don't know how many fathers I have." The child was brilliant for her age. Suddenly tears shined in her eyes and she started sobbing. "Why she wants me to leave this place ?" she asked as hot salty water spread down her cheeks.

Nishi looked dumbfounded. He wanted to cuddle up the child and comfort her but that act might intimidate the girl. So he chose to remain where he was.

"You are right Suchita," Nishi spoke in a grave tone, "I wasn't your father but I will be your father now."

"No, I don't want to come with you." At that instant Nishi though it useless to say anything as the child looked invincible. But suddenly he remembered the barren desert that his life was without a child.

"What should I do to be your father ?" he asked in a manner which was hopelessly desperate. Suchita simply refused to comment.

"Do you know what your fellow children are doing ?

They are living with their new mom and dad just like everybody in your school. They play, they study and they enjoy. Tell me, why don't you want to become like them ?"

For a moment serene atmosphere prevailed in the room. And then Nishi casually took a toy car that lay on the mat and struck with an idea.

"Have you ever sit in a car ?" he asked.

Suchita raised her head with the mention of a car and involuntarily shook her head. Nishi got surprised at her impetuous response to this query. But naturally, because this man was unaware of Suchita's strange obsession with the cars. Everyday she would watch them for hours. Particularly the white Ambassadors used to maker her crazy beyond limit and often she demanded rides in it.

"If you become my daughter, I'll give you a real car", Nishi placed a tempting proposal. He was ready to gamble, anything that day. But this time his suggestion didn't seem to impress Suchita. Finally, Nishi disconsolately accepted his defeat.

"OK I won't take you with me, still I give you a chance to have a ride in my car. Will you come with me ?"

The girl plainly looked at him which could mean either 'yes' or 'no'. Nishi assumed it 'yes' and asked Sister Clair to carry Suchita to the car. Soon Suchita found herself in a sky blue fiat along with Sister Clair, Sister Margaret, Nishikant and Saudamini. She looked relaxed in the company of Sister Clair, but once the vehicle moved she received some sort of a kick and her joys acquired maniacal proportions as cold breeze rushed inside. Suchita clapped and clapped every moment a vehicle would storm by her window. Vehicles kept bombarding from all sides. Nishi set the car in full speed, by heavily burdening the accelerator and Suchita screamed with frenzy. She liked the pace of the vehicle and the spectacular sight of huge buildings and vehicles moving past them, ensured her enthralled state. For a moment she remembered something similar to that experience.

That car, that nerve wrenching speed, that handsome driver whom she called papa and that heavenly splendour, her dear mummy. At that instant she felt like walking on air, exulting like never before. And once finally the car manoeuvred the return cruise and came to a smooth finish near the St. Joseph's, Suchita forgot that strange feeling which had taken grip over her mind throughout the ride. But one thing was sure, now she was finding himself as exuberant as a lark, she didn't know why. Sister Margaret and Sister Clair could not believe this girl behave like that. They had never seen her so excited and jocund. With all of her shoulder long hair spread in every possible direction and her face excluding uncontainable freshness, her mood elevation was starkly on display. Hardly anybody could judge why this enormous change had occurred within a five minutes of ride, because nobody could trace the life history of the girl who inherited this tremendous passion for speed from the man who showed her the light of the day, who gave her the vitality and vigor of life and who perished only due to his excessive craze for speed.

"How was it ?", Nishikant asked Suchita after parking the car in its right place.

"Incredible !" replied the girl tightly shutting her eyes at the exclamation. And she ran towards the mân and clasped his legs with her little arms, delighted to find someone who came closest to her father and yet didn't boast to be her real dad. Nishi's genuinity had finally made him victorious.

"Want to come with me ?", he asked as he jumbled his fingers through her hair.

"Sure," she didn't hesitate to announce. It was a single word that brought consolation to the hearts of everybody. But alas ! There was an exception. That unfortunate person obviously was Saudamini who put in a lot of efforts to persuade Nishi against adopting a girl child. But her husband refused to budge. Thus she had to bite the dust on yet another front that left her wondering what right she enjoyed in their marriage being an equal partner.

Sister Margaret rubbed off Suchita's name from the record, which she believed to be for the last time. Suchita was a cause of worry for the St. Joseph's administration for years. Now everybody was happy and satisfied that she finally got her proper destination, that too with her own consent. And when she left the place in her grand, sky blue fiat, many faces were left confronting with the tears trying to spurt out from their eyes. Sister Clair broke down heavily on Sister Margaret's shoulders as Suchita bade a tearful adieu. Sister Mary and Sister Samantha couldn't stand watching her say good-bye and ran inside while Bhiku stood gazing at the car, silently wiping out tears. This has always been a strange fact of life. You worry if something doesn't happen and weep once it takes place. "Now at once stop shedding tears and go back to your jobs", a stern Sister Margaret instructed the girls, "whatever happens, the show must go on", she recited her trademark quote, and herself got back to her task of finalising the list of requirement for the impending month.

✣✣✣

Suchita liked her new abode, the third floor apartment at Santacruz, the spacious balcony of which presented a fabulous view of one of the busiest roads in Bombay. She sat there in a chair enjoying the cool breeze and watching the hustle and bustle of the vehicles running like insane animals. With her chin resting against her right hand palm, she was thinking why she felt so exhilarating in her new house. And why she didn't feel bad even after losing the shelter of St. Joseph's. Why she didn't experience that sense of fear and loneliness she had to cope up with, everytime she was driven out of St. Joseph's ? Why she found herself so relaxed and secured, contrary to what she used to expect earlier. Although her immature brain couldn't point out the exact reason behind it, it came somewhere very close to that one. It was the sincere manner of Nishi alone which could break the intransigent attitude of this girl and forced her to put a great trust in him, trust which latter was to take the form of faith.

Suchita's eyes avidly searched for her father in that crowdy road but the sky blue fiat was nowhere in sight. Nishi was out celebrating his newly found daughter's arrival among friends, ever since he dropped Saudamini and Suchita home. Suchita didn't know why he didn't carry her along with him. She waited for him, continuously staring at the road below, even as darkness loomed large. Finally he came, but he came too late, when Suchita was earlier laying deep in sleep, and he came perfectly drunk in a fashion exactly similar to the day before. It was a shocking reality for Saudamini which was very hard to digest. Even after yielding to his pressure for adopting a child and accepting a girl child as per his wish, this man didn't seem to improve.

"You drank again ? I thought you would quit drinking once you have a child," Saudamini taunted her husband who had dashed against the sofa as usual.

He laughed at Saudamini, an act which was more powerful in sarcasm.

"You were a fool ! I didn't say anything like that, did I ? Did I promise you ? No !", Nishi defended himself without raising his head from the sofa and without opening his eyes.

"Yes I drank. I drank because I'm the happiest person in the world, today. Nobody can object to what I do and anyway who the hell are you bloody ?"

Nishi climbed down to his barbaric language, that sent tremors down the spines of Saudamini.

"I'm your wife," she said coldly, "I'm, your life partner."

"That's great ! But still you shouldn't say anything regarding my drinking. I drink with my own money. Your *** father doesn't provide bucks to me."

Such an ugly and unnecessary reference of her father irked Saudamini.

"Hold back your tongue Mr. Joshi", Saudamini couldn't hold back her own. Without caring for the consequences she went ahead.

"Don't pull my father into our matters. He is a gentleman and not the like of you who deserve such a nasty remark."

All barriers were crossed again and the fluidity of the situation reached such an extremity, that the flashpoint looked imminent.

With overpowering rage, the man struggled to stand erect which however seemed to be a futile effort. He couldn't move an inch this time.

"Damn you and damn your father, damn the whole family of yours", he kept on murmuring, the narcotic effect of the liquor cementing him to the sofa. It was hard to believe he could behave like that. In fact nobody should have damned except for the liquor. Liquor which was eating up his body and soul. Liquor that took charge of his body mechanism like a parasite virus whose only aim seemed to be destroying its host. And it had done a great job out there. Ingeniously, it had reduced an excellent professional into a third grade human being. Especially it was so pinching for Saudamini to watch him in that state because otherwise, there couldn't have been a better person than Nishi. She repented that she only was the one who dragged this man into this murderous trap. Now it was beyond her capability to snatch him back. She was helpless. Yet she tried to put up a brave face for quite a few moments. But Nishi's outrageous comments cracked the shell of her resistance. And Saudamini broke down with her head resting against the door, chewing one end of her saree to reduce any sound that might evoke further responses from the crazy husband. Slowly her frame slipped down the door and she sat down on the floor weeping like a kid.

At once Nishi caught the sound of her sobbing and moaned at her.

"Stop there you daughter of a bitch. No funeral is going on here, you understand ? Bloody you have a rotten mind. I know, you don't want to see me rejoice. Look here I celebrate and there you weep as if someone has passed away. To hell with you dirty women, to hell with your dirty brain. I had certainly been cheated by your parents, they presented me such an ugly stuff like you."

Nishi went on hammering, irrelevant and ununderstandable words on Saudamini each causing deep wounds to her heart. He was totally out of any voluntary control. His body seemed to have consigned all its decision making abilities to the alcohol. And the alcohol like a cruel invader exploited that right to full apogee. It forced the man in him to wear the skin of an animal. And under its tantalizing predominance, Nishi indeed acted like an animal for quite a few minutes. But suddenly his captivated mind remembered something that applied a strange gentle touch to his tongue.

"Saudamini," It was the same lady who was the daughter of a bitch not long ago, "where is my child, Suchita ?" Amazed at his down to earth tone, Saudamini pointed towards the bedroom door. "She is sleeping in the bedroom." She managed to let out the sentence with some efforts.

The drunk man rose up from the sofa, which consumed good deal of energy and somehow reached the bedroom door after skillfully balancing his paralysed body, swinging here and there and dragging his feet forcibly. His dear daughter lay there on a bed, very peacefully and delicately and the fragrance of her body filled the entire room. The purity of her soul and her very existence mesmerished the surrounding like never before. Nishi pulled his body near the bed and watched the child with overwhelmed eyes. It was a sight, he was dying to imprint on his mind. In a moment, all the alcohol was washed away with tears that gathered in his eyes. He might have behaved like an animal but even animal loves its offspring. In the process Nishi captured the most beautiful picture he had ever seen, a child adoring her home. He felt thankful that he was a man, for a man doesn't have to give birth to anybody to shower affection. Natural or adopted a child is same for him as long as he wants to be its father, simply because in any case he isn't the one who wore it for nine months and experienced mind boggling pain during its birth. Therefore, for him it makes hardly any difference whether the child is his own blood or somebody else's. Nishi gazed at Suchita with eyes full of moisture for a few minutes and then fell on the floor. By that time Saudamini was overtaken by sleep on the sofa and Nishi met his sleep on the floor. Suchita on the other hand, enjoyed her carefree slumber in the foambed. An exotic day had come to an end in an outlandish fashion. Only sweet dreams were what in store for Suchita that night. This had been a D-day for her, atleast she might have thought like that. But in that case she was terribly inaccurate. Her D-day was yet to arrive. It was scheduled to be after some three years of her becoming Suchita Joshi, when she was going to have a brother, when her mom Saudamini was going to produce a son and seal the fate of this girl.

Eight

Summer had never been so blazing. Mercury never been so enthusiastic. It shot up and thermometers failed to contain it. For centuries together sun had never seemed so devastatingly ruthless. An uncontrollable heat wave had ripped through northern India reducing most pieces of land into outright inferno. People were unable to pull through the drought as wells all dried up and great rivers took the shapes of humble streams. Human misery looked at its best while the animal clan underwent complete nemesis. Skeletal remains of domestic as well as wild life on bone dry, cracked surface of land formed the most common sight those days. Thirsty throats struggled for a single drop of water and dehydrated legs covered tens of kilometres to find a puddle. Water was less, tears were many.

Delhi being Delhi had no scarcity of water but destructive sunrays didn't spare any part of it. Days passed by and people were baked like bread loaves in a hot oven. Streets lay deserted except for some rich people travelling under reposing shadows of their four wheelers, or some poor rickshaw-wallahs roaming aimlessly, somehow agglomerating their share of wages. But students seemed to be everywhere, pedalling their bicycle to examination halls. Battling with heat was something harder than the hardest test they appeared in. Finally when it all got over the boys and girls were as if out of a rigorous punishment. Their faces showed it all.

A whopping sense of relief had overwhelmed a bubbling group of teenagers outside the Maurice High School. Their secondary examination was over for good. A decisive chapter in their life was closed. They had crossed a milestone. And what an examination it had been ! A test of their knowledge as well as physical and mental endurance. Coinciding with the worst ever famine that had hit this part of the planet in centuries. Hence the complacency was deep rooted. Many parents had turned up to assist their kids morally and they were no less chilled out.

The students engaged themselves in long conversations before parting. Indeed there were chances that many of them would never revert to this place. This was the point in their lives from where many roads laid ahead causing their directions to change. The path on which they had covered a protracted distance had finally been exhausted. But it wasn't a dead end. From this scaffold the path had given out so multifarious branches to seek diversified lives. Prospective plans were being mooted among boys and girls and smiling faces were getting sketched in brains to stock somewhere in the memory.

And up there on the second floor of the school building a young girl stood binding her forehead to the concrete parapet, screening her face with palms. Leaning from her waist to counterbalance her weight she cried with smothered gasps that contrived light jerks in her body. Her shoulder long hair were disoriented, partly blanketing her back, shoulders and arms, while a few of them hung from sideways. Plenty of water had flown through her eyes and it had stuck to her handkerchief, sleeves, her hands, and everywhere as the girl undertook to wipe off the tears with whatever she could think of. Finally she clasped her forehead in right hand, closed her eyes, and allowed the water to flow at its will. And flow it did! Like water rushing from a ruptured dam. Her white shirt, grey tie, and grey midi turned wet in a jiffy. It was still two odd hours prior sunset and hot air ruled like an autocratic tyrant. 'Furnace' could be the best word to explicate the surrounding. This heat as if was not sufficient for this teenager. She had bathed herself in hot water, partly tears, partly sweat. Her clothes stuck to her skin, her hair stroked her face and she herself slanted against a concrete pillar.

In the crowd below Bipasha Dasgupta a 16-year-old girl hunted for somebody. Even while jostling with other friends she kept on hovering her eyes for that particular person. After about ten minutes Bipasha came to a firm conclusion that 'that person' was nowhere to be seen.

"Oh my god ! Suchi !" she thought, "where is Suchi ?"

And then as if all hell broke loose, Bipasha hastened towards college building after feebly uttering 'excuse me'. Others gazed at her in bewilderment. Bipasha pulled all her might and dragged herself, covering concrete steps in desperate haste. Within a minute she was drawing near the girl crying outside a closed classroom.

"Suchi !" Bipasha snatched the girl by shoulder. She in turn stopped for a while, stared back flashing her large dark eyes and again resumed weeping as if nothing had happened.

"Suchi. Don't be stupid. Just stop it and come with me."

Neither of the two options was followed.

Bipasha moved Suchita's lean frame by tenaciously grabbing her shoulders and came face to face with her. Suchita sensed some opportunity here and clung to Bipasha's body. The lifeless concrete pillar was substituted by warm human flesh. And what a difference did it make ! Suchita let out intense sobs while Bipasha consolingly moved her hands on Suchita's back.

"I know Suchi. It's awful. Everybody is feeling like that. But see nobody behaves like you. It's just life Suchi. Many new members drop in your company, many old ones go. It's law of nature. No one can change it. Not me. Not you. So better accept the reality. I know you are particularly upset over me. Again I'm a bounded person. Bounded to my family. When my father is getting transferred I can't stay back. He won't allow me even if I insist."

"You can't leave me alone Bipasha." The girl spoke in a timid voice. Bipasha couldn't muster enough courage to say anything. Inevitably she too broke down.

"Believe me Suchi. I'll write to you every week, every day."

Suchita shook her head.

"You know I'm a mental wreck. I need your help. Please have mercy upon me." Suchita pleaded.

"I don't think you are a mental wreck. Only mentally assaulted. Still you are a brave girl. I'm sure you will fight. In fact you always do."

"I don't want empty words from you. You are very well aware about my ground realities. I'm, I'm like an aged tree. Someday I might give in. Or somebody will force me to surrender."

Bipasha looked at her grimly, eyebrows stretched like arcs.

"So what do you want me to do ? Stay back ?"

Suchita stood still.

"No, I know you are not a grown up person who will support me. I was just a fool to overlook your helplessness. I'm sorry. I asked for your help only because you are my best friend. But I only want to convey a small thing now."

"What is it ?"

"Next time you come to Delhi, don't look for me."

"Why ?"

Suchita stared at her legs with no intention to speak.

"Why ? Why do you talk like this ?"

"That's because I've no plans to continue this, this..."

"What ?"

"This wretched life." Suchita informed positively.

Bipasha froze to a statue. Never had Suchita shown so much confidence and unflinching firmness in her statement or behaviour.

It was like a lesson in first standard. "I'm a boy, you are a girl." Suchita made the things look that much easy.

"No plans to continue life ? This girl is sure crazy." Thought Bipasha.

"Listen to me Suchi," Bipasha held her hand resolutely, looking squarely in the eyes," what you said just now is the simplest thing to say. Everybody faces tough situation in life. Some way or other. More or less. But fighters fight back and cowards commit suicides. Those are real winners who conquer difficult moments. So it is unwise to accept defeats very easily."

"When are you supposed to accept defeats anyway ? If it is painful journey till death, why not to reduce the pain by dying early ? And as far as winners and losers are concerned, I'm not so keen on winning. If winning squeezes out every drop of blood you have, better lose."

Suchita had every reason why she should commit self-slaughter. Bipasha didn't have a single one why she shouldn't. But naturally she bowed out of the argument.

"Will you please give me a chance to raise my point afterwards ?"

"Afterwards ? When ?"

"We are moving to Dehradun tomorrow afternoon. I can still visit you in the evening."

"Really ?" Suchita asked, excitedly "I'll wait for you."

"But promise me one thing, you are not going to follow any foolish step right now."

"I promise."

Cool breeze swept her hair as Suchita roamed across the terrace with the folded hands. There was nobody there and she felt like the queen of the moment. The world was literally at her feet as she stood on the top of the five storied building. She welcomed the easy going air into her open arms and embraced it. Clad in light green top and blank suspenders, she found herself free of any worldly restriction. That afternoon's depression looked so diffused as if blown away by a cyclone. And she had rejuvenated herself with new vitality.

Suchita's mom was out somewhere and the girl grabbed the golden opportunity to flee. Leaving her ailing father at home she climbed to the top to keep her date with Bipasha. As per her pledge Bipasha turned up at 7 pm. Thrilled Suchita held her hand and lead her to a big concrete slab where they settled finally. Then suddenly Suchita grew meditative, realizing the fact that Bipasha would have left her by tomorrow.

"I've a good news for you Suchita," Bipasha zealousy kicked off.

"Don't crack hoaxes, please."

"I'm not kidding, I swear."

"You do ?"

"Yes I swear by you. Look, Suchi my parents are familiar with your problems. You know, I've kept them informed regularly about you. And you've also opened your heart before my mom."

"So ?"

"We have a plan to save you from this ... this ..."

"Dungeon."

"Well as you put it 'Dungeon'."

"What is that ?"

"You will come with me to Dehradun and my father would adopt you. Do you believe it ? You will be my sister."

"What a clever plot !" thought Suchita. "My mother would throw everything in tantrums." She took a long pause.

"Suchi, you didn't say anything ?"

"Let me think for a while. You know it's a bit too risky."

"It is better than suicide my dear."

"No. Suicide is far better. It will end everything once and for all."

"But what's the problem ? Why can't you accept this proposal ?"

"How can I leave my father ? He's dying." In a moment Suchita choked herself with grief. "And what about Shrikant ? He loves me so much."

"If I were you, I wouldn't have given importance to step broth..."

"Please stop it ! Please, he is my real brother. Understand ?"

"OK," Bipasha shrugged. "It's up to you to decide. I'm offering you a chance you won't find everyday. That's all I can do for you. Try to think Suchi. Both the families whether it is yours or mine, both are alien to you. It doesn't matter if you choose one for the other. I would have rather picked up the better one that's mine. No wicked mother ! No drunk father !"

"Bipasha !"

"I'm sorry but it's a fact. You want to find mental peace and that lies with us. Please accept my family Suchita. You won't commit a mistake."

A tempest of thoughts prevailed in Suchita's mind. Thunderous sea waves crashing against hard rocks could have matched the violent stirring of her heart. A better life or the worst life ? A loving mother or a vampish stepmom ? A supportive father or a dying drunk ? A loving friend or a real stepbrother ? A life or a suicide ?

"Tell me Suchita. Before your mom arrives this matter should finish."

Suchita was in no mood to answer. She grew deaf, dumb and blind. Her senses ceased to cooperate. What a great task for a 15 year old ! If she decides against quitting her fate was clear. But what if she joins a new family ? In such a case she stands to lose two things, namely her father and her brother. And people said her father would die ! But she couldn't care less. To her he was always a dead man. Never away from bottles, never close to her. Still his smile had a great magnetism. For Suchita he was always a good man ravished by her evil mother. He was destroyed all the same. So why worry for him ? Soon he would escape this trauma. Soon he would rest in peace. So why care for him even if he remains one agonizing knot in her heart ? A rescue who never was ! He couldn't free himself from liquor; it was too much to ask for his help. Why to shed tears on somebody who nursed big dreams but never actually fulfilled ? Let's end this association once and for all. Perhaps he will be a better father next time. Just pray for him Suchita and leave him at once.

And Shrikant, that sweet faced three year old devil. He is immature. He doesn't know who you are. He would love you till he realizes your true identity. Remember he can never go against his real mother for a stepsister. You are not even a stepsister, only adopted one. So why depend on him ? Why should he bring peace to your life ? And by the time he would be in the prime of his youth, you would have already crossed your peak years. Don't forget this kid is worthless to you. As worthless as you are for him.

Suchita thought in a devastatingly selfish manner. What else she could do ? Cruel time was running out.

"I'm coming with you Bipasha " she told in a not so sure tone.

"Is that final ?"

"Of course."

A mystique figure riding on a horse, zooming past the horizon. The animal gallops unfurling a cloud of dust that scintillate in yellow beams of the setting sun. The man drives it with phenomenal energy, focussing his attention on the path, never losing control. His face is covered, his frame dynamic. Tall, extraordinary built, commanding. That's what it seems because he is going away, towards the west as if to invade the territory of the mighty sun. As if to conquer this giant fireball and proclaim himself the emperor. Will he really disappear ? Without exposing his true identity ? Without bursting the balloon of suspense ?

Oh then ! Something befalls and he alters his direction. Now he points straightaway towards you. The dark figure gradually grows bigger. It clearly emerges out of obscure surroundings as if the mist has been removed from a glass window. Soon the dark picture assumes fascinating colours. That magnetic animal, that god of ardour possesses dark, shimmering fur that looks to be the best replacement for satin. Its chest is formidable, thick and muscular, while legs are skinny yet supremely stout. Eyes are gems studded in the skull, slightly watery. It's speed and attitude is fiery, undoubtedly proving itself the best animal a man ever rode.

And the man in charge of this beast looks anything but ordinary. As he gets closer, he pulls the ropes to bring down the tremendous speed, in the process compelling his horse to raise its forelimbs in air. The animal howls, balancing entire weight on hind limbs as the silver sword of the man, stretching out from his right hand flashes in sunshine. At this moment, you are certain, this one is a real monarch, a crowning prince. After this marvellous act delicate dancing steps follow before the royal figure comes to a halt before you. Without a slight hitch our prince gets down in a grand style. There he is for you in a full view, walking briskly like a ceremonial elephant. Exuding irresistible power and personal charm. Over six feet, built like a rock. His attire is a characteristic blend of a warrior suit and a princely wear, with extravagant use of gold and steel. A solid metallic armour to shield the body from any onslaught supplemented by heavy weaponry, a sword, a javelin, a bow and copious arrows. An imposing headgear with gold decoration and one of the finest pieces of diamonds mounted directly on the middle of the front portion. Other ornaments emblazoning the prince include earrings of the richest pearls, one golden ring on each finger except thumbs, studded with precious gems, gold bracelets and number of gold chains. In spite of this heavy load his sturdy frame stands upright like a great cliff. If you don't fall prey to that kingly grandeur and piercing eyes there must be something terribly wrong with you. He comes forward and your heart starts ticking like a clock. He removes the cloth that efficiently hid his face, ultimately coming out of the camouflage. Check whether you are still normal or unconscious. He then smiles at you, the most destructive one on earth and throws his long and robust hand towards you. And ...

Unavoidably dreams are broken when climax seems to be at stones throw. More so if your dream is really a sweet one. And you wake up to a dark reality. How you wish to experience it all over again ! Recollection of everything you saw is one hard dask. But one thing you are sure about is that, it was all so fabulous. And you really loved it. How often such an event constitutc the fantasy of a girl who gradually progresses from confusing adolescence to prudent maturity ? Very often indeed !

At least for Suchita it was a recurring dream, always making appearance whenever she felt glad. And today it showed up once again in the early hours of dawn. So, she must be very delighted and she herself concluded like that. This was the dawn of a new era she was very eagerly waiting for.

Suchita quickly got up, recited a prayer as she always did in the morning and started waiting for an early passage of time. Gradually, the day broke out. Little Shrikant rose up soon as usual and threw himself in Suchita's arms. She helped him rinse his mouth, fed him chocolate milk and commenced playing with him. To look after this kid was the only refreshing thing Suchita could do in that house. The little boy had charmed her always and he too liked the company of this big sister. Due to her examinations Suchita couldn't spare much time with him recently. But today she was free and Shri looked exceptionally playful and joyous. Suchita knew it was her last day with him, and she had only few minutes before their mom woke up.

Her mom ! She had almost forgotten about this lady. People said she used to be quite nice. Suchita always wondered where she had lost that virtue. What she was accustomed to was the ugly face of her mom. Saudamini Joshi. Her mere presence was a jeopardy. And she had that notorious habit of hammering irrelevant abuses, an art, as Suchita rightly believed, obtained and perfected from her father Nishikant. The only difference was her father needed a dose of liquor for that purpose, her mother required none. Behaviour wise there wasn't much to choose from both. But the dissimilarity was in intention. In Suchita's opinion, her father had a handicap that could be cured. For that he needed a complete rehabilitation and endorsement of teetotalism. Her mother, however was in demand of a psychological therapy. Both were not going to have their respective treatment in lifetime. So the problem persisted forever. What really perturbed Suchita were the rumours of an adulterous relationship of her mother with one Mr. Sethi, a colleague of Nishikant. She badly wished it was not true. But circumstantial evidences pointed towards the worst she feared. As a result Suchita's hate for Saudamini converted itself into a murderous rage. Suchita felt so ashamed she almost went insane. Then entire base of their family eroded like a rusting piece of iron once they transferred to Delhi from Mumbai. Whole situation was unpleasant and extremely unbearable for Suchita. She seriously started thinking about suicide. Then Bipasha made that startling offer, forcing her to start thinking in positive direction again.

"So, when I said get up quickly, you mean it was for playing with Shri. Am I right Suchita ?"

Some sharp, spiky words collided with Suchita and at once she got alert. It was Saudamini, her mom. Every year her voice attained new heights of savagery and unpolished sarcasm. Her personality had become nothing less than perilous for Suchita. The last five years of their association had been a strained prototype of human relations. Initially Saudamini carried a weird charm with her, now at the age of 36 she was no less than a grisly witch. Having had retained most of the original physical features, what she actually lost was nobleness of heart.

"At this rate," thought Suchita, "she would beat the devil by the time she turns 60."

"Are you listening to me, Her Highness ?" Saudamini furiously attacked. "What do you think ? I'm mad ? Can't you hear what I said ? Where is your attention lately ?"

Suchita tried to open her mouth, but her words faded in Saudamini's blitzkrieg.

"I know, I know. Our pretty Juliet has found a Romeo, hasn't she ?"

"Please mom..."

"Shut up ! I don't want to hear anything from you. Now just take that broom and start sweeping the floor. I want every room cleaned before 8 o'clock. The Chopras will be here anytime after 9."

"Chopras ? Who ?" Suchita dared to ask.

"My foot. Understand ? Now just go away. I should not repeat what I told you earlier, should I ? OK. Clean up the rooms, make this boy ready, Shri I mean. Then breakfast should be on the table by 9. Take a bath yourself, OK ? I don't want any mess around here. If I find any rubbish, you know very well how I tackle you. Now don't stand like a dumbo. Go ! Hurry up."

"Britishers couldn't have been any worse," Suchita thought and began executing the stringent orders. She didn't mind anything at that moment. Exhilarating freedom had already summoned her. What remained was passage of some time, and those bad days would fly away like birds.

Dutifully Suchita dealt with the work. Once a crowning princess now no more than a petty maid, an innocent victim of a wicked somersault of time.

❖❖❖

"Ruhi ! How nice to see you !" Suchita heard those loud words as she just finished taking bath and dressed up neatly as per Saudamini's instructions. She knew Chopras had arrived. Quickly Suchita carried Shri to an adjoining room and watched the proceedings from behind a curtain. A middle-aged couple was standing at the door. The lady particularly looked very close to Saudamini as they hugged each other repeatedly, held each other's hands, and laughed uproariously. Suchita was anything but amused.

"Come in, please. Please Mr. Chopra. Come in Bobby darling." Saudamini seemed to say. There was one curious young boy with them whom she called 'Bobby darling.'

"Seems to be their son," thought Suchita. "Well, interesting family ! The Chopras !"

"Oh ! How to sweet, Sau. Your flat is too good." Complemented Mrs. Chopra.

"Thank's a lot Ruhi. Still I think it needs renovation." Saudamini boasted.

All four of them took their seats. Incidentally the lad Bobby sat exactly facing Suchita. As soon as he settled in the sofa there was an undeliberate eye contact between him and Suchita. The boy smiled from the corner of his lips and Suchita instantly hid behind the wall. Inexplicably her heart started pounding.

"Oh Sau, I'm so delighted to come here. It's been 15 years we didn't meet."

"I'm too Ruhi. I tried to attend your wedding but I couldn't make it somehow."

"By the way, where's your husband ?"

"Husband ? Oh, he is in marketing field you know. He has to travel a lot. Presently he is not in Delhi."

"Then who is sleeping out there ?" Suchita angrily asked herself. She didn't like the way Saudamini neglected her father. No doubt he was guilty himself, but Saudamini had no right to disdain him, the man who earned money for her fussy lifestyle.

"And what about your children ?"

"I've a son, Shrikant."

"Where's he hiding ?"

"He's playing inside," Saudamini loudly called for Suchita at this instant asking her to bring the child. In a moment Suchita appeared before them carrying Shrikant in arms.

"Oh, you've a daughter too !"

"She isn't my daughter," Saudamini snatched the little boy from Suchita and scolded her.

"Why are you waiting ? Go inside."

"No, no let her stay here." Mrs. Chopra said and Suchita stood where she was.

"She isn't your daughter ? Who's she then ?"

"She's... she's... I'll tell you later on."

Saudamini made a wearied face.

"Whoever she's. She is beautiful. Isn't she Karan ?"

Mr. Chopra swung his neck in affirmative.

"What's your name honey ? Suchita isn't it ? Sit here beside me. Sit. Sit."

Suchita bashfully followed Mrs. Chopra's wish. Now suddenly she had taken a centrestage. Mr. Chopra and Bobby continuously stared at her.

"What a cute baby you have Sau." Mrs. Chopra cuddled up with Shri. "But he's a bit small. Don't you think ?"

"You know it was much late. There was some medical snag actually."

"Oh so sorry. Still something is better than nothing."

Now it was too much for Suchita. Since morning she had been waiting for Bipasha and here she was in the company of strangers. Strangers who really were strange ! Suchita quickly became aware of the piercing looks of Bobby and Mr. Chopra and that was driving her increasingly uneasy. Through the corner of her eye she stole a glimpse of Bobby. He was about 18, aggressively built and had a sly, deceitful smile on his face. A thin moustache and a raw beard indicated that he hadn't shaven for once. His lips carried an impression of chain smoking habit. In short Bobby seemed like a civilized vagabond, suitably civilized, suitably vagabond. Slowly these hawkish eyes procured different dimension as Suchita's heartbeats shot up. She was well familiar with those looks, looks following the slopes and contours of her body, looks threatening to penetrate her clothing. Suddenly she found herself unsafe in that company. Nervously she grabbed both of her upper arms with opposite hands.

"Bobby what do you say about Suchita ?" Asked Mrs. Chopra.

"Ultimate stuff !", Bobby obscenely pushed his tongue out and then suggestively flutlered his eyes at Mrs. Chopra.

"How dare you," Suchita fumed inside with insurgent rage, but couldn't verbalize anything. She didn't know why but she badly wanted to kill that Bobby.

Fortunately, the doorbell screamed at that moment and Suchita felt the mounting tension recede. She definitely knew it was Bipasha and she knew it correctly. Saudamini opened the door and as per their plan Bipasha called Suchita outside. She did the same but not before clutching her brother in arms and kissing him. That startled everybody. Leaving them like that Suchita madly ran out closing the door behind. Bipasha firmly held her hands.

"Now be quick let's move," She declared.

"Just a minute. I'll see off my father."

"Don't go inside again. Please. Don't make a blunder."

"He isn't in. He's inside that nearby flat. It's empty. You know, whenever any visitor comes my mom keeps him there. She thinks he's useless. You wait for me. I'm coming, don't move."

Suchita frenziedly opened the door of a side by flat and disappeared inside. On an humble cot there, slept Nishikant Joshi, her father. The man who pulled her out of one grave only to put into another one. The man she neither loved nor hated. He slept there like a dead man. Suchita unknowingly sobbed at the sight. A man completely defeated by a non-living fluid. A stark symbol of weakness of human mind. Mutely, Suchita went ahead and kissed his cheeks. Nishi slightly opened his eyes. A dark shadow of death was situated deep inside. His lips moved a bit, not producing any voice whatsoever. "Daddy I love you so much." Suchita held his right hand and let out of her tears, for it was impossible to contain them. She remained there for over a minute, then collected herself and with a firm determination came out of the room still sobbing. Hand in hand Bipasha and Suchita started descending the stairs as fast as they could. Once getting down they moved straight for a while, then vanished in a leftward bound lane. Suchita although in a hurry, felt a soothing calmness enveloping her soul. Finally it was all over. Saudamini could never have found her.

Within two minutes, the girls, badly panting, slowed down. It was now safe to catch a taxi. So they stopped and looked for a taxi. Suddenly a fast moving jeep abruptly halted very close to them. Before they could realize anything a young man got down and smiled at them. Suchita almost fainted at the sight. It was Bobby. What's more, from the other side none other than Saudamini showed her presence. Suchita began wobbling at the spot as her piqued mom launched burning bombshells. Her mouth clenched as if she suffered from epilepsy. By sternly issuing a warning to Bipasha, Saudamini drove off with Suchita. Poor Bipasha collapsed in tears. Their plan had failed disastrously. Suchita was separated from her forever and perhaps it was suicide option again for this friend of her.

Nine

"See you pal," Caption Jatin hoists his hand from his motorbike as he departs from one of his colleagues and takes a swift right turn towards the direction of his house. Within a minute or two his two wheeler retards and comes to a smooth, effortless stop in front of the front gate.

He gets down and removes his sunglasses. The man acquires an incredulous look as he beholds some fellows in the neighbouring house which belongs to Ma, Mrs. Kamal Sareen. Not that the people do not call upon this house, they do, but they are essentially women. That's why Jatin's sharp sight recognizes the discrepancy when it spots some males in there. Hurriedly he parks his bike inside the fence and without entering the house reaches for Ma.

While getting in through the front gate he encounters some unknown faces most of whom are males. That leaves him wondering about what must be going on inside. Well, nothing much seems to materialize actually as he watches Ma comfortably sitting on the sofa with a magazine in her hand.

"Ah, there you are I was waiting for you only Jatin," says Ma keeping aside the magazine.

"Who were those people I saw just now Ma ?", Jatin asks as he positions himself on a divan.

"Well, rest yourself properly my boy. I'll tell you about them soon," says Ma.

Just then, by sheer intuition, Jatin realises somebody encroaching them from inside and tilts to have a glance on it. What he sees could only be seen in dreams. And that throws him in such an astonishment that he gets confused whether it is reality or some kind of hallucination. A young girl, who does not seem to be more than 22 years, walks in gently, with her body draped in a thick Kashmiri shawl. Even then she shivers with cold as if she was stationed on the north pole. Her eyes are almost closed and her head drooped down just like a newly wedded bride melting with profound shyness. Her shoulder long, slight curly hair seem to be wet as if she was caught in a heavy torrent. Her creamy face glistens in a bath of brilliant sunbeams originating from the topmost window of the room. Amazingly thought it seems, she still shivers from head to feet and in addition her body produces intermittent convulsions. Some tiny water droplets manage to come out of her hair and rest on her forehead, brightly glittering like pearls. But their venture to pose a happy picture of the girl doesn't seem to succeed, as the girl appears to be in a real deplorable condition.

She havers at the sight of Jatin and looses control over the shawl. Her frail hands try to recapture it but it slips down her shoulders and spreads itself on the floor. Occurrence of this incident puts the girl in further embarrassment as she shudders due to the loss of the protective shelter of the shawl. Jatin rapidly realizes that the girl is clad in one of Ma's sarees, a plain violet one and a black, cotton blouse that sticks to her body as if her own shin. Her shining cream complexion is far from being clandestine because of the helpless robes. No wonder, in those clothes she looks ethereal, simply irresistible. As soon as her shawl goes down, she gives an evasive look to Ma and her large, dark eyes fling a prominent impression. In the meantime she desperately clasps her arms with folded hands to forestall slipping of the saree.

"Take it easy my child," this remark from Ma finally breaks the web in which Jatin found himself enmeshed for some moments. But his mind is far from being retrieved from the magical spell and he covets it to stay on, if possible, forever.

Even before the girl could stoop down and handpick the shawl Ma reaches to the spot, gathers the shawl and envelops the girl in it. She extends support to the visibly upset young lady by delicately clutching her shoulders with hands. Slowly Ma brings her near the sofa and helps her to sit there. The girl does so by occupying minimum possible space. She almost contracts herself by tightly pressing her hands, again by closing her large eyes. Her body shivers like a hell.

Still not in a position to identify this young lady, Jatin fosters his eyebrows at Ma interrogating about her in a sign language.

"Jatin, I know about her as much as you do. That means I no nothing," replies Ma. "You must be kidding Ma. Here is one lady sitting beside you, wearing your own clothes and you say you don't know who she is ?" asks Jatin.

"Believe me son, I found her near Shrikrishna temple. She was drowned in the Yamuna river but fortunately some good fellows brought back her from the jaws of death. She looks to be in such severe shock, she hasn't spoken a word since then. Somehow I could manage to bring her here with the help of the same young men. Now let's know about her address and then it will be your responsibility to dispatch her safely on your motorbike," asserted Ma.

"Well, as you wish," Jatin shrugs off at that. Ma, then turning her face towards the young lady and lovingly patting on her back asks tenderly, "Where do you live my child ? Don't you want to go home ?" Surprisingly the girl shakes her head vigorously, expressing a clear 'no'.

"O.K. Will you please, at least let me know about your name ?"

This time an easy approval comes, again through the media of shaking head.

"Suchita !", her high frequency voice exudes ultimate femininity.

"So, you don't want to go home. Where do you want to go from here then ?" Ma fires the second query.

"I want to die," says Suchita sobbing like a little girl, why did you save me ? I'm fed up with life."

"Goodness Gracious ! You mean you deliberately plunged yourself into Yamuna ? A suicide attempt ?" Ma is wonderstrucked, so is Jatin as Suchita nods her head.

Ma looks at Jatin and the young man flickers his eyebrows questioning the validity of her decision to bring this lady home. Ma in her turn and through mild gesture asks him to keep cool.

"Don't be in a hurry to dismiss your life like that my child. It is no joke being a human being. Besides don't you think such a behaviour only serves to prove that you are a coward who prefers running away from life instead of fighting for existence ?"

"I agree I'm a coward," the girl speaks in a voice trembling like a wave, "and I agree that I lack fighting spirit. That's why I opted to commit suicide. If I don't have a privilege to live my own life, at least my right to put an end to it should not be denied."

She speaks and then breaks off abruptly as the fervency of her sobbing increases. She does not unlock her eyes for a single moment as if it hurts doing so.

"And what compels you to take such a harsh decision like that ?" ask Ma.

"That's a lengthy episode. I don't want to share my sorrows with anybody," Suchita laments curtly. But Ma isn't one who could be defeated so easily. She does not retreat a single inch.

"Don't be silly," this is how she offers affection on anybody. "Today destiny has brought you among us and believe me, nobody is going to harm you here. So please feel very safe my child. If you still have any doubt look at this man," here she points towards Jatin, "He is an army officer. If you are really scared of anybody just tell us his name and we will make sure that the person goes behind the bars."

Suchita slightly raises her head with the mention of Jatin and opens her eyes. Jatin gazes deep into her large and dark ones. The next moment she lowers them timidly.

"You definitely look to be a major one Suchita and so you have every right to choose your own way of living. Just open up a bit and select right kind of people to be with. I bet within a year you will laugh at your wish to end your life. And you being here, we will certainly offer you help in that direction."

"Oh, thank you very much for your generosity," Suchita can't ward off the free flow of tears through her eyes. Time and again she met people like Ma in life, but regrettably her stay with them was terribly succinct.

"How should I refer to you ?" Suchita finally comes to term with reality.

"Call me Ma and he is Jatin, my son".

"I'm Suchita Joshi," Suchita comes up with a better sounding voice this time, "I used to be an orphan and the circumstances have rendered me orphan once again. I guess this single word summarizes atleast half of my sufferings."

"No, you are wrong Suchita. You have some kind of negative approach when you think like that," pinpoints Ma, "look at Jatin, incidentally he is also an orphan," Now it's Suchita's turn to be surprised, "I'm his Ma but I haven't given birth to him. Even after being orphan like you he never talks rubbish like what you said. Committing suicide and all that."

Ma's remark puts Suchita into predicament and she looks more pathetic than ever. But quite amazingly help comes to her from an unexpected quarter. Jatin steps forward to defend the girl.

"It's a ridiculous comparison Ma," he reasons, "We don't even know what kind of situation she has faced. I wasn't one of the unluckiest of orphans. Perhaps she might be. Besides, she is a girl and her mind is supposed to be more tender and sensitive than mine. Am I wrong ?" Here he asks opinion straightaway from Suchita who readily agrees with him by shaking her head, thus completing a whole circle of one to one communication between the two for the first time. Suchita is overwhelmed to watch Jatin say something like that. And Ma is not surprised at Jatin taking a stance against her even if it seemed for a moment that it was Suchita who had spent so many years with Jatin and Ma was just a new acquaintance, but she never minds it. In fact she is happy that Jatin looked congenial and forbearing towards Suchita because it wasn't a good idea to take to task a person who came very near to committing suicide.

"I think what you say is correct Jatin. It won't be proper to form an opinion without knowing everything about anybody." Quickly Ma admits her fault. "I'm sorry Suchita. But please tell us about yourself as elaborately as possible so that we may understand how badly you have been hurt."

"What's the hurry Ma ? Let her breathe some fresh air. Let her be free with us and then ask what you want." Jatin comes to Suchita's rescue once again. "And how about a hot cup of coffee after being soaked in cold water ?"

"Coffee, oh dear ! I had prepared coffee for us. But I forgot about this once this naughty kid of mine arrived." Here Ma gently hits Jatin's upper arm. "I'm so sorry honey. I'll be back just in a moment" and the old lady hurries her way towards the kitchen.

Suchita wonders why these people looked so much concerned about her. The old lady's treatment was exactly like a mother and the apparently tough young man actually was so soft at heart. Suchita wants to have a glimpse of the young man who could trace her mind so strikingly and spoke the very same things that she wanted to convey. His sympathetic behaviour seemed to be so genuine, they appeared to be good old friends.

It took almost five minutes for Ma to turn the cold coffee into a hot one, once again and bring it to the table in front of Suchita. But during her absence not a single word was spoken and the two young people never stared into each other eyes. Suchita remained steady, with her head and shoulders drooped down while Jatin stood confounded, not knowing what and how to say.

"Just have this hot coffee and you'll feel energetic," Ma pours the fluid into cups and passes them over to Suchita and Jatin. Indeed, the coffee does wonders and Suchita looks more commodious as she sips the warm liquid.

"I was in the St. Joseph's orphanage until I was 10," Suchita begins narrating her life history after savouring the coffee. However, she still looks feeling sceptical. But after deciding to commit suicide, you have hardly anything to lose. So she doesn't mind opening herself in front of strangers like Ma and Jatin.

"When I was 10, I was adopted by Nishikant and Saudamini Joshi of Santacruz. They said, initially I was very reluctant to leave St. Joseph's. In fact, they were some fourth or fifth couple who expressed their desire to adopt me. Earlier people didn't succeed in their attempts but I bowed down to the Joshis at last to become their daughter. The whole credit for breaking my stiff attitude goes to my father, Nishikant. In fact, he was the only one, genuinely interested in me. As for my mother, she was opposed to any kind of adoption. Even 8 years after their marriage she was ready to wait for a natural baby. But till then my father had lost all the patience. Medical reports also confirmed his fears that the possibility of a natural baby was very remote. Hence he decided to go ahead with his plan to adopt a child even against the wishes of my mother. That's how I became Suchita Joshi. At last, I got some identity, some recognition and a precious extention to my first name. But I had to pay a heavy price for these privileges." Suchita stops here and gives out a heavy sigh. Perhaps she thinks, she has talked too much.

"What wrong price are you talking about dear ?" asks Ma, in an obvious attempt to suggest that she had, in fact, talked too little.

"Well that's the whole tragedy !" Suchita sighs again. Her face turns grave serious, with the spontaneous single worded description of her life.

"My father was a great charmer, the kindness and grace personified. Frankly, I couldn't have got a better father than him. Yet he had a darker side to his personality. He was a heavy drinker. The liquor entered into his life because of my mother and remained with him forever. My father was a marketing officer in a multinational company, so we could afford a good standard of living, well above the average. But my father's obsession with whisky, heralded a decline in our lifestyle. Everyday he would return home dipped in alcohol up to the neck. Naturally, it was my mother who had to bear his wrath and his scolding and arguments over petty things. But sober or drunk, my father used to be startlingly loving towards me. The very sight of me would make him humble like a cow. He simply couldn't stand my wishes being ignored, he couldn't stand myself being criticised by anybody. He would always defend me fiercely against any mental or physical attack. I still remember, once I cut my palm accidentally by a knife. I couldn't sleep through the night that day due to unbearable pain. And my father sat beside my bed without shifting his attention for a single minute. I felt the knife had only slit open my hand but in the process it had slit my father's heart. I still remember his every gesture of love towards me. At the same time I also remember that distinct smell of liquor irritatingly reaching my brain every time he would hug me. I always fail to understand why such a good person had to take the shelter of that bad thing. If only he could beat his addiction."

At this juncture Suchita suddenly turns ruminative. Tears threaten to come out of her large, dark eyes with every mention of her father. Ma quickly catches her feeling and comes forward to console the pitiful girl.

"Well, that's human nature Suchita. It's all a part of the game. You are living in fools paradise if you expect a person to be as fair as the god. That will be very unfair indeed." Ma quips in her inimitable way.

"I don't know" Suchita puts it wryly. "What I know is, my father's craze for whisky took a very heavy toll. Every night he would irritate my mother, sometimes he used to beat her even. And in her turn she would inflict her avenge upon me. Whenever she would find me alone in the house, she used to treat me like a stray dog. She used to make me perform such duties which were not meant for me. Playing with friends was prohibited. Steping out of the house, except for going to school was ruled out. Even studying peacefully was not possible for me. Whenever I used to sit reading books, my Mom would summon me to help her in kitchen. Although we had home servants to do all the household jobs, just for the sake of punishment she would ask me to wash the dishes or cut the vegetables. Only I know how I managed to get through my exams. Naturally my rank in the class used to be quite lower than I actually deserved. I was terribly shocked at the way she behaved with me. I felt like a parrot arrested in a golden cage. In my case the cage was not golden either.

My mother used to rebuke me over trivial matters. It was a routine. Sometimes I used to be unlucky enough to get beaten by her. It was a new horrible experience for me. Just imagine a life sandwitched between a kind father and a ruthless mother. I was afraid of complaining against her because she used to threaten me often just to prevent me from opening my mouth in front of my Dad. There was no use doing it either as most of the time he used to be indecisive, thanks to his dear whisky. Sometimes, however, he used to quarrel with my mother over my issue, but that used to result in more and more hardships to me. My tender mind was brutally butchered several times. The very foundation of my life, my fertile adolescence, was destroyed by none other than my mother. No wonder I'm yet to recover the trauma, no wonder I think in a negative direction. Am I to be blamed for my attitude then ?" Suchita asks this question in a harsh manner unsuitable to her disposition that takes Ma and Jatin by surprise. She tightly clings to the shawl and stares at an indefinite point. Although her movements become free, the melancholic affairs of her face remain intact and doesn't seem to alter atleast for the near future. In a sharp volley of words Suchita presents a grim picture of her misfortune that is far from being turbid. She creates such an effect that Ma doesn't find a word to react.

"Same things have persisted till today ?" Finally she gathers enough courage to engage the wounded girl back into the conversation.

"More or less," after a sudden rush of adrenaline Suchita comes to normal tone again. "But many events have occurred within this period. Once such major incident was the birth of my little brother, Shrikant. He is thirteen years younger to me. Once my mother could produce her natural baby, her hate for me only intensified. I had come to be an unwanted outsider, an itching thorn in her bouquet. She used to make me know this fact very clearly through her cruel words. Her each taunt was aimed at condemning my useless presence in her house and it used to demolish my heart like anything. All through the nights I shed tears, silently over my misfortune. I forgot how peaceful sleeps were. Whenever I used to sleep, I would wake up terribly frightened at the end of a nightmare, with my face covered with sweat. There was only one person who could have saved me from that merciless trap. It was my Dad. But unfortunately liquor was dearer to him than any helpless child. Here I would cry desperately distorting my nerves and there my dear Dad would argue with my mother not even hearing a single bit of my appeal. Sometimes I felt my Dad and myself were similar in some respect. Both were battling with my Mom. The only difference was, he had his bottle of whisky with him. And I was alone !"

This simple proclamation 'I was alone' was the motto of this vanquished life. It became evident as the conversation proceeded. This motto could only change its tense but not the substance. So she would say 'I was alone,' 'I'm alone', or 'I will be alone.' Suchita firmly believed that she was the most unfortunate person in the world. This, however was not entirely wrong. She had thousand reasons to defend her declaration.

"My father had always been an intriguing character for me. I try to hate him because he was the one actively involved in bringing me from St. Joseph's. Naturally, I always blame him to open a whole new chapter of distress and misery in my life. But he was too good a person to be hated. I think, the script of his life was wrongly written by the destiny. Indeed, his life was a result of some kind of miscalculation on her part.

Even after the birth of my brother his trysts with the liquor continued. I guess, it was some kind of a curse. Obviously too much involvement in drinks was bound to hamper his efficiency level. And exactly something like that happened. The person who never used to waste a single second to execute his boss' order, started arguing with him over trivial matters. Soon his well established and well-nurtured good reputation crashed down heavily. He was left with quarrels at home and quarrels at works. That cascaded into his getting more and more support from the liquor. You know, such a thing forms a vicious circle and freeing yourself from it becomes impossible. There is hardly any way to escape.

Finally my father's boss decided to get rid of him somehow and transferred him to Delhi. That's how we came here. I was 15 years old then. Thus we changed our residing place but nothing else seemed to change. Same routine continued in life. Same drunkard father, same ruthless Mom. New addition was my brother. He was instinctively generous in his attitude. Although he was too small to distinguish between a real sister and an adopted one, I always appreciated this little supporter of mine. Obviously because my brother was the only one who understood me. Most of the time the job of looking after him was enthrusted upon me and I was ever ready to accept it. Perhaps it was the only thing I did with full sense of interest. Rest others would come to me as hardships.

It was a period when I shed all shells of childhood and entered a new phase of life." She was referring to the period when she put on all the characteristics that makes a girl a woman. "Until then I had sailed through my matriculation and entered into college life. But that transition was the toughest one to face. In the year of my matriculation my mother turned unimaginably hostile from the day one. Keeping undivided attention on the studies was not possible at all. That was the period when thoughts of suicide crept into my mind. I didn't know what mistake I had done. My mother was upto destroying me mentally and physically for the reasons I couldn't point out till now. She did every trick she could think of, to devastate me. And mostly she was successful in the attempts. Everyday's harsh treatment would find me tottering to stand erect. My self-esteem plunged to the bottom low. Her crude remarks on me and my existence used to flood my eyes with tears. Am I so unimportant person that anybody would drop in, in my life and kick me around ?" Asked Suchita and she couldn't speak anymore. The blanket she held around her body grew wet with liters of water surging ahead through her eyes. Ma instantly moves and grabs her by hand and pats on her back softly.

"Don't lose heart my child," she bargains on her sweet voice to flush out the emotional clog from Suchita's heart. "If you feel uneasy don't narrate your story. We know, you had been through difficult days."

Not far away from this young lady, Jatin looks unsteady, unable to withstand such a grim state of her. For a moment he feels like himself trying to heal her wounds. But then, he reminds himself that he is just an outsider like any other man and not authorised to make such advances.

Ma's efforts yield some result as Suchita recovers herself quickly.

"I'm OK" she asserts "please don't stop me now. I want to empty out my heart. It's too congested in here." She sweeps away her tears and continues, "as if my torture at home was not enough, I started getting annoyed from the outside front. Day by day as I grew up, I found myself getting more and more attention from the people on the road. Every time I got out from house I used to get surrounded by eve teasers, those spoilt boys. They used to accompany me from the house to the college and back to the house. Naturally, other girls were afraid of sharing my company just to avoid those dirty eyes. And I had to remain alone tolerating all those nasty remarks. More often those remarks used to be uglier than those made by my Mom. And I had nobody to complain. I had nobody on my side. Whole world was against me and I was alone. I believed in my Dad but he was out of senses. I also believed in my brother, but he was too small to understand anything. The situation got even worse when my Mom heard about my association with rowdy boys through the media of some useless women. Still today I wonder, how you don't do a bit of wrong and still become notorious in this world. Anyway, this matter was sufficient to ignite my mother's wrath. It was quite volatile you know. Consequently, she threatened to put an end to my education. She spared me only when I promised her, I wouldn't step out from the house, even for attending the classes, I studied under such circumstances and I studied on my own without getting proper coaching. Naturally, the exam couldn't fetch me good marks but I still managed to get through."

"But you look thoroughly educated. Aren't you ?" Ma interrupted Suchita.

"Yes, I'm. Despite all these difficulties I managed to earn a degree in commerce. That was in last year itself. But before that I received such a terrible shock, I still find myself unable to come to term with reality."

"Well, what was that ?"

"You can guess it. It was my father's demise. I was in junior college then. Although it was a tremendous blow for me, medically it was a fair judgement of nature. Surely, you can't survive much when you have already damaged your body beyond repair. That's what happened with my Dad. His entire body was as if drenched in alcohol for years. One day it was bound to give in. But it happened at a crucial time. I lost him when I needed him most. Although he was absolutely of no use as far as my life was concerned, he used to give me some sort of psychological edge, you know. I always used to think, there was somebody who might rescue me from all that drudgery. But I lost him and I lost all purpose. I'm shattered. I'm orphan again. There is nobody who understands me, who appreciates my feelings. I'm left alone. I'm alone."

Completely submerged in the deep sea of anguish, the girl grabs her forehead with hands and her tears never stop. Her personality looks diminished and overburdened with grief. Her condition is simply hopeless and capable of moving any sensitive person. The reference of her Dad, unknowingly triggers a chain reaction of sentiments in her fragile mind. And even Ma gets confused, how to sort out this tricky situation. She again clutches Suchita by shoulders. The girl cries like a child who couldn't find its mother for a long time. Over a big period of time, weeping like this has become her necessity. It has become an integral part of her life. For last so many years she has not spent a single day without moistening her large, dark eyes. It was as if her basic requirement along with food, cloth and shelter.

"After his death, we were about to leave Delhi. And I was sure my mother would have thrown me on the road. But one strange fellow, Mr. Sethi, who worked in my father's company put a marriage proposal in front of my mother. She gladly accepted it. My new father didn't have objection to my presence, but he was totally indifferent towards me. He allowed my mother to take every decision about me. And that made her my sole mistress. I began working like an ancient slave. But still I don't know how she allowed me to continue my studies. Perhaps she feared, if I wasn't properly educated she wouldn't find a husband for me. Well, that was her ultimate aim, somehow getting rid of me. In all these years, after my father's death, I looked upon my brother as my only sympathizer, which he was. And this fact used to perturb my Mom greatly. So, slowly she started poisoning his little mind and then snatched him away from me. Now he too, hated me ! Again I was rendered alone, this time really alone. Thoughts of attempting suicide again started getting roots in my mind. But I prevented myself from succumbing to it on many occasions. Because I still had a last hope ! Perhaps, by sheer chance my husband could be good enough to understand me. So, I waited patiently for my wedding to take place. In the meantime, I had to endure many cruel incidents and mental torture. And I braved them all. How could I be I without sorrows and pains ?" Suchita asked something which was no less than a riddle, a jigsaw puzzle.

"Finally after I completed my degree, my Mom began searching for a suitable boy for me. And I was sure, he would be the most unsuitable for me. I was quite right guessing that one. My Mom came up with exactly similar package what I predicted. He was a perfect vagabond you know. Just by looking at him you could have discovered the cheapness in him. I was frightened at his sight, I plainly refused to have him as a husband. And then started the sheer execution of me. I was beaten up several times. I was threatened to kill. It was brutal ! It was so awful ! You wouldn't wait anybody to set you afire. Would you ? It is better to die a death of you liking. So I opted for the only option left for me. I immersed myself in Yamuna ! But I'm so unfortunate, even dying peacefully is not allowed to me. Why did you rescue me ? Do you know, you didn't actually save me, you have thrown me into more trouble. Where should I go from here ? What should I do now ? Wasn't it better than sustaining knife wounds on body ?"

Suchita wept ! This time uncontrollably !

Now it became very difficult to handle this lady. As difficult as inserting a thread in the needle hole in dark. You don't know where the needle is, you don't know where the thread goes. Ma was in the same dilemma.

"You are not a helpless child my dear. You just tell us who the culprits are. We will have them in police custody." Ma tried to provide a solution.

"What purpose will it serve ?" Suchita shot back, "who will give me shelter ? The question is not achieving revenge, I'm hardly interested in it. The problem is about my future. Will anybody accept me as a wife ?" Queries came after queries.

"Why not ? Somebody definitely will," answers were also ready.

"I don't want uncertainties. I'm sick of them. All these years I was troubled by bleak future. I don't want it anymore. I'm determined. I'll die."

"How if I agree to marry you ?" The young man who was silent for a long time startled both the ladies. It was a daring revelation ! Suchita suddenly stopped doing anything. Her mind as if hit by a thunderbolt. She thought she was trapped in a dungeon full of killer snakes and somebody came forward and informed her that they were all fake. She held her breath in utter disbelief. Indeed, it was as surprising as a frog turning into a handsome prince.

"Heard what he said ?" Ma patted her shoulders, "that's what I was going to suggest. Now respond to his proposal. Will you accept him as your husband ?"

Suchita looked deep into the eyes of Ma, still unrecovered from the shock. Then she closed her large and dark ones and approvingly shook her head. At that instant Ma embraced her and tears continued emerging from Suchita's eyes.

✣✣✣

It could have very well been a 'mirage', a well calculated deception on the part of nature. An illusion. But it was true all the same. And Suchita was very much a part of it. To her jubilant, ecstatic soul, it was nothing less than crisp ending of a fairytale, absolutely uncanny yet very, very real. It was a unique experience, something that she believed, would never be a part of her life even if the world turned upside down, even if deers turn man-eaters and tigers, pure vegetarians. And how simple it was, not a single stone shifted its position, no holocaust occurred, not even a tiny insect bothered that it was taking place. And she thought it impossible ! As impossible as an ice remaining ice on a hot oven, flesh remaining flesh thousand years after it was catapulted into flesh-hood.

Suchita, with her family tree untraceable was going to wed Captain Jatin Mittal, the irresistible army officer.

"Name ?" the registering authority in the courtroom asked.

"Jatin Mittal."

"And yours please."

"Suchita, Suchita Joshi."

"Put your signatures here."

"Could you please wait for sometime. My important witness is yet to come." Jatin observed and the gentleman there posed an annoyed look.

Suchita couldn't guess the person who Jatin termed as an important witness as Ma was already with them. Her suspense didn't last longer. A middle aged lady rushed in with great rapidity, her leather purse bouncing over her shoulder with each step. She looked simply formidable but still her baby face picturised her younger than what she actually was. Suchita couldn't have believed, had she been told this lady was 40. Jatin's face sparkled like a cracker at the instant he realised her presence.

"Suchita, she is... well she is no less than my elder sister. I call her Didi. And Didi meet my wife, Suchita, Suchita Mittal."

"Caught the prey at last, you naughty boy," Didi gently squeezed Jatin's nose and then quietly hugged Suchita.

"May god bless you" she said as she kissed Suchita's head. The younger lady naturally remained doubtful about the other one.

"Well, don't get confused," Jatin as if sensed what Suchita's mind was reflecting. "As Ma is my mother, Didi is my sister. Rest I will tell you later. But let us first sort out this Job" He laughed.

And one by one Jatin and Suchita signed the legal documents that solemnly declared them as 'man and wife.' It was followed by the customary followed in Vedic marriage, they garlanded each other. Ma and Didi clapped gently, while Suchita ensured that it was no dream and there wasn't any earthquake taking place either. The two witnesses viz. Ma and Didi finished the further formalities by signing the documents. And they greeted each other. The whole simple affair did not last even ten minutes, but a lifelong relationship was born. It was a strange union of hearts and it was truly an outstanding family. They did not have blood relations but the bond that tied them together was as strong as any natural one. Ma and Didi, those irreplaceable ladies in Jatin's life, could feel the satisfaction overcrowded in their hearts. Their worries had ended, their search for a suitable bride for Jatin unexpectedly brought rich rewards.

❖❖❖

Thanks mother nature ! I thought you were my enemy. I thought you were my destroyer. I thought you take great pride in snatching away minute joys from my possession. I thought you were reckless enough to strip off everything that went in my favour, that put forth opportunities for me to breathe freely. But how terribly mistaken I was ! I suspected the credentials of my creator, the universal mother ! How could I know that, secretly she was planning a rich and bright future for me while I went through severe trial of mental strength ? But now, as her true colour unfolds and lay bare in front of me I'm but surprised. So this was in store for me ?

It is so heavenly, I'm yet to recover fully from this sweet shock. It will take years for me to come to terms with such a fabulous reality. As for now, I feel like a carefree eagle wandering all across the deep blue sky with currents of fresh air filling my nostrils. There is no end to my journey, there is no horizon to restrict my flight, because whatever seems like horizon, keeps an expanding with each stroke of my wings.

I'm totally in control of myself. For the first time, I'm rising such towering heights, the whole world is looking up, stretching its neck muscles, straining its eyes under blinding sunbeams.

I could ask for nothing more. Throughout my life I remained alone. But now you have granted me a lifetime partner. With this soul flying beside me, I'm sure I can beat the world anyday. I'm simply thrilled at the prospect of living such a magnificent life like this one. I'm turned on by the romanticism with which it is enriched. Glorious is the spring like appearance of the nature. Glamorous is its existence. Cold stream of water, full of life and dynamism, tracing its path in its inexplicable hurry. Its water tastes sweet like honey. And how should I express the outstanding beauty of the rose garden that encompasses this little stream ? Shining array of bright colour on serene background of green texture ? Honeybees humming around the blossoming flowers, extracting delightful, delicious juices. Well, listening to this marvellous symphony is nothing less than lending your ears to a musical masterpiece. And in the midst of this lively rose garden stands a huge mango tree providing cottage to hundreds of tiny birds singing happy tunes. This tree is a prominent manifestation of nature's bounty, always blossoming with ripe, succulent fruits and shining green leaves. With the enormous expanse of branches it provides such a tremendous coolness to one and everybody taking shelter in its comfort giving shadow that it ends up receiving millions of prayers for its well being. From one of its many branches hangs a tiny nest belonging to a beautiful pair of tiny pigeons. They are far from being concerned about the hustle and bustle outside the rose garden. They remain involved and indulged in their miniature life. They love each other. They love their nest. They love the rose garden.

Sounds very nonsense but the names of these birds are Suchita and Jatin. Their life is flourished with the kind blessings of mother nature. Please, please allow them to live like that. And don't ever let my childish dream to become superficial, worse artificial.

Oh, have I gone crazy ? Possibly yes ! Because I'm not accustomed with such high intensity joy. My goodness, things are exploding everywhere and I can hear loud chants. What are they shouting ? What do they say ?

"Suchita thy name no more is misery, it is gaiety, it is ecstasy."

How true ! How true !

Thanks once again 'O' Mother nature. Thank you very much.

Ten

"Good morning Bhabi."

Suchita opened her eyes with these words. She was almost half-slept, half-awake since morning. An unidentified young man stood in front of her, sporting a huge corner to corner grin. Suchita, still under anaesthetic effect remained largely confused. Immediately she got on to gauge the surrounding. White bed, green curtains? So she must be in a hospital. Reason? Heck, forgotten everything? That bulging tummy. Those nine months. And that unendurable agony culminating in a sweet cry. The cry of an unblemished piece of flesh.

Suchita slightly turned her head and looked at a small bundle of white cloth. A little innocent head popped out of it. She sighed at the sight and momentarily closed her eyes with a great sense of satisfaction.

" I said good morning Bhabi" Same voice spoke again. Same unidentified face with a broad grin lingered on her vision-line.

" I can't recognize you," Suchita murmured.

"You won't. I bet. I'm Captain Sameer Pande."

"Oh, Mr. Sam?" Suchita smiled.

"You got it."

"Hey Sam could she identify you?" A familiar voice came forth from behind the door. It was Jatin.

"Nop. I think they've given her a heavy dose yesterday. Well, let's see if Mr. Mittal junior does it correctly."

"I would be grateful if he recognizes Mittal senior at least. Ha Ha." Said Jatin and both the friends moved closer to the baby.

" You sure it's a boy?" Sam inquired.

"I haven't seen it for myself. Yet you should trust the doctor and nurses."

Both of them lightly touched the baby's cheeks.

"I'm sure it's a boy." Sam declared.

"How come?"

"There is one simple test. They say if he wets your cloths it's a boy. If she wets your cloth its a girl." Suchita couldn't help laughing at that.

"How did you know? Your cloth are n't wet yet." Jatin pointed out.

"That's why I didn't apply this test. I used another one."

"What's that?"

"When we touched its cheeks it frowned. So it must be a boy. Had it been a girl it would have cried."

"Well, that's more logical" Jatin agreed and at once started giggling, " and what do you say about your Bhabi?"

"Oh, what can I say? She's simply gorgeous! You are a lucky fellow Jatin. What big eyes, what fair skin. My goodness! I wonder how she was before this pregnancy."

"Well, well. No flattery please" Suchita commented shyly, her face still wrapped up in a scarf.

"And Suchita, how is my friend Mr. Sam?" Jatin asked.

"Exactly how you used to project him. Smart, lively and outrageously witty."

"Should I say no flattery please? And if Jatin had projected me rightly then may I know why I wasn't identified?"

"That's because I was sleepy. Still I'm so sorry."

"Don't worry. I'm accustomed to these insults. Is it not true Jatin?"

"Well yes. Quite right I mean" Jatin shrugged off.

All three of them broke out into laughter. At that time Suchita was beaming like anything. She looked so cheerful and pleasant. Her newly acquired motherhood had presented her with a powerful glow and as a result her face shined like a full moon. As if arrival of her baby wasn't sufficient, the evergreen Mr. Sam appeared to increase their felicity. Suchita found him extremely entertaining and she developed an instant rapport with him.

"You know Bhabi. I'm very very angry on both of you."

"Say why?"

"I'm the best friend of Jatin. Or that's what I believe. Still I wasn't invited to your marriage. I suppose this amounts for a big treachery."

"Does it?" asked Suchita. "But it would be better if you ask its explanation from your friend."

"He says it was urgent. Actually you were very desperate. Is it true?"

"Yes."

"Why? Jatin couldn't have run away had you waited for some time."

"Basically it's my fault I agree." Suchita didn't know how to explain everything. She wanted to avoid reference of her suicide attempt. So she kept silence.

"I see. I understand," Mr. Sam sensed her difficulty as Jatin had spelled out everything to him. But Suchita couldn't hide her crestfallen face, enshrining her past days.

"Do you know Bhabi? Once there was a snail," Mr. Sam quickly began his damage control exercise. "It was invited by a friend to attend his marriage. And you know what happened? By the time it reached the place it was baptism ceremony of his child. I'm just like that snail. I was supposed to attend the marriage but I'm celebrating childbirth. Anyway! It's not bad at all. But do you know what I would have done had I been that snail's friend?"

Suchita shook her head in negative.

"Well, I would have invited the snail for my engagement!" Said Mr. Sam and Suchita smiled again.

"OK Bhabi. See you in the evening. I've got some important work."

"You are leaving? Where?"

"Ah ! how should I say? Central jail."

"Central jail?" Suchita asked a bit loudly and with a big question mark on her face.

"Yes, I'm always in some jail. Smaller or bigger. Presently I'm in a jail at Pune."

"He means his workplace," Jatin clarified for Suchita.

"And what's Central Jail?"

"That means Army Headquarters Delhi."

"Oh! Nice terminology!" Suchita offered a praise.

"Well thanks. See you then."

Sam stylishly waved his hands and left the room with Jatin.

✣✣✣

Mr. Sam had been in Delhi for more than eight days now. By that time Suchita was back home with her child. Obviously, Mittal household had flaired up itself with ear splitting cries of the baby boy. And incessant chats of Mr. Sam.

"You know Bhabi," Mr. Sam would begin in a typical evening." When we were in NDA we had a great fun. There was one Maj. Chinappa. He used to be our supervisor. And believe me, he had such an awful attitude towards me. Totally prejudiced. If somebody broke a tea cup, it had to be me. If somebody cut the wire fence, it had to be me. I was held responsible for any misdeed occurring in our campus. And despite being very close to me, Jatin was regarded as a very sincere fellow. A future chief of staff! That shows how my bosses were biased towards me. I don't deny my involvement in some incidents. But it doesn't mean that I was there in all cases. Finally it became too much for me. So I decided to teach him a lesson. You know Bhabi what I did?"

" No, I really don't know" Suchita used to inform honestly and chortle.

"One day I broke the window of Maj. Chinappa's room and entered inside at midnight. Then I cut his moustache with scissors. I made him Charlie Chaplin."

Entire house would fill itself with thunderous laughter. Along with Suchita and Jatin, Ma would also join this club. Occasionally Didi would also spare her graceful presence.

"But this move boomranged." Sam used to display a tragic face.

" Oh, what happened?" Ma would ask with great concern.

"Next day Maj. Chinappa made a Charlie Chaplin out of each one of us. As usual Jatin escaped this punishment. This clever chap had no moustache at all. So, for some days our barrack was full of Charlies. Maj. Chinappa didn't remove his moustache and he didn't permit us to remove ours. But after this episode I never bore a moustache."

"And whatever happened to your rivalry? Is Maj. Chinappa still with you?" Didi would ask.

" Ya. He's with me unfortunately. He's a colonel now. As far as our rivalry is concerned, we made a pact after some days."

"What pact?"

"I promised him I wouldn't trouble him any more. In return he has ensured I should always be in trouble."

"How?"

"He made me his son-in-law."

"How come? How come?"

"Actually it was my condition in the deal. But as usual this move also backfired. My wife, the same girl whom I loved so much is a bigger problem than her dad. Believe me, she spies on me. If I throw a glance on any girl, the news reaches her in seconds. That's not enough. She doesn't do anything but partying around. I was a fool to marry with somebody like her."

"Ha Ha. Your story should make a hit comic movie." Suchita would remark.

"It's not comic Bhabi. It's full with tears and agony." Sam's histrionic skills would drive them crazy.

"And why did you choose a career in arm forces?" Some inquisitive lady used to provide him a chance to lecture on a new topic.

"Quite a nice question!" Thus goes Sam's appreciation. "Why did I join Army? I will tell you a story for this. There was a boy in America. He joined US navy because he found the ships so cleaned and polished. After spending many days on a ship he wrote to his mom. Mom I joined navy because the ships looked so clean. Now I know why. He used to clean it day in and day out. I'm like this boy. I joined army because of its grandeur and honour. I don't know whether I got it or not. What I've is Col. Chinappa's daughter."

Sometimes Mr. Sam's train would ride on a track of philosophy.

"Plato has said life is worthless. I believe in same thing. But Plato has got a name for his prophecies. I'm ignored like anything. After all what we expect from others? Some appreciation, some recognition. Now I'm not Captain Jatin Mittal. Some people are very lucky in their lives. They get attention from others even if they don't try for it. Jatin is like Taj Mahal. You have to accept his uniqueness. But I'm no Taj Mahal. Taj Mahal isn't made of bricks. Is it? So what should I do? How should I make myself important? I do a simple thing. I laugh with people. I try to make them happy. I tease them. I make a mockery of everyone including myself. That's why people enjoy my company. Because I try to make the atmosphere lighter. If you don't behave like that you are going to ruin yourself. If there is anything in life, it is this joy that you can always share. Otherwise, as Plato has said, life is worthless."

Sam's philosophy was simple; laughs, laughs and still more laughs. Suchita couldn't believe such a creature exists on earth. A man capable of dismissing greatest worries of life with a carefree remark or two.

"Jatin was like a tortoise," Sam would raise many eyebrows with comments like these, " And I was like a rabbit. I was fast. But

I had this bad habit of sleeping. So I would always lose the race. I never had a patience like Jatin, I must admit."

Suchita's aversion to politics was well known to Jatin. But when Mr. Sam literally bared the politics involved in politics, in his fun-packed narrative she too got preoccupied in the discussions.

"Someone has rightly said," he went, "a good politician is one who predicts the things that are going to take place in future. And later on explains why they couldn't occur. He is a person who tries to construct a bridge when there is no river. In politics there are no friends and there are no foes. If friends are any they are rich. If foes are any they are poor. These people are multicoloured. Like a chamelion. I would say the breed of honest politicians is almost extinct from this land. What do you think Bhabi?"

" Well I don't know much about politics. But I agree with every word you've spoken. It's high time Indian people should rise in revolt."

"Revolt? A bloody coup you should say. Like French Revolution. Hang the bastards."

Mr. Sam goes on making one controversial statement after another.

"Then what remains the fate of the democracy in India?" Jatin thought it essential to intervene. After all, Indian democracy was at stake.

" Democracy is supposed to be people's government my dear friend. Not handful of people's. Americans know it better. Britishers know it better. We are still learning our first lesson."

"You mean overthrow elected government? Army intervention?" asked Suchita.

"I never said so. Just do away with the politicians who are corrupt."

"How?"

"There are many ways."

"Like?"

"Like defeat them in polls."

"Anything else?"

"Police prosecution. Forge police complaints against them."

" Hmm." Clearly Jatin was not impressed. "Is it that simple? What a helpless fellow can do against a powerful leader? One who has got big nexus with big businessmen and big Mafia alike? Do you think Captain Sameer Pande, the bulk of the Indian population is educated enough. Educated enough to identify and segregate the politicians who are bad and defeat them en masse? And how many police officers are competent enough to push the criminal cases against these people to their rightful places? And taking into account the manipulative tactics of the politicians how many people would actually go behind the bars?"

"Don't get so excited Capt. Mittal. There is always an ultimate solution. If you fail on all fronts, just try this one. Get a 0.29 bore pistol and stuff the guy with bullets."

"Nah. It's horrible." Suchita immediately deprecates. Ever since the birth of her child she almost every time registed possibilities of death. Murders, assassinations, slaughters, genocides, butchery, homicides, massacres and killings are strict 'no'. Suchita repelled these words as if foul matter. When nature has so many ways of terminating life, why find new ones? She had reasonable reasons to buttress her viewpoint.

Mr. Sam senses a flickering opportunity to divert his gossips to a new subject 'Death'. But this move is stiffly resisted by Suchita and the young man abandons his plan. The earlier argument too goes unnoticed.

Although Suchita's mind deleted large chunk of her political parley with Mr. Sam, she vividly recollected two definitions given by him. The first one was of Home Minister who as per Mr. Sam, is Home Minister only when out of home. The second one throws light on Defense Minister.

"A Defense Minister," Sam told Suchita, "is one who has elaborate plans to defend the country from the most dangerous foe. But he is clueless when it comes to saving his skin from his mother-in-law."

Eventually Mr. Sam wound up his stay. He came like a vortex of energy and left everyone in a whirlwind of laughter. His approach looked impractical and indeed very exaggerated in many cases. But he had a raw charm that riveted almost everyone to his unstoppable tittle-tattle. After their marriage Suchita had come across many of Jatin's friends and associates. But nobody except Mr. Sam could garner a stamp of instant acceptance from her. They had their wavelengths perfectly matching. Therefore, long after Mr. Sam had gone his memories assiduously lingered. Some people when they come close to you, give a new perspective to your outlook. You get new glasses through which to see the world, new ways to adhere to and new thoughts to give a thought. In a way, it's possible to identify a philosopher no less learned than a Socrates or Aristotle in every person you meet, provided you have the willingness to do so. The most important thing that Suchita could extract from Mr. Sam was the simple fact. "Laughter is always better than tears." It's a boon, generously showered by the creator on mankind. All animals can weep but hardly anyone besides man can laugh. What a day it would be when this animal learns to use this potential to maximum.

✣✣✣

The busiest entity in the universe is time. You simply can't impede it. Time just moves on. Without giving a shit to the hurly-burly of human life. Time machine rolls on without jostling over new births, without mourning unpreventable deaths. In India summer is followed by rainy days when conventionally it should rain cats and dogs. Sometimes it rains neither cats nor dogs. They call it a draught when life comes to a naught. But good old time never stops. Winter precedes rainy days when temperature takes a nosedive. But time never freezes. It remains undeterred like a saint. Then comes summer. Even with its brute heating capacity it cannot vapourise time. The old man that time is never dies. He is immortal. He is like a wheel with different seasons as its spokes. And this wheel advances limitlessly.

Quietly Nil came into the life of Mittals and took over their hearts. The initially bound to bed baby slowly learned to creep and then stood on its own. Ran frenziedly here and there, tiring not himself but his mother. Chattered a few honeyed words. And chewed whatever his tiny hands could reach for. Tore the newspapers and broke the glasses. Threw the articles everywhere. Ate only biscuits and chocolates and refused everything else. Then smiled and laughed and danced. Fell down and got up. And cried. Cuddled up his mom. And having soothed by her blew kisses on her. The sweetest ones on earth!

It was hard to perceive how two years went by. Like a shooting star these times disappeared into the vast ocean of history.

One evening Jatin returned home, beaming like a sunbeam. As usual Suchita, waiting for him on the stairs, threw a vivacious glance on him and smiled. Before Jatin could park the motorbike, she stood up with an explicit intention to go inside.

" What's the hurry ma'm. Let me come." Jatin signalled her to stop. Amused, Suchita loitered in the door. He then quickly took out a big polyethene bag from the dickey and moved. Spreading one arm over Suchita's shoulder Jatin escorted her inside.

"What's the matter Captain Saab?" Suchita teased him. "Feeling very great?"

"Of course. Of course. I always feel great. Today I'm feeling great great."

"And what's that?"

"Great great ! Like great great grandpa."

" Oh. So, you are feeling doubly great. Say why?"

"I won't tell you so early. Where's Nil?"

"He's playing with Ma."

"I see. Anyway I've a very good news for you."

"I know. It's quite obvious."

"Guess what?"

"Let me see if I make it." Suchita thought for a while. " My husband is no more a Captain. He's a Major. Am I right?"

"Yess you got it" Jatin leaped in air like a kid and struck his right fist against left palm.

"I'm now a Major. Major Jatin Mittal." He told an ecstatic Suchita.

Then all of a sudden Suchita found herself lifted from the ground. She missed a heartbeat as Jatin held her in his arms at least three feet above the floor.

"Jatin, don't do it. Keep me back, somebody will come."

"I don't care. This is my house." Declared Jatin. And abruptly he came back to normal tone as Suchita gazed closely at his uniform.

"I'm so happy," Jatin mused.

"Me too." Suchita joined him. For next few second they became pensive. Suchita softly touched the coloured bands on Jatin's chest and gently caressed his uniform. She looked so proud. Involuntarily Jatin grabbed her drifting hands.

"Lt. Col. was the highest rank held by my father." Jatin said in a moving voice. " Once I match it I would die peacefully."

At that Suchita forcefully jammed her hand on to his lips.

"If you say anything like that in future, I won't talk to you."

"Agreed."

"And will you please put me down Maj. Mittal?" Suchita pinched his nose.

This time Jatin obliged. He slowly lowered her body until she safely touched the floor, her hand tightly in his palms.

"Do you mind if I hold your hand like this ma'm?"

"Nop. It's yours anyway. I never mind if you pick me up forever. But if somebody comes in, he certainly will."

" OK. Forget about it. But it's customary to celebrate good news with sweets. Don't you think?" Jatin said suggestively.

"There is no doubt. Let's go out and purchase plenty of sweets."

"I'm not talking about those sweets. I've brought them with me. I mean real sweets."

Suchita understood the latent meaning, protested emphatically, and finally acceded.

✣✣✣

That night the Mittals commemorated in a manner that was nothing less than grand. Firstly they went to a cinema theatre and enjoyed a James Bond movie. Jatin pleaded so vigorously that Ma also joined them at the show. It's another thing that she didn't quite like it. Nevertheless the motion picture went down well with Jatin and Nil.

"So far so good." Suchita opined.

Then to the dinner.

"Continental, Chinese or Indian?" Jatin asked with a menu card in his hands.

"I'd prefer Indian food. Nothing's like that." Suchita retorted.

They dined on Indian dishes. Jatin couldn't take exception. Deep in the heart he was one henpecked husband. However Suchita didn't consciously worked towards this end. But it was Suchita's bewitching charm that always forced him to accept her decisions. And Jatin joyfully valued her wishes.

Throughout the movie and the dinner Suchita taunted and ridiculed and derided her husband on whatever he did. She was so gratified. Finally there was a person whom she treasured more than her life. His thumping progress and his foray into elite class thrilled her greatly, as he was nobody else but herself. Her soul. Her other half. She strongly believed and advocated the theory that marriages are fixed in heavens. A single spirit is broken into two. One is given a male form and the other a female form. Then they are sent down to earth where they randomly search for one another before getting bonded in a marital reunion. Thus every accomplishment of Jatin was in fact, Suchita's achievement. His every victory was Suchita's triumph. So it wasn't Jatin alone who was promoted to the rank of Major, Suchita Mittal was also party to it. And hence she rejoiced like never before.

This was a new Suchita for Jatin. Buoyant, relishing and still very mature. Enjoying every bit of life. The celebrations in her life could be counted on fingers. But now she was able to transform his whole life into a glorious celebration.

✣✣✣

Jatin never had a doubt on the smashing elegance of his wife. But today he felt as if his heart would stop pumping blood at the murderous grace that was Suchita. The occasion was special. In the honour of the army-men who climbed one step up the ladder of the Army hierarchy some enthusiasts arranged a party. Suchita, too coy to attend public ceremonies, declined to join her husband for the bash. But Jatin insisted and she couldn't say 'no' anymore. With this green signal Suchita broke her tradition to shun gatherings. Children could have made a mess of the function, a thing hated by disciplined army-men. So it was suggested to keep off children from the party. Rightly then, Nil was sent to Ma and put to sleep. As evening approached Jatin cleaned his motorbike, immediately got ready himself, and waited for Suchita. Well she took her own time and after a prolong delay appeared before Jatin, who was engrossed in reading a newspaper.

There she was, in front of him, at a few yards away, bright and starry, utter epitome of beauty. It could have been a Herculean exercise arresting the sight in frivolous trap of words. Suchita defied every logic and every limit when it came to the display of physical assets.

Instead of tying the hair in tails or keeping them free altogether, she had bounded them together with a single fancy bow as advised by Ma. That's why they formed a curvaceous bend before leisurely sweeping her back. Naturally, on the head the hair rested tightly while they flew at will on the back. The tall 5'6" frame fitted nicely in a stunning sky blue saree that Jatin had presented her on their third wedding anniversary. The glittering chiffon, however faded pathetically in the neighbourhood of her skin. Her skin was all cream! The greatest surface nature could create in its capacity. It could reflect light like a milky white snow. It's texture, its softness, its radiance and irresistible enchanting power might as well secure its position in the greatest wonders of earth. Enveloping in its folds her great symbols of femininity was her half sleeved and frilled blouse with superb hexagonal neckline in the front and a semicircular one at the back. Bright, silvery design imparted a royal look to the garment. An amazingly brilliant ruby socketed in a gold chain adored her chest. A matching sky blue dot filled the gap between her eyebrows.

Jatin observed her in awe as if his sight was bolted to her face, the vertically oval piece of ivory. Eyes deep dark as ocean, encompassing hundred mysteries within. Extraordinarily large for this dimension of face. Arches of thin eyebrows perching from above. Delicate projection of nose sloping uniformly and culminating into a sharp point. Moderately thick and luscious, juicy lips required no application of artificial colour. A crimson red tinge always marked its presence. The smooth curve of chin shown a slight depression at the tip. The entire face wore a stainless sheet of flesh, no erratic outgrowths, no unwanted indentations. A slender neck held the head above torso. Her fragile build stood offset by wide shoulders. Moving down further, her body converged towards the waist with minimal flesh. Then expanded below it like mermaid's bottom. Her slim arms terminated into long, tapering fingers.

Jatin stuck to where he was, as if nailed down to the chair. Surely he wasn't watching this lady for the first time. Still there was something awfully intoxicating about her. A sorcerer's magic? A witch's spell?

"Hey, mister, what happened?" Finally Suchita asked herself. "Aren't we going to the party?" she hung her purse to her right shoulder.

"Am...... oh yeah! Sure, sure."

"Then? What are you waiting for?"

"Nothing I suppose. You are looking very great."

"Oh thank you" she shyly looked down.

"I mean you always look great. But today there is something different. What've you done to your face?"

Suchita frowned. "Nothing. What makes you think like that?"

"Well I've not seen you like this before. This much good looking I mean."

"Now please stop it and let's go."

"I swear! You've to tell me your secret."

Now Suchita got annoyed.

"The secret is this my dear. My only hubby has become a major in Indian army. That may have affected my body too."

"Really?" Jatin asked unbelievably " And how has it affected me?"

"You are a born general Jatin. This simple elevation won't affect you much. Still I think your eyesight has changed. Now the world has become more beautiful to you."

"You are right Suchita. Probably we've both changed for good."

Jatin got the answer finally. The rise of husband's stature definitely affects wives. This law worked quite well for their case.

As they cruised along on the motorbike now it was Suchita's turn to ponder over Jatin. He had not undergone revolutionary metamorphosis. There wasn't much difference between today's Jatin and yesterday's. And Suchita always fantasized him in army uniforms only. A towering frame, slightly below 6'. Fair colour, imposing build. Nicely and in his own words 'forcibly' cut small hair. Brownish gray eyes not so large as Suchita's. Stout forehead and thick eyebrows. Slightly pentagonal face with a cleavaged chin. Somewhat bigger but shapely nose and sufficiently pronounced lips. A forever clean-shaven face. Suchita could identify him even with her eyes shut. That's due to the fragrance of his after-shave lotion that blended perfectly with his deodorants and body odour. What Suchita liked most about Jatin were his handsome looks which when coupled with his tall, muscular body produced an astounding result. Something like a Hollywood action hero, strikingly macho.

Lot many army heavy weights turned up for the party along with the rank and file of Indian Army. The lengthy list included chief's of different commands besides the all important chief of staff himself. Most men were accompanied by their better halves. And the programme truly came alive by the impeccable presence of these highly educated, modern women most of whom were staggeringly voluptuous.

When Jatin and Suchita arrived the mood was already upbeat. A big section of the crowd contained men and women with various kinds of masks shielding their faces. Many of them rushed to Jatin and encircled the couple, screaming and clapping. Suchita tamed by this sudden hullabaloo clung to Jatin who looked very confused but thoroughly entertained. One particular chap came too close to Jatin, pulled him by arm and forced him to dance. Music, dance, laughter and drinks completely stimulated the atmosphere. Suchita however, made friends with like-minded ladies and retreated to a corner. Anxiously, she kept a watch on Jatin. That peculiar masked fellow haunted him everywhere, she couldn't guess why.

The party began to flow with games and dances and climaxed with dinner. Meanwhile the people in whose honour the party was organized were felicitated. These fortunate men then posed for the photographs with wives. Ultimately a joint snap was shot after which the place errupted in wild clapping and noisy cheer ups.

"Children couldn't have made a better mess," Suchita whispered sarcastically. Jatin asked her to keep the mouth shut.

Already irked by this lively show Suchita almost got agitated over the masked fellow who chased them throughout the party. Finally on her insistence Jatin requested him to uncover his face. He merrily did! And surprise, surprise he was none other than Mr. Sam. For a few seconds Jatin and Suchita stood dumbfounded. As one loyal friend Mr. Sam had kept Jatin's company by himself achieving the badge of Major. There wasn't any communication between these two friends as Jatin found himself too busy with celebrations to contact him. While Mr. Sam deliberately kept his promotion a secret. In the party too, Sam made a complete fool of Jatin, as he couldn't recognize him till end, even while Sam was accepting a bouquet in his honour as his name that was being announced, languished in the deanfening noice of the crowd. Mr. Sam bowled over Jatin and Suchita on yet another time when he introduced them with his lovely wife Naha, fondly called "Mrs. Sam." That pleased them greatly.

In the end when all of them sat together at home, Suchita poked her forefinger in her ears, tightly sealing her eyes and clenching her teeth as Mr. Sam ebulliently went on,

"You know Bhabi..............."

✣✣✣

Eleven

Dr. Khatri is a big name in medical circles, that's for sure. His grand therapeutic accomplishments and surgical feats earned him a great name and helped his reputation grow as a wildfire. With popular appeal automatically come momentary benefits and riches. All his wealth is aptly on display at his plush three-storey hospital at Karol Bagh, may it be palatial design of the building or lavish use of granite. A gold medallist surgeon from Cambridge University, Dr. Khatri leaves no stone unturned when it comes to treating patients. He has equipped his hospital with the state of the art machinery, latest surgical equipment and a team of brilliant young doctors. Naturally his hospital overflows like a packed theatre. With the aid of his marvellous gadgets and alert subordinates this man can execute miracles. No wonder the most complicated case in the capital lands in his hospital.

When Ma suffered a massive heart attack, the conclusive choice for Jatin was Dr. Khatri. He wanted to repair whatever wreckage had been done to Ma's heart because of the attack. He thought it substantive in order to evade any further complications. And the old lady who bragged to have a doctor son was admitted to Khatri hospital.

Last Tuesday was a fateful day for Ma. As she prepared to resign for an afternoon nap a telegram arrived. Curious, Suchita rushed to her to share the news. Well it turned out to be a grief stricken affair. Ma's five-year-old grandson living in Chandigarh had developed a tumor in the brain and succumbed to brain haemorrhage. Such a sudden demise of this child gave a solid impact to Ma. It was a shock that couldn't be assimilated especially because her daughter and son-in-law had kept her in dark about the child's malady. With the telegram still in hands Ma's body pump gave in. It was only with the assistance of the postman that Suchita could sprint for medical help and sought immediate contact with Jatin. Jatin in his turn intercepted them in the middle of the route and directed them to Dr. Khatri.

It was her seventh day at the hospital and the doctor had agreed to discharge the patient. Finishing a hectic day at work Jatin made his way to the clinic. After parking the vehicle he almost ran towards room no.18, that's where Ma had been accommodated, room no.18, second floor. In last seven days Jatin had become so habituated with the surrounding that he needed no reference to locate the room. His legs automatically propelled him.

The door was barely left opened.

"Suchita must be in," he thought, "she had promised she would also come."

Without actually intruding in to the room he just pushed his head through the opening and asked.

"Please may I come in?"

Suchita looked back, hearing the familiar voice while Ma sat resting against a pillow with a doughy smile. But no one reacted as promptly and sharply as Nil. He vaulted out of Suchita's lap and raced towards Jatin bellowing 'Daddy'.

"Yeah, my little Captain," in a slick movement Jatin grasped Nil, kissed his cheeks and hurled him in air. The next moment Jatin was sitting on the bed, beside Ma and Nil clung to his back.

"Well, ready to go?" Jatin asked Ma and twinkled his eyes.

"I guess."

"Still not sure? If you want you may rest for few more days."

"Good lord! Why to engage a bed when doctor allows you to go home?"

"Ha ! Ha ! I was just kidding. Well what do you say Suchita, My dear ol' wife?"

"I agree with Ma, Jatin my dear ol' husband."

Suchita rejoined and they all broke into laughter.

"OK, before any doctor or nurse shows up, let's get out of here." Jatin commanded as if playing an army officer heading a cavalry at the front.

Suchita assisted Ma to get up on her feet. With her help the old lady languidly descended the stairs. She walked so sluggishly, Jatin caught up with them even after concluding the formalities at the hospital office.

"Any order Captain?" Jatin asked Nil as the boy sat on the frontseat of the bike slightly speculating over something.

"Well officer, the female regiment should catch a taxi."

"And what about the male regiment, Sir?"

"Ahm. Well bike is not bad for them."

"All right."

Soon Suchita and Ma headed for their house in a taxi. The male regiment however looked at ease on the motor bike. As soon as they were on their way Nil, sitting in front of his dad grew restless.

"Anything the matter Captain?" asked Jatin.

"Well, officer, You had promised me something in the morning. Remember?"

"Oh yeah. You had demanded one AK-47 for you."

"Has the gun been delivered yet?"

"Well to tell you the truth Sir, it's in the dicky."

Nil turned his face and gazed at Jatin with sheer joy.

"I want it now. I got to kill some real terrible guys."

"No, not here."

"Please my dearest Daddy."

"When I said no, it only means NO. Understand?"

Disappointingly Nil turned his face. Anger showed on his face as the child repeatedly struck his hands on the metallic handle of the vehicle. When he finally realized the futility of the act he stopped doing so.

"Have you told Ma about your birthday?" Jatin asked.

Nil didn't answer.

"Nil, do you want me to hand over the gun to you, of course when we go home?"

"Yes," he replied curtly.

'Then tell me what I asked."

"I've not told anything to Ma. Mom had objected to it."

"Good. You are a nice boy."

"But Daddy why should we keep it a secret?"

"Because we want to give her a surprise."

"Oh!" Nil agreed to the point.

"Nil. How old are you today?"

"Three. Just three."

"That means you've grown up."

"No, I've not grown up. I can't drive a bike like you."

"Agreed. But you are older than what you were on last birthday. How old were you on last birthday?"

"Two. Because before three it's two."

"That's right. So you are three years old. Now you will go to school after some days. There you will learn many good things."

"So what?"

"So you have to start learning some good things immediately. I don't mind you playing with toys. But at the same time you should learn counting, you should learn new words."

"Yeah. I know counting up to 10. And I know new words too. 'AK-47' isn't it a new word?"

"You naughty! It is just a name of the gun. There are so many words that you don't know, learn them from your mom."

"Ok agreed. But not now. Today I'll play with my AK-47."

"Hmm." Jatin sighed.

✣✣✣

Virtually dragging her by shoulders Suchita and Jatin helped Ma sit on a bed. The old lady almost collapsed on the Divan as if she were a crumpled page of an old book. She looked hopelessly pallid. After many days a Punjabi suit formed Ma's attire. Despite being a die hard Punjabi, she found herself comfortable in sarees and she had been using them extensively. However, in these troubled days at hospital she preferred convenient Punjabi apparel to cumbersome sarees. Her silky white hair, fair skin and white suit stood in sharp contrast with dark shadows encircling her eyes.

"Your medicines Ma," Suchita appeared carrying a mouthful of drugs.

Ma smiled feebly. And after a long long time.

Suchita fed her the tablets, one by one, helping her swallow them with water, smoothly massaging at her back. When it was done, Suchita turned to go back.

"Suchita," Ma tried to pull her with hands.

" Yes Ma."

"Would you please sit here for a while?"

"Amm why not? What's the problem? Aren't you OK?"

"Perfectly. I just want to talk to you."

"Well no problem," Suchita shrugged and sat beside Ma.

"Suchita you looked so tired. I know you didn't get enough sleep. You were there with me for all the seven nights.'

"Big deal" Jatin spoke from somewhere, clearly to tease Suchita.

"I wanted to call my daughter..." Here she started coughing. Again Suchita rubbed her back.

"I'm OK. Well, Jatin said it would be too much for her if we let her know about my health problems. She is already suffering from her child's loss."

"I know. Why are you telling it to me now?" Suchita asked.

"I feel concerned about you. You've suffered a lot because of me."

"Ma' please..."

"I had asked Jatin to call my son-in-law, but I don't know why he went back so quickly. Yes Jatin, why did he leave early?"

Jatin who was neck deep into newspaper was all ears.

" I myself asked him to go back."

"Why?"

"Because when a son and a daughter-in-law are so close, there's no need for any son-in-law to care even slightly."

Ma couldn't think anything to say of. Suchita looked at her triumphantly. Jatin had made the point an awful lot clear. Without giving Ma any chance to protest Jatin went ahead.

"Finished thanksgiving? I know Mrs. Sareen, now you are going to go to your piggy bank and say look Jatin this is your money. You have spent a lot of bucks on me. And if you are really going to do it Ma just forget about it. The last thing I'm going to do is to accept money from you. No way. Sorry. If at all you want me to accept anything from you, there is a big package with me, that is to be handed over to you. Just count. A huge amount of love you spent on me before and after my marriage. Again there is lot of love spent on Suchita and Nil separately. In addition you found a life partner for me in Suchita. And when she was pregnant you were with her day in and day out. You've suffered heavy losses in terms of time, sleep and money on countless occasions like this. For me, for Suchita, and for Nil. There wasn't a single illness in this house that didn't bother you, that didn't need your power to cure. Have you ever imagined, how many hours you've spent for putting Nil to bed? Or how much time you spent playing with him? Or cooking food for me when I was a bachelor? If I convert this debt into money the figure would run into millions. And if you ask me to pay it I would be bankrupt in no time. If you try to return back whatever small amount I've spent on you, it will only show how far we are from each other despite being so close physically. Ma, you know myself and Suchita were not blessed enough to have a mother. Before you came, we missed her badly. And when you came, I thought finally I've got one right here with me. Look at this girl, Suchita. Throughout her life she had come across more bad people than good. But finally she thought she had some really wonderful companion. An elderly lady, so loving and so kind. Don't you remember how badly she depended on you in initial days? She sought help from you in every difficulty she faced. You have guided her to raise this small, beautiful cottage of our love. You taught her everything from cooking to bringing up a child. You taught her to be able mother, able wife and able woman. You've given her a new lease of life. How come you deny her humble service to you when you badly needed someone like her. It is just beyond my understanding."

Tears showed brightly in Ma's eyes. Actually she had not mentioned anything about returning money and clearing account with Jatin etc. But she was going to raise this issue sometime in near future. Jatin, however rightly anticipated Ma's move and made his stance intelligible. He knew very well the ins and outs of her nature. So, before she could say anything about it, he delivered this lengthy lecture. In doing so, nonetheless Jatin forgot many things. That Ma was recovering from a heart attack, that she was suffering from her grandson's death, that emotionally she was very very fickle.

"Please stop it! Please don't derive any untoward conclusion out of my behaviour......"

She coughed badly. Suchita astonished by such a backlash from Ma surged ahead to provide support. There ensued a long interval during which Ma coughed very menacingly. Almost four five minutes went past as Suchita and Jatin tried to help her rest suitably. Eventually the old lady managed to soothe herself. Due to excessive coughing water rushed from her eyes and under its influence some silky white hair stuck to her cheeks. Suchita rubbed her face with a towel to make it dry. Soon Ma retrieved back her normal state.

"I don't want to stretch the matter too far." She said in a husky voice. " Still I want to make my stand clear. See what's happening in this house, it happens everywhere where two generations operate face to face. I'm one old person, my one leg is already in grave. So, I'm beyond this money matter. My only needs are food, cloth, shelter and emotional support. Money never figures in my thoughts at all. So whatever excess I have, I spend it on my dear ones. Then why should you refuse accepting money from me? Why do you deny a thing that gives me satisfaction? Aren't you mistaken when you call it a thing separating us, although it is in fact a representation of our closeness? What do you say Suchita?"

"I think, I should keep off from this argument. Let both of you come to an agreement." She giggled.

"No, I'm asking your opinion as a neutral party."

"In that case I would say both sides are quite right."

Suchita played a diplomat. Ma and Jatin couldn't help laughing at that and tense situation rapidly plummeted.

"You certainly deserve to work as UN mediator," Jatin commented. " You would agree with both sides and ask them to fight with each other."

"But in our case Jatin," said Ma, "her opinion is correct."

"That's right Ma." Jatin agreed.

"So what's decided?" asked Suchita.

"It will be sorted out in near future. We'll stop for a while." Said Ma and Jatin nodded.

By that time Nil was in their vicinity with his voluminous AK-47. He came charging in directly on his parents.

"Hands up. You are surrounded," he screamed. "You move a bit and you are dead."

"That's not how you behave with mom and dad, dear. And what is that? A new toy?" Asked Ma.

"It's not a toy. It's a gun."

"Oh goodness! A new military fatigue too?" Ma stretched her eyebrows in amazement.

"Ha Ha. This is Nil, Captain Nil," He executed a classy salute.

"But what for all this? Anything special?' asked Ma as Jatin and Suchita just stood smiling.

"Mom when will we eat all those sweets. I know our fridge is full with them." Nil went on.

"Sweets are also there? What's the occasion after all Suchita?" Ma was dying to know the worst kept secret.

"Don't tell her." Nil intervened, "and don't give her any sweets. Or else I'll shoot you," he ordered.

"Why so abhor for this old woman? Why shouldn't I eat sweets?" Ma inquired deploringly.

"Because," Nil said, "Mom says doctor uncle didn't permit you to eat sweets. That's why."

"Oh" Ma gulped. She still looked befuddled." Jatin, are you at least going to tell me what's special today?"

"Well Ma" He came forward. "There are two causes for this celebration. One our Captain Nil is turning three today."

"Really? My god! I had completely forgotten."

"Yes it's his birthday. The other reason is this grandma has come back home after seven days."

"I see," Ma's face glowed like gold coins, "but no balloons, no decoration, no children, no cakes? Even the house looks a bit untidy. Why?"

"That's because Captain Nil's mother was busy. You know his grandma was admitted to hospital." Jatin spoke in a playful tone.

"Oh dear ! He should really shoot his grandma"

"And Nil had promised his mom, there wouldn't be any celebration until she returned back."

Ma couldn't but be flabbergasted. She felt remorseful.

"What's a birthday of a kid without kids?" She asked."Now I'm back. We can still have a birthday party."

"But it's 7.30 already Ma" Suchita informed nervously.

"Let it be Suchita," Ma's dynamism stood reinstated.

Consequently there was a huge merrymaking at night. Ma spent thousands of rupees for celebration, for toys and snacks and lighting. Jatin dared not utter a single word against it.

Time runs so fast when everything looks normal. When life is at its best. When this journey is meaningful and enjoyable genial. When the path is bed of roses. When companions are loving and trustworthy. When atmosphere is placid, warm. When sky is limpid and wind is gentle breezy When laughter is in air and contentment is at heart. When rapturous youthfulness sweeps across the land. When sweet aroma rules the world. When affection is the language, when faith is the anthem. When values are cherished and dignity respected. When love is loved and hate is hated. When charity is admired, scornfulness loathed. When forgiveness is human and mankind divine.

The time clock doesn't like such a world. When this order takes its shape the time clock as if governed by Satan, runs madly. And then suddenly tremendous change is brought about. Black clouds cover the sky and serenity of the atmosphere is blown away. Gentle breeze becomes a hurricane. The path is cleared of roses, replenished by dry, unemotional thorns. Laughter gives way to tears and satisfaction to anxiety. The land falls prey to unending darkness.. Thinking about the world gives rise to nausea. 'Hate' becomes the prime word, treachery snatches the rein. Values are bundled and shown dustbins. Saints are hanged and rapists are adored. Love goes extinct and charity remains in religious books. Forgiveness is forgotten and divinity diminishes.

Oh, why does the time run so fast?

Yesterday it all looked so fabulous, today it seems as if the earth is cracked below my feet.

This is how Suchita thought when Jatin gave a startling news to her. As usual he returned home from office in the evening and looked so charged up when he took his wash, singing and whistling merrily. Then he played with Nil as Suchita started preparing some snacks. Some moments later Jatin sent his child to Ma and he himself went to kitchen where Suchita battled against heat and suffocation even as the exhaust fan tried to provide some solace.

"Where's Nil?" She asked.

"I've sent him to Ma."

"Why? I wanted to give him food. He was so hungry."

"Well he can have anything at Ma's house. I've sent him there because I've an urgent work with you."

Suchita stopped for a while, smiled and said, " I know your urgent work. But I'm too busy for that. And just look at me. Don't you think I should take a bath?"

"No fooling around please. I've a really important work and I need your appointment Ma'm."

"OK. Let me finish this. I'm just coming. Please wait for sometime."

Jatin rushed to the front room and Suchita followed him in few minutes. She stared at him teasingly. For the first time in their long association Jatin seemed to be grave serious. Suchita smiled at him in order to cheer him up as she settled beside him.

"Suchita how much shock can you absorb?"

Suchita watched him blankly at that, totally puzzled.

"I couldn't follow you." She admitted flatly.

"Even if it's not true, if I say I'm going to die soon. How would you react?"

Smile faded from Suchita's face.

"Why to consider any case when it is not actually happening. And please don't ask me anything like that."

"Suchita you have to answer my query. Only for once. What'll happen if I say I'm going to die?"

"I'll die at the same instant. Before you could die in front of me."

"Hmm. And what would you say if I tell you that I'm not sure to die but I may die?"

"Jatin what's this going on?" she asked irritatingly, " I will die, I may die. Will you please stop this for heaven's sake."

Suchita tried to rise up and go away. Jatin immediately grabbed her right hand. She knew at that instant, there was something terribly wrong with them. She looked back, her dark eyes puncturing into Jatin's. Her heartbeats racing to exponential speed.

"Don't shy away from the inevitable," Jatin spoke in a hoarse tone.

Suchita mutely obeyed his wish.

"Say you won't hesitate to accept anything good or bad. Because you are party to every joy and sorrow and every hardship that comes with my life. Remember you are my wife, my half soul. Would you be reluctant to accept anything?"

"No I won't." Came a sterner reply.

Jatin lightly touched Suchita's hands and caressed. She closed her eyes, feeling the warmth of the flesh. She expected some harsh words to explode. But surprisingly nothing seemed to happen. Finally Suchita opened her eyes and gazed at Jatin. He was there with his head dropped down. And then all of a suddenly he broke into a roaring laughter. Suchita couldn't make anything out of it.

"Oh my god!" Jatin couldn't control his laugh, "I've, I've never been so weak. Just think of it. The son of a war hero. Believe me, I couldn't have taken so much time to march into enemy camp. And I'm afraid of breaking a simple news. In fact a very good news."

"What is that? Suchita asked, now completely relieved.

"They have selected me for the IPKF."

" You mean the Indian Peacekeeping Force? Same thing, you were talking about?"

"Yes, yes. Before that there will be a training session for three months.'

"And then?"

"And then? Off to Sri Lanka!"

"For how much time?"

"Don't know."

Some tense moments of silence followed.

"You mean it would be forever?" An innocent question was fired.

"Silly girl! It will be until normalcy returns to Sri Lanka."

"What if it doesn't?"

"Well then we'll shift our house to Sri Lanka."

"Please I'm talking honestly."

"Normalcy will definitely return to Sri Lanka. We are going there to establish order."

"Is it a risky affair?"

"No, not so risky as one may think."

"Then how much risky?"

"Do I need to quantify everything?" Jatin asked annoyingly and rapidly calmed down. He judged the situation was volatile. "Life itself is a big risk my dear," Jatin said in a softer tone. "And its uncertainties are truly glorious. One more thing, if parting is painful, reunion is unbearably pleasant. I promise you Suchita, I'll come back after three months, not a single day more. But by that time you should prepare yourself for a bigger separation. May be one year. May be not. May be only six months. Only god knows. There is ample time to groom yourself for it. There is enough time to judge its implications, its repercussions.'

Suchita's vision glued to his face, her eyes moistened, her hands throbbing.

"Do you remember Suchita? All the promises we made before marriage? All the beautiful dreams we saw? All the lovely days we imagined? We swore by each other to keep going together, through light and darkness. Through heavens and hell. Through fire and water. Through joys and sorrows. I asked you to share my life and you said yes. I told you, I can take on any challenge if you hold my hand and you agreed. You promised to accompany me in days and nights alike. I made you an apple of my eye, a force that driven me in every walk of life. I know the bond between us is very strong. So strong nothing can break it. Even the god himself. Then what's the worry? Do you think our love is not capable of sustaining these blows? When you said you'll cope with every adversity with me, did you actually mean you'll fumble at any point?"

"No." Suchita's voice arose out of a choked throat. A minor provocation now, could give rise to a flood of tears.

Jatin pulled her towards him, her head finally seeking shelter of his chest. Bodily contact rapidly paved way for uncontrolled emotions. Salt water eagerly sought exit via her dark eyes. Jatin's comforting hands gently wandered all over her back.

"Suchita, won't you agree with me if I say that this phase is temporary?"

Suchita shook her head.

"Then may I assume, you would stand firm?"

Same reaction followed. For next few moments both of them didn't say anything. Suchita sniffed at times while Jatin fondled her hair. Suchita managed to overcome the original shock with the reassuring touch of Jatin.

"When are you leaving?" She asked.

" On day after tomorrow."

"Where?"

"Dehradun."

"Please contact me from time to time."

"I would telephone to you everyday, OK? And I'd write to you twice in a day."

"No need to show that much courtesy." Suchita mocked at him.

"Then how else shall I inform you about what thing I'm eating for breakfast? And at lunch and dinner? And which soap I use? And when do we sleep and... say... who shouts at me day in and day out? And what heavy work we do? And where do we go? And when is our holiday? And whom do we meet? Civilians I mean. And how many of them are girls? And who is the most ravishing among them? And..."

"Amm." Suchita beat her fists at Jatin's chest and together they broke out in a heavy laughter, eventually melting into a deep embrace.

Twelve

"Any word from Jatin ?" Ma inquired, as if customary.

"No, he hasn't written yet. I don't know why." As usual Suchita replied woefully.

"He'll write. Definitely. He won't forget you dear. You take it from me."

"How much time does it take ? He can't spare a few minutes for me ?"

"Suchita don't lose heart."

"I can't even contact him by phone. That's the whole trouble."

"He must be really busy." Ma tried to defend Jatin.

"I don't know. How should we know ? There must be some correspondence."

"OK, OK. Calm down. Now you are getting upset. That's not good."

Suchita looked dismal. She gave a disappointing jerk to her neck and heavily sighed. Then slightly lowered her face. She seemed so worried; Ma had no idea how to brighten her up.

"Believe me Suchita he'll send a message."

"When ?"

"Very soon."

"How do you know ?"

"My heart says so."

"My heart doesn't speak anything ?" By this time Suchita had amassed a huge bulk of tears. Before they could burst out has gone she had already found a hideout in Ma's arms.

"Silly girl," Ma swept her hands over Suchita. " I know it's almost one month since he has gone. But still he's on duty. Let's give him a chance. May be another month. That would be fair."

Suchita kept mum.

Ma too, didn't know what to say. It had almost become everyday's practice. Same troubled questions and same comforting words. One thing was sure, it wasn't going to continue for long.

Even Ma started suspecting wrong things. Still she had to remain a picture of strength, a mighty force to reckon with. She knew if the pillars crumble, walls can't survive. If a gigantic tree collapses there is no scope for the creepers dwelling in its shelter, to breathe normally. That's why Ma always stood there, spreading warm happiness and pointing towards a distant ray of hope. She would plant a seed of faith in Suchita's mind. A faith for goodness. A faith for Almighty. A faith for whatever is divine in this universe. She insisted and indeed very confidently believed, all was going to be well. For, it was just a test of their resilience. And if they gracefully overcome this period, there stood a benevolent time ahead. A time of fulfillment of dreams, a time of drastic tranquillity and thriving rosebuds. For that they had to wait patiently with steel will and uncompromising courage.

"Mom let's go to a movie," Suchita almost lost her balance with this unexpected loud voice. It couldn't be anybody but Nil. He approached his mom jumping like a monkey. Obviously the kid was very glad.

"Why movie ? And why now ?" Ma asked.

"That's because a very nice movie is running these days."

" No movie. Nothing doing," Suchita announced.

"Please mom. Rahul has seen it yesterday. He says it's so good. There are tigers, elephants, and rabbits. It's fun mom."

"So what ?"

"Today Minu, Nitu all are going. Monty also."

" I said no. Can't you hear that ?" Suchita's wrath erupted. "Just take out your books and start reading."

Ma was shocked to see Suchita so much infuriated. In fact she had increased her voice to this level, for the first time. This chiding produced the most expected result. Nil started crying loudly as Ma nabbed him in arms. Suchita gyrated her face entirely away from Nil, burning like a hot coal. Her evaporable mind had fallen prey sto Nil's obstinate demand.

"Mom's bad," Nil seemed to say in between his sobs.

"Dad would have shown me the movie. Ma where's dad ? When'll he come ?"

Ma tried her best to contain his boisterous movements.

"Mom's bad. She doesn't love me." He reiterated.

"Nil, don't say like that. She's your mum. She loves you more than anything else."

"Then why does she shout at me ? Why can't we go to the movie ?"

"Because this is no time for that. When your Daddy comes back, he'll show you lots of movies, OK ?"

"No. Call him back now. I want him. I don't want to live with mom. She's bad."

By that time Suchita had stooped her head and almost chewed her fist. Tears gathered in her eyes like a heavy tide of seawater. And Nil's repeated remarks did the job. She started weeping in muffled sobs as if a heavy weight had been kept on her chest quelling her normal breathing. Ma pitifully rushed for Suchita with Nil still in arms.

"I'm bad ! Aren't I ? I'm bad," Suchita recklessly pushed and pulled the child by his tiny jersy. She repeated this exploit a number of times, as Ma peered at this fanatic behaviour of Suchita with a numb attitude, being too stunned to do anything. She virtually became immovable for that moment. Then suddenly Suchita seized him in arms with whatever power she could muster. And kissed him madly.

"Yes I'm bad. I'm bad," she spoke the painful words.

⁂

Sensing the tense and moving atmosphere in the house Ma decided to spend that night with Suchita and Nil. As usual the kid went to sleep in Suchita's arms. Placing him on bed, she too closed her eyes, still sitting in a chair. What she needed was an undisturbed sleep.

Ma just watched the whole drama hopelessly. She felt so bad. Despite being the eldest one, she couldn't control Suchita's rage and Nil's stubbornness. These two had caused themselves and Ma a great deal of emotional trauma due to their immature conduct.

"What would have happened in my absence ?" thought Ma.

Nil had wounded Suchita's earlier lame mind, harming and damaging it severely. Suchita on the other hand always looked for an emotional support in this child. That's why by calling her bad Nil provoked a sharp reaction from his mother. But now the situation was safely under control. Suchita was mature enough to understand and forgive Nil's act. And Nil, well he was a small kid who could not have lived a single day without Suchita. So, no doubt, the issue was settled. Ma sighed at the thought and began preparation for meal. Hearing some activity in kitchen Suchita too reached there.

"Take a rest honey," Ma smiled at her.

"No. I'm OK. I'm sorry Ma."

" Now forget about what happened. Just make it a point. Don't get angry on a person so small as Nil. He is absolved even if he does anything. You are not. Because he's a kid, you are not. Understand ?"

Suchita rapidly shook her head.

"Now stop whining about anything. Don't feel guilty either. Now go, wash your face."

Suchita obediently followed Ma's instructions.

✣✣✣

The troubling incident had a sweet end at last. Suchita herself fed her little son that night with a love only mothers are known to flaunt. What's more, she promised, they were definitely going to watch the movie. Nil in his turn, vowed never to breach his mother's wish. Convinced, all of them retired for sleep after dinner.

It was half past ten. Nil had already gone to bed. Ma and Suchita after a stretched out deliberation felt an urge to sleep. Accordingly, the lights were put off.

Within fifteen minutes or so, Ma started feeling giddy. A twiching sensation on left side of the chest saw her move uneasily to and fro on the bed. And at once she gasped for breath with an acute pain emerging from beneath the rib cage as if she was hit by a sharp blade penetrating deep into heart. The pain aggravated quickly and her face grew a layer of sweat.

"Suchita," her mouth issued a forlorn call for help.

Suchita, who had not been completely sleeping was by now completely on guard after picking up some movements from Ma. With this call she sprang up in a second and rapidly switched on the tubelight. Frightfully, Suchita watched the old lady wrestling with pain.

"Oh, my god!" Suchita deathly exclaimed.

It was a sight that could panic anybody. Ma tried to ram into chest with both her hands, her face shrouded in an inexplicable expression. Clearly she was faced with extreme agony. Her legs wildly moved from one end of the bed to another. Suchita almost fastened herself to the spot as if her blood turned icy cold and froze in her blood vessels. It was more gruesome because she could speculate what was transpiring. Ma was being subjected to a heart attack, a second one in a row and if Suchita was not at fault in assessment of its potency, it was real overbearing. There wasn't much she could do except for curbing her adrenalin secretion. Her earlier exposure to Ma's heart attack was quite beneficial in that direction. Suchita mollified herself and assisted Ma rest in a more preferable position. She quickly served her water and fed her some tablets that were specially prescribed for such contingencies. She then dialled the number of Khatri Hospital and solicited for an ambulance. At this terrible hour she badly needed Didi's help. But there wasn't any source to communicate with her. Happy Home couldn't afford the overhead cost of telephones. Also it wasn't much of a requisite. So, the government had immediately turned down a scheme for lending telephone facility to the orphanage. That's why Suchita resolved to go there herself.

The ambulance arrived in a little while after a brief, unpleasant period that seemed like years. Appeased, Suchita attended Ma in the vehicle. There was no point in waking up Nil. Therefore she locked the house from outside with a heavy heart. She didn't know what would happen if Nil was to rouse up while she was away and discover himself alone at night. But then she had little time to think over it and also likelihood of Nil waking up at midnight was rare. Nonetheless, Suchita's heart throbbed savagely and her mind was as if caught in a typhoon of thoughts.

In the hospital she left Ma, once handing her over to doctors and set out for Happy Home. It was almost 11.15 p.m. Ma, desolated in hospital made every effort to get back her rational body control. Nil slept softly in a house shut from outside. And Suchita, that young lady who never had a doubt about her timidity was out on the forsaken streets of the capital. For someone as novice as Suchita the situation wasn't quite pleasing. Once stepping out of the hospital, her senses grew numb. The darkness appeared abysmal and unending crackles of crickets gripped her brain as if a heavy shot of marijuana. Suchita felt an enormous pressure building up in the heart, so intense she feared it might burst out like a balloon full of water. Fortunately, it didn't. She was too overwhelmed with anxiety to understand what was happening actually. The trouble wasn't with her body, it was with her psyche. And for the time being it was out of her dominion.

So, finally Suchita was out in open world. With all its refinement and malignancy, it was ready to imbibe her. Instantly everything turned alien. The street that brought her to the hospital manifested itself to be a carpet of red-hot coal. The cold air advanced toward her face like thousand needles. The descent, illuminating lights on the poles seemed so bright, they almost blinded her. An occasional vehicle that drove past, as if roamed the roadway with the sole intention of pulverizing her. And a few passerbys stairing at this lady would turn out to be insane serial killers.

For one split second Suchita had an earnest urge to die. The next moment she thought of Nil and Ma and Jatin. So, unwillingly she had to pull through.

"Taxi," Suchita screamed at a vehicle, shaking her hand wildly. The cab promptly halted before her.

"Kantibhai Daga Road," she told briefly and occupied the backseat.

The cab driver with a stone cold demeanour didn't even shake his head. Smoothly the wheels rolled over. Suchita closed her eyes and threw her body entirely on the seat positioning her head horizontally. Then consciousness hit her mind.

Alone at midnight with a stranger ? Does it make any sense ?

Suchita stared at a mirror that projected the face of the driver. A stout skull, brown colour and a thick beard. In that lonely hour he looked appallingly offensive. Could it be a serious mistake taking help from somebody like this guy ? Is he honest ? Wouldn't he try to reap some disgracing advantage out of her vulnerable situation ? Wouldn't he try to establish his masculine superiority over a defenceless female ? When you grow suspicious you could doubt even a naïve infant. A grown up taxi driver is too old anyway.

The eternal fears sucked Suchita in their mammoth trap. Fundamentally, men are supposed to be afraid of death, women of rape and death, not necessarily in that order. As usual, however the feminine gender stands at the receiving end. In a sweeping wave of mistrust Suchita eyed that cab driver as the most heinous human being. She could think of no reason why she should continue travelling in his cab.

"Please stop it. I say..., will you please stop it."

"What happened ?" The driver cut short the ride and looked back.

"I want to get down," Suchita had already unlocked the door.

"But you said Daga Road."

"No. I'll stop here."

The driver shrugged off in surprise. He could read Suchita's face and judge very easily that the lady was in some hassle.

"You sure you wanted to come here ?"

"Yes," Suchita searched for money in her purse.

"How much ?" She asked.

"I would suggest ma'm. You shouldn't stop here. It would be a foolish move."

He knew it better! It was the worst of all localities in Delhi. Suchita disagreed then and then, thrust the money in his hand and made her way quickly. She didn't know where she was. But now she was away from that dangerous taxi driver. She was safe and sound. At least she thought like that.

Incidentally a group of three young men standing below a Banyan tree, tracked down every movement of Suchita since they spotted her taking out money from her purse. They waited till she passed by and walked some distance. Then attacked from the back, impinging like hungry vultures. In a moment, she found both her arms twisting at the back, a sharp, imposing knife dangling before her eyes and her purse confiscated. She realised her fate in no time. Without a bit of resistance the poor lady submitted herself to her tormentor's will and closed her eyes.

"Please let me go...," she repeated as tears ran over.

"Where's the cash ?" the person who snatched the pouch from her, desperately tore it open to gain access to the money.

"Bloody bitch! Tucked in inner pocket ? We aren't nuts." She heard him saying.

And then something happened. The man, markedly their chieftain whacked her by his dense, rough hand. In a single stroke Suchita's face pointed towards her right shoulder, having relocated itself at a right angle, some of her hair eclipsed the left part of the face. Her cheek ached like anything. If it was an act of terrorizing, it was hugely successful.

"Hey, Tony. What are you waiting for ?" The man shouted at the one carrying knife. "Take out her earrings. I say take out her earrings." He yelled.

Tony threw the weapon to his boss and started plucking out Suchita's earrings as the person at her back held her tighter than ever, her arms crossed and ground to death. She felt, she would certainly dislodge her shoulders in the process.

"Please! For god's sake." Suchita's frugal appeals died in air.

Hardly had Tony done with his business when a sound of moving four wheeler made its presence felt. The next moment a taxi suddenly surfaced from nowhere and bumped against the leader of the hooligans. Within a fraction Suchita sensed the pressure on her body easing itself. She dared open her eyes as a tall and bearded man ruthlessly beat two of the ruffians. The third one who had captured Suchita and by now loosened his grip, ran away altogether setting her free. Suchita was thus, back to sanity after a terse spell. She could identify the taxi driver, the same chap whom she had relegated as someone who came closest to being a rapist. Now he fought valiantly and simultaneously with two men for her sake. Suchita felt ashamed. She was one stupid woman who could have tarnished her image by such an erroneous judgement of human nature.

Within two minutes the place was cleared off robbers as they resorted to fleeing. Suchita stood in front of the cab driver, her head going downhill with unbearable shame.

"You want to go to Daga Road, don't you ?" He asked.

"Ye...yes." Suchita's lips moved a bit.

"So why did you get down here ?"

"I'm sorry. I was afraid of you."

"Afraid of me ?" The man boomed with laughter. "That's the finest joke I ever heard."

Suchita tried to smile but found it a difficult task.

"I would have loved it, had my wife admitted like that. I knew from the beginning, you are one faint hearted fellow. That's why I decided to follow you for sometime. But I think I came a bit late. I was busy counting today's earnings. That's why. OK no problem now. But are you alright ?"

Suchita nodded.

"Don't make a mistake like that in future. Let's move now."

When Suchita eventually disembarked at the Happy Home it was 12 midnight. She didn't know how to remunerate the cab driver. The man, after knowing her identity as a wife of a major fighting on a distant battleground, declined to accept anything. He even tried to return the money he had taken earlier but kept it on Suchita's insistence. He could appreciate Suchita's plight better. After all he himself had served in the Army.

"The whole episode could have been averted," Regretted the driver. "You didn't read what is written on the back plate 'Retired Soldier' ".

Suchita could only curse herself for this folly.

The first thing she did on landing at Happy Home was to take refuge of Didi's arms and cry her heart out. She wept until she thought, she was satisfied. Then with mutilated cloths and bruised body, accounted entire incident, apprising Didi about Ma's heart attack and the blood curdling near to death experience. And oh! She remembered about Nil. The boy imprisoned in the house. Suchita got shaky again. Without wasting much time the two women started off and rushed for the Mittal household on yet another taxi. Luckily Nil was found enjoying sweet dreams. Suchita, relaxed to be at home and that too with Didi, vigorously got on to finish the last item on her agenda. She straightaway contacted Dr. Diljeet Sareen, Ma's only son residing in Montreal, Canada and his sister at Chandigarh, by telephone.

❖❖❖

"This report comes from Colombo." Suchita read out from a National Daily. "The IPKF that resumed its peacekeeping operation last month seems to be enjoying a lucrative beginning, as the Tamil Rebels sent out signals of far reaching lull in their activities. The soldiers have comfortably taken charge of the situation and Indian Army has occupied many strategic points in order to overcome the deadly combat capacity of the opponent. After their deportation to Sri Lanka Indian soldiers have assimilated themselves well into the conditions widespread in the island nation. They also seem to have a big following among the local public as huge gatherings were seen in many parts lending vocal support to the Indian effort. As per the news reaching the capital the moral of the army is very high and it is confident of emerging as a lead player lest the ongoing effort of engaging the rebels in negotiations fail. Meanwhile, both the Indian as well as Sri Lankan government is making an all out effort to persuade the guerillas for the peace talks. A senior army officer, however, speaking on the condition of anonymity has warned, a heavy offensive could be required in the aftermath of failure of talks. It would be a foolish thing, underestimating the striking capability of the tigers, he was quoted as saying."

Suchita folded the newspaper and placed it on a table.

She looked contended.

"Well that's a good news," said Ma.

"It sure is," Suchita readily agreed.

"I think it should end your worries. Shouldn't it Suchita ?" asked the old lady.

"To a great extent," Suchita childishly twisted her arms and shoulders and chuckled.

"If I'm not spoiling your mood, may I make a request Mrs. Mittal?" Dr. Diljeet, who had immediately airdashed to Delhi after receiving Suchita's call, also sat with them, along with his wife and children.

"Anytime Dr. Sareen," Suchita had sprouted like a fresh rose.

" I don't know how to put it," he looked indisputably puzzled. "You and Maj. Jatin and Nil. All are so important to Ma. Even more than me. You've looked after her as your own mother. I....I don't find words to express my gratitude."

" So it's thanksgiving program, isn't it ?" Suchita asked.

"Not at all. Not at all. But you know about her health. It's badly deteriorating. She has already had two heart attacks. I mean it's really a distressing situation for me. I live thousands of kilometres away. I can't fly to Delhi very often. Also Ma will need constant attention now, medical attention I presume."

"What do you want to suggest exactly ? Just call a spade a spade." Suchita kept no restraint while talking about Ma. After all she had equal right over this old woman.

"Honestly Mrs. Mittal, I want her to accompany me to Canada." Diljeet detonated a bomb. And it exploded violently.

"Accompany him to Canada ?" Suchita had that gut wrenching feeling. " It makes no sense. It makes no bloody sense." Her heart cried out even as she mutely watched Dr. Sareen, too wonder-struck to say anything.

" I know it's not fair," Diljeet continued, " Leaving you alone when you need a support. But just imagine yourself in my position. I've no option left but to take her with me. I say it with great pain Mrs. Mittal. But it has to be like this only, I'm so sorry."

Suchita turned her face to Ma, her eyes brimming with tears. The old woman silently rested on her cot without any apparent reaction. She had no eye contact with Suchita. Then suddenly she spoke in a voice as creeking as an old cradle.

"I opposed his decision, but he's not listening. Whether in India or Canada I'm one useless person now. I won't possibly survive two or three years. I thought about this over and over again. And I found, Diljeet is quite right. I don't want to be a burden on you. I just need a few peaceful days before death. And I don't want to trouble anybody during this period. Suchita, I'm sure Jatin's coming back safely. I pray to god everyday and I'll pray in future. I'll pray for you and for Nil. But please do me a favour. Please, please let me go. Please."

Suchita couldn't say 'no' or couldn't think of any plan to foil this move. Moreover Diljeet didn't seem to budge a little. And he had slapped valid reasons in support of his argument. Worse, Ma didn't have any reservations about this decision. So, it was Suchita who was going to give up. And she did.

"If both parties are agreeing on this point I've no problem," she packed a great deal of confidence in these words. She wasn't going to leave even the slightest hint that she might suffer due to this action of Ma. Although it was as true and as stark as anything that she would. At the best she could try to eliminate any reaction that might suggest her displeasure and in turn force the ailing old lady into double mind. Suchita scored a great victory here. She had no complaints about Ma. But sometimes in the near future she had to settle her scores with her stars. Those bastards had ceased favouring her anymore. In a matter of two months her booming family had disintegrated into several fragments, an overall destruction before her eyes.

"I believe it's final," Suchita spoke hoarsely to no one in particular.

Ma nodded gently.

"What about this house ?" she asked to Diljeet.

"I've contacted a broker," he informed. " He has promised he'll fix a deal within two days."

"Anything that I can do ?" Suchita offered her aid.

"Don't trouble yourself. Thanks anyway. Even if it takes a few days to finalise the agreement your part doesn't come into picture. My brother-in-law will take care of this matter."

Suchita sighed lightly and excused herself. As she dashed out Ma and Diljeet watched her with great concern and pity. They couldn't help being gravely sympathetic about this young lady. Diljeet had bitter sentiments of guilt. And Ma was so deeply moved, she would spend a whole night feeling sorry and spilling tears.

⁂

"Yeah, story, story, story." Nil scrambled over Suchita's knees. After quite a while his mom had conceded to his demand to narrate a tale. Suchita had spread out herself on the bed with her legs folded, while the kid mounted himself on the projection thus formed, tilting towards her. Suchita clasped Nil's hands separately and upheld his balance.

"But what should be the story ? A magician's ? A demon's ? Or a princess' ?" asked Suchita.

" I like demon's stories."

"No. They are scary. You won't sleep at night. I'll rather tell you a princess' story."

Surprisingly Nil readily approved. Very sincerely the child acquired a position beside his mom as per her directive. Suchita acknowledged the change of attitude by her son with a proud glance.

"Once upon a time." Thus went the story, "There was a big kingdom ruled by an old king. This state was prosperous and people were peaceloving and hardworking. The king had only one daughter. She was so lovely, people swore by her beauty."

"What was her name ?"

"Hmm. Let's call her Rose. Because she was as delightful as a rose.

"OK."

"So people called her princess Rose. Once the princess was playing with her friends in her royal garden. Do you know what happened ?"

"No," said Nil.

"There was one ugly monster. He saw the princess and took fancy on her. The monster forcibly grapped her in arms and flew away."

"Was he very powerful."

"Yes, yes. He was. Now this news spread everywhere. The king was so worried. He didn't know what to do. Finally he announced whoever brings back the princess safely would marry her. Automatically, he would take over the reins from the king. People heard the news but nobody dared to accept the challenge. The monster was a real, terrible menace."

"No one went to save the princess ?"

"Wait wait. There was a young boy called ... called say Nil."

"Ha Ha."

"This Nil was a very good boy. He worked in fields and looked after his old parents. But they were poor. So, he decided to accept king's offer. His parents resisted initially. But later on permitted him somehow. So, Nil sought blessings from his parents and the king and set out to beat the monster. On his way he met a fairy who was also troubled by the monster. The fairy gave him exact location of the monster and told him that he could be killed only if his left eye is crushed. Nil thanked her and proceeded forward. He reached the appropriate place and loudly shouted at the monster. Angered by this act the monster came out. Nil informed him, that he was one warrior of a distant state who had come to rescue Princess Rose. He told him to accept defeat. Nil said, that even if he looked so small, the monster couldn't lift him up. Terribly insulted, the monster straightaway lifted him up to prove his might. Nil wasted no time and stabbed his left eye with his sword. The monster died instantly. Nil went back carrying Princess Rose with him. Finally the princess was reunited with her family. Moreover, she got a prince too. As per the king's promise Nil married to Rose and became a king. And they lived happily ever after."

"Wow fantastic," Nil got on to his feet applauding.

"The princess was really lucky, don't you thing Nil ?"

"Ya. But mom what would have happened, if the monster had defeated Nil ?"

"I don't know. The princess could have died weeping."

"Oh, that could have been truly sad."

"Liked the story ?"

"Very much."

"Nil, don't you remember your dad ?"

"Who ? Dad ? Why to worry about him ? He's on duty. When his work finishes he'll come back."

Suchita impressed by these words looked at him admiringly.

"Who told you all this ?" She asked.

"Ma."

" What else she told you ?"

"Ahm. She told me I'm now a grown up child. So I should behave properly. I shouldn't quarrel with my mom. I should obey her every wish. I'm the only man around here. So I should behave like a man. Under my supervision my mom won't weep. I'm here to take care of her. I've promised this to Ma."

Suchita felt an unexplained comfort catching up her heart. She badly wanted to burst into song and dance. Unknowingly, she buried Nil tightly in arms and kissed him a lot muttering 'I love you' everytime. She thought she had met her destiny at last. She begged for an instant death. If there was any appropriate time for that it was now.

Nil fell asleep in Suchita's arms. She carefully placed him on the bed, kissed at his forehead and got down tyding up herself. Slowly Suchita moved towards the window and stood there slightly touching the steel frame with hands. A lonely house shown feebly in weak luminescence of moon. The familiar light always reaching her through its glass windows was prominently missing. It now burned at a far off place called Montreal.

Thirteen

"Life in jungle couldn't have been more dull than this," Major Jatin Mittal dashed his right hand against a huge tree as he inspected the area around their camp.

"I agree with you Major," Sergeant Kishanlal promptly joined his boss, "The only preys for our guns seem to be these tiny birds." He pointed towards wild sparrows sitting on a branch.

"Birds, birds everywhere, not a single tiger to kill", merrily sang Kishanlal and Jatin couldn't inhibit a laughter.

"I bet the tigers are afraid of our guns," Jatin remarked confidently. He mounted on a big lump of mud and with his palms on his waist surveyed the adjoining area through his ultralens.

"I think we better return back Kishan. There is no point spending so much time for a bird watch." Jatin proposed. "I again agree with you Major," chirped Kishanlal.

So both the armymen set out towards their huts. It was almost two and a half months since they arrived at the Sri Lankan forest but they didn't get a solitary chance to test their aim. That was quite frustrating for the young blood that ran through their bodies. They felt like handling a grocery shop where not a single customer turned up for months together.

Until the two got to their station and washed their hands keeping aside their weapons, all the eleven members of their team had piled up at the spot from different directions.

"Any news guys ?" asked Major Jatin as he came out, bending through the short door of the hut, wiping his hands with a towel.

"Nothing serious Sir," Munna, the ammunition specialist jumped forward, "Even animals don't dare to penetrate this forest."

"I agree, even I'm coming to conclude we are no less than fools who keep on beating these bushes suspecting a snake is there. No sober mind will make its way through these woods, I'm damn sure about it." Jatin exhibited his displeasure.

"Wait a minute Major," It was Kishanlal, "I saw some mysterious bootmarks while we were returning."

"What ? Why didn't you tell me then ?" Jatin fumed over Kishan.

"No worry Major, close examinations have revealed that they were created by our own shoes," quickly he burst the balloon that sent a laughter wave and Jatin was also a party to it.

"Naughty Kishan !" Major Jatin patted on his back. "You always remind me of Mr. Sam. He is as professional in cracking jokes as you are.".

"Well, that's an honour to be compared with the likes of him, Major," said Kishan, badly suppressed due to this hearty compliment from his boss.

"Well boys no need to get slackened due to the lack of challenge," said Jatin. "Just thank the great God that the chances of our going back alive have multiplied. So keep strict vigil over maximum possible area and hope that nothing risky happens and unnecessary blood is shed."

When Major Jatin spoke they would lend their ears with the eager and curiosity of a child. They had tremendous faith in the young man and his ability to visualise the things. His remarkable prowess to analyse the situation and make tactical moves. He was the sole administrator, the supreme authority as far as their tiny group was concerned. His good verdicts were going to make them a victorious brigade and at the same time his single misjudgement could dig their tomb. Jatin knew it, that's why he always warned his comrades against any kind of looseness in their assigned activities. He was the one who always played his cards cautiously.

After the strict and exhaustive survey of their neighbourhood areas, the armymen sat on a rough mattress that they spread on the ground in front of the hut. Two of them, viz. Amarsingh and Shankar Choudhari were up on the watch tower ever since they had dispersed for inspection. It was according to the shift schedule prepared by Jatin for the round the clock check over the surrounding area. As the men continued discussing among themselves, T. Ganesh or Tirupati Wakkal Ganesh, their special cook in the mission placed his sturdy aluminium tea pot on the hot clay oven that unleasned red hot flair from within. 'The light brigade' as they called themselves, couldn't charge unless it consumed this hot fuel supplied by T. Ganesh.

"Sir, I have a doubt regarding the planning strategy of the mission," Asif Ali, Jatin's think tank and expert adviser raised a question which troubled him for months.

"Go ahead", Jatin singaled a green light.

"I'm still confused over the way the whole planning is done. I don't think it was a very clever more to make so many fragments of the Army to tackle such a cunning enemy. Instead, we could have cobbled together to pose a strong and united defence."

Jatin smiled at Asif as he casually helped himself with some wild berries placed in front of him.

"What you say is correct," he remarked, "But only when the battlefield is a plain desert like the one we have in Rajasthan. Or atleast it should be such, that the free movement is possible. But the situation here is altogether different. You know very well how toughly we have managed to camp in the jungle, although we are very few in number. Now imagine a big infantry. How are you going to make sure of a rapid forward or backward movement in the woods ? I will say it is just impossible !" Here Asif readily approves Jatin's argument. "Besides, our enemy is not known to possess a big army. So it is very unlikely that they will attack us in a concentrated manner. No ! Do you know what they mostly rely upon ? They take advantage of their knowledge about these woods and their experience in quick marching through dense forest. No matter how big army you are. They can make you eat the humble pie with the sole asset of their mastery over guerrilla warfare. That's why our bosses have come to conclusion that the only way to survive their attack successfully was to break up our massive power and dilute it with the woods, so that whenever the enemy strikes we can squeeze it from all direction. Such a thing will give a deathblow to them. This strategy of defeating an enemy by entangling it from all sides was successfully used in the past by Alexander, the great. Do you know what he did ?" Asif nodded in negative. He would have said no even if he had any information regarding it, because he didn't want to lose any great military advice coming from his learned boss. Jatin was fond of talking endlessly about great ancient warriors and military generals. Alexander, the great was one of his favourites.

"Those days the battles were face to face and not like what we fight today," Jatin began from the preliminary stage." Once Alexander faced a stiff challenge from an army far greater than his. But he had a readymade plan in his mind to take on such a challenge. Initially, both the armies were in front of each other forming two strips of soldiers. But as the battle broke out, Alexander suddenly pushed a big number of soldiers in the middle of the enemy strip and quickly shattered the enemy strip into two. Once it happened, he ordered rest of his men to surround these two enemy blocks and tightened the grip over the enemy. Finally, the helpless foe had to give in to the military genius of Alexander. That's real awe inspiring, how by using his brain he could beat on army far superior than his. In our case, we are the part of one of the five best arm forces in the world and our enemy is one who takes shelter of woods. You can guess who will be the winner," Jatin's confidence was a thing to experience.

"Asif, your doubt over our planning reminds me of a joke regarding yet another great general in history, the formidable George Washington." Jatin's talkative mood continued as T. Ganesh handed over cups of steaming hot tea to his associates and began climbing over the ladder, carrying the tea kettle to serve his two friends on the top.

"Once the United States governing body brought a bill for discussion, which suggested that the American army be broken into groups of 20. Commenting on this funny resolution, George Washington advised them to first pass a bill. It should ban any enemy, invading USA. in groups comprising more than 20 men," Jatin cluckled and his men joined him.

"One thing is sure, George Washington had a great sense of humour", said Jatin, "very similar to our Mr. Sam."

Bip ! Bip ! Bip ! The radio receiver set inside the hut gave out signal indicating that someone was on line.

"Excuse me gentlemen", Jatin quickly kept aside his tea cup and stood up to attend the call.

Within no time he reached for the receiver.

"Hellow, Major Jatin Mittal here. Over."

"Major Sameer Pande reporting to you sir, over."

"I see Mr. Sam is calling me. So take the name of the devil and the devil's call is here ? OK, what do you say ?"

"First you clarify whom you called devil. If I'm Mr. Devil, then devil's buddy isn't Mr. Angel, mind you."

"Ha ! Ha ! OK, I'm so sorry. But please don't get irritated like this man."

"Major Mittal, you must understand one thing, that the radio set was not provided to us for the sake of chitchatting. You must talk business and no rubbish. Understand ?"

"OK, sir let's get on to our business."

"Hey, you are getting serious buddy. I was just kidding man."

"I know, I know, tell me frankly, when are you not kidding ? You do only two things in life. You sleep and when you don't sleep, you indulge in kidding. That's all."

"Now common, don't be so harsh man. I think you forgot my eating. How can you survive without eating something ?"

"No, you can't. That's why you are eating up my brain over the radio set, presently."

"Alright, I disconnect the call."

"Aye. Don't do that. Let's be serious and exchange our reports as usual. Or Col. Choudhari will order us to walk barefoot into the enemy citadel."

"You are 100 per cent right. Well, as for my side there is no news. You know very well, not a single person was spotted since we arrived here. So no chance of confrontation with the enemy yet. However, we are maintaining hard patrolling. You see, you simply can't afford to be ignorant in the foreign woods like this one. Well, what about your team. Everything OK ?"

"Yes. The life is reduced to only patrolling as usual and nothing else. But when everything looks normal I always find something fishy. It may be the serenity before actual storm. I'm afraid, it will be like that only. So be alert my friend. You are towards north, nearer to the enemy camp. If the tigers leap forward, don't loose any time. Straightaway contact me. I'll attack from the back."

"No worry, we are all supposed to help each other only. And that's the main purpose of providing radio sets. If the enemy raids your camp, you too don't wait for a minute. The very first thing you will do is to contact me. See how we crush them within no time."

"But it will be better if such a matter doesn't arise."

"I agree with you Jatin. Well, by the way how's life buddy ? Any news from Suchita Bhabi ?"

"She keeps on writing man. I only don't do it often. But I'm so worried about her. She is all alone."

"Never mind ! Things will improve fast. Well, anything else ?"

"No."

"OK, then, Report everything to Col. Choudhari. I'll also contact him. Anyway, keep in touch as usual and call me tomorrow evening. See you. Over."

"Bye. Over and out."

Now it was Jatin's turn to call somebody, i.e., his boss Col. Choudhari. As he dialed the code, within a fraction his massage in the form of the invisible radio waves ran through the air and reached Col. Choudhari's pocket receiver about 150 km east of Jatin's camp producing the peculiar 'bip', 'bip' sound from the gadget.

"Hellow, Col. Choudhari speaking, over".

"Maj. Jatin Mittal reporting to you sir. Over."

"How are you Maj. Mittal ? Anything serious ?"

"No, not yet Sir. As for the situation stands today, there is no movement whatsoever from the enemy side. But we are keeping strict vigilance and not allowing the boys to lack motivation. Yesterday Cap. Datta from the southern camp and today Maj. Pande from the northern camp contacted me. Everything looks fine according to their observation. And I also fully agree with them."

"That's great Maj. Mittal. Just keep it up !"

"Thank you sir. Any news from the top level efforts, sir ?"

"Well, both the governments are trying to persuade the rebels for ceasefire and peaceful settlements. But till today there is no improvement. Perhaps our adversary wants to extract more advantages before any deal is struck. And if, the talks fail there might be a heavy bloodshed in offing, mind well."

"We are ready to face any emergency, sir."

"That's the spirit Major ! But one thing all you young officers should note, and it is, the key to every successful mission is effective communication. So make use of your radio sets as frequently, as possible. Don't let any small thing skip and bring it to the notice of your colleagues and seniors. I warn, any minute tactical error and the whole system collapses like a bungalow of cards."

"We don't let it happen sir"

"Good ! All the best and keep informing. Over."

"Over and out."

By neatly restoring the radio receiver, Jatin came out of the hut and saw his men bursting into laughter as Shrihari Jadhav, that newly wedded young man reticently tried to hide a piece of paper under his shirt. The boys repressed themselves as Jatin approached the group.

"Any new Major ?", asked the only man who referred Jatin as Major. Unquestionably it was Kishanlal.

"Not really. The same everything O.K. massages". Jatin sat in between Darshan Singh, the landmine specialist and John De'soza, the hand grenade champion, spreading his arms across their shoulders.

"Well, it seems something funny was going on when I was attending the call. May I share your joke guys ?" He asked and his men started looking into each other's eyes. Nevertheless there wasn't any problem is sharing the joke with their young boss who always treated them like friends.

"Shrihari has written a letter to his wife." It was Lalit Patel, their medical man, "We were guessing what could be its content."

"I see, the job is quite interesting", Jatin remarked satirically.

"That's an injustice sir," complained Shrihari.

"Almost everybody has scribbled a letter in last two three days, but nobody wants to discuss the matter in them. I don't know why I have been made a scapegoat."

"Is it so ?" asked Jatin sympathetically, "But why such a spurt in letter writing ?"

"Don't you know sir, tomorrow is the second Monday of the month ?" It was John De'soza, "The army postman will be visiting our camp."

"Darn it ! I had forgotten it in all the haste." Jatin struck his right fist on the left hand palm. "Well, I should also give a try with pen and paper." He smiled.

"But don't ask for its contents. I won't tell you." Here Jatin winked his eyes on Shrihari. Laughter went off in the camp like a bomb.

And then out of the blue like a whimsical madman, Jatin stood up and precipitately made an entrance into the hut. He looked capsized in all respect, almost angry over himself. All his men were worried about their families they had left many away but this man was so busy in his endeavour and planning that he almost forgot about those people close to his heart. This was the situation when status quo was all well. He couldn't think what he could have done had there been bloody warfare or even frequent firings. At the moment, Jatin castigated himself like anything. But as he opened his suitcase his face was imperturbable and poised, although his mind was as if caught in a blizzard. Swiftly his hand took out a photograph from one pocket that depicted Suchita carrying little Nil in arms. It was a picture shot by Jatin himself on Nil's first birthday. He ran his photograph for a moment, touched those smiling faces deftly with fingers and slipped it back into the pocket. He at once felt like running away from the jungle and catch the very first flight to Delhi. But his hands were tied and his mind was is a fix. His indignant eyes searched for those two letters sent by Suchita, the only two means through which she had tried to communicate with him. Circumspectly, Jatin pulled those pages from beneath his cloths and flipped them tenderly. Suchita had deplored the frequency of the letter consignment which was so shabby, she had to bear many burdensome days without the exchange of a single word between them. And for a person like Suchita it was too acrimonious a punishment to bear. Prodigious sinful feeling crept into his mind. He was guilty of not paying attention to his dear wife whose every breath spoke out his name. He was guilty of overlooking, though transiently the petite child he was responsible for bringing into life. Alarmingly bedeviled, Jatin took hold of a letter pad, lacerated his pen on its back to make sure that it was superlatively in order and hurriedly got out of the hut. His mind became a ghastly, violent sea of thoughts which made their way haphazardly through his pen and appeared on the paper in equally haphazard manner.

'Dear Suchita',

Don't forgive me for so much delay in drafting this letter. Indeed, even capital punishment will be very mild for the crime I have committed. When I read your last letter, i.e., the second one, my concern for you grew thousand times. Believe me, I couldn't sleep properly for two days.

My heart sank the moment I heard about Ma. I don't know how you must have faced the days after she suffered heart attack. But as the tone in your letter suggests you must have reacted fiercely. And I appreciate you for your courage. The way you handled the situation and swiftly contacted her son and daughter, was really incredible. No doubt in this process you have repaid Ma's every debt and favour. But now that Diljeet has taken Ma along with him to Canada you must be very lonely. And that throws me into a puzzling situation. I don't know what I should do. Until Ma was there I had no worry about you. But now as she is gone, I'm restless. Probably that's why I always tried to remove your thoughts from my mind because it stings like a needle. Frankly, I never felt so helpless and weak in my whole life.

I feel terribly sorry for Ma also. I don't know whether I'll get a chance to see her again. Canada is too far and as for now even Delhi looks equally distant to me. Only heavens know what is in store for us.

Suchita, I may sound somewhat negative in my thinking and approach and you will definitely blame me for raising doubts about your ability to live alone, even when you have demonstrated that you can. But it's not me, it's my blind love that keeps on creating such complexities. Just as you must be praying for me and my well being, my subconscious mind unknowingly devotes itself to your thoughts 24 hours a day. And it is precisely this habit of it that generates so much anxiety is my mind and it becomes extremely hard to digest realities.

Well, I was always a follower of the 'hope for the best and prepare for the worst' motto. In our case, I find it necessary to elaborate what the terms 'the best' and 'the worst' specify. This is just to make everything crystal clear and remove all cobwebs that might block your true vision, leading to misconception and confusions. As the situation stands now, 'the best' thing for all of us will be any kind of peace treaty with the rebels that will break this impasse somehow and make it possible for the peacekeepers to return back. We hope for it. And the 'worst' thing for which we have to prepare ourselves, is our solid washout at the hands of enemy resulting in complete debacle of the Indian Army which is not possible even if a single Indian soldier survives. It won't be unfair if I declare in the same breath that is the remotest possibility, that our top brass will straightaway dismiss as sheer nonsense. But as frontline fighters we accept this eventuality, and make up our mind in that direction. Again, I may sound very pessimistic here, but considering the odd against us, it is not farcical argument.

Well, you should not get baffled by what I said right now. We were just talking in terms of possibilities. But the fact is, we will emerge ultimate champions in these jungles and I will be right back to provide you, the once in a lifetime opportunity of welcoming a victorious husband. Nevertheless, he might have a bullet shot is his arm, but you should take it sportingly. At least, that is expected from the wives and family members of the warriors.

I don't want to entangle yourself and me in so much complications of words. So now let's be straight and speak out directly from heart, without allowing our damned brains to interfere even slightly. Next time when you will write a letter, write it very frankly and in minute detail so that I may get a clear picture of how your life is going on. I have come to realize from your earlier letters that you have tried to give an impression of 'all is well' by smartly concealing whatever is not well. But I know you are under tremendous pressure. For the first time in life you are attempting to stand alone. Moreover you have our nice little child at your discretion who must be ensuring that you don't get required quota of sleep. Mind well, this is not the time to run away from the situation. This is the time to act. This is the time to capitalise on all those things sowed into your mind by Ma and myself. Suchita this is the time to fight back and I'm sure you will. Never mind Ma went to Canada and I'm in Sri Lanka. You are not alone. Whenever you feel lonely just go to Didi. She will be of great help to you. Remember Didi handles a situation far trickier than yours. So your extra burden won't bother her much. Besides, she has a raw power in the form of young boys and girls. So if in any worst condition you require physical protection, don't think twice to go to the 'Happy Home.'

Finally about Nil, ask him to forgive his unfortunate dad for not being with him for so long. Suchita, in case of any eventuality, i.e., if I don't return, I wish to see my lad to grow up into an honest man. Don't prefer an army career for him, although deeply within my heart I'm eager to watch him follow the footsteps of the senior Mittals. But at the same time I feel that our useful stint in the army should be over for good. We should think more in the direction of peace and love and hope that no wars are fought in the future and casualties of innocent lives occur in all these baseless rivalries. It does not mean that my approach is non patriotic, but...'

The pen almost slipped out of Jatin's hand as a mind boggling sound erupted from some nearby place, accompanied with desperate human shrieks. It was as if some volcano had emerged from within the ground vomiting dazzling, hot, molten lava. The sound was followed by a loud 'Whoooshhhh' and something fell down heavily as if the ceiling of the sky was broken and its pieces struck the earth. These two events occurred hardly within a second that left everyone surprised and shocked. Jatin instinctively jumped away and turned to look what actually had happened. What he saw made him freeze at his spot. Their watch tower had collapsed on their hut forming a huge lump of debris. It was a partial fall triggered by hitting one end of the compartment by some unknown thing. The impact was so drastic, the strong branch of the tree which supported its one end was blown off leading to slopping of the compartment in downward direction with most of its inner material, including the two guards crashing down heavily on the hut down below. Very few things managed to survive the slide and clung to the branch of the other tree hanging like wild nests.

For a moment all the men stood still, their mind refused to accept the reality and their brains couldn't think of anything. As if this accident was not enough, smoke started coming out from the heap of their destroyed huts. Within half a minute Jatin's mind regained some composure and his brain started deriving implications from the event and rapidly he arrived at conclusions.

"Don't stand like spectators", he shouted at his stunned men, "Get them out, Amar and Shankar. Don't forget Ganesh."

Yes, that fat boy Ganesh, was also caught under the garbage along with his clay oven that caused the dry wood to catch fire and emitted black smoke in the process. It was a cruel way to disrupt one's cooking process.

"Asif, pour some water on it," Jatin ordered, "Don't let the fire spread. Otherwise we are doomed."

Nobody knew about the root cause of all this, but nobody questioned their boss and quickly started clearing the rubbish. Jatin's brain stretched its thinking power and started relating the series of incidents. It was hardly two minutes after the tower hit the ground when quite instinctively Jatin turned back and moved a few yards away from the place. He was searching for something which might provide a clue whether it was an accident or a sabotage. It didn't take much time to confirm what it was. At about 50 yards from their hut, he got the torn away branch of the tree on which rested their fallen compartment and with it was a red hot burning piece of metal ! What was it ? Jatin's head spun as his military mind drew fast inferences. It was a missile hurled right on target ! At once Jatin sprang up on his feet. All the while his incomplete letter fluttered in his hand. He calmly put it in his pocket, tied the pen to his shirt and moved fast.

"Hurry up boys, we are being attacked," he yelled at the top of the voice, "Lalit move the injured towards this end," here he pointed towards the direction where he stood with respect to the hut. Boy ! He had not noticed one thing until then that he sat facing the enemy territory and the missile was shot from backside. That means they were attacked from exactly opposite side. It was surely a big jolt to their calculation. This fact suggested that Jatin's camp could might just be surrounded by the tigers. Were they playing an Alexander on him ? Jatin got furious as this possibility struck his mind. He couldn't comprehend how his enemy could break the formidable wall of Indian Army, but there was no need to panic. If that really was the case, he could still turn the tables and score a winning edge over the enemy, Jatin knew how. He worked exceptionally fast.

"Now everybody grab the guns and take positions". Atlast five minutes after the missile attack Major Jatin ordered his men to be ready for the battle royal.

"John and Darshan quickly take out the weapons and Kishan you will help me search for the radio transmitter." He wasted no time in assigning the duties.

"Shrihari, get the lens, climb over a tree and keep watch on the enemy movements. Go report me quickly," saying this Jatin rushed to the radio set.

In the meantime, Lalit, Asif and Munna pulled Amarsingh, Shankar Choudhari and T. Ganesh from within the heap. Now their task was to pull them out from the jaws of death. Out of the three, Amarsingh sustained sharp injuries due to his fall on the pointed rifles and solid hand grenades kept on the ground, while Shankar was relatively lucky and escaped with a broken hand and a bruised body. Ganesh on the other hand, had to bear solid impact of the stumps that were used to provide the framework to the huts. The poor man was grounded into a pulp and he suffered suffocation due to the smoke generated from his oven. Immediately Lalit got on to revive these men even as their combrades began preparations to face the acid test they were expecting for months.

On another front, in a frantic effort Maj. Jatin managed to recover the radio set from the vast pile of military equipments. Unfortunately, it was in too bad a state. The sudden dash had forced open the gadget, tearing apart its electronic components and spreading them all over the place. Jatin himself and Kishan a master electronic manipulator tried to get back every missing element from the junk. But introducing life back into the transmitter looked almost impossible.

"Hang on Kishan. You can do it," Jatin encouraged his exasperated fellow. He was very tough to give in so easily. Ironically, the radio transmitter which he always considered to be his last resort had taken the form of his first priority. He had not many options left after having three of his men badly injured and an enemy who struck from the back. Escaping away from the spot was out of question for this proud officer of Indian Army. Thus he was left with fighting a battle which was half lost as the enemy had established an advantageous beginning.

Kishanlal gave early signs of disappointment as his efforts went abortive. But he still tried to put together different pieces of scrap just because he was instructed to do so by his boss. Till that time, i.e., seven minutes after the missile attack Shrihari Jadhav was up on a big tree, starting at the surrounding area with his ultra lens by carefully concealing himself within the vast expanse of leaves and branches. The sight was so horrifying, he almost stumbled down the tree. Somehow, he collected himself and quickly got down.

"Sir, sir we are trapped by the Tigers," he came panting towards Jatin, "There is a gun pointing towards us from almost every corner. But there is some place left for escape, towards this way." Here he pointed towards north-east direction. It was a suggestion least expected by a determined military marshal.

"Shut up you coward," Jatin took him to task the way only he could. "If you want just run away in that direction. You understand ? Save yourself if you can you, you dirty mind." On very few occasions did Jatin use to lose his temper. But this time he was enveloped in an overpowering rage nobody had seen earlier. His eyes instantly turned red as if the whole blood in his body had gathered in his eyeballs. His body shuddered with fury. He seemed so very enraged, it was impossible to recognize him. But he knew he was angry more on himself rather than on Shrihari. It was frustrating act of a leader who sensed the situation slipping out of his hands. It was nervous reaction of a lion helplessly left with struggling to free himself from the cruel net of a hunter that threatened to end his reign and his liberty. It was a desperate cry of a man who saw many dreams of tormenting evil forces for the sake of the motherland in his childhood but when the actual situation arrived, found himself totally off hand, not having the slightest clue as to what strategy to adopt. It was as if his hands were slashed off from the shoulder and he was demanded to fight with a demon having a sword in each hand.

At the unusual reaction from his boss, Shrihari stood at the same spot dropping down his head with shame.

"You think I'll run away," Jatin asked him sarcastically. "Look, look at them," he pushed Shrihari by arm and directed his forefinger towards his men who by now were ready with their guns, forming a human wall surrounding their camp.

"I'm proud of them. India survives only because of such fearless men. Give me thousand of them and I can conquer the world." Jatin could feel the hot blood surging ahead through his blood vessels.

The sight of his brave compatriots poured unimaginable enthusiasm in this young man. "Do you think they don't have anybody dependent on them ? But when you have taken up this holy duty, just keep aside everything. You don't have a single family to protect, you have millions of them, spread all across the country. If you can fight for them, nothing like it and if you don't, die like great warriors. Don't let them down, don't show your defeated faces to them. It is better if we perish in these battlefields. Millions will pray for our soul. You will book your place in heaven, young man. Understand ?"

Jatin gently patted on Shrihari's back as tears rolled down his cheeks.

"I'm, I'm sorry sir," he said in a choked voice. Suddenly the man wiped out his eyes and maddeningly ran towards the heap of weaponry, picking out a fine long range rifle.

Just then the enemy opened fire from the eastern end, exactly opposite to the earlier attack. This is where Lalit was providing treatment to the ailing members of the team. Within fraction of a second, number of bullets gushed in and penetrated through his body as if it were a sieve, instantly rendering him lifeless. It was Jatin's duty to ask this man to shift towards a safer position in the middle, as soon as Shrihari came up with the news that they were surrounded from all sides. Instead, he wasted time chiding Shrihari. Result ? They lost their medical man and with no success in establishing radio contact with the headquarters, further medical assistance was completely denied.

"Shrihari, go, save the injured men," Jatin screamed hysterically and Shrihari jumped to execute the order. Without caring for anything his rifle started shooting bullets in the bushes from where firing was started. Suddenly the attack from the enemy end ceased. Quite evidently, the men who killed Lalit were also assigned the same fate. Very calmly Shrihari kept aside the rifle and pulled T. Ganesh. Till then Asif and Munna reached the spot to help shift the other two. From the responses of Ganesh and Amarsingh it wasn't very hard to judge that they were no more. Unfortunately enough, Jatin's casualties rose to three. And with the slight flickering of eyes, Shankar Choudhari suggested that it was as good as four.

Clearly, waiting for further attack from enemy could prove absolutely fatal. There was no point in wasting time anymore and make the enemy take bolder steps. It was a time to retaliate. It was a time to prove that offence was the best form of defence. So, with his feet resting on shaking ground but confidence steady as a rock, Jatin ordered John De'soza to make use of hand grenades. Shrihari, having seen all the enemy positions was an ideal person to guide him in the task. Moving fast as per their boss' orders, within minutes five Indian men stood ready with heavy shells in hand, facing towards different directions. As soon as Jatin raised his fists up directing towards the sky, deafening sound rose in the jungle. The charge of the light brigade had begun !

Till that time darkness had gripped the dense forest but the defiant explosives overshadowed its effect. The enemy, however, by virtue of being a veteran of bloody encounters was already expecting such a daunting aggression from the Indians. That's why within no time their machineguns ran riot giving rise to heavy downpour of burning mental pieces that pierced through the thick sheet of trees separating the two opponent forces. Surely when you can't fight the enemy face to face, it is better not to take chances and hit whatever seems like an adversary. The tigers followed the same tactics. Out of thousands of bullets fired, atleast some were bound to demolish human flesh and that was enough ! Taking full advantage of their superior position and mental victory the enemy shot down another three Indians. Munna, Asif and Shrihari fell prey to the fiery reply of the tigers in the bloody exchange of bullets and shells. But there was hardly any moment to shed tears on the departure of these martyrs.

"Major, Major the radio is working," Kishanlal came tumbling, saving himself from the fierce battle. He had done something, least expected by his boss at that stage. And after losing about half of his team Jatin sensed a minute chance of bouncing back. Springing up on his feet, instantly he moved towards the transmitter and established contact with Mr Sam as Kishan grabbed a machinegun to protect his boss.

"Sam, we are in deep trouble, six men down. Rush quickly and inform Col. Choudhari." He could afford no more time than to utter those frenzied words. The man was left with horror as the opponents gunned down two more, John and Darshan in this crucial period. Within five-six minutes the Indians were reduced to two and the tally was about to complete. Nobody could be more unfortunate than Jatin. He had sought help from his army to protect the men who were no more breathing life. But the fight had to go on. The Major had nobody with him except Kishan in that pathetic evening. They had lots of guns but no men to push the triggers, they had lots of shells but no hands to throw them.

With tremendous fury the two men battled with their recoilless machineguns. It was a fight for survival. It was an attempt to keep the enemy engaged till the help arrived. But with the resistance from the Indians decimating to two frantic array of bullets, the tigers tightened their grip in order to suffocate and foil any further onslaught. They marched forward as Jatin and Kishan maddeningly fired at every possible direction. But the enemy was too strong for a two man army. Impulsively, a sudden shower of bullets burst from every corner. Out of them a sharp, burning metal piece shattered Jatin's back. Then came another one through the shoulder. His face got covered with a heavy spray of blood as a third bullet gushed through his right chest. Instantly everything turned hazy. But he could see Kishanlal's head pounded with shots from atleast three corners. This witty companion dropped dead in front of his Major without giving a slight cry. In a moment Jatin's brain visualised every moment of his life. His mom, his dad, Ma, Suchita, Nil, Didi, Mr. Sam, his motherland. A proud contended life reached its peak. He rose to the occasion. He never let his ideal stumble. Only the time didn't help him. That's why each stinging wound made him smile at himself. He was the most fortunate Indian, a brave son of soil. History was going to sing his song. Poets were going to immortalise him in the hearts of millions. Never mind he left back his dear ones, never mind he made irreversible blunders, never mind he lost his battle, he still managed to carve out a golden figure of himself. Not blessed with the love of natural mother he accepted the love from the ultimate mother, the motherland and devoted his life for her honour. That's why today, he felt very happy as his sight grew weak and slowly but steadily and calmly his soul left his body after a final decisive blow at head. The strong 5'11" body collapsed in a dash. The real tiger was dead. The inimitable Mittals had added another feather to the cap. They had offered another flower to the motherland. Major Jatin Mittal ceased to exist.

Fourteen

Velvety comfort of the foam sofa was not a very delectable thing for Suchita. It was as good as any other surface meant to sit on. But she liked resting herself on the cushion, shutting her eyes and shutting herself from everything and remain there with a perfectly blank mind. It used to be like performing an act of yoga. As usual she had dispatched Nil to his nearby Montessori school and returned back. And as usual she had no idea how she was going to shell out so many hours without him. Ever after Ma left for Canada her life had again thrown itself into the dark seclusion. She again started getting the smitten by her life before marriage. But the formidable presence of Nil was a titanic breather for this lady. Once he got back to home she would consign every painful thought that might invade her mind to oblivion. Other way was to preoccupy herself in some enterprise and that was what she tried to do. Once Jatin had gone to Sri Lanka, her interest in the situation there and the politics that revolved around the whole problem, had increased. She would read out entire newspaper everyday in her quest of updating her knowledge about the Indian peacekeeping operation on Sri Lankan soil. But of late, she couldn't gather enough courage to go through the newspapers simply because the reports were getting more and more discouraging. If the things were going to be what predicted by these reports hitting the headlines, the situation was very near to a flashpoint. The political solution of the problem, i.e., through peaceful dialogue seemed a distant reality. In the words of newspapers "there seemed to be a political stalemate in Sri Lankan ethnic crisis". That's why, the whole troubling scenario forced Suchita to isolate herself from the news breaking in, in the newspapers and television, just to avoid herself from getting disheartened.

Suchita opened her eyes and had a glimpse of the newspaper stacked on the teapoy, but she didn't dare to bare its pages. Once more she fused the eyelids and went back to her harmonious state. That was a more likeable state of her mind rather than having a stormy and rough one that it could gain after reading some disturbing news. It was half past nine and that meant, she had been sitting there continuously for two and a half hours and still she had no intention of abdicating the job. Overtly because she had already taken her bath and next item on her agenda, i.e., cooking the lunch was far ahead. She had a momentary urge of visiting Didi at 'Happy Home', but left the idea because it wasn't a good move to go there too often and have a share of Didi's precious time. But whenever Suchita felt terribly bad the first thing she would do was to get proximity to Didi. After Ma's exit Didi had become her light house that guided her through stormy nights. She was the only one whom Suchita trusted and sought advice from.

'Ting Tong'. The door bell rang interrupting Suchita's reflective state. Rashly she transformed into a wary woman. A visitor at such an odd hour? She couldn't guess who on earth was willing to drop in. Well it might be the milkman wishing to have advance payment, just to tackle some emergency. Or it might be the electric or water bill making inroads into the house. OK, it could be anybody who wouldn't be detrimental to her. Suchita dragged herself sleepily towards the door and she couldn't believe her eyes as she gazed through the sight hole. It was Didi! In a frantic moment Suchita brushed aside her laziness and opened the door.

"What a pleasant surprise, Didi!" she exclaimed excitedly. "Just now I remembered you". She gave her glorious smile at the lady who didn't seem to be much impressed with the welcome. It was in sharp contrast with what Suchita had imagined. Indeed, she would have grabbed Suchita by arms and slammed a funny comment or two at her and laugh wholeheartedly. That was her way of showering love. But this time she returned a meek smile and nevertheless kissed Suchita on forehead.

"God bless you," she muttered unsteadily and walked in. Keeping her purse on the teapoy she settled herself on the foam chair.

"Don't bring water", she said as Suchita was about to go to the kitchen for the same purpose. Didi was fully accustomed to each and every habit of Suchita.

"Sit here beside me. I have something to say". Didi spoke calmly. Although her appearance was much the same, it had remained similar to when they met for the first time but the brightness of her face was prominently missing and her disposition had attained a strange dullness.

"You look very weak Didi. Any trouble with health?" asked Suchita.

"No, I'm perfectly alright", she said even if she couldn't hole up her swollen eyes and the reddish tinge in them.

"I don't agree with you", Suchita remarked."You look pathetic Didi. Why did you come here? You could have rested and consulted a doctor. If there was any urgency you could have sent a message. I would have visited you instead. No, I won't hear any excuse, let's first go to a doctor".

"No Suchita I'm saying I'm OK." Didi responded firmly "What I have come to convey you is more important".

"OK, just say it", Suchita said in a complaining tone. By her voice she could very well be a four year old girl.

"How are you my child?" asked Didi.

"Now come on Didi you have not come all the way to ask me how I am", Suchita laughed, "I'm also alright, very fine indeed! I suppose we have met not long ago. Only seven or eight days back. And nothing serious has happened within this period".

"When is Nil supposed to come?" Didi fired another volley which looked a bit extraneous in the context.

"He won't be back before 12.00 o'clock".

"I'm afraid, we will have to pick him up early".

"Be very clear Didi. I'm not getting a word of what you say. Are we moving somewhere?"

"Ya, you have to come with me. Where, I don't tell you right now. It will be a surprise".

"Well OK. I won't ask you either. I'm also getting very bored sitting alone in the house. It will be a nice experience to be with you somewhere. I guess it will be a zoo or a movie." Suchita tittered impishly. "I will be back in a moment, I've to change my sari", saying this she went in, in breakneck hurry.

✣✣✣

Some half an hour later Didi, Nil and Suchita were heading towards an unknown destination in a taxi. Nil looked overjoyed because he got an early freedom from school. Moreover, he was out enjoying with his mom after a gap of so many months. At that moment he was a joy personified. Suchita too felt so exhilarated and carefree. It was Didi's company that made the whole difference. Suchita forgot every angst and every convoluted thought. But she couldn't conceive why Didi appeared so sullen.

Ultimately the taxi pulled up in front of a big, staggering construction, the expanse of which was impossible to judge. It wasn't a braintwisting task to identify that concrete structure. Suchita had heard its description at least about a million times from Jatin. Well wasn't it the famous 'Central Jail' of Mr. Sam? Or the one and only 'Indian Army Headquarters Delhi', Jatin's workplace? But why had they come to that spot which was bound to remind them of Jatin? Suchita found herself outwitted.

"What's our purpose of visiting Army Headquarters?" She asked.

"You will come to know soon", Didi answered concisely as she handed over money to the taxi-driver and briskly snatched Nil by arms. As they walked down the road Suchita found it difficult to keep pace with this energetic lady, who looked in no mood to elaborate on her comments. But it was a time Suchita started smelling something fishy.

Corridors after corridors passed behind as Suchita coyly watched groups of young men, some in military outfits, some in civil. A few gentlemen even bowed down at the sight of Didi as a mark of esteem. Clearly the lady was a well known figure in these premises. Suchita had so many troubled queries to ask, but Didi wasn't very keen at attending them. She got further intimidated at the sight of some old couples and young ladies who also seemed to be traversing along the same path as theirs. And why they looked so distressful? And why some of them were overwhelmed with wet eyes? And why they didn't look normal? And why they looked rickety? And why all of them had come together in the army headquarters in the first place? Why? Why?

"Didi !" A devastated scream echoed from the shining walls of the building. It was a solid female voice that hit the interior surface of the corridor and transmitted itself towards the stunned individuals nearby. Its intensity was so profound it couldn't have been possible to quantify it in decibels. The next moment all eyes altered their positions to target the spot from where this shriek had originated. There stood a young lady oscillating like a stroked string of guitar. You won't be able to induce such a tremendous vibration in a human body even with a chilling, frosty weather. Even then her head remained firm like a rock and her large, dark eyes stretched their muscles as if with horror.

Terribly astonished to hear such a heart tearing call from Suchita, Didi turned back and unknowingly Nil slipped down from her arm.

"Please, don't make a fool out of me", Suchita pleaded, joining her hands together. The affairs of her body was as poignant as hopeless ruins of a majestic palace. "I won't move a single step further if you don't say everything is well. I want to know why we are here. Tell me the truth Didi, tell me the truth", Suchita violently shook Didi's shoulders.

Nil stood dumbfounded to see this insane behaviour of his mother. Surely it heralded some bad omen.

"Say something Didi, say something", Suchita clasped Didi's arms with whatever power she could collect. But Didi remained silent. She attempted to pose a normal picture but eventually her own emotions burst every false appearance that she tried to wear. Defeated in her act of pretence the senior lady lowered her head and started sobbing. By that reaction Suchita could judge something. "You are right Suchita. What you guessed is absolutely right. Jatin's no more".

A lightening struck with those words. Suchita could feel herself torn into millions of pieces with something blasting in her head and its death like pain dashed against each and every recipient nerve cells that carried the signal to her brain. For a moment her entire body froze at the spot with no movement whatsoever. But her talkative eyeballs popped themselves in horror. She was unprepared for accepting this eventuality. She had hundred per cent confidence that it wasn't going to befall. But calamitously it did. Like all those incidents that confiscated her right to live a normal life, this one also occurred when she had not the slightest hint that it could. The nature had betrayed her on yet another occasion. Her body crumbled under this influence and her mind cracked like a nut. Momentarily everything turned bleak and she felt the surrounding spinning all round her body. A feeble 'my god' emanated from her mouth as her right palm partially covered her open mouth. The next moment she lost all her control over the body and it fell pray to the gravitational pull. Anticipating such a reaction from Suchita, Didi had already surged ahead to balance her body weight on her own. And that pretty kid Nil, watched everything that threw him into perplexity not knowing what had happened and why it had happened.

❖❖❖

Strange as it may seem Nil Mittal, the cuddly five year old boy and the one and only son of late Maj. Jatin Mittal had striking similarity with his father. Both were born to army officers and both lost their fathers when they were not able to stand on their own. But strictly speaking Nil was more unfortunate because in his case, he was so small, he had learned the art of speaking not quite long ago. But one thing that went in favour of him was, he had his mother with him although completely demoralised and completely defeated. The solid presence of that unshakable lady called Didi in the life of both Jatin and Nil was yet another resemblance. She still stood with Jatin when he had lost his life and returned from the battlefield in a coffin.

It was a sight not many dare to see. The slain body of somebody you have watched to grow from a seedling to a tree. Didi remained composed as she tightly held Nil against her and tentatively moved her fingers through his hair. About 20 years back she was standing exactly like this with Jatin when he was to collect the medal of bravery won by his late father. Unknowingly Didi's eyes moistened and her heart jerked. It was the same child, brought in front of her with his body mutilated with number of ruthless bullets that reduced his awesome frame to a sheet of dead tissues. It was the same child who would turn to Didi and sleep in her arms when a nightmare used to horrify him. Now he had become so brave, he never retreated an inch when it rained bullets from everywhere. It was same Jatin who managed to squeeze out tiny droplets from Didi's eyes with his unanswerable questions about life. And he was still making her cry. It was the same child whom she protected like a tender lotus flower. But she couldn't save him from those unbearable agonies he must have gone through before completing the last breath. It was same Jatin who rushed to Didi every time he found himself in trouble. Now he had left her in deep anguish. It was the same child for whom Didi had passed so many sleepless nights. This time he didn't give her that opportunity. And he returned like nobody else. He returned perfectly victorious. Some men are like that only. They perish so that the civilisations may survive. They bear heart bursting moments so that others may rest in comfort. Jatin was one of them. And Didi was proud that Jatin was one of them.

"Ma'm, if you wish, you can have a glimpse of his face", an armyman suggested and Didi's heart started throbbing. Did she have enough courage for such an act? She certainly didn't have, but she could amass it somehow. Why to lose an opportunity which was never going to come again? Dumbly Didi grabbed Nil's hand and moved forward. She shut down her eyes until the voice of the opening coffin ceased. And slowly her eyelids opened. It was Jatin sleeping in that congested wooden compartment. His face glowed like thousand suns. Didi felt as if he was smiling even the bandage wrapped around his forehead implied where the final bullet was hit.

"Hey Didi, you are alone? Suchita didn't come to see me off? Oh well, my little captain Nil is here at least", he said.

"Young man, I have begged in front of your wife but she wasn't ready to come here. She says she wouldn't stand your sight", Didi said coldly.

"Ha! Ha! She sure is a nonsense. Look, here her husband comes all the way from Sri Lanka to meet her and she remains inside home by shutting the door.

"Never mind I'll convey your message to her. But tell me Jatin does it hurt being there?"

"Yep! Those bullets are pretty heavy stuffs for our bodies. I really esteem the chap who invented them. There is nothing like receiving a bullet at the chest" He said in a cynical tone.

"And what should I say to Suchita?"

"tell her, I'm so sorry. Well, she could always find another gentleman".

"Shhh......Jatin. Please don't say like that. Don't question her commitment to you".

"OK. Sorry. But ask her to be brave and relentless. Any way! As along as you are with her, I've no worries about her. And yes, last but not the least ask her to raise captain Nil the way you raised me. Is that all?"

"I'm afraid, yes".

"Carry my good bye to Suchita. Of course, goodbye to you. Goodbye Captain Nil" Jatin again became motionless as a stone. His eyes sealed. Gently Didi touched his cheeks with her shaking hands. She then lifted Nil by arms. The child joined his hands and saluted his dad. Tears sprinkled down Didi's cheeks as the armyman closed the coffin. Nil looked at her, with his eyebrows stretched to the limit and face in an inexplicable state. And then suddenly he jumped into her arms letting out a devastating cry. His father had gone to Sri Lanka without taking him into confidence. But still Nil didn't think he could go that far. He had crossed all limits, without kissing him goodbye.

There were no rituals, for nobody was there who could perform them. So in a simple affair Jatin was cremated in Army's electric cemetery in presence of invincible tanks blasting fireballs into air as a mark of respect, just to proclaim that yet another Indian warrior had fallen. And that proud tricolour, which he tried to hoist in the battlefield bundled up his body. Flowers and wreaths from army bigwigs, government officials and political leaders were laid all over his body. Soon the flesh went in and in a moment the ash came out. An earthen pot containing that ash was handed over to little Nil. He was to immerse it in Yamuna river as per the Vedic sacrament.

✣✣✣

"I can't sleep. No, I can't", Suchita lodged her touching grievance. She seemed to have extraordinary strife while talking. Something like that is bound to happen when you spend a whole day trickling down tears.

"Don't be so stubborn honey. You are no child" Didi leaned over Suchita's body and slightly massaged her head. She couldn't stomach the pitiful sight of this young lady whom she saw so much gladdened a day before. Now she had come to be a human mess. Her eyes were turgid and the skin immediately surrounding them grew dark. She hurt her throat whenever she attempted to speak and she broke down after every few minutes. Suchita had changed sides on so many times while in bed, her hair sprawled on her forehead and at whatever lengths they could reach. But she was not aware about their presence.

Suchita remained the only wife that day who didn't attend her husband's funeral. Jatin had promised her to return back and he kept his words while Suchita couldn't follow her part of welcoming him proudly. Unpretentiously she didn't have heart to watch him sleep in a coffin. That's why she refused to be threat at the funeral. When she fell unconscious at the Army Headquarters, Didi admitted her to the army hospital where she spent the terrible moments while Jatin was being consigned to the elements. But how inevitably she had been cursing herself for making such a foolish decision. It was, in fact a golden opportunity which she sorely missed. Now where was she going to find her prince in flesh and blood? No wonder she couldn't sleep.

"What happened to Jatin? I want to hear about him. I want to hear about him." Within 24 hours she had almost made it a habit to duplicate sentences. As she spoke every time the muscles of her forehead contracted themselves and tears flown down her cheeks as if eternally.

"This is no time for it dear. It is half past eleven." Suchita moved her head vigorously on her pillow as a firm disapproval.

"Nil has slept?" She asked, partially disconnecting her ponderation over Jatin.

"Yes, certainly he is matured than you." Didi remarked.

"I know, I know, I'm the weakest person in the world. But don't deviate from the matter. Tell me about Jatin", she said forgetting the fact that she herself had deviated by enquiring about Nil. But Didi didn't mind such eccentric behaviour of Suchita. She knew her mind was fully paralysed.

"Actually before leaving for Sri Lanka Jatin had met me, that you know. At that time he told me, he had given my name as his nearest relative to the army, so that in case of any eventuality the news should first come to me. Obviously, he was worried about you because he could not guess what your reaction would be to any such news. He gave me this responsibility to carry such message and safely make you know about it. But it seems, I have failed in my attempt. However I've promised Jatin to look after you and Nil till you come out of this bereavement. And I will keep it. May god give me enough courage for this purpose." Didi's voice was no less chocked, her eyes no less moistened. She dropped down her head and squeezed Suchita's hands. "Why do you worry my child", she covered Suchita's cheeks with right hand. Suchita grabbed it firmly and broke down heavily.

"He was too brave" Didi asserted.

"I know, I know", Suchita seemed to say but she was so overwhelmed with weeping she couldn't produce a sound but a feeble hush.

"Nobody knows what exactly happened that night. But it seems they had some trouble with their radio transmitter. The enemy rose up unexpectedly and caught them unprepared. They fought fiercely but the opponent were big in numbers. Maj. Sameer Pande has said, he received a message from Jatin when his team was almost reduced to half. That speaks out for some technical failure in the transmitting mechanism. When Maj. Sameer reached the spot the enemy was about to leave the place along with the bodies of our soldiers. Nevertheless, they were also half a team down after their battle with Jatin's men. Maj. Sameer turned so furious at the sight, within five minutes he shot down all the opponents. In a press release yesterday he said, he used excess bullets to kill the enemy. They shot twice or thrice at head to ensure that.everybody was dead. We should thank this man. It's only because of him, we could get the dead bodies intact."

"Intact? For god's sake, was he really intact?", asked Suchita.

"I should say. Although he received some six bullets, one even went through his head".

"Oh god! How awful it might be" Suchita sniffed, "Just how painful is it if you prick a needle into you? And he received so many burning metal pieces! Tell me Didi wasn't I supposed to be party to every joy and every sorrow of Jatin? Then if they fired six shots, how come not a single one smashed through my brain?"

"Will you please stop thinking about him now?", Didi almost thundered "Is there any sense burdening yourself with wicked thoughts like that? I'm also going through the same phase my child. I lived with Jatin for much more time than you. I understand, you cannot escape yourself from these cruel thoughts. It hurts and it stings like a thorn. Do you think, I don't suffer? I'm as devastated as you. I'm literally shattered. But some how, you have to find some way-out. I know it is terrible for people like you and me. I don't know why such things keep on happening in our lives. I'm sure god must be mighty indifferent. He doesn't know how many blows should be given to one's credit. He is testing our strength since our birth. But we should never crumble down under such loads. If we want to survive, we must show fighting spirits. No matter, you are up against the lord.

And don't just look at the negative side Suchita. There is always a positive dimension to every thing. You will go through severe depression right now but time is a great healer. Finally someday you will accept the reality. And the sooner it happens, the better. Then you can think about the future. And there is hardly any doubt in my mind, the future is bright. Consider it as a great opportunity to discover yourself, to judge your inner power. You might be thinking that you are not blessed with grit, but you are. In fact everybody is. I don't mind you, getting sad at this stage. But by no means, it should be perpetual.

And never ever forget that little legacy of Jatin. Of course I'm referring to Nil. When you have somebody like him with you, you cannot pretend to be alone. You simply can't run away from the situation. I know he is too small to be considered. But when he'll grow up you will sense the potential of his existence. And today the need of the hour is, you should concentrate wholly on his development. Prop him up, he will reach the sky".

Didi spoke and she spoke like never before. For some moments Suchita stood hypnotized. She consigned her grief, to oblivion, she omitted Jatin from her mind. As Didi insinuated she pondered slightly over the future and willy nilly her crippled mind came up with a frightening query.

"But how do we survive? You need something for your bread and butter. Don't you?" By now Suchita had almost bathed herself in tears, but they kept on coming.

"That's the point" said Didi "That's where lies your fear. But do you think Jatin never had a tussle with this eventuality? Believe me, he had thought over every possibility before leaving you behind. And that's why at least for near future financial problem won't bother you. Jatin has accumulated enough money in the bank account and for at least two years all problems are solved. Besides you don't have to spend a single penny over Nil's education. That is because, on account of Nil being a son of a martyr, the government will bear all these charges. Then remains the question of, what will be your own course of action. There are two options. Although it's not a time to suggest this one, but as per Jatin's wish you should find another suitable hus..."

"Please" Suchita interrupted fiercely, "Please, that might be his wish. But I can't follow it. No I would rather break his wish." Disappointingly Suchita closed her eyes. Her sorrow was unbearable.

"I knew, you are not going to respond positively on this matter. Well the other alternative is to stand on your own. You are well educated and you can always find a fitting job. That will be more constructive and productive approach. Think about it and carefully decide what you really intend to do. Don't forget I'm always there with you and you can always count on me for support. Understand?"

Suchita pressed her lips and vigorously shook her head.

"I'm leaving for happy home tomorrow. I wish I could stay here a bit longer. But I have a big responsibility there. You are just a single person, but there I have 50 of them, waiting for me. So I must go. And you have to digest this blow alone. But don't forget whenever life becomes a burden come to me, my doors are always open for you. And please don't get discouraged. OK.?"

Lovingly Didi enveloped her in arms.

"Now its time you sleep, Suchita".

"No, I can't" Suchita reiterated.

"Well I know one thing that will definitely put you to sleep. Just a minute" saying this Didi reached for her purse and took out some tablets.

"What are those?" Suchita enquired.

"Sleeping pills. I need them sometimes. Just try it. It will help." Didi uncovered a pill and handed it over to Suchita. She gulped it with a glass of water and stretched herself on the bed with her eyes closed. The strange medical recipe worked faster than Didi could have imagined. Within minutes deep sleep cast its shadow over Suchita.

✣✣✣

Night! Darkness! Evil spirits! Hideous monsters! Ghosts! Snakes! It is called a chain reaction. It originates in the minds of children. When they are alone at night! When they are alone in deep jungles, where visibility is stark zero. Strictly speaking there is some visibility. Eerie and supernatural! Breaking every barrier between the tangibility and intangibility. Otherwise why one is able to see those horrible faces and sharp, sparkling images? Glinting eyes! Half skeleton, half flesh? Flesh decaying with time, flesh producing sick odour? And ugly human skulls, trickling warm, red and sticky blood through numerous pores, bathing themselves in its pool? And wicked witches generating shrill, deafening screams that escalate with so extreme rapidity, it can destroy the very foundation of your hearing mechanism. And what about those ghosts popping enlarged eyeballs out of their sockets, eyeballs having red, zig-zag blood capillaries, very similar to the path traced by lightening? Face, if you can, the piercing, chilly sight that can dig a hole right across your head with its stupendous power.

And not to mention those abnormally strange creatures called bats that might emerge from virtually anywhere and dash against you, flapping around its wings wildly in an obvious attempt to make you know about the impending terror. Can you free yourself from deadly poisonous cobras and vipers encircling you in huge numbers with their cold, coiling, slender bodies clinging to your frame? Can you wait for their lethal venom to get injected into your blood by penetration of their sharp, pointed teeth into your skin? Not to forget that dirty pair of hands, dipped in thick, dripping blood that recede slowly exposing rough, black skin some where and white broken bones at the other places. And its only aim seems to be advancing towards your neck and suffocate you by squeezing it. Can you sustain the pricking sensation of its hard nails?

Remember those nerve wrenching footsteps? That mysterious knocking at the door followed by the creaking sound of its opening? An experience so very clear and so very subtle. Can you withstand it all? Can you? Can you?

Suchita desperately locked her eyes. But there is a queer speciality of darkness. You can feel it with open eyes and it still haunts you when you close them. So by whatever means you are in danger. Suchita used to go through such horrible experiences many times in her childhood and even in her adolescence. But today after so many years the nightmare struck again! It was as if a defeated response of her nervous system to the hostile and aggressive input from the nature. Within minutes her face developed tiny sweat droplets and still her body shivered. Ridiculous was the state of her affair. A tiny five year old slept peacefully in his mothers arm and the mother didn't know how to escape the dreadful thoughts. Presence of her son, on the contrary helped to whisk away some fear out of her mind. With her heart throbs accelerating, soaring sky-high the lady got down from the bed, still very very overwhelmed with unidentified, frightening feeling.

Instantly her legs turned numb and she almost bumped against the wall. Somehow, but not without collecting substantial efforts she managed to fulfil her aim to find the electric switch board. And when it appeared to be within reach, the lady frantically pushed whatever button she could touch. Suddenly, the entire room bathed itself in milky white shine of the tubelight, and Suchita suppressed a spontaneous, helpless sigh by pressing her right hand palm against the mouth. It was to prevent any big noise that could have disturbed the deep sleep of her child. The fragility and the infidelity of her body didn't allow her to stand erect for much time and consequently she found herself resting on the floor, with her limbs folded, drawn near and pressed against her breasts, her chin resting on knees and eyes searching for a suitable spot to fix its vision line on. Strands of her hair remained in perfect disorder, her saree as if worn just for wrapping something around the body, completely off the shoulder. Eventually she caught sight of Jatin's photograph hanging on the wall and rueful sobbing was what to follow. She attached her left hand, just below the wrist, to her lips, slightly tilting her head and squashed her eyes extracting warm drops of tears. It had come to be her normal life, a routine. Her eyes simply forgot to remain dry!

Today in the morning Didi left for Happy Home and Suchita faced what could best be described as the worst day of her entire life-span. The morning newspaper flashed her photograph with Jatin and Nil and scanning newspaper, her way of mind detraction, in turn embroiled her back into thunderous state. Throughout the day she remained unstable, almost volatile, shutting the door as if, even the outside air would harm her. Not long ago her dreamlike abode used to bear smiling faces in remarkable number. Now black melancholy had proved itself dominating, wickedly taking possession of the house with its octopus like tentacles. And Suchita found herself grounded into pulp, thrashing into millions of pieces. But naturally! As she had been subjected to so rapid changes in circumstances. Even stones cannot sustain such drastic alterations in external environment. They invariably crack due to nonstop bombardment of heat, cold and rain. No wonder Suchita's tender human mind gave in to the cruel and unfaithful time. It was squeezed, torned, broken, crushed, mutilated, tortured and finally burned. What remained were ashes, as dead as grave, as barren as a desert. Mysterious fear kept hovering over Suchita just like deadly vultures in search of their victims.

Dash! Within twinkling of an eye a sharp stone burst the window pane producing deafening sound and finally hit the forehead of an innocent life called Nil. If happened within a fraction and there was no clue suggesting who hurled that stone. But the effect it managed to generate was enormous. Suchita almost sprang up with the blast, her muscles grew stiff and her fingers contracted themselves forming tight fists. Suddenly the window glass grew a big hole and the removed glass took the form of tiny pieces showering themselves on the floor. In a moment Nil was awake, his forehead in blood and eyes in tears. His painful scream was followed by his mothers. It was a moment when Suchita could have fainted at the spot and she almost did. But the mother in her was far stronger than herself. She almost jumped towards Nil and held him with whatever power she could gather. With surprising agility she grabbed her child in arms and carried him to the front room almost running. It was a berserk effort of a mother to move her son to a safer position, away from any mischievous attack. All the while Suchita pressed the wounded forehead of Nil with her saree and gripped him entirely with her body. The little boy could hear his mother's heartbeats even as his forehead spurted red droplets. During this brief period Suchita's eyes remained dry as if the continuous supply of tears was cut off momentarily. But once she escorted Nil to a safer place tears rained again. This time with full flow. The violent collision sent tremors down her spines. She couldn't relate this horrifying incident logically and her brain remained sluggish, unable to contemplate about anything. Then at once Suchita released her child from embrace.

"Don't move honey, I'm coming, I'm just coming", she whispered in Nil's ears as she delicately laid him on the sofa. She could watch the bloody scar on his forehead in the deem light reaching from the other room and something went piercing her heart. Suchita missed a heartbeat or two. What was his crime that somebody had punished him so cruelly? She didn't have time to ponder and hurriedly made her way to the bedroom even as Nil tried to prevent her with his tiny hands. Suchita hesitated at the sight of the broken window and that emotionless piece of stone laying on the floor after doing its duty with precise accuracy. For the first time in her three decades of existence Suchita turned so furious her blood almost started boiling, simply because she contained a powerful mother inside. Not withstanding the frightening sight of the broken glass she reached for a drawer taking out an antiseptic liquid, some cotton and bandage.

Soon Nil got his first aid as Suchita placed a cotton piece soaked in antiseptic on his wound and enfolded the bandage around his head. The child was yet to recover from the shock but his weeping ceased and got reduced to occasional sobbing. Eventually he fell asleep in mothers arms without uttering a single word of protest. Indeed right from the day his father left the house this child grew more matured and considerate. Suchita placed him back on the sofa as water rushed vehemently through her dark, large eyes. Till then she shed tears for Jatin alone. Now Nil too had claimed his share. That's why the water flow doubled and her cloths grew wet under its effect.

Once Nil achieved his tranquil state of sleep, Suchita's mind started reflecting again as if the wheels turned in its machinery. Mother in her had surged ahead and conquered. Now the vanquished woman in her rose up and she found herself caught in the trap once again. Her body turned itself into an edifice of concrete as she couldn't move a single step anywhere. She forgot, not long ago she had ventured into their bedroom bravely. Now she dared not look at the door, lest entering the room. The soothing tubelight penetrated her eyes with the intensity of hot summer sun rays, blinding her vision, retarding her vigour. High frequency vibrations stemmed from within her body but her brain still worked. It started drawing inferences from the episode. Somebody had sprang up as her adversary she couldn't guess who. Otherwise who on earth was going to harass the troubled life of a war hero's widow?

Clearly staying away from reality was not going to solve the problem. In turn it could enhance its intricacy. Nobody was ever so fool so as to throw a stone that could accidentally break a solemn house's window. The assault was intentional and there was no doubt about it. The question was who did it and why? But Suchita was not a person who could amass enough courage to investigate into it, to peep out through the window just to see who was hanging around. In such matters she was as good as Nil could have been. Or worse, lesser than him.

It was an act of intimidating her with a well calculated plan. If she was to fall prey to it then she had had it. If somebody was really interested in tormenting her then the path was simple as this lady was known to buckle under any pressure, even slightest. And what if the unknown person went on ambushing her not of course by stone pelting, but by any other mean? That could mean the summit of her demoralisation and a life uglier than the hell, worse than the death. So it was better to sort out the matter quickly. If the blunder of bending in front of such a person was made, there could remain no way out.

Thus finally and decidedly Suchita stepped forward overcoming her scared state. Once in a while she could act like that because her brain was too intelligent to let the fears always take charge of herself. Calmly she reached for the switchboard and lit the front room, neatly worn her saree and tied the hair together. Although her demeanour looked steady, her heart throbbed and her head ached. Hiding herself from anybody that might be curiously searching for her through the broken window, Suchita went into the bedroom once again and put off the light there. Now she moved softly towards the window from one corner and gazed through the broken part. There was nobody! The road lay deserted. Smoothly Suchita shifted her position and got to the other corner. She spotted somebody standing beside a street light pole. Remember the face? Not long ago she was proposed to marry this man, that rowdy chap, a professional rogue! After hitting the five year old child with a stone that bastard was whistling merrily placing both his arms in pocket. Suchita turned red hot at his sight, but she was deeply hurt after realising the fact that ultimately he succeeded to find her. How he could do it was as simple as ABC. Morning's newspaper bearing the photograph of Mittal family was responsible for this rendezvous. Suchita's worst fear turned true. At that moment she cursed the day she attended the party organised by the army and she cursed the photographer who shot the snap and now handed it over to the press without bothering to inform her.

In a moment she ran towards Nil, her legs treading heavily on the glass pieces scattered all along the floor about which she forgot in her frenzy. Sharp, pointed pieces pierced her delicate skin and she cried in pain. Blood oozed out from wounds and she struggled to suppress the spontaneous voice. Blood and tears were what her life was getting reduced to. That night both the mother and son lay wrapped up in bandages on the sofa, with the former having consumed her tranquillizer, the sleeping pills which, of late had come to be the most kindly thing for her. Never mind a barbaric animal keeping watch on her after having broken her protective shield, never mind her only son sustaining wound on forehead and she herself on legs, never mind all fears and nightmares, she slept and she slept peacefully. The sleeping pill is a great wonder indeed !

Fifteen

Dear Nil, here is your ruinous mother who wants to convey her genuine feeling to her only offering, i.e., you. I can't write it on paper because my fingers won't sustain the weight of the pen for that longer. And my child you are also unable to read something to the extent I want. I can't say it to you orally either because you are so small you won't understand the complex thoughts that spreads across a grown up mind. Irony is I can't wait you to grow up and understand what I mean to say. I have no other option left but to put my thoughts silently within my heart and if the great god really exists, he will extract them out of my soul and plant them into your mind so that whenever you grow up, you will be able to comprehend what your poor mother wanted to tell you. It will be the revelation of ups and downs, mostly downs of my 28 years of stay on earth.

My dear child after getting defeated on so many occasions in my life, I really wonder what exactly was the purpose of the creator to give me humanhood. Throughout all these years I have searched and searched to find out what could have been the reason behind my suffering. Believe me, I could find none. I have suffered only for the sake of suffering as if to satisfy somebody's wicked whim. I have suffered only because we human beings are puppets in the creator's hands and live this life of blood, flesh and bones for the sake of his amusement. That's why for no substantial reason persons like me crush themselves below the giant arms of destiny. Tell me what else could justify my hardships?

I'm such a hopeless person my son, I can't tell you my origin. What I know is, I was found in the footpath and only heavens know who kept me there and by what intentions. I could have very well been an illegal child, a fruit of any unlawful combination. An illegitimate! But to be on a higher moral ground I always objected this possibility. But time and again such thought would mushroom in mind and coerce me into ineffable misery. My self worth would become a big zero on such occasions and I can tell you there is no equivalence to lose your self esteem, the only ray of hope that remains afterwards is the prospect of death. You won't be surprised when I'll say that my life was plagued by such lacerating moments but I always showed stiff inclinations to stand erect and thereby subjugated most of them. Only once did I relinquish my patience and tried to end this life, but fortunately or unfortunately I was salvaged. I wonder what good this extra piece of life has done for me. It certainly handed out me unbelievable happiness that I never thought I was worth for, but if you consider the average life-span of a person was it more than four or five per cent of that?

After getting married with your father and being one of the members of our blissful family, I thought finally I had reached my ultimate fate. I thought, that was the end of the instability in my life. But it was not going to be like that. The loss of your father was very very hard to cope up. Our life became as directionless as a ship would be after the loss of its navigator. I know ours was not the only family facing such a destiny. Indeed there were many more. But the shock is more pronounced in our case, may be because of the lack of a continuous comforting face and of course, my weakness and my inability to handle such a gruesome challenge. You like me or not I'm like this only. Cowardice is what I stick to most of the time and failure to face adverse moments is my lifeline. That's why when you got injured, hit by a stone on forehead my reaction was rather subdued. The women, however are known to shed all their inhibitions at any such occasion and retaliate against these aggression with the spirit and ferocity of a tigress. I defied this law by locking myself in a fine shelter instead of attacking the savage man forthwith. Now I'm so ashamed of myself. I can't express the disgusting feelings. If I can't stop a small piece of stone aimed at you, how am I going to save you from larger obstacles in life which I'm very well acquainted with as indispensable? If I'm not able to discharge my duties as a mother what right I have to call myself one? Apart from giving birth to you what else I have done that would grant me a right to say proudly that I'm a mother? And with no father and no mother you are but an orphan my child. Just like me! Just like your father!

Today I'm going through such horrible experience. I feel as if hundreds of crawling leaches have taken charge of my body and they are sucking my blood at their will. And within some time period my body is bound to be emptied out. My pain is so obnoxious, I'm again reaching the peak of depression.

You will readily agree, the days after that stone pelting incident, posed an acid test of our patience. And you know very well how that cruel rascal, called Bobby or something, kept on pursuing his mission of terrorising us days after days. You lost so many days of school, honey. Remember, for four five days we almost locked ourselves in the house as if we had been sentenced to prison. It was only after I braved to go to Didi somehow, that we could get some relief. No doubt we have sent him behind bars by laying a trap with the help of the police but for how many days is he going to remain in the custody?

Some day or other he will be free and who knows he won't strike again? He definitely will! The incident has starkly exposed the vulnerability of our life. He knows we are unprotected, unarmoured. We can't pose even the slightest of resistance even if he enters our house by forcibly breaking open the door. We will still be disabled if he pours some combustible material on us and strike a match. It is a detestable anticipation but it is not impossible either. The world is full of such human animals and nothing can be predicted about their behaviour. Sometimes they can beat the devil by their evil designs. So there is no harm in foretelling such an outcome of this battle.

Many times I ponder about the worthiness of myself being a wife of the likes of Jatin. Was it an meticulous unification or a perfect mismatch? I've seen wives and family members of many of Jatin's friends. They have the same exemplary power and strenuous spirit of their soldiers. Do I possess even a tinge of these qualities? Right from the childhood I have remained extremely coy, reasonably timid girl who always repelled hollow darkness and frightening loneliness. I never exhibited that remarkable 'never say die' attitude which could have brought me somewhat near to your father.

I always believe, your father was too good a person for me. He accepted me the moment he recognised my helplessness and my desperate need for a shelter. He was born considerate and had a generous heart capable of sprinkling affection endlessly. But moreover he was a man of iron will, somebody possessing what I call a multi-layered personality. Peripherally such men are as soft as a flower could have been, almost feminine. Below it is a tough layer, a core of steel that allows them to be so stiff at times, they remain unbaffled even when the whole world takes animosity of them. And lastly at the centre, there is a soft matter once again, which symbolises their membership in the vast animal kingdom as human beings. That precisely was his quality which turned me on. Other thing was his zest for life, his unambiguous approach towards the manner in which your days are to be spent so as to make every moment absolutely meaningful. Ironically, my personality is devoid of anything that could have made me move closer to that of Jatin's. But perhaps such a discrepancy in our characters made it possible to unite our souls simply because the opposite poles attract. Or do they? Because in our case one of the poles has moved farther and ascended greater heights by breaking all the limitations of human body, while the other one is left at the same earlier position waiting for the day when they will combine once again.

Just keep aside this subject for a moment. Because the more I engulf myself in Jatin's memories, the more I get disturbed. At this juncture I want to share with you the reminisces of my childhood, which always brought a sense of incompleteness to me, due to the absence of my parents. As a little girl I joined St. Joseph's Orphanage which was very lively in all respect. And I was very fond of it! At that time, if my memory doesn't betray me, I too possessed some residual liveliness that degenerated over a period of time and the lack of it stuck to me as a lifelong deformity. Even if I had gone through some kind of drastic change in my life on account of loss of parents I retained some urge to live life. Although it is a tough job remembering everything about that period for, I used to be very small, I distinctly visualise the faces but their names I know by heart. I feel very nostalgic about my stay there, you know. I had heard a lot about ones blood relatives your parents, grandparents, brothers, sisters, cousins, uncles and aunts. And I tried to imagine what could have been my relationship with them, its nature, its compulsions, plus points and obligations, just by looking at the world around and hearing descriptions from my school mates. Then I used to relate those hypothetic people with those who were around me. In the process I used to create bonds.

When I left St. Joseph's these bonds suddenly vanished as if cut by sharp scissors. But my short sojourn has remained a golden patch for me. I lust for those days. It's a great pity, I had to bid farewell to such a delightful home. I wish I could visit it for once to see what has occurred to St. Joseph's since I left. I guess Sister Margaret would be either dead or she must be counting her days in late 1980s.

Bhiku surely must have died. Probably sister Clair would be heading the orphanage with the aid of sister Samantha and Mary. Some new governesses must have entered and they must also have filled Bhiku's place. I'm sure new children are definitely adoring St. Joseph's as the supply of orphans never stops. At last the God is yet to become so kind. Every thing must have transmuted but for the fragrance in its air and the joy in its atmosphere. Frankly, I repent, I left that place.

And ever since I decided to leave St. Joseph's I crave for the easing lifestyle there, which I never managed to acquire later on. It was only when I met your father, quite accidentally and we tried knots that I could forget about St. Joseph's somehow. The period between these two events was quite testing. I'm so seek of it, I avoid its mention here. But just by this gesture of mine you should understand how awful it must have been. The only thing I can say is that it taught me practical explanation of Darwinian theory of 'the survival of the fittest' and how big fish eat smaller ones. If you want to live a respectable life here, you have to be strong. Strong enough to demolish any force that might strike you, to cut any hand that raises arms against you, to devastate anything that threatens to destroy your future. If you are not strong enough, better be ready to get humiliated, to be treated like domestic animals, to be a slave at the hands of superiors. Once you accept such a life you cannot complain. If at all you want to, there is nobody to listen to you. Don't expect the great God to leap forward and make you free. He won't, simply because he doesn't lie anywhere else but within you. If at all you can flare up yourself, ignite the gigantic power dwelling in you and make yourself stronger than the strongest you will survive. You can't but survive. Paradoxically I was a huge failure on this front and failure here means failure everywhere. No wonder, I lived like a humble cow who never protests even if her owner doesn't feed her, yet provides abundant milk to the same chap. This period was a big bad patch wherein I lived a life of total surrender just like a helpless destitute or an abused prostitute. I was robbed of every human pleasure. In this matter I was poorer than a beggar. I was treated as if my heart was carved out of stone and my brain was incapable of thinking. My surroundings took pride in forgetting my place in human race, in forgetting the tenderness and sensitivity of my heart. Cleverly they forgot that a human mind is so weak and delicate, it can break easily with a single word stabbed like a knife. And I was bombarded with hundreds of them every minute, every hour, every day. I have shed litres of blood on account of these sharp incisions, the symbolic blood that is. Worse I've lost actual blood too, through the actual wounds created by actual physical assaults. It was truly a disgraceful life I had. I'm ashamed of being myself, all because of sins committed by others. I've screamed, I've shouted at the top of the voice and I've shrieked. Is there anybody who'll explain what's wrong with me? I've two eyes, a nose, a pair of hands and a pair of legs just like you. I've a brain that works like yours and I can express my feelings with my vocal chords and exhibit my emotions of joy and sorrow with laughter and tears. I too get jubilant when somebody appreciates me and pat me gently or stroke my hair with genuine love. I too get proud when somebody calls me good looking and charming and I too like to dance in the first monsoon shower just like you do. I too get depressed and frustrated at every failure and I too want to cry hiding my face in mother's arms when my mark-sheet doesn't show a descent aggregate. I too get scared at the sight of darkness and fire and ravaging sea. I too weep in pain when any sharp thorn breaks in, into my leg. I too get bothered by the shape of my future. I too get infected by various diseases as I'm not immune to the germs, the viruses and the bacteria, just like you. I too feel embarrassed when my cloths accidentally expose some body part. I too get greedy at the sight of precious diamonds and brand new cars.

When there is so much similarity between us, why you are a human being and I'm but a trivial animal worth feeding on grass and toiling in fields? Why you adorn resplendent thrones and I lay in mud, with subsiding strength in my muscles? Why you enjoy rich moments and exotic days and I venture through nightmerish nights? Why you can get sumptuous meal and wet your throat with grapefruit juice everyday and I have to strive for a stomachful of food with an humble glass of water? Why you wear cloths of gold and silver threads and I struggle to hide my skin by attaching patches here and there? Why you ride on majestic horses and luxurious cars and I'm left with covering my rough path barefoot? Why you reside in marble palace and my roof leaks and water floods in when it rains? Why you get resounding success at every walk of life and I fail miserably at each step? Why smile is marked permanently on your face and I'm cursed with never ending gloom? Why your bag is full of gold and what I have is a penniless pocket? Why your fields blossom with rich harvest and mine is left starved due to lack of water and nourishment? Why your tears are tears and mine plain water, your blood is blood and mine a useless red fluid? Why you are what your are and I'm what I'm? Why? At last why?

Nil, I might sound a born pessimist which, I can assure you, is an incorrect notion. Here I'm just a representation of all the oppressed and poor and downtrodden and 'you' is that favourite person whom the god has blessed with every bounty in excess. It is not that his tremendous prosperity stings in our eyes, no. We just want a share of such fate. We just want to be acknowledged as humans with due recognition of our needs and wants. We just want some help from destiny to guide our lives through a meaningful path. But the reality is different. The god looks down on us. 'Inferior' is what he might describe our creed as, forgetting suitably that he himself has made what we are, that he himself runs a machine creating human beings and writes what it is likely to live, a contended, complete life or an unforgivable punishment. That we are happy only because of him and he only should bear the blame if we are sad. But these words seem like a mutinous leader's speech in an unequivocal dictatorship. Here justice is the least expected thing, and further torment is always round the corner.

But there is always a simple solution to all the suffering. Very elementary! Yet very provocative! Nil, you must be wondering by now, about such a frank thought sharing of mine with you. It boils down to the same elementary thing I just mentioned. Son, this poor mother of yours wants to abscond from all the worldly hardships. My stock of patience has been exhausted, my stiffness has run out. Now I want to escape away. Far away, crossing all boundaries and overcoming all the limits. You guessed it right, I want to free myself from this beautiful body once and for all. This disclosure might come to you as a big surprise but for the likes of me it is the first and the last option. The sole option. Call me a chicken hearted fool, I'll accept every criticism, every nasty comment. And you are the most worthy person to ridicule me. Because nobody is bothered whether Suchita Mittal is dead or alive. It only matters to you. The loss will be yours, you will feel the heat. Don't let this shock hammer your body and soul. Consider it very natural, very trivial, just like the death of a stray dog at the next corner. No faces should bathe in tears, no condolences should be entertained. It will mark the end of a matter which didn't matter at all. Make it as simple as that. Why to create a fuss about an absolutely unimportant turn of event? Simply because my being with you doesn't make much sense as I will but be a burden on your shoulder and so you are better off without me.

Nil, you cannot guess how I'm feeling at this moment. I feel as if thousands of strange insect larvae are eating up my flesh from inside. I'm getting sucked into a hollow nothing and my blood is getting icy. Perhaps I'm the only mother taking such a drastic step when she has a child to look after to. I know I'm committing an irreversible sin, an unpardonable crime and a well planned blunder. What I can say? My birth itself was a blunder on the part of nature. I'm just trying to make the record straight by countering it.

I know what you are going to think about me in future when you grow up. You will curse me every moment and even refuse to call me a mother. I won't blame you. You were an abnormal blend of characters, my boy. On one hand you have the blood extract of war heroes and brave warriors and on the other hand a contribution from this timid lady, i.e., me. But don't ever let this bad tendency of mine take control in you. Destroy it and throw it away in garbage. People like me are not suitable to grace this world. We make it sound foolish and expect it to be a sort of fairyland which is an absurd proposition. So emulate your great father and not me. Nil, my dear child, if my wish weighs some importance, if at all I have some divine accumulation of power, I pray for a complete satisfactory life for you. May you live thousands of years, as young as 20 years old. May success embellish you like a precious diamond on a prince's crown. May you have the courage and determination to guide your own ship towards your destiny, to sail it through the ocean however turbulent and hostile it may be. May you be the king of your fortune and may you be so extremely powerful so as to tilt every moment in your favour, to forcibly change the patterns of the stars and to change, create and rewrite the lines on your palm at your will. May the nature bestow upon you the health, the wealth, wisdom, fame, serenity of mind and unbounded happiness. I know I was her enemy, but sportingly she should accept you as her friend. But keep one thing in mind, when you will become strong and powerful, don't let your mind to fall prey to greed and hypocrisy. Chivalry is what you should abide by. Always keep it in mind that being powerful becomes meaningless unless you utilise your superiority to protect the cause of the unfortunate, poor and needy. Strangled and defeated. Just like me! Just like your poor mother!

I've nothing else to offer you than these good wishes. I'm simply starved of resources my son. And finally pardon me if you can. Pardon me because I gave birth to you. Pardon me because I raised you on my contaminated milk. Pardon me because I rejoiced in your soft touch, your imaculate smile, your faltering speech and your mischievous deeds. Pardon me because I took pride in you, calling you my legacy. Pardon me because I made you a subject of my inspiration. Pardon me as I received huge quantum of energy from your soul day in and day out. Pardon me because I didn't confirm to your requirement of a mother. Pardon me because I was not eligible to carry such a responsibility. Pardon me because I said , 'Sweet my child I live for thee' when they brought home your dear dead father and now leaving you abandoned in this race.

But I won't let you roam aimlessly on street. Now onwards your home will be 'Happy Home' where your dad grew and prospered. And Didi will be your father, mother, brother, sister and friend. That's why I have called her here tonight. Although, I mentioned no reason, it must have become clear by now. So, move forward and daringly embrace your new life while I embrace my death. Goodbye my son, Good luck.

Suchita slowly opens her eyes. Considering her fragile state, this job is pretty toiling. She puts in great effort in stretching her eyelids and separating them away from each other so that the gap between them widens and the faint glow of the zero watt bulb casts its presence. Somehow she manages to lift her body by applying force on her frail hands and positions herself on the bed. For a moment she rests by shutting her eyes again and leaning on a pillow that she held against the wall. Each organ of her body cries due to acute pain and she experiences a burning sensation on her skin. Frequency of her heartbeats soars disproportionately and she almost suffocates due to want of oxygen as if she had run a marathon race.

Finally she sits on the bed with her legs down and looks at Nil, sleeping beside her. Her child seems like a newly born baby, his faultness face bringing fourth tears in her eyes. At the other corner sleeps the one and only Didi. Her extraordinary fascination about the Mittal family remains an intriguing fact. Despite knowing the reality that coming to Suchita means sharing a stockpile of grief, she responded positively to every call made by her. For Suchita, Didi is greater than the God, because the God remained in his well defined position even if Suchita burned herself in blazing flames of life but

Didi always reached for her in the form of cool showers and comforting air currents removing all the blisters that broke out on her skin. Soothing her mind. Luxuriating her soul! Today also, when she invited Didi for no proper reason, the lady didn't repudiate. In spite of the tremendous responsibility and workload, she respected Suchita's call.

"Now Didi", Suchita thought, "I've troubled you for the last time".

And then an inconceivable energy took possession of Suchita. Hot blood flushed out whatever laziness her body had and a raw power surged ahead through her blood vessels. She grabbed something on which her life had come to depend on. Those marvellous sleeping pills! Right after the day she heard about Jatin's death these tablets had become her real friends as dear as Jatin himself could have been. Those were something that snatched away every agony, every distressful thought from Suchita's mind and offered her carefree, enlivening freedom. She loved that limited departure from the ludicrous human life and she always thought about the means to extend that peaceful stage to even greater period and if possible forever. That day had finally arrived. It was going to mark her release from the materialistic world, her release from the dungeon. And ahead lay a fabulous period when her soul could meet that of Jatin. And most importantly it was going to be unending, eternal. A sad smile appeared on Suchita's face because her quest for this everlasting bliss was plainly going to prove her claim that she was a coward. But that was the last thing she cared for.

Steadfastly she tear opens the cover and plucks out a tiny white tablet. She holds a glass of water in the right hand and lifts the tablet by the left one. Even if her heart runs unsteadily she involuntarily consumes the pill. Then goes the other! And...

Her attention shifts towards Didi as some damped sound originates from her. But Didi is not awake, her body only turns side. As soon as it becomes ostensible that Didi is not awake Suchita gets back to the business. Third pill is swallowed. And then fourth, fifth, sixth, ... Soon the twenty tablet pack becomes a part of wastage.

Dizziness sets in as the wonderous medicine immediately gets on to its work and grips the lady in its anaesthetic effect. It marks the beginning of the end. The end of a tussle. The end of a saga. The end of an epic. The gates of heaven lay open inviting her in its spread arms.

Come my child. Come my little girl. Your punishment is over. Your jinx that you are ill-fated no more holds good as a divine asylum awaits you. Come embrace your heavenly abode. Come join this band of overjoyed soul and enkindle their spirits. They were waiting for you from the moment you had been sent to earth because they knew the earth is no place for you. Their forecast has been proven to be fitting. You have already gone through crushing defeats on earth. Now its time to be victorious. Now its time to rein like a queen. So come fast, hurry up, hurry up. Pack up your bag and baggage. Don't forget you are heading towards heaven.

Suchita looked coldly at Nil, the inseparable piece of her heart. And she felt herself crunched in a colossal jaw, its teeth digging wildly at her head. OK. she had reserved her place in heaven. But what about this tiny lad? Knowingly and unknowingly she had helped writing a similar script of his life, similar to her own. Rendering him alone at the useless world's behest. To be severed into pieces. To be tossed into air like a lifeless cricket ball. And to be deprived of every right a person is supposed to delight in. And after inflicting such a harsh future upon Nil what the hell she was going to do in heaven? Watch a high intensity drama? An action packed, thrilling act?

Looking at this child, struggling to stand erect while having fun with delicious feasts and luxurious lifestyle? Shame on you Suchita. You were so mean! You were so selfish! If at all you were so doubtful about your capability of raising a child, why did you bear one? If at all you couldn't protect him why did you boast to be his mom? Agreed you were a coward but by cheating your tiny son you have exposed another dimension of yourself. You are unfaithful. Suchita, you are a traitor!

Conscience is an amazing manipulator. Sometimes it can manage to persuade even ruthless out-laws to think humanly. So making a sensitive mother to reconsider her decision of committing suicide, for the sake of her child was in its best capacity. But alas! Things don't change just by thinking alone. You don't find a sweet, congenial lake in a desert just because you are thirsty and want it badly. You don't live a life you always dreamt of just because you dreamt it. The facts always remain true and the facts don't change. And the fact was that Suchita had herself hit the final nail to her coffin. She had already devoured a heavy dose of sleeping pill and the death started tightening her throat.

Hey Suchita! What are you up to now? We are sick of your strange behaviour lady. It's all over. Your cursed stay on earth is over. Now don't get entrapped in any alluring compulsion. Just stop worrying about your child. Remember what happened to you when you were of his age? Still you survived. Look he is in a far better situation. And if at all he has a tough time in store for him let him face it. Nobody is without pain here. So no more excuses, come quick.

Angels of heaven! They are the impatient angels of heaven. So good looking. So handsome. They are standing at the earth heaven intermediate boundary. Waiting for Suchita's response.

But her response is not enthusiastic. She is overwhelmed with madness, overpowered with motherly love. "I won't come' she says 'I won't'. I'm happy on the earth with my child. I'm not so greedy just as you think. I'm not so fool, to be fooled by you. Now don't trouble me any more. Leave me at my own discretion. And just go away. Please."

The angels turn furious at such cold shouldered welcome by the lady. They are angry because they had been invited by Suchita herself. Now flatly she refused to come along. It was an insult. It was sheer disrespect. The net effect of this bargain is catastrophic. The angels start changing their appearance. Out goes the fairness, in comes the black shed. Their beautiful faces transform themselves into ugly masks. They grow hideous feline teeth and formidable bovine horns. Their eyes start burning and turn red hot like a molten mass of iron. Instantly one of them grabs Suchita by arm.

"You idiot! We are messengers of death. We can be good enough at times to sympathise with the humans. But you are not worthy for that. You are to be dealt with like this only."

He pulls Suchita forcibly as she cries at such a horrifying reversal of roll. 'Nil!' she screams "Save me, hold my hand my child. NIL! DIDI!." Her voice doesn't produce an iota of effect. Nil sleeps peacefully. Didi too. Suchita's grave mistake digs her own grave. She falls in a well fabricated by her own. Darkness reins and remains as the sole entity. Hollowness follows suit. Suchita commences her journey through this media, where everything is nothing and nothing is everything. All hurdles fell apart, all barriers collapse. Smooth cruising is what remains. Cruising through a deep space, so deep things don't show up for ages. Infinitely deep! Cosmic bodies glitter at unfathomable distances. Suchita battles away till last, in a bloody encounter and crumbles down.

Nil Mittal has a good time with deep midnight sleep and his mother laying beside him turns lifeless.

✣✣✣

One would call it a mere coincidence or a sheer chance. But it was something more than that. The confounding similarity between Major Jatin Mittal and his son Nil Mittal was on downright display. Same hypnotic, magical atmosphere on Delhi's Azad Maidan. Same patriotic, hysterical crowd, same tricolours fluttering wildly with the sweet smelling wind, same terrific enthusiasm and of course same day, 15th August. Even the stone cold voice on the microphone seemed to be similar to those who had captured the earlier occasion in 1973.

"Ladies and gentlemen", the microphone spoke mechanically, "Some 17 years ago a little boy called Jatin Mittal was standing here at the same position wearing a medal of bravery. But that medal belonged to his father. Today, he himself has brought the honour. As we know he had earned same fame and recognition with his gallantry and dedication to our nation. He reached the similar fate like his father. That is he, too perished in the battlefield, while fighting bravely. Maj. Jatin Mittal was a part of Indian peace keeping mission to Sri Lanka. On 12th Feb. this year he lost his life while leading a battle against Tamil rebels. On the auspicious occasion of 15th of August we remember his great sacrifice and show our gratitude by presenting him the medal of bravery. Just like his father, his award will be received by his son, Nil".

Same modesty but same dash, marks the walking style of little Nil Mittal. Entire crowd blows up into wild clapping as he is endowed with the medal upon reaching the dais. The dignitaries present pat on his shoulders. That serves as a breaking point, as if the sponge is pressed, water rushes through his eyes. But his face smiles as he clutches the medal in his right hand. It is a proof of his royal identity. He is a descendent of lions!

With Nil on the stage the programme ends with the rendering of National Anthem in unison. About twenty yards away from the stage a lady soaks her handkerchief in tears. Then, by way of silent signals she advises Nil, not to venture through the crowd and remain on the stage. She knows, it is difficult for a child like him to rush through the dispersing mob. She had a prior experience of the fact when she stood on the same spot along with Jatin 17 years ago. She works in the orphanage 'Happy Home'. Her name is Nilam Didi. Finding her own way through the vast collection of men, women and children Didi manages to reach the stage and hugs the little son of Jatin named Nil, after her name, i.e., Nilam. And she blows a kiss on his forehead. The two wait patiently for the mob to recede as Didi holds Nil's chin with her hand and stands at his back. She feels as if time had travelled in opposite direction. She feels as if she had just turned 23 and taken charge of 'Happy Home' not long ago. She feels, the boy standing next to her is called Jatin Mittal who has joined 'Happy Home' after his father's death in 1972 war. Unknowingly she keeps on filling her eyes with water and her handkerchief keep on wetting itself.

Some five minutes later the duo jointly reach the main road and climb up on a city bus. Within another twenty minutes they get down in front of the Happy Home. In a peculiar repetition of history bravery award returns to this orphanage. A complete circle has been traced. Such situations are quite tricky you know. People fail to decide whether they should cry or laugh, mourn or exult. On one hand you have the grief of your dear one's departure and on the other you have the proud feeling about the laurels and accolades they have brought. If possible you can have tears in one eye and a sparkling glint in the other. You might wish to walk on air and at the same time break down in tears. You would like to share your joys and achievements among one and all and simultaneously dampen the grief within. It doesn't happen with too many. But those who go through it are extraordinary. Nil Mittal was one of them.

All the Happy Home joins hands together to welcome this pretty kid. He is not only their newly found brother but an inspiration. Although his contribution towards claiming the medal is hardly anything but his graceful acceptance of it is no less than a courageous deed. The steps he covered before receiving the medal while fighting with emotional outburst are praiseworthy. And the fact that he is a predecessor of one of the bravest son of soil makes him more lovable. That's why he commands great honour, trust and loyalty at such a tender age although dramatic tides in his life has rendered him subdued and shy. At this particular instant these qualities of him are rather more pronounced. Didi, on the other hand looks quite relaxed as her burden is vastly reduced. Recently the Defence Ministry has honoured her by awarding a permanent membership of 'Happy

Home'. Moreover with her request she has been relieved of her duty as the head of the orphanage. Now she works here as a senior member of the 'Happy Home' family whose wealth of experience is utilised in running its affairs. The government has appointed a new head at her place who has fast managed to gain control over the administration. Today this lady has organised the ceremony to mark the 'Independence day' and Nil Mittal's felicitation. She has large, dark eyes and a cream complexion. Meet Mrs. Suchita Mittal, the new indomitable 'chief-in-charge' of Happy Home. People say she is a suicide specialist. Bust as usual she doesn't give a damn to them.